D0975600

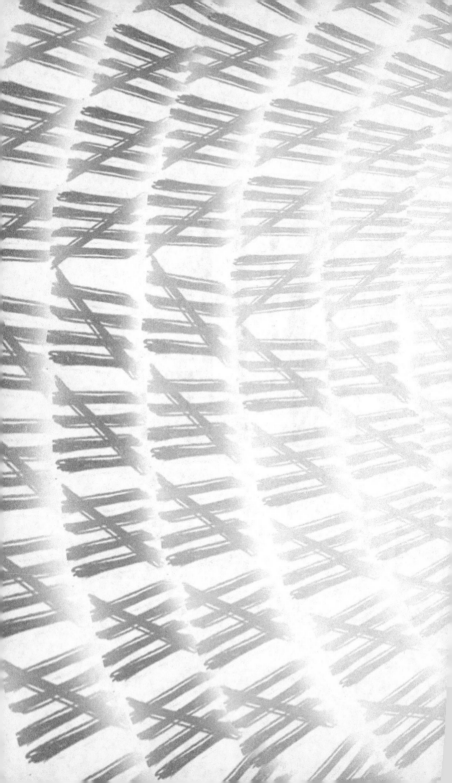

LYNNE MATSON

NIL
ON FIRE

HENRY HOLT AND COMPANY | NEW YORK

Henry Holt and Company, LLC
Publishers since 1866
175 Fifth Avenue
New York, New York 10010
fiercereads.com

Henry Holt® is a registered trademark of Henry Holt and Company, LLC.
Copyright © 2016 by Lynne Matson
All rights reserved.

Library of Congress Cataloging-in-Publication Data is available.

ISBN 978-1-62779-295-0 (hardcover)

Our books may be purchased in bulk for promotional, educational, or business use. Please
contact your local bookseller or the Macmillan Corporate and Premium Sales Department
at (800) 221-7945 ext. 5442 or by e-mail at MacmillanSpecialMarkets@macmillan.com.

First Edition—2016
Printed in the United States of America by R. R. Donnelley & Sons Company,
Harrisonburg, Virginia

1   3   5   7   9   10   8   6   4   2

FOR STEPHEN, ALWAYS

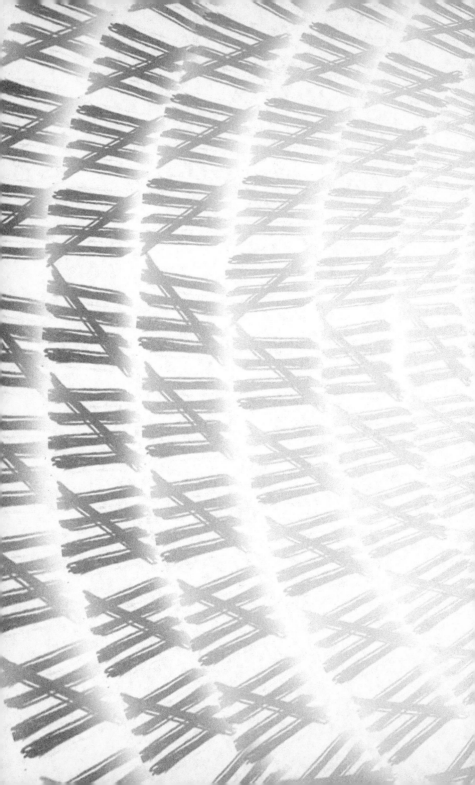

AND NOW THESE
THREE REMAIN:
FAITH, HOPE, AND LOVE.

BUT THE GREATEST OF
THESE IS LOVE.
—1 COR. 13:13

CHAPTER 1

Paulo blinked, slowly, his consciousness returning in crisp frames filled with color and scent and sound.

He stood alone on the black rock platform. The acrid smell of death filled the air, accompanied by the distant crackle of flames. Above him, the sun burned like smokeless fire, still high noon. But over the carving, the gate was gone. Skye was gone.

His chance to leave was gone.

Reality set in, stark and devastating.

I failed, he thought.

A cry ripped from his throat like the wail of an injured animal. He dropped to his hands and knees on the harsh black rock, landing so hard that pebbles raked his palms, drawing blood, but he was too consumed by his growing terror and overwhelming bewilderment to care. How had he missed the gate? He'd waved to Skye, grateful she'd made it, knowing he was last and that the timing felt right—the completion of a circle begun three months before, the end of a cycle begun years before he or Skye were ever born. Only he'd hesitated, for reasons that he couldn't explain. For reasons he couldn't *remember*.

He'd lost time, mysterious minutes stolen by an invisible entity.

And now he was alone on Nil.

An angry tear welled in his eye; he wiped it quickly, already pulling himself together, knowing he wasn't truly alone. There were lions and hyenas and pumas on the island too, and he was very aware that he did not sit on top of Nil's food chain. He coughed, then choked, tasting smoke and salt. The thick air billowing up from the meadow snapped him to attention like a hot slap to the face.

He needed to get away from the mountain. There was nothing for him here, not now.

Not for three more months, to be precise.

Paulo stood, and with one last look around the silent black platform, he stepped back. Then, even though there was no escape, he turned and began to run. Down the steps, past the fiery meadow.

Around him, the island burned.

The island let him go.

It would wait.

It was accustomed to waiting. Once it had waited for centuries. Time wrapped the island like an invisible sheath, fluid and constant, both armor and weapon.

The island was weakened but not broken.

The male kept running, through smoke and flames and blood as the island settled in to watch. And to wait. And above all, to renew.

And so it began, again. Only this time, the island would not show weakness.

Or mercy.

That era was over.

CHAPTER
2

SKYE
MAY 21, MIDDLE OF THE NIGHT

I'm not crazy. I'm not crazy. I'm not crazy.

I think I might be crazy. If I'm not already there, I'm definitely hovering on the brink.

Rives and I flew into Madrid yesterday afternoon. We landed eight hours ago, almost to the minute. I'm still acutely aware of *time*. Sometimes I think I should stop counting, stop noticing as each day vanishes into the past. But other times I think counting is my way of *remembering*, of reminding myself that time is fleeting, and precious, like life.

So I count.

It's been three weeks since we said a tearful farewell to Dex under a fiery Hawaiian sunset among friends, and almost nine weeks since we last touched the strange island of Nil. Nil, a place that still exists, a place where you have exactly 365 days to escape or you die.

Rives and I did it.

We escaped. We saved as many as we could, and we left Nil's ticking clock behind.

But something came with me through that final gate, something powerful; I feel it. It whispers to me in the nighttime darkness. It's a distant whisper, one I don't want to hear. One I can't block out.

One I fear is stronger than me.

My dreams began the night we got back. First I dreamed of raging fire, of choking smoke. Of blood-soaked hands and cruel smiles and the crushing pain of leaving a friend behind even though he was already gone. Other dreams focused on Paulo, a different friend, one who had inexplicably chosen to stay. I dreamed of him racing through fire and fear, only I never saw where he was running *to*, or what he was running *from*. I never saw what haunted his back—but something was there.

Just like I know something is *here*. In my dreams, in the dark.

Now I dream only of blackness: the sightless, yawning blackness found between gates, cold and consuming and frighteningly *endless*.

But not empty.

It's never empty.

Something lives in that blackness, writhing like invisible fog, something dark and chilling and *real*. It reaches for me, whispering without words, clawing at me with charcoal fingers; it invades my daydreams and haunts my nights, its grasp almost finding purchase in those moments my mind is dark, and unguarded.

I won't let it in.

But I can't shut it out.

I haven't told Rives. Then again, I think he knows. I see it in his eyes when he looks at me: the worry, the fear, and the love. The same love that pulls me back, the same love that keeps me sane. Because at that frightful moment when I'm trapped in the darkness—when I'm seconds away from breaking, a breath away from *slipping*—I reach for Rives. I always find him, or maybe he finds me. Either way, he brings me back.

Every time.

I'm not crazy.

~~I'm not crazy.~~

My name is Skye Bracken, and this is the truth.

CHAPTER 3

RIVES
MAY 28, ALMOST MIDNIGHT

Look around. Pay attention.

   Notice what others ignore.

   My dad's classic advice, advice I painfully honed during my 365 days on Nil. Advice locked in my head for life, advice now second nature. Advice I couldn't stop following if I tried.

   I took it all in: the shadows beneath Skye's eyes dulling her skin like bruises, the way she anxiously tugged on her raw diamond necklace when she thought no one was looking.

   But I was always looking.

   And when it came to Skye, I noticed *everything*, especially the problem she seemed hell-bent on ignoring.

   It was the elephant in the room, big enough to screw with her sleep. Regardless of where we crashed, Skye tossed and turned, her nights restless and full of dreams. Her days weren't much better. More than once in the past few weeks I'd caught her completely zoned out, her eyes unfocused and distant. I didn't ask where her head was; I didn't need to.

   It was Nil-related. It had to be.

   And it seriously pissed me off.

   The island had already taken enough, from both of us. We'd served our time, paid our dues. We'd survived. We were *done*.

Forcing myself to relax, I pulled Skye close, feeling her cheek press against my chest. *She's safe*, I reminded myself. *We're safe. And we're together.*

She actually seemed asleep. Steady breathing, lips closed but soft.

I slowed my breathing to match hers. Moments like these made me feel invincible, like *we* were invincible. Nil wouldn't steal another minute from us. Nil was my past.

Skye was my future.

Is she?

The amused whisper sliced through my head like broken glass, cruel and cutting. I froze, willing myself to chill out, grounding myself in the *now* until the flash of memory passed.

An instant later, Skye cried out, her spine twisting. "Rives!" Her whisper was choked. Her whole body shook; her skin had turned ice cold.

I held her close. "I'm here," I whispered, gently stroking her hair, willing her trembling to stop. "It's okay. Just a dream."

"Rives," she said again, her voice full of relief. But her heart still raced, like mine. We lay like that for a long time. Me, stroking her hair, Skye, fighting to let go of her demons.

When we'd left Nil ten weeks ago, I thought we'd won.

Now I wasn't so sure.

CHAPTER
4

This one was strong.

He came from a land of ice, but his spirit was made of fire. He fought valiantly to stay conscious as he traveled between worlds, clinging to awareness up to the very limit of fracture, much like another human who had come before: that one a female, a descendant of a visitor from an earlier time. Only where she had truly been familiar—her flesh, her blood—this one was new. Nothing about this human felt familiar except his innate strength; it touched every part of him, a current running so powerfully through his being that the island had sensed it through the fibers of space, of time . . . making him the right choice. The necessary choice. It had nearly exhausted all of the island's fading strength to reach him, to call him, but he had answered.

He would do well.

He would need to.

The island watched as he rolled out of the gate and spilled onto the black sand. The island waited as he stirred and blinked, as he raised one hand to block the bright sun. Fear lanced through his heart with the fierce light. For an instant, he stopped breathing.

And then he sat up.

Slowly, his muscles on high alert like his senses, all fog cleared from his consciousness with one deep inhale. He breathed, steady and calming, lowering his heart rate by will, an impressive show of strength as he gazed around.

His body turned slightly north, he stood, looking toward the place where others once gathered. His thoughts were clear, organized. Most centered on people he had left behind, on statements he wished he had made, but a few thoughts lodged here, concerning his own safety and well-being.

He was not afraid.

His swift and selfless reaction pleased the island. The island needed this one, like it had needed the one before. But then, it had failed.

It would not fail again.

The price was too great.

Hafthor stood in a semi-crouch, unaware anyone—or anything—was watching him. To his left, the ocean stretched without end into a cerulean sky; he found no hint of Icelandic gray among the rich blue. Over the water, the sun shone brightly, free of clouds, its rays warming his bare shoulders, the salty breeze brushing his skin without bite. He wiggled his toes. Beneath his feet, the coarse black sand churned cool under the top layer of warmth. To his right, lush palm trees stretched tall, surrounded by spindly trees he'd never before seen. Clumps of shrubs huddled against the sand line, forming the island's first line of defense.

He peered more closely at the foliage. A kangaroo regarded him with curiosity, arms high and still. Like the animal, Hafthor didn't move; instead he stared at a spot just past the kangaroo. A few meters inside the tree line, something linear stood out: a makeshift shelter, a triangular shape too symmetrical to be natural. He moved toward the trees, still on the sand but close enough to startle the kangaroo. The animal hopped away, retreating into the tangle of green.

Upon inspection, the shelter appeared old. Abandoned.

Unwelcoming.

No, he thought.

He would not hide, not here. Not until he understood where he was and why he was here. He would seek help, and this shelter offered none. He had nothing—and no one—but himself, but it was enough. *As long as you know who you are, you can never be lost,* his father would say. He touched the tattoo on his shoulder, summoning courage.

I am Hafþór, he thought. He had no one to rely on but himself—and so he would.

Dropping his hand, he backed away from the shelter and carefully looked around.

In the distance, a black cliff rose toward the sky. It matched the cliff at his back, the pair bracketing the beach where he stood.

He scrutinized the cliff to the north, arms crossed but relaxed.

Then, like the barest brush of a silken feather, Hafthor felt a gentle push at his back, the island breeze urging him forward. He didn't know he was being guided, or that it drained the island's precious reserves to do so.

North, he thought. *I will go north.*

And so he did.

Farther north, at the edge of Nil City, Paulo stood before the Wall, feeling very much alone. There was no one else in the City, just ghosts. He stared at the names belonging to people who had once cared for him, who had kept him alive and safe when he couldn't care for himself. Names like Skye, and Rives, and Dex. He stared at Skye's name, grateful for her friendship, saddened that he'd let her down, even though he still didn't understand why. Slowly, he raised his knife and methodically carved a check. One for Skye, then one for Rives. Then another check, and another. Jillian. Brittney. Zane. One mark at a time, he completed the story of the people who had been here before him, of people he'd outlasted, people with seasons served fully and people with seasons cut short. He saved Dex's cross for last. That mark would not be forgotten, or forgiven.

On his life, he vowed it would not happen again.

He would not let the island take another.

He stepped back, satisfied. Before him, a few spaces glared back, still empty, spaces he'd chosen not to fill because they belonged to people he'd never met, with fates he didn't know. A few names seemed conspicuously absent: names like Rika, and Maaka. If their names were here, Paulo would have given them a check, for he knew their fate. He knew they'd survived. But they'd chosen to make their way alone, to not join the City, and Paulo would honor their choice.

His choice would be different.

He walked over to the last name, Brittney, no longer seeing her name or her check; he was intent on the empty space below. A blank slate, a new chapter. Lifting his knife to the Wall, Paulo carefully carved five letters: *P-A-U-L-O.*

The time to survive alone was over.

The ghost of a smile crossed his lips because right now, he *was* alone. He was a City of one—and possibly an island of one as well. Oddly enough, in the weeks since Skye had left, Paulo hadn't seen another living person; he'd only seen animals. Wild animals falling out of equally wild gates, docile animals falling prey to the deadly. He had the strangest sense the island was waiting . . . for something, perhaps even some-one. Or perhaps Skye's theory had been correct: that without people, the island's strength was compromised. Weakened.

But he was here.

So life continued. The *island* continued, and with its existence came the cold truth: Paulo would not be alone for long. It was only a matter of time. For all he knew, he already had company.

Turning away from the Wall, Paulo faced the City, then looked back at Mount Nil.

I am here, he thought, standing still, and straight. *I am no longer afraid. When the time comes, I will meet those you send and we will fight.*

That is my *choice.*

And then he got to work.

CHAPTER
5

NIL
NOON

Each noon brought the promise of fresh blood and pride and power. The island's appetite had grown insatiable. Once it had sampled the incredible might of life and death on a grand scale, and it thirsted to do so again. It ached for more; it needed it.

And it would have it, soon.

Today's prize would be tomorrow's power.

Coated in blood that was not her own, this female radiated vitality and fury in equal amounts, the electria coursing through her body so ferociously that the gate required minimal strength to open; the island simply used hers.

Took it, used it, reveled in it.

Delicious.

She didn't cower when the gate took her; instead she reflexively lifted her knife with one blood-splattered hand, thrusting the wet blade toward the iridescent wall as it rushed to devour her. Her slashing movement had been instinctive, her natural response being to save herself, even if it meant harming others.

The warm blood coating her weapon testified to that.

The island had wisely left the other human behind, closing the gate with force, preserving its power, and hers. Once it had allowed two humans through simultaneously, but the split in focus between the two had been disastrous. The island could not transfer both, and had lost immense amounts of energy attempting to do so, but the true cost of that unfortunate transfer had been the loss of both prizes. Both humans had been lost between, and with them, their electria: power the island craved. Power the island needed. That day, the island had learned the necessity of restraint, and the power of balance: one gate, one human. One transfer at a time.

The island would not make the same mistake twice.

It had learned that from the humans too. Mistakes were not to be repeated. They were to be prevented. And remedied.

And this female would be key to correcting the island's last mistake.

This one was lethal. Angry.

Absolutely perfect.

Even when she lost feeling in her physical form as she traveled between worlds, this one fought the transfer with all she had left, revealing a depth of resilience and resistance greater than anticipated, a welcome surprise.

Better still, in the crucial seconds during transfer—in those precious moments when her unconscious mind lay raw and exposed—the island discovered that she would fight until her time's end, honing the innate strength she already possessed. And the island would let her. The island would provide ample opportunities for growth, and would force her to become as powerful as she could possibly be—but it mattered little, because in those same precious moments, the island had already chosen her fate.

The fight would be delightful.

Time to wake.

Carmen woke, instantly on guard.

She hopped to a crouch, feeling naked without her knife. Then again, she *was* naked, which made the loss of her only means of protection that much worse. Around her, tunnels of water snaked through the rock; the ocean crashed close enough to hear even though she couldn't see it.

What in the world? she thought.

Still crouched, she turned slowly, feeling the cool sea breeze brush her skin, the constant stickiness of Colombia conspicuously absent. She completed a full rotation, absorbing her quiet surroundings, the lack of people, of anything remotely familiar. In the distance she was fairly certain a zebra stood at attention, watching something. Maybe her.

She'd never seen a zebra before, except in books. She'd never been to a zoo. She'd never needed to go; her father had simply brought the animals to her. A petting zoo, he'd called it.

She had no interest in petting a zebra.

And if it threatened her, she'd kill it.

Where am I? she wondered, taking stock of her surroundings carefully. A spike of fear reared its head; she crushed it instantly, without hesitation. She had no time for fear, or the vulnerability it brought.

Standing slowly, Carmen backtracked, replaying the last memories she had.

Ice.

Heat.

Pain.

Not all the pain was hers. At that, she smiled.

The last thing she clearly remembered was surprising Carlos, an older boy who thought himself more attractive than he was in every sense of the word. He'd thought he'd surprise *her*. He'd thought he'd corner her in private, and teach her a lesson. He hadn't liked her repeated refusals, and he'd liked her mockery even less. But he hadn't expected her skill, or her speed. And there was no way he could have known that her father had trained her himself—to *protect* herself—especially from boys like Carlos who refused to take no for an answer. In the end, it was Carlos who'd learned a lesson. The slice down his cheek would leave a scar.

She had been the stronger one when it counted most.

Father would be proud, she thought, lifting her chin. Only he wasn't here, and she'd no idea where *here* was.

But there was one thing she knew in the depths of her soul: she was Carmen Medina, youngest daughter of Juan Felipe Medina, the owner of the largest construction company in Bogota and a self-made man who'd risen to wealth and power one smart move at a time. She had his genes, his ruthlessness, his cunning.

She might be alone here, but she wasn't afraid.

She wanted answers. She wanted clothes. But more than anything else, she wanted a weapon.

A weapon, the female wanted. The island would see that she found one.

It had let her acclimate long enough.

Summoning heat and air, the island pushed at the female's back. The island wanted blood, and when it was time, this female would spill it.

Until then, the island would play elsewhere.

Turning inward, the island reached for the seam. The island found it easily, focusing on the invisible wedge left behind, a weak point preventing the seam from closing completely, a remnant of the past that had grown over time. With calculated precision, the island leaned on the wedge, widening the rift between worlds: a razor-thin gap that should not be open, not now. Not after the crucial hour.

But it was. Open and unguarded.

Under the island's pressure, the seam expanded a mere fraction. A surge of power rolled through the island in a delicious ripple. Through the seam, the island sought the one who had escaped, one it had desperately wanted to keep: the female, Skye. If it couldn't have her, it would break her.

It was almost time.

CHAPTER 6

SKYE
JUNE 2, LATE MORNING

Holy crap. *The darkness.* It's gaining strength, feeding itself, pulling power from a place I can't see, from I place I haven't dared look.

But when I woke from my last nightmare, I *knew*: I need to confront the darkness, *now*, before it's too late. Because as the darkness grows stronger, I'm growing weaker, probably because I don't sleep—at least not well. Sleep is a full-on war, waged in the dark. Waged *with* the dark. Something has to give, and I don't want it to be me.

If the darkness wins, I'll lose.

I'll lose *me*.

I'll be gone, lost to the infinite blackness, to the darkness *between*—like Sy, like others I never met. Now I know that the Wall wasn't always true. That a check didn't always mean that person made it back, or made it *through*; it just meant that person caught a gate. Sy was proof of that.

So many things we thought were true on Nil were wrong, or at least not completely right.

But me, I'm still desperate for the truth. About Nil's past, about why Paulo stayed. About what lives in the darkness. Maybe my curiosity is genetic, like my recklessness, because now I can't help wondering what will happen if I turn *toward* the dark, rather than away from it. Maybe if I reach into the darkness on my terms, maybe I'll see what's calling me, and why. And then I can beat whatever it is, because I'll finally know what I'm up against.

Part of me knows that's insane, like lock-me-up-in-a-padded-room crazy.

But the other part of me thinks it might work. Even better, I'll make my stand during the day. Confronting the darkness in daylight seems safer than a meeting held in the dark. The light will be *my* edge, my weapon. So today, when the sun rises, I'm going to face the dark. Maybe I'll even figure out what it wants. Because the darkness wants something; I just don't know what.

It wants you, my subconscious hisses.

No. I play my own devil's advocate. *But maybe it wants something from me.*

The distinction seems critical, like the answers. Knowledge brought more than power; it offered freedom—at least it had on Nil.

The only thing holding me back is fear. And not just any fear, one in particular: I fear I created it, that the darkness actually comes from within me, born of the void created by Dex's death. That the darkness is a manifestation of guilt. *That it's all in my head.*

I fear that if I look into the darkness, I'll see *me*.

But the calm, resilient part of my mind reassures me I'm sane, and the fierce part of my soul—the part that helped me survive Nil—agrees. Somehow I'm certain that the darkness of my dreams is real: that it's foreign and lethal and not to be ignored. *That it's a remnant of Nil.* One I brought back with me, a shadow of that last gate.

So maybe, in the end, I just need to acknowledge it and say goodbye. Because if I'm the one who brought it back, then I need to be the one to let it go.

I have a plan. It involves a nap. And it's happening today.

As soon as Rives leaves for Marseilles to see friends, I'll banish the darkness for good. End of story.

I feel better already.

My name is Skye Bracken, and this is the truth that will set me free.

Two hours later, I knew I'd made a terrible mistake.

The darkness poured in just as I knew it would, a greedy blackness writhing with life and invisible whispers, begging me to come closer. I crept to the edge, sensing the invisible line, taking the utmost care not to cross it with any shred of myself. All I could see was black. Endless, terrifying black.

Before I could look deeper, I felt the line bend.

The darkness surged with victory, reaching for me with sinewy claws, spilling across in roiling ribbons of sentient blackness—and the instant the darkness breached the line, the whispers turned deafening. I lurched away, too slow, too late. The darkness brushed my shoulder with icy fingers and the profound depth of it was shocking.

I *felt* it.

The whole of it. The essence of it. The *want*.

It wanted *me*.

The darkness held me in place, binding me with invisible ties. I screamed for Rives, but the darkness absorbed the sound; it devoured my desperation, my plea, *everything*—even the timbre of my voice, as though all were a preview of the full course of me.

A pinprick of light flared.

I was the bug under the microscope, caught between the light and the dark, a microscopic speck in time and space and something much greater than me. I could still feel the line, still feel the edge of me. I could almost see that crucial boundary, reflected in the wisp of light.

The light pulsed, once; the chorus of voices converged into a single clear tone: desperate, and unquestionably human.

I leaned closer, trying to see—and abruptly, the line thinned. The darkness snarled, the light faded, and I had a moment of complete clarity that if I fully crossed that line, *I would not come back*.

Like I'd flipped a switch, I fought with all I had, lashing out with muscles and bone and blood and *will*. I broke free; I woke up. I lay alone on the bed in the sun-filled flat, covered in a thin sheen of sweat. Still shaking, still wanting.

Now that I'm awake, why do I still feel it?

CHAPTER
7

RIVES
JUNE 2, MORNING

Each step away from Skye felt loaded, like a magnet fighting its pull.

Don't leave her alone.

The quiet thought made me pause. I almost turned back, retraced my steps.

But I didn't.

Skye had asked me for space, for time alone. I kept moving, kept walking. Kept going through the motions. I boarded the train, took my seat, but my worry weight was too great to shake.

She's fine, I told myself. After all, this girl was the same one who'd taken down a ninety-kilo cat with nothing but a rock and piece of twine.

That clear truth made me relax.

But the moment the train left the station, the whisper exploded in my head like a scream: *DON'T LEAVE HER ALONE.*

Too late, I thought, jumping to my feet.

I already had.

CHAPTER 8

NIL
AFTER NOON

That one did not listen well.

His mind less guarded than hers, he heard but did not listen, not even to himself. He had left his mate, leaving her vulnerable.

Power had shifted, like the seam itself. Like the focus of the island, reaching there and here. Perhaps the shift was meant to be, since she was the one who had caused it.

Indeed, she was the one.

The island saw it so clearly. The end was written; the future spilled like the light of a thousand suns, bursting with brilliance and flaring into the now.

Now, it would be up to her: his mate, the one called Skye. The one with the power to listen, and to hear, and above all, to survive.

In the meantime, the island must choose wisely, both here and there, with what little power it had left. Here, the island had developed an affinity for the one called Hafthor, a male who was potentially worthy of the Sight. Usually the island gifted the Sight to females, but there had been exceptions. It was too soon to judge.

For now, the island would see through Hafthor's eyes. Occasionally, human sight had proven useful, even insightful, and the island would utilize every advantage it could.

Through Hafthor's eyes, the island watched.

From behind the largest thicket of palms, Hafthor studied the girl. Long black braid, sharp cheekbones. *She would be beautiful,* he thought, *except for her smile.* It hinted at cruelty.

And she was a thief.

As he'd watched, she'd strolled into the empty village, past the wooden wall packed with names—some of which looked recently added—and strode into a small thatched-roof hut as if it were hers. And yet, he knew that it wasn't, just as he knew that the rope she'd walked out with wasn't hers, or the cloth bag bulging with gourds.

The hidden people would not approve.

He'd met no one else here, but he knew they existed: he saw their fingerprints on the empty beds carefully made; he heard their voices in the wind and their whispers in the trees; he felt their dead lying still in the field of flowers.

He felt the hidden people everywhere, and they demanded respect.

Perhaps this girl felt them too, because she didn't linger in the village. After poking her head out and glancing around, she walked straight toward his hiding place, a look of satisfaction on her face. He shrank back, blending into the palms. She passed him without a glance, too intent on looking over her shoulder, her satisfaction shifting to caution, as if she sensed she was being followed.

Hafthor silently observed as she headed south.

Seconds passed, weighted and thick.

Then he followed, taking care to stay concealed, which was not an easy feat given his size. She, on the other hand, was lithe and nimble, and exceptionally stealthy. Hafthor lost her trail within minutes.

Now he stood alone on the black sand beach, south of the City, in the place he'd first begun. *Full circle*, he thought, taking in his surroundings, *a message to begin again*. To go a different way.

He pressed his fingers to the tattoo on his shoulder, then crossed his arms. Closing his eyes, he listened.

South, the sea whispered. *Go south.*

Without hesitation, Hafthor went south.

CHAPTER 9

NIL
MID-MORNING

Paulo stood inside the Arches, facing the mountain. It towered over the island like a silent giant. He knew in the deepest part of his soul that he was not alone on the island, even if he was the only human. But surely by now there must be other people.

So why hadn't he seen them?

Pawns, he thought abruptly. *We're part of a game, pieces to be played.* Perhaps he *was* the only pawn in play, perhaps not. But it mattered little to him. He had no control over others, or the island. But he could control himself.

Or could he?

How long had he been staring at the mountain?

Frustrated, he ripped his gaze away, his thoughts drifting to that last day with Skye. To his failure. His eyes fell, and when they landed, he startled.

Etched into a small flat rock at the base of the smallest arch, Skye's initials stared at him. *S. B.* Above the two letters hung the words *Search* and *Look Inside.*

He read and reread the words, searching for meaning. Had Skye left this message for him? Had she known he would stay?

What had she known that he didn't?

He stared at her initials until his neck ached, then he turned away, the rising tide calling him down from the rocks. With ease, he worked his way down the jagged black cliff, not missing a foothold. At the bottom, he paused. The skin on his back prickled as an unseen hand dragged ice down his back.

Run, whispered the sea.

A shimmering gate vaulted into the sky. A wild gate, the kind that still filled Paulo with unease.

He ran. Up the black beach, away from the gate, cutting and swerving as he stayed ahead of the leading edge until the glittering wall collapsed. Finally, it winked out. Gone.

Paulo dropped his hands to his knees, his chest heaving, but his eyes stayed alert as he began counting.

One.

Two.

The air thickened.

I said run. The breaking waves rumbled like laughter. A second gate appeared meters from the demise of the first, shooting skyward, then rolling directly toward him.

No, Paulo thought with force; he was already sprinting. *Not today. I'll go on my own time, of my own free will.*

I *control* me.

A black cat popped its small head out from the scrub brush, ears twitching. Without missing a step, Paulo cut right, grabbed the cat from the bushes, and spun around; he threw the cat directly into the shimmering gate. Rainbows of glittering light washed over the cat. Paulo staggered toward the sea, triumph warming his face as the cat vanished. *Let the cat take this wild gate,* he thought with pleasure, *a ticket to an unknown place. My time has yet to come.*

Paulo had business to finish, and the will to see it through.

The gate winked out; the sea breeze kicked up without break.

Noon was over.

Paulo rested his hands on his hips as he tilted his face toward the mountain. *Nice try*, he thought, a smile pulling at his lips. *But I'm still here, still fighting. And I'm not done yet.*

From his vantage point in the trees, Hafthor watched the dark-haired boy with interest. For the past few minutes, the boy had darted and dodged two separate walls of glistening air, walls identical to the one that had captured Hafthor back in Iceland. The boy's speed and agility were remarkable. Equally remarkable was the expression on the boy's face: determination, and peace. He had no intention of touching either of those walls, and he hadn't.

He knows something about this place. Hafthor eyed the boy's clean white cotton shorts and the tribal tattoo on his bare shoulder. *Something important I don't.*

This person was one he needed to meet.

As the boy turned away, Hafthor stepped from the trees.

"Hallo," he said, lifting his hand in greeting.

The boy swiveled back. He didn't look the least bit surprised to see him, nor did he gape at Hafthor's bedraggled palm-frond skirt. Instead, the boy smiled. A kind smile, one that inspired trust.

"I'm Paulo." The boy walked up and offered his hand.

"Hafthor."

They clasped hands briefly and let go.

"Tell me of those walls." Hafthor pointed back to where the shimmering walls had vanished. "They brought us here, yes? But they are dangerous?"

"Yes, and no." Paulo glanced at the mountain. "Let's head to the City. I'll fill you in on the gates and everything else I know. And we'll get you something more comfortable to wear." A wry smile twisted his mouth. "Welcome to Nil."

The thrill of noon had passed, and the lack of conflict was utterly dull. As the pair turned north, the island turned away. It turned inward, toward the seam, the fissure between worlds, because this world needed more humans. It was time to search for another, one more like the female, Carmen. But until it found the right choice, the island would toy with the one that got away: the female, Skye.

She hadn't broken yet, a pleasant surprise, for when she did, the pain would be exquisite. The fight itself was proving to be as much fun as the break would be. And the snap of her mind would come; she was so much like her predecessor from years before, a male, Scott. He had thought himself a match for the island.

He had been no match at all.

But this female was different. Special. She fought, hard, with an intensity that was admirable, but in the end, she would bend to the island too. And then she would break.

They all did.

Perhaps she wasn't special after all, the island thought with disappointment. After all, she was only human.

Abruptly it tired of her.

It wanted to break her, now.

CHAPTER 10

SKYE
JUNE 5, AFTER NOON

Something has changed.

The day I got too close to the edge, the fragile balance between me and the darkness shifted, and not in my favor. Now I know I *can't* win, not if the darkness brings all it has to our battle. It's bigger than me, *stronger* than me, and suddenly, more intent on *me*. On *consuming* me, as crazy as that sounds. But the defiant part of me refuses to accept that the war is already lost. Maybe it's not the strength of the fighter but size of the heart that decides the victor.

I don't think the darkness has a heart.

But I do.

It gives me a chance; it must. It's what I tell myself to give myself hope. Because there's always hope, right? It's what I told Paulo, once.

Paulo.

At first I thought the voice belonged to Paulo, asking why I left him behind. Then I thought it was Dex, asking why I chose him. Why I *didn't* choose him.

Now I know it's someone else entirely. Someone as trapped by the darkness as I am.

The voice belongs to a girl, and my instincts tell me she's in trouble.

That makes two of us.

My name is Skye Bracken, and I'm still here. Barely. This is the sad truth.

CHAPTER 11

RIVES
JUNE 7, DEAD OF NIGHT

I'm losing Skye.

She lay beside me in the dark, my arm curved around her waist. Her last nightmare had just faded; her trembling finally stopped.

But she wasn't asleep.

Not by a long shot.

Lately she barely slept at all. She was a walking ghost. Pale, eyes rimmed in gray, drifting through the day, a shadow of herself.

It made me furious, because I was so damn helpless.

Skye relaxed, then to my relief, she finally drifted off. She'd barely slept five minutes before she tensed.

"No!" she rasped, her entire body rigid, her fists balled tight around the sheet.

"Skye," I whispered. "It's just a dream."

I caught the wisp of a giggle. A cruel cackle, cloaked in the dark. But it wasn't Skye laughing, and nothing about the night was funny.

It was a remnant of Nil.

You let us go, I thought. Fury ripped through my veins. *It's over.*

You left, came the thought, cold and amused. *But I never let you go.*

Fifteen minutes later Skye's nightmare roared back.

Wake, dream, scream, repeat.

When the day broke, I shook off the dark. It was time to get Skye help, *now*. And I knew exactly who to call.

I slipped onto the balcony and rang Skye's dad.

He answered in seconds. "Rives?" Concern rippled through his voice. "Is everything all right?"

"I need your help." I paused. "Something's wrong with Skye, and it has to do with Nil."

CHAPTER 12

NIL
AFTER NOON

This one may have been a poor choice.

The sense of him during passage was profound, both his strength and flaws. The island waited for him to wake, knowing that the time to choose a different one had passed. Time was the one element out of the island's control.

Now the male was here.

The rest would be up to him.

In recent weeks, the island's capacity for guidance and protection had shrunk dramatically, especially with the energy constantly directed toward the ones beyond the seam, an expenditure of electria both necessary and debilitating.

More precious electria had been required to sustain those humans already here.

The last of the island's waning power had been needed to acquire four-legged creatures rather than two-, for the humans did not bring enough to sustain themselves. However, the behavior of such creatures and the humans' reactions to them were as unpredictable as the humans themselves. Sometimes the humans saved the creatures, sometimes they killed them, their choices bewildering at best.

The island marveled at the humans' capacity for compassion and cruelty in equal parts. It was amazed by the depth of love and hate and passion and callousness, of selfishness and selflessness. Never before had the island experienced such a range of emotion, such a boundless capacity to destroy, and also, to save. And to hope. Each arrival held a seed of faith—in themselves, in others, in their future, in something greater. Some seeds were larger than others, but all were to be nurtured, for with that growth came strength.

And the island needed the strength desperately.

But it would not take more than it needed, for there was strength in restraint, too. A strength born of free will, another lesson the humans had taught the island. Now, choice remained the island's best hope, and of course, hope itself. Hope that the humans would see what must be done, both now and in the days to come.

The male stirred.

Withdrawing, the island waited.

Calvin groaned, his head clearing abruptly. Within seconds, he was on his feet, running.

Around him, black rock stretched for miles, an eerie land, foreign and silent. Rock as charcoal black as the soundless tunnel he'd just passed through, with a doorway he'd barely seen. He'd been stalking through the parking lot, pissed off at having to run laps after Coach called him out for slacking off, as if he hadn't already proven that he was the best. The best sprinter, the best athlete on the team—the best athlete in the *state*, period. After all, he'd won the Mr. Football award as a junior, solid proof that he was the best. Hell, he was the best running back the state of Alabama had ever seen. He knew it.

He also knew that right now, he was seriously screwed; he just didn't understand how, or why. Darkness had appeared in front of his face, then swallowed him whole. Darkness that had seared his skin like an invisible brand, so painful that when the fire turned to ice, it still burned. And it stayed unnaturally black.

And now he ran, across charcoal ground like an ancient firepit of giants. No matter he'd already run six miles before the air swallowed him, no matter that his thighs still ached. He pushed himself across the open rock, not sure where he was running to or what he was running from. He was six feet two, with muscles cut from stone, shaped by his father, a former defensive back for the Chicago Bears and the pride of Dothan, Alabama. He hadn't been afraid to stand up to his coach, to tell him he was wrong. To tell Coach that he, Calvin Jackson, had the best legs on the team and Coach was damn lucky to have him anchor the 400-meter relay. He hadn't been afraid, not then.

But now, as he ran over the rocks, he was terrified. He'd never been afraid, not like this. Despite the blue sky, all he saw was black.

Swirling blackness coursed through his head, a churning, seething darkness that seemed a direct reflection of his feelings in the moment the hot air engulfed him.

It's not a coincidence, he thought with fear. *I'm being punished.*

And he ran on, desperately, not sure what he was searching for.

The one called Calvin certainly enjoyed the feel of flight.

He ran, his electria flowing through his veins and muscles and tissue with impressive force and endurance.

But the depth and breadth of the male's fear was highly disappointing.

Fear opened the door to darkness; sometimes fear was the door. The island accepted the unfortunate possibility that fear would dominate this male, a counterproductive development. Fear wasn't inherently negative, but with these humans it certainly could be.

Perhaps the island had chosen in error. Perhaps the island had been drawn to the wrong sort of strength. It had happened before.

But as the one called Calvin ran on, the island reserved judgment. Perhaps he would surprise the island. That had happened before too. Regardless, he was strong. And he was here.

Despite the new blood, the island still wanted her.

It needed her, the one called Skye. The island understood her like no other, as she understood the island.

But the island could not understand why she had not seen.

The island felt the weight of time, the inherent intractability of it. The island had reached for her over and over again, pushing the limits of both the barrier and her mind. Still, she remained frustratingly out of reach, even after the shift in power she had brought upon herself. It was a reality the island could not help but admire. Her force of will was strong as iron, forged in a cauldron not of the island's making.

That must change, the island decided.

Her will must bend for the island, not against it. Because if she did not answer soon, the time for her to answer would pass and the consequences would be disastrous. The island's reserves leached out like time, with time, bleeding power with each hour that passed. Soon the island would not be able to call her at all, or keep the seam intact.

Yes, the island decided, watching the male run, thinking of her. The time was now. A new card must be played. It would not be easy, or without pain, but the one called Skye was strong. She could bear it.

And so it would be.

With all the force it could muster, the island summoned the past to win the future. To win her.

Skye.

CHAPTER 13

SKYE
JUNE 10, MORNING

Skye.

Look at me, Skye. Look at me.

She sounded closer than ever before.

LOOK.

Fine, I snapped. *You win.* She'd been begging me all night. *I'll look.*

I turned toward her voice and was shocked to actually *see* her; she was extraordinarily clear. A girl my age stood in the darkness, as real and alive and tired as me; she didn't float inside the darkness but rather seemed bound by it. A sense of kinship washed through me as she reached out, her blue eyes desperate. She was as trapped as I was; we shared a nightmare from which I couldn't wake.

Help me. Choose me.

I stepped closer. I needed to help her, to pull her free.

Maybe she would free us both.

The thought brought a sense of hope I hadn't felt in weeks.

The darkness didn't move. Her lips did.

Skye.

SKYE.

Rives's voice drowned out the girl's, which was odd because he wasn't shouting and I couldn't see him. But I could hear him, in the dark, in this faraway place where I hadn't heard him lately at all—and then I felt him. His voice wrapped me in warmth, pulling me close by a velvet thread. He was my tether, my grounding force. I would not be lost, not with Rives. The tether went taut.

The girl faded; the darkness surged.

Panic rose. Rives shouldn't be here, not this far into the dark. The darkness's greed seeped into the marrow of my bones: it wanted Rives, too. Suddenly I was terrified—for me, for Rives, for the girl . . . for all of us fighting in the dark, together but very much alone.

Rives! My shout vanished without an echo, blackness filling my mouth in the wake of my words.

I woke, abruptly wrenched into the light, gulping air.

Rives's name lingered on my lips, but the real flesh-and-blood version sat beside me on the couch. He looked sick as he studied me.

"Are you okay?" I reached for his face, but he intercepted my hand.

"Stop," he said. "What about *you?* You were dreaming. And screaming. I had to shake you awake, Skye. Ready to talk about it?"

"I can't even remember." I stretched, smiling, taking pains to slow my breathing.

Rives stared at me. "You're an atrocious liar, you know that? Like the Oscar-winning performance of a bad liar." Lines of sunlight streaked across his face from the open shutters, but his eyes stayed shadowed. "Your nightmares are getting worse, Skye. You can't ignore them anymore. We have to deal with it. If you won't talk to me, what about Jillian?"

I looked away.

Stop, a tiny part of myself said. *Stop pressing. Don't make me go there in the day.*

"I already talked to Jillian, remember?" I offered casually. *She's got her own demons to face*, I wanted to say. *She doesn't need mine, too.* But instead I said, "And I've talked to Charley a ton. I'm good."

Rives watched me, his expression grim.

"C'mon, Rives." Reaching up, I wound my fingers through his hair. It had grown longer since Nil, long enough for me to pull him gently to me, to pull his mouth to mine. I kissed him with all that I had, this boy I loved so deeply it hurt.

Please let it go, my lips said.

"Don't worry." I murmured this plea against closed lips.

He tipped his forehead against mine. "It's not that easy, Skye."

"I know." I sat up quietly, then glanced around for my shoes, purposely avoiding his too-intense gaze. Sometimes Rives saw more than I wanted him to see; sometimes he saw meaning in little things I missed myself. But even if he saw it, I didn't want to dwell on the darkness right now, or the girl invading my dreams. "We're going to Lake Como today, right?" I said brightly.

"Wrong," Rives said decisively. "Change of plans. We're going to Gainesville. We're booked on an afternoon flight."

"What? Why?"

"Because we've got to figure your nightmares out." He ran a hand through his hair. "Maybe it's some sort of post-traumatic island stress, but whatever it is, you don't sleep. And it's scaring the hell out of me. It's gotten worse. And you won't talk to me, Skye. Won't let me in your head." His voice cracked. "Maybe your dad can help. It's worth a shot."

The hopeful expression on Rives's face nearly brought me to tears, but I wouldn't cry. It drained me, and I needed every bit of strength I had left. And now that I considered it, Rives had an excellent point. My dad was the only Nil expert we had. For all I knew, he'd helped Uncle Scott back in the day, and if there was one thing I knew, it was that my dreams were linked to Nil.

"Okay," I said slowly. "Fine. We'll go to Gainesville and talk to my dad. Maybe he can—"

Rives dipped down and kissed me as fiercely as I'd kissed him, derailing my train of thought, a desperate kiss full of want and relief, as if he'd expected me to fight his plan. His lips lingered on my throat, then he groaned as he cupped my face in his hands. "I'd better stop if we plan to make our plane."

He hopped up and began moving around the room, gathering his things, his steps light. "You'd better get packing too, my Skye." He pointed a rolled-up T-shirt at me. "We leave in two hours."

"Aye, aye, Captain." I saluted as I stood.

"So we're pirates now?" He raised an eyebrow, grinning. "Or is it once a pirate, always a pirate? I do recall you commandeered a canoe once."

"And aren't you glad I did?" *Otherwise I wouldn't have met you.*

Dropping the shirt, he swung me around, then deposited me on the floor with a swashbuckling kiss. "You have no idea how glad," he murmured.

"Actually I do." Tracing his jaw, I thought of all that Nil had shared with us in our last moments on the island. "And you know I do."

"True." He kissed me again. "An honest pirate, you are. Now get packing, matey."

"So bossy, Captain," I said with a smirk. But I couldn't stop smiling. I gathered my clothes as Rives did the same. We joked and laughed and things between us and around us felt both perfect and perfectly normal for a blissful few minutes. Somehow I knew everything would be okay; it had to be.

I had to be.

We'd come too far for me to lose it now.

Still, at the airport, I bought a Red Bull and chugged it in one fell swoop while Rives was in the restroom. I didn't want to make a big deal of it but I desperately needed the caffeine.

I didn't dare fall asleep on the plane.

CHAPTER
14

RIVES
JUNE 10, NOON

We buckled into our seats at noon.

Beside me, Skye pulled a book out of her backpack. At least it wasn't her journal.

I looked out the window, rewinding the hell of last night. A night that was no different from the ones before—and that was the problem. Watching Skye battle her inner demons all night long sucked; it was worse than patrolling Nil City's perimeter in full dark. At least back on Nil, I felt like I was doing something. Guarding the City, guarding people I cared about. Here, I was more than useless. I couldn't help Skye. All I could do was wake her up.

It was why I'd called her dad.

He'd listened quietly as I'd detailed Skye's rampant insomnia, her daytime distance, and her brutal night terrors. I'd even tossed in her recent energy drink addiction. She thought she was so stealthy, but she couldn't hide the empties from me.

All she could hide were her thoughts, which sucked.

I used to be able to read her mind. Literally hear her thoughts; they drifted through my head through some potent connection forged in our last moments on Nil. A connection forged *by* Nil. But lately that connection had weakened, because Skye had blocked me out. More like *locked* me out—of her head, out of her thoughts. Where Skye's mind used to be was a Nil-black wall. Maybe it was self-preservation, maybe it was to protect me. Either way, I hated it.

We used to protect each other.

I glanced over. Her snack sat untouched, her book unopened. She'd actually fallen asleep. Lips slightly parted, eyes closed, Skye breathed in a slow but steady rhythm. Considering the Red Bull she'd downed earlier, the fact that she'd crashed out upright was impressive.

Sleep, I thought, willing the moment to stretch out long enough for Skye to score some solid REM. Surely the shadows under her eyes would fade with rest, the crescent moons banished once and for all.

I'd no sooner had that thought when she jerked. Her hand gripped mine, her nails digging into my palm. "What do you want?" she croaked. Her voice sounded constricted, like she was underwater.

"Skye." I brushed her cheek with my free hand. "Wake up."

Skye's eyelids flew open, her chest heaving, her hand holding mine in a death grip. She turned to me and my heart stopped. Her steel-flecked eyes were packed with fear and desperation and something else, something potent.

Want, I thought. They were packed with *want*.

But it wasn't want for me.

I held her gaze. "Who are you talking to?"

"No one." She averted her eyes.

"Skye. Look at me. Please."

She did. Haunted eyes, packed with Nil ghosts.

"Are you talking to Nil?" I asked bluntly.

To my relief, she shook her head.

"Then who?"

She did that chew-on-the-inside-of-her-mouth thing that she always did when she was thinking—especially when she was deciding how much to share.

"A girl," she said finally. "I hear her, Rives. Every night. Every *nap*. Every time I fall asleep. She won't leave me alone."

I frowned. "A girl? Like, someone you know?"

"No. I don't know her, but she knows me. She knows my name." She hesitated. "I think she's in trouble, that she needs help. But how can I help her?" Her haunted expression gave way to frustration. "I know it took me longer than normal to come through that return gate; Jillian told me that. Which means I was in that darkness longer than anyone." Skye met my gaze straight on. "Do you think Nil did something to me during my last gate trip, while I was in that darkness between? Something that makes me hear people in trouble? People in trouble *here*, in this world?" Skye looked at me like I might have a clue. Like she *hoped* I had a clue.

I had nothing.

Would I ever stop being wholly pissed off with Nil?

"Quit being all mad and think, would you?" Smiling, Skye squeezed my hand.

God, I loved her.

I refocused. "Of course Nil did something to you. To me, to *us*. But, do I think you can hear people in distress, in this world or dimension or whatever?" I shrugged. "I don't know. It's a stretch. But I wouldn't rule it out." I regarded Skye thoughtfully. "This girl," I said slowly, focusing on the key problem keeping Skye awake, "have you seen her? Or do you just hear her?"

"I used to just hear her. But . . ." Skye twisted one wild curl of her hair as she spoke, a nervous Skye tic if there ever was one. "Now I see her. She's so real. I have a clear picture in my head of what she looks like. I don't know if I'm just imagining it, or if that's really her. Or if I made it all up." She gave a weird laugh. "Maybe I'm losing it."

"You're not losing it. I believe you. And maybe if you think about her, I'll see her too."

Hope lit Skye's face, erasing the ghosts. "That's a great idea." She took my free hand in hers. Holding both of my hands tight, she pressed as close as the armrest allowed and slowly touched her forehead to mine. "Close your eyes," she whispered.

I did.

The other passengers faded away; awareness of Skye filled me like light. Like life and blood and bone and breath. Eyes closed, hands tight, I felt our connection, solid and real, far deeper than the press of skin between our palms, but when I reached for Skye in my mind, all I found was blackness: an unyielding black wall as solid and massive as the one I'd hit when I sucked down deadsleep tea on Nil.

But we weren't on Nil; we were on a plane. And I'd given up dead-sleep tea months ago.

The disappointment tasted as bitter now as the tea had then.

Pulling away, I opened my eyes. Skye's expression was eager, her eyes overly bright.

"Did you see her?" Her hopeful tone crushed something deep inside me.

"Skye." I chose my words carefully. "I think you've been shutting me out for so long that you can't let me in. You know how when we first got back, you could hear my thoughts and I could hear yours?"

She nodded.

"Lately I haven't heard anything from you. It's like your mind is closed off. I just hit a wall." I smiled slightly. "But I'll give you credit, Skye. It's an intense wall. Pure black. Impenetrable. You don't do anything halfway."

Skye froze. "What did you just say?"

"That you don't do anything halfway."

"Before that. About the black."

"Each time I reach for you here"—I tapped my head—"I run into a solid wall of black. I can't tell whether you're locking me out or locking yourself in."

Skye had gone white.

"No," she whispered. Then she sighed. "Crap. It's both, I guess. I *have* been blocking you out. I didn't want you to know about my nightmares, I didn't want to drag you in." She laughed humorlessly. "But I guess I already have."

"I don't follow."

Skye looked at me with her no-holds-barred expression. "Every night I dream of blackness, like the darkness between gates, Rives. Every time I *sleep*. It's alive, Rives. I know it. There's a speck of light though, too, and I think that's where the girl is, inside the darkness. But the darkness—" She fought a shiver. "It's real and powerful and it wants something from me, just like the girl."

The darkness is real and powerful and it wants something from me.

Dread flooded my gut. The darkness sounded bad. Like demon-spawn-of-Nil bad.

"The darkness." I forced myself to stay calm. "Can you show me? Can you let me in, not that you're not intentionally locking me out?"

"I'll try." She closed her eyes.

Rives. Skye's thought, calm and clear.

A summons.

An invitation.

A mental lock clicked, a wall shifted. I was holding Skye's hand; I was following her *through*. An expanse of black filled my head; it slammed me back into my seat from the sheer scope of it. Before I'd only brushed the edge, like touching the tide at the high-water mark. I fully grasped that until now, Skye had kept me out. Held me back.

She had protected me.

But now, I saw it; I *felt* it. It was yawning and hungry and full-on Nil black. And it desperately wanted *her.*

How could she not see it?

I'd never felt so afraid, because I didn't understand. Or maybe I did. My flash of insight brought a whole new level of terror.

"Did you see it?" she asked. Still hopeful.

"Yeah." I swallowed, still reeling from the onslaught of black. "It was—" I grappled with the word to sum up the darkness, and failed.

"Intense." I looked at her. "No more, Skye. Don't lock me out. We're a team. You don't have to do this alone, whatever this is."

She nodded and exhaled, her relief clear.

Looking at our hands, Skye traced a swirling line on my palm, a path reminiscent of the Man in the Maze. "What you saw?" Her voice was as soft as her touch. "I know it doesn't seem that bad but it's so much worse when I actually sleep, Rives." She flinched. "When I sleep," she continued, "the darkness is alive. It reaches for me even as the girl calls to me. The more I try to listen to her, the harder it is to fight the darkness. It's like I can't have it both ways. And when I fall asleep, I'm scared I won't wake up. Ever." Her voice had dropped to a whisper.

"That won't happen." I pressed my palm against hers, leaving no space between them. "I won't let that happen. Next time you fall asleep, I'll be there. With you." I didn't know how—hell, I didn't understand what was even going on—but I refused to lose her to invisible demons, especially demons born of Nil.

She nodded. "You always are, you know. You always bring me back. But lately"—she looked away—"you don't hear me."

My blood chilled. "What do you mean, I don't hear you?"

"You don't answer." She bit the inside of her cheek.

"I don't answer," I repeated.

I'm failing her.

The thought made me furious. Where was my fighting chance? My fair shot? How the hell was I supposed to be her mental knight in shining armor when I'd no clue what I was fighting? We were pawns in a game without rules, or with rules we didn't know. I had the sick sense it was the latter. Nil-created, perhaps Nil-directed. A Nil tendril, in this world.

"Rives." Skye's voice was quiet. "It's not your fault; if anything, it's mine, and not just because I've blocked you out. I think I go so far into the darkness that you can't hear me. So far that it pulls me in farther than I want, far enough to pull me away from you. For those few seconds, it wins." She closed her eyes. "And that's when I scream, and you don't answer."

Merde.

It was a nightmare reaching into the light, full of fangs and claws. If I could see it, I'd punch it in the face, beat it back. Beat it to death.

But I couldn't see it. And that was the problem.

I focused on the solution. On *Skye*. On what mattered.

"Skye, listen. This thing, this *darkness*, it doesn't win. Ever. You're in control. You're stronger than whatever the hell this thing is. Remember, it's in *your* head. And if you locked me out, you can lock the darkness out too, right?"

"I guess." Skye didn't sound convinced. She sounded exhausted. She rested her head on my shoulder as I wove my fingers through hers.

"It's going to be okay," I said adamantly. "We'll get through this, whatever this is. And if Nil did something to you, we'll work through it, together. That's why Nil gave us that gift, right? Our connection. So you don't have to do this alone, okay?"

"Okay," Skye whispered. For a long moment she didn't speak. "I'm so tired, Rives. And I feel like I'm failing the girl. How can I help her if I don't know who she is?" Her steel-flecked eyes glittered behind a slight film of tears. Skye rarely cried. Only when she was angry or flat-out spent, and right now, I knew it was the latter.

She was beyond exhausted.

And the mystery girl was partially to blame. Maybe if we could get the nightmare chick to leave, she'd take the darkness with her and let Skye sleep.

"Try again," I said suddenly. "Show me what the girl looks like. Now that you're not consciously keeping me out, maybe I can help. Two is always better than one, right?"

"Right." She sat up straight and squared her shoulders, Skye-fierce. "Close your eyes," she said. "I'm going to focus on the picture I have of her in my head. Don't think of the blackness, okay? Focus on the girl's voice. It's what works for me."

I thought of Skye. Of her smile, her laugh, her passionate *I-will-take-you-down* look that she faced Nil with every damn day. I thought of the girl who made me want to breathe and live. The girl who took on the blackness in her head and gave it a cold shoulder.

I thought of *us*, of our connection. A golden thread linking us both.

The darkness washed through my head with a powerful iciness, pulling me deeper as I held Skye's hand in mine; our connection pulled taut, a potent thread that I couldn't see but could feel. A light flickered, like a bulb on the brink of failure. I focused, and it brightened into a beacon. Into a tunnel. No, a halo, a flash of blond. An outline. A face.

A girl. A voice.

No.

And I knew that voice.

I knew *her*.

A face flashed full and crisp, a high-def nightmare made real.

My eyes flew open; I couldn't breathe. *This is not happening.*

"What?" Skye leaned close, her eyes full of hope. "Did you see her? Blond hair? Big eyes?"

"I saw her." My voice sounded remote.

"You saw her," Skye breathed in wonder. "She's real. So maybe we can save her."

I shook my head. "We can't save her."

"Why not?"

"Because she's already dead," I said flatly. "I buried her, on Nil. Her name was Talla."

CHAPTER
15

NIL
AFTER NOON

It would be so easy, the island marveled with delight, relishing what lay ahead. Their connection was so strong, so entwined, that breaking one would break the other. The island would shatter them both, a reward of two for the effort of one.

Perhaps it had been wrong to focus on her all these weeks. Perhaps he was the one to break.

The one who would break, the one who could be broken.

Yes, the island reasoned, reviewing the history of the male, Rives. He'd nearly broken once, over a female, the one with electria so powerful it had taken all the island's restraint not to take her on her Day 1. How fun—and unexpected—to bring this male to the point of fracture again, to push him beyond. And this time, he would take the female, Skye, with him. Their connection would be their undoing.

Abruptly the island's focus shifted.

Like a scent on the wind, darkness called, demanding attention. Still reaching beyond the seam, the island pivoted toward another male, a different one with no connections worthy of interest. The stench of his pride tainted his soul, a window to the darkness within. There was always darkness, and the island was drawn to it. The island was drawn to him.

The gate caught him unaware.

He was easy to find, easy to take. He would be easy to manipulate.
The island trembled with the rush of new blood.

Ace woke slowly, disoriented.

Blood leaked down his cheek from where he'd scraped his face on the ground, but he didn't wipe it; he was too intent on his surroundings, fighting a slice of anger and a bigger wave of annoyance. He had plans for today and this detour wasn't a part of them.

He'd always hated surprises.

Ace hopped to all fours as he looked around. Charred ground surrounded him, unfamiliar and eerily quiet. Something terrible had happened here; he felt it.

Something that now involved him.

He had the freak thought that he'd brought this upon himself. After all, he'd just ratted out Mikey, a classic jerk move if there ever was one, but it wasn't Mikey's butt on the line now; it was Ace's. And technically, Mikey had taken the money. He was the muscle; Ace was the brains—and the beauty. His perfect abs were pure icing on the Ace cake, and girls loved it. Loved *him*.

Mikey had never had much of a backbone, and Ace had never had much of a conscience.

But damn, even if karma had kicked him here, this scene was messed *up*. And by the standards of his world, that was saying something.

Suddenly Ace knew.

Someone kidnapped me—to send a message to Dad. Ace half smiled, knowing if that was the case, his dad would come bail him out—or send someone who would. His dad knew people. But first his dad would set things right, or make things right with the right people. Which meant, for now, Ace was on his own.

The breeze rustled at his back. He turned to find a blackened corpse resting a few feet away and he froze. Something had burned here, and some*one*. Even though it was long gone, he could practically smell the burned flesh. That scent wasn't new for Ace, but the lack of total control was.

I'm out, he thought abruptly. He stepped quickly, moving away from the charred body and scorched earth, not sure where to go except away from death. *Never get your hands dirty*, his dad had taught him.

He left the dirty work to others—just like his dad.

And now his hands were coated in soot.

Ace frowned.

The island was so captivated watching the first male, it nearly missed the second. A rare mistake.

The second one whimpered.

He bled, too, christening island dirt with his DNA, weeping from a slash on his forearm. He'd landed out of sight of the first male, their view of each other conveniently blocked by the surviving thicket. Fresh blood pumped through the second male's veins, shock mixing with panic and pain.

The island breathed deeply, inhaling the scent of fear.

The second male cowered in the island breeze, retreating into himself as if he held the escape route inside, which, the island pondered, was not altogether untrue. The island examined this male carefully; it sifted through his thoughts, catalogued his reactions, isolated his fear. Like the first male, he had not seen the gate coming. Then he had been surprised; now, he was terrified. He did not move. His fear had shut down his reactions. At this rate, this male would perish before ever reaching anywhere close to his full potential, his true electria wasted.

A test, the island decided. To determine whether the second male had potential for growth, or whether his weakness was an inherent flaw too ingrained to change. It was illogical to wait to take power that would never develop. The test would begin, now.

The island breeze whipped in a new direction, blowing the scent of rotting meat toward the far corner of the meadow, along with the smell of fresh blood.

This male's blood.

Past the burn line, two heads pricked above the grasses. They sniffed once. Moving in tandem, the pair slunk forward. Acting on instinct, the hyenas parted ranks, cornering the injured male with predatory precision.

The male had yet to move, panic rendering him powerless. Still cowed in a frozen stance, his eyes flicked around, landing on the hyenas one heartbeat too late. Snarling, they attacked without mercy, a flash of fur and teeth and blood.

The male's last breath came quickly, his electria flowing from him to the island in a rush. He was no more, as if he had never been.

The island jerked with the surge of power, pleased.

The ground shook under Ace's feet, then stilled.

Earthquake? he wondered. He glanced around.

To the east, what looked like a pair of hyenas were attacking something with gusto. He didn't know a single thing about hyenas, but interrupting any animal while eating was a bad call, so Ace quickly walked the other way. Every bone in his body screamed for him to run, but he didn't want to risk the hyenas making takeout of him. His pulse pounded in his ears, making it tough to think. And he needed a clear head to get out of the nightmare of whatever the hell this was. *Wherever* the hell this was.

But where and what didn't matter.

He'd thought his way out of every mess he'd ever been in; he just needed to find the right angle, the right mark. All Ace knew for certain was that it wasn't behind him.

Striding forward, Ace wondered where his clothes had gone. Same for his wallet full of cash. The loss of money pissed him off; he couldn't give a rat's ass about his jeans. He didn't care who saw him naked. He looked good without clothes and he knew it. But the money hurt.

He'd worked hard for that. Sort of.

He stopped, taken aback.

Ahead of him, a rhino snorted beside a small group of spindly trees. An elephant stood a football field's length to the right. *How in the world did I end up in Africa on a solo safari?* Someone was messing with him. His dad would be royally pissed.

Then Ace squinted. A girl stood on the black rock, looking like a *Sports Illustrated* vision in the flesh. Tube top over a nice rack, full hips covered by a tight skirt, caramel skin, long black braid, full lips. The knife in her hand was the perfect accessory.

Ace smiled, fear giving way to calculation.

As the new male strode toward the fighter, the island observed his posture, and his posturing. The fighter, Carmen, stood ready; she was observing too. She was the island's trophy; he was the toy.

The fun had begun.

Those beyond the seam could wait. They would wait, suffering as the seeds already planted took root, growing until they fractured the foundation. And the two beyond the seam would no longer be one.

The island would feel the moment when they broke, and would revel in it.

Until then, these two demanded the island's full attention. And they would have it.

CHAPTER 16

SKYE
JUNE 10, EARLY AFTERNOON

It's not every day you find out you're being haunted by your boy-friend's ex-girlfriend. I guess today was my lucky day. The girl in the darkness was Talla, a girl Rives might have loved. A girl Rives had buried. And not only was I seeing Talla, *in my freaking head*, I was hearing her. She knew my name.

She knew *me*.

No wonder Rives looked so shaken. He was as pale as the clouds outside my window, his body unnaturally still. His eyes had an emptiness I didn't like at all.

"Maybe it's memories," I said stubbornly. "Maybe I'm pulling them from your head."

"You don't really think that, do you?" he said. Same emotionless tone, like he'd passed some critical line and was shutting down. But he gripped my hand so tight it hurt, as if he were afraid I'd vanish in midair.

"No," I admitted. "But how can I hear her, Rives? I never met her. It makes no sense."

"Nothing about Nil does," Rives said, his face like stone. "Not then, not now. We need to talk to your dad." He leaned his head back against the headrest, but he didn't let go of my hand. "I love you, Skye. More than

I ever knew it was possible to love someone. If I lost you—" He broke off, his jaw working as he swallowed, fighting to stay in control.

"You won't." I leaned over and kissed his temple.

He said nothing.

A weird, wired silence fell between us. Around us, business went on as usual. The flight attendants moved smoothly down the aisle, passing out cool beverages with warm smiles; a woman with her hair twisted up and speared by a pencil worked furiously on a laptop, totally intense; a balding man leisurely browsed the front page of a newspaper in a language I couldn't read; a boy sat beside us, headphones on, rocking out to tunes I couldn't hear. Nothing out of the ordinary, *except the fact that Rives's dead girlfriend was in my head.*

It was as extraordinary—and as extraordinarily creepy—as Nil.

I tried not to picture Talla, but with Rives beside me, I had no choice. His mind was in overdrive, so naturally, mine was too. We usually only heard each other when the thoughts were specifically directed toward the other, or when the thoughts were rich with emotion. And now that I'd consciously let Rives back in, our mental connection had resurfaced full force. Now Rives's thoughts flew through my head without break, flashes of another Nil. Another *time*, one painfully real and just, well, *painful*.

Talla, the girl trapped in my head, fully alive with Rives.

I'd never seen her so clearly.

Talla sprinting down the beach, her face in hard profile, her long blond hair swinging behind her; Talla strapping on a glider harness, her chin lifted and abs tight; Talla talking to Rives with sparkling eyes, an angry bruise on her face; Talla holding a spear in her hand, a dead rabbit in the other, her expression cool; Talla paddling out on a surfboard, her eyes bright, looking like there was no place she'd rather be; Talla closing her eyes in Rives's arms in the darkness, her smile relaxed; Talla lifeless in Rives's arms in the daylight, her eyes closed forever.

I couldn't block her out, couldn't stop the flow of memories; they rode cascading waves of Rives's lingering pain and growing fury. Soon it was too much. Some things I didn't want to know, memories that weren't mine but hurt as if they were. And if it was too much for me, it was killing Rives.

"Rives." I turned to him. "You're torturing yourself."

His jaw spasmed. "And Nil's torturing you."

"Not really."

He laughed harshly. "How can you say that, Skye? Nil won't let you sleep, and now you're hearing the voice of someone I buried."

"How?" I asked, my eyes searching his. "How is this even possible?"

He shook his head. With his free hand, he pinched the bridge of his nose, breathing shallowly; his other hand still held mine tight. "I hate it. I absolutely *hate* it, Skye. We made it. We *left*. So why is the island still messing with you? With us?"

"I don't know." My voice was soft. "But until we talk to my dad, talk to me. Tell me about Talla. Maybe if I know more about her, I'll know what to do. What was she like?" *Besides apparently a very fit blond badass.*

He half smiled. "She *was* a very fit blond badass. She was the most competitive person I've ever met." He paused. I knew he was turning his feelings into thoughts, shaping his thoughts into words. "She was a swimmer," he said quietly. "She'd placed second in the US Nationals in the four-hundred-meter free not long before she landed on Nil. It killed her to be second. She wanted to win. To be the best, at everything she did. She dreamed of the Olympics." He sighed. "But Nil stole that from her." He looked out the window, visibly struggling to keep himself together. "Talla the girl? She wasn't exactly warm and fuzzy. But she was incredibly honest and loyal to a fault, like someone else I know." He rubbed his thumb across my palm. "I don't know if Jillian ever said anything, but there are certain things about you that remind me of Talla. At first it kind of scared me, to tell you the truth. But then I got to know you, and fell for everything that makes you Skye. Including the parts that reminded me of Talla." He said this all matter-of-factly, but I felt the rawness of it.

"She was Jillian's best friend on Nil." A statement, not a question.

"She was. But Jillian also was close to Charley, and Macy. And later, you. But we buried Talla, Skye. And we said good-bye." He turned to me in disbelief. "I can't wrap my head around this. Or maybe I just don't want to." His last words were quiet.

"Me either. But we're going to have to."

Rives nodded, but said nothing.

There was nothing else to say.

An hour after we landed, my dad couldn't wrap his head around the situation either. And the expression on his face told me he liked Talla's voice in my head even less than Rives did. Rives had gone for a run, giving us some space, probably trying to find some space in his own head. I wouldn't mind going for a run myself. I wouldn't mind running until I was too tired to dream, think, or be haunted.

It was wishful thinking.

Dad still looked shell-shocked. He hadn't moved from his makeshift desk in his temporary office in Mom's guest room. I maneuvered around a towering stack of books on the floor to stand directly in front of my dad.

I waved my hand in front of his face. I needed him thinking clearly, and back on track.

"For the love of Nil, focus, Dad. Did Uncle Scott have dreams about darkness when he got back? Or dreams about any person in particular?"

My dad didn't answer immediately, but at least he looked coherent. "He did have dreams when he got back from Nil," he said finally. "Nightmares, too. I remember him waking up. Sweating, sometimes talking. We shared a room, so I witnessed that myself. From what I recall, he mostly dreamed of Jenny. He called for her in his sleep, doodled her name on paper. You know that from the journal. He thought of her constantly; he told me that point-blank. And I know he went to find her." Regret flashed across my dad's face. "He had other dreams too, Nil-related I'm sure, but he never mentioned dreams of darkness.

55

However," he added quickly, smiling supportively, "that doesn't mean he didn't have them."

"What about dead people?" I asked bluntly. "Did he dream of them? Of people buried on Nil? Or one person specifically?" My voice rose with each word, bordering on hysterical. I teetered on the edge; I could go either way *because I never slept.* "Because I'm not dreaming of just any-one, Dad. I'm dreaming of one person. The person Rives cared for most on the island, the person whose death affected him most. I hear her, Dad. *Every night.* She talks to me. Begs me. Pleads with me. I don't know what she wants, but *she won't leave me alone.*" Tears pricked my eyes.

"Oh, honey, come here." My dad wrapped me in a hug, the sort that made me feel like everything would be okay even though every brain cell in my head screamed otherwise. He held me long enough for me to get myself under control. Then he dropped his arms, and gently rested them on my shoulders.

"Skye, you're the toughest person I know. My girl who has stars in her eyes, but feet firmly on the ground. You're going to get through this, get *past* it. I know you will. And you have Rives. He's part of it too."

"But what do we do? What do *I* do?" I searched his face for a clue.

"I think," he spoke slowly, "you're going to have to listen to her. The girl. But I don't believe it's really who you think it is. It's not Talla you're hearing. I fear that Talla is merely a voice. A face. A conduit. I'm afraid you're actually hearing Nil."

The truth of his words hit me like a cold slap. *Nil.* I was hearing Nil. *Nil* was in my head, *Nil* was talking to me.

Of course it was Nil.

I'd just refused to see it.

"How?" I whispered, frightened on a whole new level. "How can I hear Nil? How can this be happening?"

Dad shook his head. "I don't know. But I don't think the *how* is as important as the *why.* There is one thing I *do* know." He smiled. "You're strong enough now, just as you were then. Trust yourself. Trust in your strength, in your own sense of self and right and wrong. It's what helped you survive Nil last time. You can do it again."

I gasped, stumbling backward, falling into a totally surreal *what-is-happening* moment. "What are you saying, Dad? What do you mean, I can do it again? *Are you saying I have to go back to Nil?*"

"Over my dead body." Rives stepped through the doorway, eyes flashing, looking every inch the furious and ruthless Leader I'd first run into on a Nil beach. "There is no way in hell I'm letting Skye go back to Nil."

CHAPTER 17

RIVES
JUNE 10, NIGHT

The room exploded in noise and heat and *oh HELL no.*

Skye turned on me, her eyes narrowing, her hands on her hips. "Do not tell me what to do, Rives. I'm a big girl. But"—she whirled back to her dad—"are you really telling me to go back to Nil? Are you *kidding* me? Because I don't think—"

Professor Bracken's exclamation competed with Skye's. "I'm certainly not telling you to return to Nil! Absolutely not! What I'm trying to say—"

"Because you don't understand the darkness, Dad!" Skye stared at her dad like he'd grown a second head. "It's horrible! And if that's really Nil, then I can't—"

"Stop."

The steel in my own voice sliced through both Skye's and her dad's at once. Silence fell like a dark cloud.

"No more Nil." I didn't care how harsh my voice sounded. "We're *done.* There is no way in any world I'll let Skye go back there." An image of Dex's mangled body in the meadow coursed through my head; it was Skye's bloody memory, not mine. "You have no idea what she went through. What she *survived.* What she did—for all of us." I glared at the professor. "A return trip for her is not negotiable. It's not happening."

The professor's expression softened. "Rives, I agree. Hear me out. What I was trying to say"—he shot Skye a look that said *let me finish*; she tipped up her chin in a *go on, you've got thirty seconds* move—"is that Skye is tough. Skye beat Nil once, and escaped. And she can do it again, *here*." He emphasized that last word, then looked directly at Skye. "I have full faith that you can get Nil out of your head without stepping anywhere near that hellish island."

"What do you mean, 'Skye can get Nil out of her head?'" I crossed my arms.

The professor spoke calmly. "Rives, obviously Skye isn't hearing Talla. It's not possible for reasons you know all too painfully well."

Because she's dead, I thought harshly. *Because I buried her, six feet under in Nil dirt.* I had the most insane thought that Nil had resurrected Talla and brought her back to life. But I knew that wasn't possible. Nil might play God, toying with people's lives, but Nil wasn't God. Stealing people's lives didn't make the island all-powerful; it just made the island cruel.

And a murderer.

All the checks fell squarely in the evil column of Nil. Apparently I was still keeping track.

The professor had stopped talking, no doubt sensing my mental drift.

"Go on," I said. "Please."

He nodded. "Skye's not imagining Talla's voice, or her image. She wouldn't be able to manufacture someone so real if she were delusional. So, if Skye's not hearing Talla, she's obviously hearing Nil. Nil is using Talla to speak to Skye. The question is, why?"

Nil is using Talla to speak to Skye.

I knew exactly why. I stared at Skye, feeling sick. She wasn't the pawn; that was me.

Skye was the prize.

"Rives." Skye's hand slid into mine. "Come with me." She pulled me out of the office and down the hall. Then outside. Onto the back porch, under the misty Florida night sky. Humidity buried the stars; only the moon shone bright. Nil was out there somewhere too. Watching, laughing. Plotting. My free hand clenched.

Skye's soft voice breathed into my ear. "I know you're freaking out. I kind of am too. But I need to talk to you. I need you."

I turned, and not caring how sweaty I was from my run, I wrapped her in my arms.

"I hate Nil." I spat the words. "I hate that place. Using Talla, using me. Using you, definitely wanting you. Why won't it let us go?" I pulled back to look into Skye's eyes, my hands finding hers. "I cared for Talla. I really did. But what I felt for her back then is like a drop in the ocean compared to what I feel for you, Skye. I'm not downplaying my feelings for Talla, I'm just stating the truth. And the island knows how I feel. How you feel. So it's using her for something." *Like a warning,* I thought. Like a *Hey, I screwed with your head and your heart once, I'm not afraid to do it again. And that was just a taste of the pain I can make you feel.*

It had gutted me to bury Talla. Ripped something open that took months to heal, leaving a brutal Nil scar.

But if I lost Skye, I was done. I didn't deserve her, but I sure as hell couldn't imagine life without her. She was my best friend and my future, the girl I dreamed of traveling the world with as a two-person team, me snapping pictures, Skye writing the stories. The fact that Nil had linked us so completely in our final minutes on the island ensured that, if Nil tore us apart, I'd have more than a scar—I'd have a crippling wound that would never heal.

"Rives?" Skye tucked her hands in mine. "Worry is pouring off you, but right now I have no idea what you're thinking."

"I won't let the island hurt you. But I'm scared, Skye. Of this darkness, this long-range Nil. Nil shouldn't be able to mess with us here, or want to. I don't know how to protect you from the invisible."

"I don't think you have to." Her cheeks flushed with hope. "I think I figured out what Nil wants."

CHAPTER
18

NIL

AFTER NOON

The one called Skye had heard.

Seen.

Perhaps even understood.

Hope flared within the island, rich and pure, a full-bodied human emotion the island recognized for what it was, an abrupt surge flowing from her and back again, powerful enough to summon a gate on that side of the seam. A gate that would seek another like her, if balance held true. But lately, the innate balance was off, the island's own essence precarious. So when the first gate deviated from course, taking another, the island accepted the shift without surprise. However, if the second gate's appearance was equally unexpected, so were the humans who arrived.

This pair was perplexing, not unlike the species as a whole.

One loathed the other and still, she had attempted to warn him of the gate. She was the stronger of the two, her own strength calling the second gate, calling her. He thought her charming, and charmed by him. His confidence was misplaced, as was his footing.

They were highly entertaining to watch.

"Bloody hell," Davey grumbled. He'd just slipped on a loose rock. The cracked ground required a keen eye, which wasn't easy given that

Molly Hargrave walked next to him completely naked, even though they'd made a pact in the first two minutes not to look at each other.

He'd broken the pact a minute later. Who wouldn't? Molly Hargrave. Naked. A man had only so much willpower.

But apparently Molly had enough for both of them. She hadn't peeked, not once. At least Davey knew he looked good. In fact, Emma had told him that last night. Wondering what Molly thought, he slipped again.

"Crap it all!" Davey groaned. This time his foot had lodged in a tight spot, making him stop walking altogether.

"Do you mind?" Molly said, exasperated. Her face was tilted away, her sun-kissed auburn hair spilling down to cover her chest. The blue streak on the left side gleamed brighter in the sun. "Look where you're going. Get your foot free and come *on*."

"How do you know my foot's stuck?" Davey asked innocently. "Were you looking?"

She scowled, then blushed, enough red shooting across her cheeks that her freckles faded, which he knew because he *was* looking.

"No," she retorted, a little too quickly. "But the sooner we get to the trees, the sooner we find help. And clothes."

It was the most she'd said since they'd arrived.

By Davey's count, they had been trudging across rock as black as coal for half an hour. He still couldn't figure out what had happened. One minute he'd been ditching lunch to surf or possibly get high—or both; the next minute Molly was screaming at him to look out.

Look out for what? he'd wondered.

And then he'd passed out. He'd woken up to find Molly Hargrave staring at him—and his bathers were gone. So were hers. They were naked as babes and just as shocked.

He hadn't decided yet whether it was a dream come true or a full-blown nightmare.

"You're an arse," Molly said suddenly.

Nightmare, Davey decided.

"I didn't steal your clothes," he said matter-of-factly. "Or you, for that matter." He winked, making her scowl deepen.

"I know," she replied, making sure her hands covered her lower parts. "I'm talking about last night. I know you hooked up with Emma. I'm telling Lauren." Lauren was Molly's best friend, and also Davey's sort-of girlfriend.

Was, Davey thought.

And Molly had no idea what she'd seen.

"What will you tell her, exactly? And when?" Davey asked, his tone curiously cheerful. "And how? Because right now Lauren's not here, and I haven't a clue where *here* is." *Or what the bloody hell we're doing here together*, he thought. But he didn't say it.

He jerked his foot free and winced.

"You're bleeding." Molly's voice was quiet.

"You are nothing if not observant," Davey said. A gash ran length-wise down his ankle. Bright red blood dripped off his foot, disappearing greedily into the black rock.

"Arse," she muttered.

He kept walking, keeping his eyes on the ground. "Molly, what were you yelling at me to watch out for? What did you see?" His voice was quiet.

"It doesn't matter now."

Wrong answer, Davey thought.

"I think," he said, "that it matters very much. I think you saw something important. Something that explains *this*."

"Nothing explains this," she said slowly. "I'd followed you outside because I wanted to talk to you before I went to Lauren, and you were texting. You weren't even looking. The air rippled—I know it sounds strange—but it rippled, and then it moved. And then it hit you. You vanished, and a few seconds later, the weird air flashed again and hit me. End of story."

Wrong again, Davey thought. *I think it's just beginning.*

He forced a smile. "Well, *this* story is feeling a bit awkward, don't you think? You, me, here." He waved his hand. "Naked."

"Awkward doesn't cover it," Molly said. "More like horrible. No offense, but if someone had asked me to pick company for this nightmare, I wouldn't have picked you."

"You know, whenever someone says 'no offense,' usually whatever follows is offensive," Davey said affably. "But I wouldn't have picked you either."

Liar, the island whispered.

Davey stiffened.

"Did you hear that?" he asked.

"What?" Molly stopped, looking around.

Lips tight, Davey said nothing. He scanned the area, inspecting the silent landscape sprawling around them.

"I'm not sure," he said finally. "But something tells me we're not alone."

"You're right," Molly said. "There's a kangaroo over there."

Davey squinted in the direction Molly pointed. Sure enough, a big red boomer regarded them with curiosity. "So we're in the outback, are we?" he mused, marveling at the size of the kangaroo staring back at him. "A far cry from Sydney. How the bloody hell did that happen?" He stared at the animal, and his pulse skipped a beat. Past the kangaroo, a striped cat stood rock still, a massive beast, its head pointed toward Molly and Davey and, naturally, the kangaroo.

Davey desperately hoped the tiger was eyeing the kangaroo.

"I have no idea," Molly said. "But maybe that guy knows." She pointed to a slight rock rise where a thickly muscled boy stood. He wore a cream-colored loincloth that looked a bit small on the boy's large frame—privately Davey thought it looked slightly ridiculous, like he was playing dress-up in too-tight clothes—but the skull tattoo on his arm was a nice touch. On the other hand, the massive *A* tattoo on the boy's forearm made no sense at all. The boy held up some cloths, and Davey realized they were *clothes.*

And his rock was in the opposite direction from the tiger.

"By all means," Davey said, already moving, "let's go say hello."

A trio, *the island mused, watching the intriguing pair approach the one called Calvin. Three brought balance, and strength of its own making, a different sort of balance than a traditional pair. A positive development, the island decided.*

Leaving them be, the island turned away.

Turned north, toward the one called Dominic, a different islander than the others. He had attracted the island through the water, but it could not take him then, nor would it have chosen to, not with the spear in his hand and bloodlust in his heart. But the next day he had attracted the island again, and in that quiet moment, the island had seen his true measure.

He would serve the island and others well.

For now, the one called Dominic stood alone, surveying the deep water, the white froth pooling around his feet. As he had done before, he stepped confidently into the sea and dove, with a full breath and no fear.

The island did not need him, yet.

But there was one the island needed now, the one who had opened her mind at last. Beyond the seam, the one called Skye had finally braved the darkness for the truth, and with the help of her mate, she'd seen.

The island's plea had been heard. A decision would follow. Until she chose, the island could do no more.

Withdrawing, it was the island's turn to listen, on both sides of the seam.

CHAPTER 19

SKYE
JUNE 10, NIGHT

"I know what Nil wants." Rives's tone was sharp. "It wants you."

"You're right and you're wrong," I said. "Nil *does* want me, and it doesn't. I think that the island wants me to *do* something, and I think I just figured out what it is. You know how the gate on the Death Twin opens on schedule, right? Every June and December, on the solstice?" I spoke quickly; my latest epiphany was so *clear*. "Well, the Summer Solstice is a few weeks away. I think that Nil wants to make sure no one goes through from this end. It's the only thing that makes sense."

"Nothing about this makes sense," Rives grumbled. He fell silent as he considered my idea.

I fought the urge to keep talking, giving Rives the minute he needed to catch up with me.

"You may have a point." He forced the words out, like the admission cost him. "But, if Nil is so hell-bent on stopping the influx of kids, why keep Paulo? And what about the random gates? Who knows how many more kids are on Nil now. What does stopping one person do?"

One person.

One person can change a world, I thought, stifling the suffocating void bubbling up inside me. *And not always for the better.*

"What does stopping one person do?" I repeated softly, hearing the ache in my own voice. "It's a start. And I'm pretty sure it's what Nil wants."

Part of me—a huge part—still believed Nil was tired. Tired of living, tired of existing, tired of taking lives. When I'd been on Nil, I'd felt the island's fatigue with a certainty that left no room for question. I couldn't imagine that level of exhaustion had faded.

Which meant that while I'd helped save lots of people, I hadn't helped the island—not the way it wanted.

Why did Paulo stay behind?

What did I miss?

Rives stared at me, a slight frown marring his beautiful features. I'd drifted and he'd let me; it was his way of trying to see where I was going. Sitting up straight, I directed our conversation back on track.

"Nil wants me to block that gate," I said firmly. "I know it."

"Then let Maaka do it," Rives said flatly. "He knows that the island has changed. He came around to our point of view, remember? So he'll be the one to keep anyone from going to Nil from this end. From the Death Twin. It's not your job."

"Maybe it is." My tone was gentle. "You knew Maaka better than I did. He chose to leave with us, which counts for something. But he didn't seem overly helpful, Rives, or understanding. I don't know that he'd say anything."

Rives looked away. His thoughts followed his gaze, and for a long moment, he was far, far away.

"I think Maaka would do the right thing to help his people," he said finally. "He was proud of his island heritage and traditions, but I think he finally understood that Nil had changed. And he strikes me as the sort of person that once his mind is made up, it's tough to change. So if I had to guess, I'd say Maaka would have told his elders about the way Nil had become twisted."

"I don't want to guess," I said. "And even if Maaka does tell the truth, what if the elders don't listen? What if the elders still support sending firstborns? Or even if they don't encourage it, what if they do nothing?

What if someone decides to go to Nil anyway? We have to make sure." Conviction strengthened my words, assuaging the ache thrumming through my veins. "We can't let anyone go through that gate. We have to stop that tradition, forever."

Relief washed over me with the certainty of my words.

Help me, she'd said. *Choose me.*

That's what she wants, I thought. *That's what the girl*—I couldn't bring myself to even think the name Talla—*the voice of the island, has been trying to tell me. Nil needs me to block the stationary gate in June and end the islanders' tradition.*

But is that enough? I wondered. Doubt dulled my relief.

"I want to talk to Charley and Thad," I said suddenly. "Especially Thad. I want them to read my uncle's journal—the one that led me to Nil in the first place."

"Why?" Rives regarded me intently. "I've read your uncle's journal, Skye. And you probably have it memorized by now. What do you think Thad and Charley will find that we haven't? And if something stands out, what would we do with it anyway?"

"I just can't help wondering if maybe there's something in that journal that will help convince the elders or the person next in line not to go," I said. "Maybe something from the journal will click with Thad's experience. Maybe he met an islander, someone who can tell us something—something we don't even know to ask. Maybe we can even find a way to destroy that gate for good, or at least keep it from ever opening again."

Rives didn't respond.

"We have to try," I insisted. "We have to ask. We have to do all we can, on *this* side."

He cursed under his breath. "What makes you so sure?"

"Because Nil is tired. Because the girl—*Nil*—asked for help. She asked me to *choose*," I said quietly. "And it's not the first time."

Confusion replaced worry on Rives's face. "What do you mean?"

"When you were on Nil, did you ever hear the island?"

We rarely talked about our time there. The best part we already knew, already shared. But this question needed an answer.

Watching his expression shift, I knew he'd say yes before he opened his mouth.

"It took me a while to realize I was hearing Nil," Rives said. "But I was. Nil called me to the Cove; it's how I found the Looking Glass Cavern." He lifted his gaze to the night sky. "The island is something I don't understand, because it's not of our world. But is it real? Is it alive? Hell, yeah. Absolutely."

Now he looked at me.

"It scares the hell out of me, Skye. I don't know how to deal with this—this *thing* that's alive. This foreign thing that's somehow messing with you, here." He kissed me passionately, almost out of control, then he pulled away, pulling himself together. As I watched, Leader Rives roared back. "Why the question about hearing Nil? We know you're hearing Nil now. At least we think you are."

I couldn't tell if Rives was in denial or just not fully convinced.

Choose me, the girl of my dreams begged. It *was* Nil, because Nil loved to make people choose—or at least, it loved to make *me* choose. My last moments on Nil swirled like ghosts, ones with murder in their hearts.

"Skye, talk to me," Rives said. "I can't read you, other than the fact you're holding something back. If I don't know, I can't help. No more secrets."

Tell him, I told myself.

I took a deep breath. "You know that back on Nil, I felt the island's fatigue. But on our very last day, there was a moment when I didn't just feel Nil, I also heard it. It was the moment Nil made me choose."

"Choose?" Rives frowned.

"Between Dex and Jillian." I closed my eyes; I couldn't bear to look at Rives. "In the meadow, when you'd already gone to the platform. The hyenas came for us. I had one rock. One chance. The island forced me to choose who to save, Rives." I was back in the meadow, making my choice, knowing I couldn't win. "I chose Jillian," I whispered. "And Dex died."

The ugly truth lay exposed. Now Rives knew what I'd done, why Dex's blood still coated my hands. I'd cried about my choice so many times that no more tears would fall, but something inside me had died that day with Dex.

"Skye." Rives voice was gentle.

I opened my eyes to find Rives's expression achingly tender. "Don't own Dex's death," he said. "Like with Nikolai, Nil had already decided Dex's fate. He'd lost so much blood. Dex might not have made the trip home even if you'd chosen him." His eyes stayed on mine. "If you knew what you know now, would you make the same choice again?"

I didn't hesitate before I nodded.

"I thought so. You saved Jillian. That was huge, Skye. But don't you see?" His tone had grown urgent. "You didn't choose yourself, Skye. You were selfless."

Live, the island had said.

The tiger had spared me, then saved me. Or maybe that was the island—once on my first day, once on my last.

Did Nil spare me because the island rewarded my choice? Or because Nil knew it needed me later, as in now?

What am I missing?

I leaned into Rives's reassuring weight. His question had released something deep inside me, something small but powerful. I *would* make the same choice again, and knowing that moment would play out the same way gave me a cathartic release that my journal never could; a powerful knot unwound a little, enough to let me breathe without pain.

"I keep wondering what we missed." I splayed my fingers across his heart. "What *I* missed. Why didn't we finish what we started?"

"We did all we could."

"Did we?" My voice was thoughtful; my hand fell. Abruptly the darkness of my dreams shifted in meaning: it was a black flag, a warning too late; it was a death notice penned by my hand, written for people I'd never met.

Call it the butterfly effect, my dad had warned me once. *A ripple in time or fate. Our choices define and shape our lives, and our choices impact others.*

Me, choosing Jillian. Me, not choosing Dex.

Me, letting Paulo go last.

My choices, all impacting others, all with ripples reaching into today. Teens with names I'd never know, with faces I'd never see, all suffering on Nil—because of me. Because of *my* choice to end Nil and break the cycle of death. But I hadn't.

I'd just made things worse.

A terrible reality set in. I began to shake. "I think that by saving those on the island with us, we left it a living hell for those who came next. We didn't shut Nil down; we altered the island for the worse." I pushed away from Rives, feeling a growing sense of horror. "It's like the greatest butterfly-effect fail ever. Thanks to us, the newcomers won't know about food or deadleaf bushes or Search or gates. They won't know how to escape. And for all we know, that meadow fire burned the groves. At a minimum, it drove the big animals out of the meadow, and they'll go where they can find food—like Nil City. And the worst part?" My voice grew choked. "The newcomers won't know about the year deadline—unless by some miracle Paulo tells them."

"He will," Rives said with confidence. "He'll set everyone on the right track. Have faith in him, Skye."

"I did," I said quietly.

But something had changed. Something had changed Paulo's *mind*, changed his choice—and maybe changed Paulo himself.

And I had no idea what this Paulo was doing now.

Choose me, the girl had said. It *was* Nil. The island had forced me to choose once; now it was asking. It was giving me the chance—and the

72

choice—to do what was right. To correct my mistake, and finish what I started.

Regardless of what Paulo was doing on the other side, I had to block that gate. I had to be on the Death Twin on the Summer Solstice. I had to stop Nil once and for all.

And I wasn't meant to go alone.

That revelation rushed through me like light.

"I want you to come with me, Rives." I grabbed his arm, speaking fast. "To the Death Twin on the Summer Solstice. You convinced Maaka once, and you might have to do it again. Or convince someone else equally determined to keep this crazy tradition going." I knew Rives would loathe the idea of getting anywhere near Nil. "I know it's asking a lot, after all you've been through. But I really want you to come with me. I don't want to do this alone."

He smiled slowly, that melty Rives smile that made the rest of the world fall away, lighting his gorgeous green eyes from within. Only this time, his eyes burned a little too bright, as if there were too much emotion threatening to spill out the edges.

"Skye." He shook his head slightly, his voice rough. "You didn't even need to ask."

CHAPTER
20

RIVES
JUNE 10, NIGHT

Nil nightmare round two had begun.

Or maybe the first one never ended.

The sick thing was, the latest installment of the twisted Nil saga had caught me completely off guard. You'd think by now I'd be used to the unexpected, but where Nil was concerned, I was more than a slow learner. It was like I had a Nil blind spot. I tended not to see the twists coming.

Not a happy thought. Or a safe one.

Thad constantly cautioned, *Eyes wide open.*

Always, I'd think.

But now? Now I worried that even with my eyes wide open, the blind spot was still there, keeping me from seeing the truth. Keeping me from seeing the danger. Putting all of us at risk. Putting *Skye* at risk. And that was the worst part. Skye was in danger, and I finally saw it, thanks to the roaring blackness in her head so large that my blind spot didn't matter. Her dad knew it too.

It was written all over his face as she outlined her latest plan to revisit the Death Twin on the Summer Solstice.

"Let me talk to your mother," he said quietly. Then he looked at me. "Rives, a quick word?"

Skye crossed her arms. "Anything you can say to Rives you can say to me."

"Not everything." Her dad's expression didn't change. "We need a guys' moment. Father to boyfriend. We won't be long."

Skye rolled her eyes, clearly annoyed.

Pulling me into his office, the professor put his hand on my shoulder with a grip so firm that movement wasn't an option. "Rives, I know Skye. And I know you do too. Which tells me that she's going to that Death Twin, with or without us." His jaw ticked. "Clearly you agree with me, because you've already agreed to go."

I nodded.

"So we'll go with her. Hopefully she's right, that blocking the gate—that changing an islander's *mind*—will end the vicious Nil cycle once and for all. But something tells me there's greater danger on that Death Twin than Skye appreciates, and you're the only one who can keep her safe. Promise me that you'll watch out for my daughter."

"I promise," I said.

Skye's dad studied me. "I hope you can keep that promise." He sighed. He dropped his hand, then ran it through his hair. "And Rives?"

"Yes, sir?"

"Whatever you do"—his voice was dangerously quiet—"you keep her away from that gate. At all costs. You understand? Do not let her go back."

Ice shot down my spine.

At all costs. Do not let her go back.

Merde.

Despite her denial, deep down Skye was considering a return trip to Nil. Her dad saw it, and now, so did I. Maybe Skye didn't see it yet; maybe she wouldn't admit it to herself. Hell, I'd barely considered the sick idea, because I hadn't wanted to. But why else would she want Thad to look at the journal?

And then it clicked.

To save Paulo.

That's why she wants to go back.

It was a miracle the Bracken house wasn't full of stray dogs and cats; Skye's urge to rescue things in distress had few limits.

She'd even rescued me.

But to go back to Nil? The idea shook me to the core.

"Rives?" The professor pinned me with his gaze. "Promise me. Do not let her go back."

"You have my word," I said.

As I walked out of his office, I fervently hoped I could keep that promise. All I knew for sure was that I'd die trying. I just hoped it didn't come to that. But where Nil was concerned, nothing was a given.

Skye sat in the living room, a look of satisfaction on her face, her phone in her hand. My gut said her plotting had reached epic proportions.

"Guess what?" She was beaming. "I just talked to Charley. Instead of meeting us in Seattle, she and Thad are going to meet us in Hawaii. They're going to the Death Twin with us."

"You're joking." I stared at her, shocked. "Thad would never agree to that. And they can't afford it anyway."

"He did." Skye smiled. "And they can. They only have to fly from Seattle, remember? And they're using money they saved for our summer trip. Charley and I have been talking, and she agrees with my idea. She thinks closure would be good for all of us."

Closure. I almost snorted.

"And Thad actually agreed to this. He jumped right in." My statement dripped disbelief.

Skye had the grace to blush. "Well, at first he yelled something in the background that sounded like *Hell, no*, but then eventually he said he'd go. Well, specifically he said"—Skye made air quotes with her fingers—" 'There's no way in hell Charley's getting anywhere near Nil without me.' He said they were a package deal."

I could relate on all counts.

"A road trip, then." I studied her carefully. "But Skye, listen to me. This trip ends at the Death Twin. No farther. We are not going back to Nil."

"You have my word," she said solemnly.

But her mind was closed, like her expression.

She was up to something, and I didn't like it.

I had ten days to figure it out.

CHAPTER 21

NIL
MORNING

Paulo stared at Hafthor, wondering what in the world this kid was doing. *Scratch that*, Paulo thought. He had absolutely no idea what this *man* was doing.

Hafthor was a hulking beast of a person, crouched over a trio of small wooden houses crafted against a black boulder at the City's edge, his blond hair falling into his eyes while he worked. Stepping back, Hafthor regarded the middle house intently. Broken white shells defined the houses' open windows and doors, all facing the sea, all slightly misshapen, like the houses themselves. Both Hafthor and the tiny houses looked incredibly out of place, a man toying with a child's playthings in a place where there were no children and never would be.

"What are you *doing?*" Paulo flicked his eyes from Hafthor to the houses and back again.

"Finishing the roof," Hafthor answered. He tenderly placed another bundle of coconut husks on top of the tiny wooden structure, a giant holding fragile matchsticks.

"I see that," Paulo said dryly. "But why?"

"Because it's not finished yet."

Paulo rubbed his forehead, wondering how he'd ended up stuck on the island with a person who not only had zero sense of humor, but who also might not be fully stocked in the sanity department either. Hafthor was a strange one. He hadn't reacted when Paulo had given him the rundown about the island, the year deadline, and the only avenue of escape: gates. Daily ones, unpredictable and wild, and the equinox gate, still months away. Hafthor had simply nodded, then walked away to digest the information that Paulo had dropped on him.

That had been weeks ago, and Hafthor hadn't mentioned any of it since.

With care, Hafthor adjusted the husk roof on the middle house.

Paulo sighed. "Why the houses, Hafthor? There's a ton of stuff for us to do. Like go find people who may need help, and hope. We don't have time for playhouses."

Hafthor's head jerked up. "These are not playthings. These are for the hidden people."

"The hidden people," Paulo repeated. He took a small step back.

Hafthor nodded. "My mother taught us the Icelandic legends, including tales of the hidden people. Hidden people are real, and you must do all you can to give them a home and make them happy." Hafthor's blue eyes clouded. "We are not alone here. There are hidden people; people here we cannot see. I feel them. And Paulo . . . the hidden people are not happy."

Paulo couldn't argue with that. He stared at the tiny houses. They were roughly a foot tall, at most.

"These hidden people," Paulo said with curiosity, "they'll fit in there?" He waved at the dwellings dwarfed by the black boulder.

"The small ones," Hafthor said, standing up to his full height. "I can do nothing for the big ones. The island is their home already."

An odd chill crawled down Paulo's spine, an icy finger pressing against bone.

"Are they—good?" Paulo hated the hitch he heard in his voice, the thread of fear. "The hidden people?"

Hafthor shrugged. "They can be."

But not always, Paulo thought.

He remembered the boy snatched in the field by a large cat; he remembered the boy fighting briefly and losing swiftly. He remembered other deaths at the hands of different predators, many of them strange. He recalled faces of people lost to the island forever, people stolen by the ultimate predator—the island itself. He never saw the face of the island; it was always hidden, cloaked in secrecy, cloaked in darkness.

It is dark everywhere here, he'd overheard Michael tell Rives once.

He felt the truth of that statement in his bones. He'd never spoken with Michael, but he'd watched him from afar, enough to be impressed with his intuition and strength. Michael had been dead right. Paulo had no interest in meeting hidden people if they were in fact here; the very idea of hidden people brought to mind dead people, perhaps people seen by his aunt Rika. Were there island ghosts here, too? The more he stared at the little houses, the less safe he felt.

"Paulo?"

He looked up to find Hafthor regarding him intently, his arms folded casually across his chest.

"Most people are not all good or all bad, true? People are—" Hafthor gestured wildly with both hands as he struggled to find the word. "Complicated."

"This place is complicated," Paulo said slowly. He thought of the island, of all the wild gates he'd seen in the past weeks since Skye left, all the wild gates he'd run like the wind to avoid. But his footing was surer now, as was his path. Ghosts or no ghosts, most things were less complicated than when he'd arrived—like the end date, a year deadline as unmovable as Mount Nil.

Paulo knew exactly when his end here would come.

This knowledge gave him a critical measure of comfort, a vital measure of control in a place where he had little. But it wasn't his time, not yet.

In this moment, standing beside Hafthor and his odd tiny houses at the City's edge, Paulo felt an abrupt urge to *leave*, to go toward the Looking Glass Cavern and show Hafthor the carvings tucked inside.

Perhaps this man with a history and culture and stories so different from his island ones—yet equally grounded in the unseen—perhaps this man could find something in the symbols Paulo could not. Perhaps Hafthor could see beyond the carvings, discerning something Paulo had overlooked that would help them all. Because Paulo still hadn't figured out what happened to him that day on the platform, the day he'd failed Skye. The day he'd lost time. Maybe the carvings would give up a secret he didn't know to seek, something to help him succeed where he'd once failed.

Maybe Hafthor wasn't crazy after all.

"You're right." Paulo nodded. "The island isn't happy, and I'm trying to figure out why. If you have a minute, there's something I'd like you to see."

Hafthor stepped away from his houses. Perhaps he felt the urge to leave now too, because he followed Paulo without a backward glance.

It never occurred to Paulo that the urge to leave was not his own, which was precisely as the island intended it to be.

The island watched, pleased, as the pair strolled north. It knew their destination, their intentions, it even knew their fears; all were found easily near the surface of their minds, all typically human. The male, Paulo, did not like closed spaces; he imagined the walls pressing in as he left the water and entered the Cove's tunnel. The island had already catalogued this fear to use if needed. The male, Hafthor, was more concerned with what lay beyond the walls, a more rational fear. As those two crept through the narrow passageway, the island felt the thud of their hearts, the pulse of their electria flowing throughout their frail human bodies as water dripped from their skin. As tempting as it was, the island would not take them, not yet.

But it would take a sip.

Of them, of time.

And so it would be.

Delicious.

Paulo stepped into the Looking Glass Cavern, blinking against the sudden rush of light and space. He inhaled, drawing a breath so rapidly that a wheeze echoed throughout the underground chamber as his chest expanded and the grip of the tunnel loosened. He'd never tasted such sweet air in his life. He'd always hated when Maaka had brought him here, not because of the cavern; it was the horrible route he had to take to enter it. It didn't matter whether he took the Cove entrance through the rock passageway above, or the water-filled passageway below. Regardless of his chosen route, his claustrophobia suffocated him to the point of near fainting. It seemed to be getting worse each time he attempted it. If he wasn't mistaken, the walls of the passageway had narrowed as he walked. As his heart slowed a fraction, Paulo made the snap decision to exit via the underwater route. At least it was shorter.

Hafthor stared at the walls coated in carvings.

"This is why you brought me here," he said. His stance wide, he crossed his arms, facing the wall, settling into himself with a comfort Paulo envied. "To see these carvings."

Paulo stepped forward, beside Hafthor. "What do you see?"

Hafthor studied the wall methodically. "History," he said softly. He glanced at Paulo. "What do you want me to see?"

"I don't know," Paulo admitted. "A clue. Something I don't, I guess." As always, Paulo's gaze went to the massive diamond, the one with the eye in the middle. It called to him, drew him in. *Pulled* him in. Time swirled through the cavern, wrapping around Paulo and Hafthor as the two boys stood still, each staring at the carving that spoke to him most, each lost in the moment. The moment passed, as did the next.

Time marched on, like the island, but the pair didn't move.

Around them, the island drank in the echoes of power, of time, faint but delectable, more a tease of what was to come than any true measure of sustenance. The island took what it could, until no echoes were left, until the island grew bored and then frustrated. It wanted more, but time demanded the island wait, at least for this pair. With supreme effort, the island looked elsewhere.

As always, the island was drawn to the fighter, the female, Carmen. Strong and predictable, the fighter did not disappoint. Perhaps today the island would disappoint her.

Carmen regarded Ace with thinly veiled contempt. He was more concerned with his abs than the stealth of his feet. *Annoying,* she thought. For the hundredth time, she wondered how, in this strange world, she'd managed to get stuck with him.

Ace smoothed his hair back, tucking a stray strand in place.

"Come on, pretty boy," she said with a sigh, her hand instinctively brushing her hip. The metal blade butting against her side reassured her that she was the one in control, regardless of what she let Ace think. "Move faster and try to be quiet, would you?"

She'd been here several weeks by her count, and so far, the only person she'd found was this fool, Ace. She'd seen lots of animals, strange ones, and more than once she'd had the disturbing thought she was an animal too, stuck in a cage for someone else's amusement.

But she was no one's toy.

And Ace was certainly not amusing. He wasn't even entertaining. However, Carmen expected he would come in useful eventually, which was why she allowed him to cling like lint. Plus, at the moment, he was the only other living soul around.

She didn't want to think about the body she'd found.

Thankfully there'd been no bodies in the abandoned settlement, just weapons and food. Located on the west side of the island, thatched-roof houses—huts so rustic they were almost charming—circled a firepit. People had lived here once, and not long ago. Recently enough that the chicken coop still housed birds, with a lovely cache of fresh eggs that Carmen had taken full possession of, along with rope, some knives and a sheath, plus clothes. Shorts and bandanas, the latter wide enough to wrap around her chest and bind it tight. She'd even found twine to secure her hair, and sandals to protect her feet.

But she didn't stay in that camp. Despite the lack of bodies, it swirled with ghosts and something evil, something that reeked of death.

The whole island stank of it, if she were being truthful. It was why she preferred to stay near the shore, where the breeze smelled salty sweet and fresh, where food swam in abundance and the animals let her be.

"You are one quiet chica," Ace said.

"My name is Carmen," she snapped.

"Touchy, touchy." He raised his hands, smiling and confident. *Overconfident*, she thought.

He tilted his head as if he could read her thoughts. Then his smile flickered for an instant, like a dying firefly. Something fragile replaced it. "Okay, Carmen, so where are we going?"

"A place where we can get what we need."

Farther north, at the top of White Beach, Molly plucked a familiar green fruit off a tree. She squeezed it gently, brought it to her nose, and sniffed. Satisfied, she handed the fruit to Calvin.

"If it smells sweet, and kind of musky, then it's ready to eat," Molly told Calvin. She hadn't eaten guava in years, but when she was twelve, for an entire year, Molly had practically lived on fruit, and guava had been one of her favorites. Fortunately, that phase had passed. Right now Molly would have given anything for a cheeseburger with extra ketchup.

"What's *musky* mean?" Calvin stared at the green fruit, then sniffed it suspiciously.

"Ripe," Davey offered. He held up his fruit and with a nod, took a bite. He showed Calvin the inside of the fruit, which gleamed a deep pink.

"You can eat the peel?" Calvin's suspicion grew.

"Totally," Molly said. "It's guava."

Calvin shrugged. "Guava," he said before taking a bite. "Tastes weird." Juice dribbled from his chin.

With a guava in each hand, the group headed south, toward the black rock cliff curving into the sea.

No people. No houses. No boats.

No docks.

No roads.

No power lines.

No sign of civilization at all.

Molly had trouble accepting the reality of the last few days. Grabbed by a mysterious force, she'd woken in a mysterious place. Something she couldn't pinpoint told her she wasn't in Australia at all anymore; a sixth sense perhaps. This same sense told her she was in as much trouble as she suspected: She was lost, hungry, out of sorts, and stuck in this strange dream until she figured it all out.

Not a dream, she thought. *More like a nightmare.*

After all, Davey was here.

She was stuck here with the last person she'd choose to have her back. She wasn't sure Davey even *had* her back, wasn't certain what he'd do in a truly prickly situation. Right now she might pick Calvin as more reliable, the friendly boy from America, but he actually seemed more terrified than her and Davey put together, which was odd since he had more muscles than anyone she'd ever met. And she had known Davey since she was four, whereas she'd just met Calvin.

So, left with little choice, she'd slept outside last night on the beach, under the stars, with—of all people—Davey King, the biggest player she knew. They'd literally slept back to back, skin touching skin—which was awkward and weird and highly unnerving in its own odd way—as they tried to stay warm. Calvin had slept a few feet away. Given the weirdness, Molly had barely slept. She wasn't sure about Davey. They'd talked a little, enough for Molly to know that Davey didn't have a clue what was happening either.

She focused on the one person here who knew more than she did.

"What have you been eating?" Molly asked Calvin as she savored the guava. She wasn't certain when they'd find more food, so this harvest of fruit might have to last. They hadn't seen another person since meeting Calvin yesterday, let alone a restaurant or supermarket, not that she had any money. She fervently hoped Calvin had something helpful to share. "You've been here for—what did you say, four days?" she asked.

"Something like that," Calvin said. "Raw eggs, mostly. I found a chicken, with a half-dozen eggs. I ate the eggs raw. They were okay." He shrugged. "And I ate a raw fish." He exhaled harshly, his huge frame rippling. "Couldn't keep it down."

"Nasty," Davey said.

"Yeah," Calvin agreed.

"And you've seen no people?" Molly frowned. "Not one?"

"Not until you two. But I've seen a lot of animals. Weird ones, too. Animals that shouldn't be together, and sure shouldn't be on a tropical island. I'm talking lions, a camel, a couple monkeys. Even a zebra. And a kitten."

"A tiger cub, more like it," Davey offered. He looked at Calvin. "Where did you say you found the clothes again?"

"I told you. In a bag."

"Just in a bag," Davey repeated in a dubious tone. "Like, a welcome package? With itty-bitty chocolates and nuts and a thoughtful note like *Hey, Calvin, welcome to paradise? Don't pet the tiger. Try not to die.* Like that?"

"No." Calvin kept walking, facing forward. "Just a bag. Lying around."

"Just lying around. And it had clothes. Which just happened to fit all of us and we all just happened to be naked."

Davey stopped walking and faced Calvin, his eyes piercing, all humor gone. "I want the truth and I want it now."

Calvin ran a hand over his head, his powerful muscles glistening in the sunlight, then shook his head, a slight movement that Molly suspected wasn't meant for anyone but himself.

"Look. I told you the truth, Davey. Straight up. I was running, and I found two bags. One had clothes. The other had some food, but it was bad. Seriously rank. And, it was hard to tell because of the rotten food, but that bag also had something that looked kinda like a pillow." Calvin shrugged. "It was weird." Then he swallowed, and blew out a nervous breath. "Okay, and—there were bodies. Two of them. Skinny kids. One white, one black. Boys, both about"—he glanced at Davey, and met his eyes—"our age. Just laid out, dead. And they were wearing clothes like these."

"What?" Molly felt the blood drain from her face. "You found dead bodies? And they were wearing clothes like these?" She jerked her head down to look at her wrap shirt as if it were ready to come alive and choke her. She whipped her eyes to Calvin. "Oh my God. Did you take these clothes off *dead bodies?*"

"Hell, no!" Calvin's eyes went wide. "Man, I'm not about to disrespect the dead. But their bags? That was fair game. These"—he gestured to his loincloth—"and those"—now he pointed to Molly's skirt and top—"were in the bags."

"Bags that were beside dead bodies," Molly said. She felt as though a black hole might come and swallow her whole any second. "Of boys," she added. "Like you two."

"That's exactly what he said," Davey said drolly.

Molly glanced at him; for a moment she'd forgotten he was there. *Such a jerk*, she thought. But Davey's predictable asshat behavior helped her refocus with less panic.

"The question is, why?" Davey continued, oblivious to Molly's cool gaze. For an instant she thought he actually looked worried, then his normal cocky expression slid back in place, marring his handsome features. "Why did they die? Why were they here?" Davey waved around his guava. "Why are *we* here?"

"I can answer that, at least in the general sense." A male voice sounded behind them. Molly turned first. Her eyes met a boy's caramel ones, set in a tanned face. He stood a few meters away on the white sand beach, a calm smile softening his angular features. No shirt, familiar cloth shorts, and tribal tattoos wrapping one taut bicep. "I'm Paulo," he said casually.

"Molly," she replied.

Calvin jerked back. "Jesus! Is that a rat?" He pointed at a boy with a blond buzz cut standing slightly behind Paulo, something furry dangling from his hand. It struck Molly that the boy appeared to be Paulo's bodyguard, not that Paulo seemed to need one. It also occurred to her that ginormous, muscle-bound Calvin was shaking.

"Yes," the hulking blond boy said, a serious expression on his face. He raised the rat slightly. "But we will not eat it. Rats carry disease, and are better buried. But I would not be so cruel as to bury it alive. Its death was swift." He frowned, glancing at the dead rat in his hand. "Still, the blood. I fear the island craves it." He sighed and turned to Paulo. "I will bury the rat while you talk to the newcomers. They are not the hidden people I fear."

He strode off.

Davey yelled, "Watch out for the tiger!"

Without turning, the blond boy raised the rat in acknowledgment and disappeared into the thick brush.

"Hidden people?" Calvin looked bewildered, then whipped his head toward Davey. "And what's with you and tigers?"

Molly stepped closer to Paulo. "What island?"

The female, Carmen, found the City empty, exactly as the island planned. The longer she was isolated from the others, the stronger she would become. The island tracked her approach, studying her, sifting through her emotions. The spare was not worth the island's time or scrutiny; he was an afterthought.

While the fighter took what she wanted from the human City, the island turned its attention back to the pair, which had turned into a quintet while the island had been distracted. One was a killer, blood still dripping from his kill. But the kill was too small to bleed power, the killer's heart too soft to be useful. Disappointing, on both counts.

Still, the island watched.

For an instant the island considered taking one of the five, absorbing their power without wait. But the island was bound by rules, unyielding rules, all crafted by time; the island was constrained by time itself and the year deadline demanded obedience. To the island's dismay, there were no feral creatures close enough to reward the island with an early prize.

The blood and power the island craved was so close, yet out of reach. After the taste of power in the Looking Glass Cavern, waiting was cruel torture for the island, and yet wait the island must.

If it could scream, it would.

But here the island had no voice. No outlet, no release. It was as trapped as the humans, and it despised the humans for that too. And yet, nothing was forever. Not here, not there. In three days' time, a new shift would come, perhaps the biggest one yet.

To soothe itself, the island looked beyond, looked ahead. A new prize would come in a few days' time, perhaps the best prize. The knowledge empowered the island, as did the passage of time. Time took and time gave, and time always was. Time ruled the island, but within its time, the island would play.

And victory was a mere three noons away.

Over the island, the crescent moon glowed like electria unleashed, and the island inhaled.

CHAPTER
22

SKYE
JUNE 18, MID-MORNING

Now it was me worried about Rives. Now that I'd stopped the downward spiral in my head—now that I *knew* I wasn't crazy—it was Rives who was struggling; it was Rives fighting his personal demons, Rives fighting the shadow of Nil. Or maybe Rives fighting his sixth sense. He was definitely fighting something. I caught him clenching his fists at weird times, often while staring at me.

Like now.

We were minutes away from landing in Honolulu, an hour away from meeting up with Charley and Thad. In two hours the four of us plus Dad would all be on a boat headed for a remote area of Micronesia, a place Rives and I had left behind three months ago. *Three months ago. Three days until the solstice. Three minutes until we land.*

Still counting, I thought.

I wondered whether I'd ever stop.

At least now that I'd accepted that Nil was in my head, the darkness had retreated. Not disappeared, but withdrawn a vital fraction, enough to let me sleep without soul-crushing fear, enough to keep me from breaking. Enough to let the girl take center stage.

She was ever present.

In my dreams, in my daydreams, in the quiet moments when I

paused to think. *Choose me*, she begged constantly. I knew the only way to get her to leave was to go to the Death Twin and stop the island from taking another.

The rest would be up to Paulo.

Better yet, the simple knowledge that I wasn't crazy had brought the release I'd so desperately craved. I was haunted but sane. Time formerly spent journaling now went into exercising and working through arguments with islanders in my mind—I was ready to go head to head with an entire team of elders if need be. I felt more like myself; I felt like *me*.

I was back.

I felt even better knowing that in three days, I'd banish Nil from my head once and for all. Because wouldn't she—the girl, Nil, whoever was begging for help in my head—leave me alone once I did what she asked?

I refused to consider any alternative.

Three days, I thought.

The plane dipped, then touched down with a rough lurch.

I turned to Rives and smiled. "And so it begins," I said dramatically.

He shook his head, his jaw tight. "I don't think it ever ended."

"Charley!"

Hearing my voice, she turned, her ponytail swinging behind her, her eyes lighting up when she saw Rives and me a few feet away. She and Thad stood near the ground transportation entrance, a striking couple who were easy to spot in the middle of the bustling Honolulu airport. Each wore a backpack and carried nothing else. Our trip didn't require much in the packing department. Rives and I each had only a single backpack too.

I hugged Charley, feeling the strength of her as she hugged me back. Now that I knew her, Charley's slow drawl didn't fool me one bit. She was a force of will and muscle.

Beside us, Rives and Thad clasped hands, then Thad pulled Rives into a tight hug.

"Good to see you, brother," Thad said, his voice gruff with emotion.

"Feeling's mutual." Rives grinned.

Relief that Thad had survived Nil hit me anew; it was Rives's relief driving mine.

Thad let Rives go and turned to me. "Skye." He hugged me as warmly as he'd hugged Rives. "Long time no see, Nil slayer."

"I wish." I hugged him back. "I mean, I wish I'd slayed Nil, or at least helped it pass peacefully." But I hadn't done either: I hadn't killed the island or helped it.

I'd just made it worse.

Thad studied me, his blue eyes intense.

"Looks like this is the last shot then, eh?" He adjusted his backpack, his smile fading. "Skye, listen. I'm not going to lie to you, and I want this out in the open from the get-go. I have a bad feeling about this trip. After all, this is Nil we're messing with, right? And the thought of being anywhere near a gate?" He raised his eyebrows. "It creeps me out. *Weirds* me out." He sighed. "I spent a year there, Skye. A full year. And barely got out alive." His sapphire gaze held ghosts I didn't recognize but knew belonged to Nil. "I just want it on the record right now that I think this is a seriously bad idea."

"That makes two of us, bro." Rives nodded.

"Noted," I said, annoyed. *Don't they realize I have no choice? That if I don't go, the girl in my head won't leave me alone? Ever?*

I wanted her *gone*, which was why I *had* to go to the Death Twin. There was no alternative, not for me. Not if I wanted to be free.

I glanced at Rives, his expression a blank mask, but his eyes were weary with resignation. *He knows,* I thought, relaxing. *He knows I have no choice.* Still holding Rives's gaze, my voice radiated calm. "It's going to be okay."

"I hope you're right," Thad said, his tone skeptical.

Me too, I thought.

Thad turned toward Rives. "So tell me. Besides this little detour, what's been happening?"

The two boys fell into a familiar rhythm, a relaxed back-and-forth about our recent Europe trip and Thad's current training schedule.

"This is going to be awesome." Charley's voice was confident. "An island road trip with you and Rives to stop Nil once and for all." She glanced at Thad, watching him laugh with Rives, her smile fading as her expression turned pensive.

"Charley, what is it?"

"Thad doesn't get it." Her golden eyes flashed. "He thinks this trip is optional, like it's a whim. It's not. Not for me." She paused. "I think because he was there a full year, he feels done. But I left early, without planning on it. I'm not saying I want to go back to Nil, not at all—for the record, I don't. But, I still have this weird sense of unfinished business; I've felt this way since I left, and it's only getting worse. Like I left Nil before I was ready, before the island was ready to let me go."

"But the island *did* let you go." My statement sounded like a question.

"Maybe. Sometimes I'm not sure." She chewed her lip, then glanced at me. "I don't know if you know, but Thad threw me into that gate. There was no going back. But I'm still not sure it was my time. So I'm totally on board with your block-the-gate plan. Maybe even destroy-the-gate plan. I can't help but think I'm supposed to help you do this, whatever *this* is."

She tilted her head slightly. "Did you know you and I were on Nil about the same amount of time?"

I nodded.

"And you know how many more days I spent on Nil than you?" She studied me.

"No."

"Ten," she said. "I was on Nil for ten more days than you were. I don't know what that means, but it means something; it must. I know you and Rives figured out the numbers, the ones that add up to ten: three, two, one, four. You were there eighty-nine days, me ninety-nine. And Thad and Rives were there for a full three hundred sixty-five. Ten," she repeated. She shook her head and sighed. "Maybe I'm looking for something that doesn't exist. But I can't help but feel that this trip is important, that you and I are here together, *right now*, for a reason. I can't help thinking that my role with Nil isn't done yet. But something big is going to happen." She looked at me. "Don't you feel it, Skye?"

Thad snorted loud enough for us to turn. His blue eyes gleamed with questions and if I wasn't mistaken, a bit of challenge. "You two are dangerous. But whatever you're up to, count Rives and me in."

"Already done. Welcome to Hawaii," Charley said smoothly.

"Too bad we're not staying," Thad grumbled.

Charley laughed. She squeezed my hand, then stepped out of whisper range, a clear signal our secret conversation was over. As a group, we made our way toward the ground transportation exit.

Thad pointed to Rives's head. "Still no dreads? I figured by now they'd be on their way back."

Rives shrugged. "Nah. Another time, bro. Another place."

Thad nodded. "I hear that." No smile now. He turned to me, his expression serious, his eyes sharp. *The face of a Leader,* I thought. *So like Rives.* "Where do we start, Nil slayer?" he asked.

My phone buzzed with a text from my dad.

At the curb. Ready when u are.

"Dad's here," I said. "He's got the car."

As I replied to my dad, Rives talked. "Skye's dad confirmed the plane this morning. It'll fly us to an island where we'll catch the boat to take us the rest of the way. We should reach the Isles of the Gods in a few days. That's what the locals call the trio of islands in the Pacific. The professor—that's Skye's dad," he added for Thad and Charley's benefit, "discovered that the locals refer to the main island as the Blessed Island, aka Maaka's homeland. It's where we need to start and, hopefully, finish. The Death Twins are a short canoe trip away from the main island. But I'm hoping not to go there."

Worry flashed across Rives's face before the blank wall slammed back down.

94

I tapped his closed fist. "Don't worry, Rives. It's going to be okay."

He shook out his fist and flexed his fingers. "Stop saying that," he said quietly. "And for the record, we are not going to the Death Twin until the day of the solstice. No earlier." *And maybe not at all if I can help it.*

Rives's thought was a shout in my head.

I threaded my fingers through his and pulled him close enough to kiss. "Rives."

"Don't try to distract me, Skye."

"I wouldn't dream of it." I grinned as Thad laughed. "But I've got to go to that island, you know that."

"There's our ride." Rives pivoted away, pointedly ending our conversation.

Following his cue, Charley and Thad turned toward the automatic doors leading outside. Letting them drift slightly ahead, I tugged Rives's hand and directed my thoughts toward him.

I have to be on that island. I have to make sure no one goes through that gate. I have to shut it down. I know I'm one person, but I have to try.

Rives's face fractured and fell, then showed nothing at all.

He heard me, I thought with satisfaction.

Sometimes it was the strength and will and determination that counted, and my thoughts were as strong as the diamonds in the Crystal Cavern.

I was going to the Death Twin, with or without Rives.

With, I hoped.

"Of course I'm coming with you," Rives snapped. Thad and Charley turned back toward us in surprise. "Merde, Skye. I just hate this entire thing, okay? Don't ask me to be all happy with this insane plan."

"It's not insane." My voice was frosty. "It's the only way to get Nil out of my head. And yours," I added.

Rives pulled me into his arms. "I know," he whispered, his cheek resting against my head. "I'm just scared, Skye. More like terrified. Of this whole thing. Of losing you."

"You won't lose me; you're helping save me." The desperation filling my nightmares leaked into my voice despite all my effort to hide it. "Believe me, I don't want to go to the Death Twin either. But unless the elders are planning to block the gate, it's up to us. We have to stop it once and for all. It's the only way we'll ever be truly free." I looked Rives in the eye. "But before we do anything else, we need to talk to Maaka."

CHAPTER
23

RIVES
JUNE 18, LATE MORNING

Me, hunting for Maaka.

Skye, trying to stop Nil.

Some things never change, I thought.

Nil was a freight train, roaring toward me, cloaked in darkness, and I couldn't stop it. Only Nil wasn't coming for me. Nil wanted the strongest survivor to play Nil's game, the same survivor that stole all of Nil's prizes but one. Sure, Paulo stayed—but Nil wanted Skye. No matter how many times she denied it, I *knew* Nil wanted Skye; I'd felt it in the darkness when Skye had let me in. Calculating Nil was up to something, and all I knew for certain was that it wasn't good.

At least Thad and I were on the same page. Neither of us wanted to get anywhere near the Death Twins or the solstice gate. Our plan was to keep the four of us far, far away. Stall, if possible. Do what we could from the main island, and leave the rest up to the islanders. It was the only way to keep Skye out of harm's way. Out of Nil's clutches.

Too late, the cold whisper at the back of my head crooned.

I stiffened.

"What?" asked Skye. Her steel-flecked eyes saw too much.

"Just thinking that we've got three days until the solstice. We're cutting it close."

A truth and a lie. We *were* cutting it close.

"True." She sounded worried. "We'll make it. Right, Dad?"

"Yes, we'll make it, Skye," he answered. "But let's focus on the islanders, on the main island first, shall we? I truly would prefer you stay away from that Death Twin."

No shit. And I truly would prefer that Nil stay the hell out of my head.

She frowned at me, then squirmed toward the backseat. "Thad, I've got something for you to see. My uncle's journal. I'm sure Rives told you about it, but it's how I ended up on Nil in the first place. I want you to read it, and look at my uncle's notes."

His acceptance was reflexive, but his face had the look of someone handed something he didn't ask for, didn't want.

"Why?" Thad's voice was flat. The journal sat unopened in his hand. "How will it help now?"

"I'm wondering if anything looks familiar to you, or stands out as important. Maybe something that will help us convince the elders to stop their crazy tradition?"

Thad glanced at the journal as if it were kryptonite. "Skye, I hear you. But I can't help you. There's nothing in here the elders don't already know, I guarantee that. So, no thanks. I can't go back to Nil. Not even through someone else's head. Sorry."

He moved to hand the journal back to Skye, but Charley deftly intercepted it.

"I'll take a look," she said.

Thad's lips were tight, but he said nothing.

For the next few days, the journal never left Charley's hands; she was as obsessed as Skye. The two of them constantly pored over the journal with silent whispers, animated hands. The freight-train-coming-that-was-Nil roared louder in my head.

"I seriously can't believe we agreed to this." Thad's eyes stayed on Charley as the boat skipped across the open water. She was intently studying a page in the journal's middle. "How the hell is this going to end well?"

"We're going to go to the Isles of the Gods, talk to the elders and Maaka, everyone's going to agree that Nil is now a bad, bad place, and no one needs to go to the Death Twin on the solstice or actually, ever, especially us. We'll all be one happy family. End of story."

Thad laughed out loud. "Right."

"You don't like my version?"

"I do, man. I do. It's just—this is *Nil* we're talking about. Nil's a wild card, always, and she loves to throw in a twist." He shook his head. "I have a bad feeling it's not going to shake out like we think."

I sighed. "Me either."

The crappy fact was, Thad had hit the Nil nail square on the head. Island rules, island games. Building toward something only Nil knew.

One day, I told myself. *Then it's over.*

I didn't react when the cold laugh echoed through my skull.

One day, I repeated silently, my thoughts savage. *And then it's on.*

"Four hours!" the professor yelled, over the sound of the choppy surf. "We'll be there in four hours!"

Tick tock.

The constant clock.

Time passed with the waves. Skye's uncle's journal disappeared into Charley's pack; our conversations vanished as well.

The rough sea bounced us around like popcorn.

Charley looked green, seriously seasick. Skye and Thad, on the other hand, looked remarkably chill. Skye's expression was calm, her face determined and set; Thad's expression was resolute, like a man previewing his funeral.

If I had to guess, my expression mirrored Thad's.

The closer we got, the worse I felt. Only the queasy feeling in my gut had nothing to do with the boat ride and everything to do with Nil. My blind spot stretched like a black hole in my head.

Skye pointed ahead. "Look!" she shouted over the noise.

An emerald mountain gleamed in my line of sight. I'd forgotten how much the main island resembled Nil. It stretched wide, boasting a massive brilliant green peak. Two smaller islands lurked in the distance, each with a small patchy green peak and black cliffs. The Death Twins. *Aptly named*, I thought, and not for the first time. Twin spires of green, one harboring a platform, a portal to death opening in a few days' time.

Nice.

I snapped a series of pictures of the Death Twins, then a few of the main island. The only person in sight was an older man on the long wooden dock. Through the telephoto lens, his dark-brown eyes were sharp. Wrinkles etched his face; crisp black ink swirled across his arms and chest. He seemed to be waiting for us.

I capped my lens and stashed my camera in my pack, an idea forming as I watched the man on the dock. We moored smoothly. The wrinkled man tossed a rope to our captain and the two of them secured the boat easily, a practiced move. Our captain—a fellow by the name of Charles—tugged the knot once, then leaped onto the dock.

"Uncle!" Charles called, grinning. The men greeted each other affectionately.

Skye's dad stepped off the boat and offered his hand to the older gentleman. "Rangi," the professor said warmly. "Good to see you."

Rangi clasped Skye's dad's hand, his smile knowing. "Interesting timing, Dr. Bracken."

"Indeed. It is the longest day of the year tomorrow." Skye's dad nodded, his eyes intent on Rangi. "This place seemed the perfect place to celebrate it."

"I think you'll be disappointed, Dr. Bracken," Rangi said softly. "We have nothing planned for tomorrow that would hold your interest." His eyes flicked briefly to the four of us, his smile slipping a fraction. "I think you have come a long way for nothing."

His eyes were back on the professor.

"Perhaps." Skye's dad smiled. "I consider myself a cautious optimist, Rangi. Perhaps it's disappointment we're looking for."

The two danced around the solstice subject like players in a chess match. Silence crackled between them, grounded in a history I didn't know. But judging from the set of Skye's face, she did. Seconds passed, time lost. The Nil train roared loud enough to rattle me.

Enough, I thought.

I stepped forward and introduced myself. "Rangi, I'm Rives. Pleased to meet you, sir."

Rangi shook my hand, his expression one of surprise as his eyes met mine, then flicked across my chest, taking in my coloring, my new tattoos. Understanding clouding his certainty. *An islander*, he'd realized. A twist he didn't expect but couldn't help but respect, a factor he didn't know how to handle. So much like Maaka.

Dropping his hand, I nodded.

"Rangi, you know why we're here. Let's not pretend. Tomorrow is the Summer Solstice, which has more meaning here than any other place in this world."

"Rives," the professor warned. *Don't press*, his tone said.

Too late, I thought.

Rangi's barely hidden haughtiness reminded me of Maaka. *Outsider*, it screamed. This was Maaka in fifty years. My idea crystallized in silent certainty.

I smiled thinly. "Rangi, are you an island elder?"

Surprise flickered through his eyes. "Why do you ask?"

"Because I need to talk to an elder. And I think you're one."

He didn't answer, so I forged onward. "I know we've been here for less than two minutes. But time is precious, both here and on another remote island, one in another world, an island some people call Nil. I know your people call it something else."

Rangi didn't respond. I waited until I knew he wouldn't.

"Did Maaka talk with you after he returned?" I asked. "Did he tell you how that island has changed? That it's not the place it once was?"

Rangi's expression cooled.

"Council meetings are private matters, young Rives. *If* the elders met with Maaka, I would not be at liberty to tell you what was discussed. It does not concern you."

"Wrong," I said. "It absolutely concerns me. It concerns all of us standing here. It concerns all the people in both worlds, those here and there, and it especially concerns the unlucky kid tapped to go tomorrow."

Rangi said nothing. He didn't even flinch.

I hadn't expected an elder cone of silence on this scale.

"So," I spoke slowly, "the elders may or may not have spoken to Maaka after he returned. He may or may not have discussed how the island we call Nil has changed, and the elders may or may not have listened to him. And based on a meeting that may or may not have occurred, the elders may or may not have made a decision whether to allow anyone through tomorrow's solstice portal. Does that sum up the situation?"

A glint of amusement lit Rangi's dark eyes. "Perhaps."

"Thanks for the help," I said sarcastically, my cool slipping. "And I bet if I ask, you have no idea where Maaka is."

Rangi shrugged. "Last time I saw him he was fishing on the island's north shore. But I don't know where he is now."

Of course you don't, I thought. At least Rangi had confirmed Maaka was here. I'd silently feared he'd fled to the mainland, so at least we still had a shot at finding him; it just wouldn't be easy.

Nothing involving Nil ever was.

Skye's fingers tugged mine.

"Isn't that Maaka?" She pointed.

Down the black sand beach, a bare-chested boy sporting black tattoos across his left shoulder, chest, and arm stood talking animatedly with a girl. She wore a yellow floral dress, her dark hair long and flowing. For a moment, I thought it was Kiera. One long look confirmed it wasn't Kiera, but the boy was definitely Maaka.

"Yup," I said, not letting go of Skye's hand. "It's reunion time."

We started jogging.

"Wait!" Rangi's voice echoed over the water breaking against the dock. "Let me show you to your house!"

I didn't turn. "Later," I said. I didn't care if he heard.

Thad and Charley kept pace behind us. I kept my eyes on Maaka; I didn't want to risk losing him, not when he was so close. I knew how elusive he could be.

Before we were in voice range, the Kiera look-alike strode off. Maaka watched her go, arms crossed, back to us. As I strode up behind him, he turned, probably because I was panting; my stealth skills had slipped, either from disuse or desperation.

"Rives." Maaka looked mildly surprised. "What brings you to my island?"

"The use of the possessive is a nice touch." I nodded. "Good to see you too, Maaka." I tipped my head toward the girl, who was getting farther away with each second. "I see you haven't lost your way with the ladies."

A smile pulled at the corners of his mouth. "What brings you here, Leader Rives?"

"You remember Skye." She waved. "And this is Charley, and Thad. Every one of us has been to Nil and back. Like you." I paused. "Or not like you, Maaka. If you recall, we flew standby while you went first class."

"But we all arrived at the same place." He shrugged.

I snorted. "That's debatable, but it's not a discussion for today. Today let's talk about tomorrow, shall we? And please don't tell me the end is already written, unless it's written that no one goes through that gate tomorrow and the island's time is up."

Maaka looked intently at me. "Paulo did not leave with us. He chose to stay. Perhaps he saw something we missed."

"I don't think so." Skye's firm voice caused Maaka's head to swivel back toward her. I had the distinct impression he'd forgotten she was there.

"You don't think what?" Maaka's condescending tone made my fists curl.

Skye smiled, a dangerous one that let me relax. "I don't think he chose to stay, Maaka. I think something made him stay. And I think he saw what it was."

"Do you?" Maaka said blandly. He crossed his arms, putting a wall of ink between him and us. A new tattoo on his right shoulder looked back at me: an eye in the center of a diamond.

"I do." She straightened. "Maaka, you left with us. You know the island has changed. It's not safe, for anyone. Please tell me you told the elders."

He looked down his nose at her. "Why should I tell you? This is not your business."

"Oh, that's where you're wrong." Her tone stayed cool, calm water hiding a deadly rip current below. "It's totally my business. I still hear Nil, Maaka. Every night. Every day. Nil called me here, and here I am."

Maaka paled. "The island called you?"

"At least someone's finally listening," Thad said pleasantly.

"Yes." Skye nodded. "It called me. Still calls me, as a matter of fact, to make sure no one goes through that gate tomorrow. It wants the tradition to end. The island is tired, Maaka."

"But Paulo stayed." Defiant Maaka resurfaced.

"Yes, we know." Skye sighed, frustrated. "We have to trust him on that end. We can't control what's happening there. But we can control what's happening *here*. And the tradition has to stop."

For a long moment, the two stood still, a clear face-off, a total déjà vu moment. I flashed back to a similar standoff on Nil. The only thing missing was the Man in the Maze as a backdrop.

"You don't get to decide," Maaka said finally. "It's not your choice. Or mine."

"Then whose is it?" Skye snapped.

"No one you know. Go home, Skye. Good-bye, Rives." Maaka started to walk away, and I stepped in front of him.

"So that's it? You're done? You're here, you said your piece to the elders, and you're washing your hands of that island? To hell with anyone else who goes? Is that it?"

Something like regret flashed through Maaka's eyes. "It's not that easy, Leader Rives."

"Nothing worth fighting for ever is," I said. "And the end of Nil is worth fighting for."

He studied me, his gaze thoughtful. Like he was weighing words, deciding trust. "Her name is Lana," he said finally. "The choice is hers. I gave her my recommendation that the journey is no longer worth the risk; I gave her my knowledge of the island as it is now, and I gave my word that I will not follow her tomorrow. I can do no more."

His word bound him, not me. Not us. It felt like a total Maaka cop-out.

"You mean you won't do more," I said.

He shrugged. "Good luck, Leader Rives. Speak from the heart." He paused, his expression odd. "Remember what I told you."

"Always." I looked sideways at him and almost laughed. "So I guess this was the middle after all, right, Maaka?"

He turned away, toward the Death Twin. "The middle," he repeated slowly. "The end. A new beginning. I don't know anymore." His tone reflected an inner confusion that almost made me feel sorry for him. Almost. "Only time will tell," he said quietly. "It does not run backward." He spun back to me, his dark eyes oddly fiery. "Remember what I told you." He offered his hand, a first for us. "Lana is my cousin. She is strong. Like her." He nodded at Skye. "I would prefer Lana not go. But her mind is set. Perhaps you can make the difference. Perhaps you will bring this cycle to an end." His eyes flicked between me and Skye, and I wasn't entirely sure which of us he was referring to.

But it didn't matter. Like Charley and Thad, Skye and I were a package deal.

I shook Maaka's hand, wondering if he'd ever man up like he should. "I'll try."

He nodded. "That's all you can do."

Maaka turned and walked away. I had the strangest sense that this was our true good-bye, that I'd never see him again.

"What the hell did you just agree to?" Thad's voice cut through my quiet revelation.

"A trip to the Death Twin tomorrow," Skye said. She sounded disturbingly cheery. "Who's in?"

CHAPTER
24

The island opened one eye.

It would rest again, but for now, it would wake. It must wake, so when noon came, it could call the ones it needed. The one it needed. Until then, it would watch those already here. Like the one called Paulo, one who shared the island's sense of anticipation, one who might even share the island's true hope. He needed no guidance, which was fortunate since the island could spare no energy for it, not now; all the power the island had left would be spared for moments it must act, and for the final moment, when failure to act would equal failure.

Time would tell.

It always did.

The sun rose over Mount Nil, twinkling with promise. Honeyed light cascaded down the peak in rivulets of brilliant gold. On the far side, out of sight, the silent platform sat ready. As he stared at the mountain, Paulo pictured the black platform drenched in light, the swirls and lines on the ground filled with glittering white sand, waiting.

It was time.

With effort, he turned away from the mountain. By the firepit, a small group sat quietly, some staring off into space, others picking at their food. He'd set a dozen whole fish to roast before dawn; he'd retrieved the full water gourds from the Cove, too. He was preparing the only way he knew how. Hafthor stood, his back to the pit, gazing toward the sea and his little houses. Molly sat near Davey, pushing a piece of fish around on a wooden plank. Calvin crouched on his feet, poking the embers with a long stick, stoking the coals. Amara sat by the fire, near no one. As usual, she wasn't eating, or talking. She was intently carving a wooden stake with cold precision.

"Morning," Paulo said. All five lifted their chins to look at him. He took in their faces, their anxiety and distress and ever-present panic running just below the surface of their expressions. Not for the first time, he marveled at the effortlessness with which he'd watched Rives lead the City before. At the time, Paulo had been so concerned with himself, with his journey. Now all these faces, all painted with their own brand of fear, looked at him for guidance. Looked *to* him.

He wasn't entirely sure that he was up to the task.

Still, here he was.

It also occurred to him that they didn't look as afraid as they should.

He cleared his throat and his head. "I'll be back in a few days," Paulo informed the group. "All the water gourds are full; I refilled them from the Cove this morning. The food stores are as full as they can be, but ration the dried food as best you can; it's all we have. We have a new chicken, so at least we have eggs. Don't waste them. Hafthor will fish each day at the traps. I would suggest that everyone work to keep the firepit going. A night watch with torches wouldn't be a bad idea either."

Calvin's eyes went wide as Molly's narrowed.

"Where are you going?" she asked. Her gaze was wary.

"There is something I have to do. While I'm gone, look to Hafthor for any questions. He's been here the longest besides me."

Arms crossed, Hafthor tipped his head in the barest of nods.

"I should be back in a few days." *Possibly with a newcomer,* he thought. The crescent moon had gleamed in warning, although he hadn't needed it; he *knew.* Tomorrow was the Summer Solstice, the longest day of the year, and the most powerful gate of the year as well. To be called to the noon gate was an honor among his people, yet he fervently hoped no one answered. But something was happening today; he'd felt the island sucking in energy for the past few days, and last night he'd barely slept, so in tune with the silent vibration of the island at its core. The crescent moon had called; he would not risk being late.

Five faces, ten eyes. All still trained on him, waiting.

He relented.

"I can't tell you right now, but when I return, I'll tell you where I went and why. You have my word."

Hafthor gave Paulo a satisfied nod; Davey looked annoyed, as usual. Molly's expression stayed intense, and troubled. Amara had no expression at all. She returned to scraping the piece of wood with a jagged black rock, her movements slow and calculating. Paulo hadn't admitted it to anyone, but he found Amara slightly frightening. Since she'd arrived, she'd focused her time on making weapons, not friends.

Calvin threw his stick into the fire and stood. "All I want to know is what animals live here, all right? Like the ones that can kill us. Because I know I saw a jaguar out there. And Davey here says he saw a tiger, which is flat-out insane. And I want to know what else we can eat because I'm damn hungry and all I've had is fish and raw eggs for two weeks straight."

"Welcome to paradise," Davey muttered.

"I saw a rabbit this morning," Paulo said evenly. "You can trap it. You also can cook eggs over the fire, or go south for coconuts, pineapple, and redfruit. As you know, guava is to the north. There are some crab traps set to the north as well; I haven't checked those lately. But." Paulo paused, making sure he had Calvin's full attention. "Avoid the mudflats; they're directly inland from the Cove. There are at least five hippos there by my last count and they're highly dangerous. There are monkeys there too, which can be more trouble than you'd expect." He fought a wry smile. "And like I first said, I don't know what other animals are here, besides us. But I know they're hungry, just like we are. Don't let the fire go out."

And with that, he left.

It occurred to him he should be more encouraging, but lately, he'd felt that reality was the better course of action. He had three months left to stay alive, to keep the others alive, and then in exactly three months' time, he'd have a second chance to try to correct his colossal failure.

But first, he had to get to the platform.

There was no time to waste.

CHAPTER
25

SKYE
SUMMER SOLSTICE, DAWN

"They're gone." Rives stepped away from the trees, his hands empty.

"Gone?" I pawed through the brush, desperately hoping our canoes would magically appear. They didn't.

"Stolen. Taken. Confiscated. Commandeered." The corner of his mouth quirked slightly. "Gone."

"Got it." I whirled away, fighting a scream of frustration.

"I know." Rives's voice was soft. He looked around, already calculating, already one step ahead. "We need to secure another mode of transportation. Pronto."

"And this is why we should've left last night," I retorted.

He stopped his visual search. "Do you really want to waste time rehashing last night's argument?"

"No." I glanced down the beach, desperately trying not to freak out.

I'd wanted to camp out on Spirit Island—the Death Twin housing the stationary gate—last night, but Rives refused to navigate the waters toward the Death Twins in the dark. He'd put his foot down, literally. I swear, he'd actually stomped. So, picking my battles, I'd opted out of that one, but now I wished I'd fought for it.

Black sand stretched in both directions, empty of people and all seaworthy transportation. In the distance, bathed in dawn's golden light, the Death Twins beckoned, frustratingly out of reach. An ocean swim was out of the question. We needed a boat, *now*.

The solstice clock was ticking.

I spun around and came face-to-face with Charley.

"We need to find a boat to borrow," I told her.

"Commandeer," Rives added helpfully.

"Whatever." Thad's dour mood sliced through the moment. "Let's just find a boat that floats and get this thing done."

For an island out in the middle of nowhere, oddly enough, all the personal watercraft had mysteriously gone missing. It took us three hours to acquire a pitiful-looking dinghy, and, with my dad's help, we finally managed to get it in the water.

"Go," my dad said gruffly. "But please be careful. I love you, Skye."

"Love you too, Dad. And don't worry. The four of us will stick together. We'll be back early afternoon."

He waved, and gave a pointed nod to Rives. "Good luck."

"Let's hustle," Thad said, paddling ferociously. "The sooner we have our gateside chat, the sooner we're done. For all we know, the girl won't show."

"That's the best-case scenario," Rives said.

"Don't tell me the worst," Thad warned. "Don't say it, don't think it. Just—don't."

No one said a word. We fell into a steady rhythm as the four of us stroked directly toward the Death Twin. I wondered if we all had our worst-case scenarios. I wasn't sure what mine was, but I knew it involved failure.

Come, the girl in my head—I still couldn't bring myself to call her Talla—urged. *Hurry*.

I fought a rising sense of panic.

One hour, I thought. One hour to get to Spirit Island, one hour to convince Maaka's cousin not to walk through that gate, one hour to break the gate. And as for that last one, I had absolutely no clue how to do it. I didn't even know if destroying a gate was possible.

"Time to bail," Rives called.

"Bail?" His words wrenched me out of my head. Dark water crashed against unforgiving rock with a vengeance, spitting whitewater froth between the two islands. We weren't anywhere near close enough to swim. "Jump out? Are you crazy?"

"Yes, I'm crazy. It's why I'm doing this with you." He handed me his paddle. "But I don't mean jump out. I mean bail, literally." He pointed at my feet, where cold water wrapped my ankles in liquid shackles. "We're sinking. And we need to get through the channel between the islands in one piece." The determined sea god Rives was back. "Thad and I'll bail while you two paddle."

"Great," I said.

"Just super," Thad agreed, scooping up a frothy handful and tossing it overboard.

Rives and Thad were a silent bailing machine while Charley maneuvered us into the slough between the islands. Massive black walls sloped away from us, glistening with water, not unlike the walls of the Crystal Cove back on Nil. Just when I thought *It's taking too long*, we popped out from the narrow passage, bursting into brighter light as the current slacked. The narrow beach where I landed after following Paulo so many months ago waited thirty feet away. There were no canoes in sight, no boats of any sort. And no people.

"Looks like a ghost town," Thad murmured.

Rives said nothing, his face chiseled stone.

Hurry, Skye! the girl begged without break; it was a deafening chorus of one.

"Faster!" I cried, digging my paddle deep into the water.

The dinghy jerked to an abrupt halt; wood splintered with a resounding *crack* near my feet as the boat ran aground on a rock. Water rushed in through the floorboard like a geyser, filling quickly. The four of us spilled into the breakwater. Half walking, half bodysurfing, we made for shore. The boat sank behind us without a trace.

We staggered onto the beach, panting and soaking wet. The weakest swimmer, I was dead last.

Ahead, the tree line beckoned. Beyond it, the foliage thickened, too dense to peer through.

Skye!

"We need to hurry," I said, moving toward the trees without stopping.

"Skye." Rives touched my arm, his jaw working as he fought to stay in control. "Stay close to me. Please?"

"You stay with *me*." I pulled his hand reassuringly. "C'mon."

Thad fell into step beside me. "Skye, tell me you've got the words ready."

I started to smile, to adopt a fake-it-till-you-make-it sort of confidence, then I switched to brutal honesty and my ghost of a smile vanished. "Thad, *I* have to do this. I hear Nil every day; I hear the island right now. Like a shout in my head. It's screaming for me to come. Like Charley said, it's closure. The island wants us here, to stop the gate from taking another."

Thad didn't look convinced.

"You don't have to come." Impatience gave my words unintended bite. "You can stay right here, Thad. On this beach. No judgment from me." I started jogging toward the trees. I didn't wait to see if Thad followed; I could barely think with the noise in my head.

Come, she begged.

CHOOSE ME.

Her words filled all the space in my head, pleas bathed in blood and hope and life and emotion as I jogged along; an invisible thread tugged me down the path I could have walked blindfolded. The leafy canopy shrank as we neared the center of the small island. Rives hadn't left my side. Thad and Charley kept pace on our heels.

"Someone's already there," I said.

"Who?" Rives asked. "Lana?"

Was it Lana? I didn't answer, because I didn't know. I just *felt.*

"I think it's a girl," I murmured. "But I'm not sure who." And I felt the presence of a boy, which made no sense at all.

Apparently I still hovered on the edge of crazy.

Abruptly the trees ended; a black rock clearing sprawled before us like a small stage, one with a single player. A crisp memory rushed back, the past mixing with the present. Paulo, kneeling on the black rock, tracing lines on the ground in the dark. Only this time it was a girl kneeling in the light. Her long brown hair fell around her shoulders; she wore a ring of white flowers around her head. More white blossoms were strewn around the platform. Sand as white as sugar filled the rings and lines cut into the ground. The juxtaposition of white on black was stunning, highlighted by the pure light filtering down through the trees.

I stepped onto the black rock, my bare toes brushing the outermost circle filled with white sand. Instantly, the invisible voice fell silent; the mental barrage stopped. I was blissfully alone in my head.

I could *think.*

"Lana." I spoke softly.

Her head snapped up, her mouth open in surprise. It was the girl I'd seen yesterday with Maaka. Her gaze swept across us and fell on Rives. Her eyes narrowed as she pointed at him. "This is *my* time, my gate, not yours. Wait your turn like the rest of us." I realized she thought Rives was an islander, like her.

He looked taken aback.

"Lana, it's not what you think." Rives raised his hands. "No one is here to take your gate or your turn. But you don't want to go. I promise you don't want to go to that island. We've all been there and it's not the place you think it is."

"He's right," I said. "The island has changed, Lana. And not for the better."

"Sure, there's fish and shrimp and gorgeous black sand beaches where you can meditate to find your inner chi or personal path or whatever," Rives said blandly. "But there's a dark side, and it's not pretty. Ask any one of us. All four of us went there, and we're here to convince you that it's a bad idea. I promise you, Lana, you don't want to go."

A small goat bleated from the edge of the clearing, followed by the snap of a branch. Zane trotted out from the trees, his bleached-blond hair falling into his eyes. Seeing us, he stopped and broke into a wide grin. "Whoa. What is this, old home week?"

"Zane!" I ran over and hugged him. I hadn't seen him since our group Nil reunion six weeks ago, and his sudden appearance *here* made no sense. He squeezed me back, then slapped Rives on the back.

"Damn good to see you, man, but these are strange circumstances," Rives said. He stared at Zane, and I couldn't help thinking Rives was cataloging the circles under Zane's eyes and the hollows of his cheeks.

Did I look as exhausted as Zane?

"What are you doing here?" Rives asked him.

"Can't stop dreaming about Nil, Chief." Zane swallowed. "Actually, I pretty much dream about Sy. Every night. He stands there, covered in blood. And he talks to me. Good times." He shook his head. "I see dead people," Zane whispered in a childlike voice. Dropping back into his normal tone, he laughed without smiling. "It's like *The Sixth Sense*, only it's not as cool when it's really happening to you."

"I'm so sorry," I said with feeling. "I don't dream of Sy, but I dream of Nil. It's why we're here too. But how'd you find this place?"

"I've been here before, remember? Three months ago?" Zane grinned. "But I would've found it anyway. It's like the island called me here, called me *back*. It's like I followed Sy's voice in my head like a GPS. I know"—he held up both hands—"it sounds crazy. Lately I've felt a little whacked."

"Probably because you're seeing dead people," Lana said not-so-sweetly.

Zane's eyes whipped to Lana. In one glance, he took in the skimpy white dress, band of white flowers in her hair, the fluffy white kitten in a basket by her feet, and the goat tethered to a nearby tree. Understanding flashed across his face like a shadow. "Looks like you cats were ready to start this party without me."

"It's not your party, it's *mine*," Lana shot back.

Just like Paulo, I thought.

"Happy birthday, Lana," I said quietly.

Her head whipped to me. Vulnerability flickered across her face before she flashed a cool smile. "It's not my birthday. Yet."

"So when is it?" Zane looked curious.

"Why do you care?" Lana crossed her arms.

Before Zane could answer, Michael exited the trees. He pointed at Zane and said, "You walk fast, my friend." Then he broke into a rare Michael smile.

Zane burst into laughter as Lana threw her hands into the air. "Is there anyone you didn't invite?"

"I was invited by the island," Michael said, turning to her. "It called me here."

"Same as me." Zane nodded. "We both got a little island invite to go along with our hellacious dreams of Sy. My mom thinks I'm on a surf trip." He shrugged. "Michael and I've been camped out here for almost a week. My dad's picking us up tomorrow if his boat makes good time."

Lana was staring at them with a slightly open mouth. Then she clamped her mouth closed, her expression clearly irritated.

"So glad I could have such a nice turnout for my bon voyage party," she said sarcastically. "But it's supposed to be a solitary exit. A quiet reflective moment as we shed the old self en route to the new."

"Gee, so Maaka of you," Rives observed. His crossed arms matched hers. "It seems like he gave you the traditional send-off, but left out the good parts. Did he bother mentioning that the island is home to hippos and leopards and other fun beasts that will eat you for lunch?" He tilted his head toward the snowy kitten in the basket by her feet. "That cat won't stand a chance on Nil. It'll be a midnight snack for a hyena. And the island likes to play with its food now, Lana. And that's you."

She glared at Rives, saying nothing.

"Lana, listen to him," I urged. "Listen to *me*. The island has changed, I promise you. You don't want to go."

"She's right," Thad said. Charley was nodding.

Lana's eyes stayed on me.

"If it's so bad, then why did Paulo stay?"

I hesitated, not sure what to say.

"Exactly," she said smugly. "*Haoles* don't understand our traditions, or the island's purpose." She paused. "Now leave."

"What?" Zane looked shocked. "Leave? Are *you* crazy? Look, Lana, all of us showed up because the island is still messing with our heads. *In* our heads. We're a flesh-and-blood warning sign telling you not to go."

"Zane's right," I said. "The island can't survive without us. Without you. And its time is over." I stepped closer to her, my hands raised in surrender. "Lana, I know this will sound crazy but I hear the island. It's telling me to stop you. To stop this." I waved my hand around.

Doubt flickered across her face. "The island talks to you?" she asked quietly, her eyes riveted on me.

"Yes. And it doesn't want you to go. It doesn't want anyone to go."

Lana looked conflicted, her certainty shaken.

"It's an end," I spoke softly, "not a beginning. Please don't go."

She was wavering, I could tell.

"The island may not even be there," Rives added. "When we left, the island was on fire. Literally, the island was going up in flames."

Lana glanced back at Rives, her expression turning suspicious. "You're lying," she said.

"He's not," I said. "We had torches to protect us in the meadow, and when a hyena killed one of our friends, we set the hyena on fire. And the meadow was burning."

Anger rolled over Lana's face like a cloud. "So this is guilt, is that it? You set the island on fire, and you feel guilty for what you did. Or maybe for not saving your friend. Well, that's your problem. I have a date with destiny."

Zane shook his head. "Dude, your date isn't going to end well, that's for sure."

Lana shot him a withering look. "So, you're a dating expert?"

Zane's grin was light. "What can I say? Ladies love cool Zane. I think it's the surfer vibe." He looked thoughtful.

Lana parted her lips to argue when the island breeze stalled.

The noise in my head exploded in the newfound stillness; it clouded my thoughts as the girl in my head screamed at me to hurry.

To stop Lana.

To *choose*.

The ground near Lana's feet shimmered, then vaulted vertically into the air.

"Please." I choked out the words. "Don't go."

Behind Lana, the massive gate took shape; it was a writhing, shifting swath of air, still tinged in black. Then the black fell away, leaving a brilliant, glittering wall of iridescence. Beside me, Charley sucked in her breath.

Rives threw one arm in front of me. "Lana!" He was holding me back, talking to her. I was a bystander, trapped by Rives's arm pressing against my waist and the girl screaming in my head. I couldn't move; I couldn't think. Couldn't find the words I needed.

Prisms of light bounced across Lana's face, her defiance turning to awe.

"Don't do this," Rives pleaded with Lana. "The island may be a burned-out husk for all we know. It was *on fire*, Lana. Hell, maybe the volcano exploded and the island is gone."

"If it was gone, there wouldn't be a gate." She pointed at the glittering air shimmering behind her. No longer rising, it writhed on invisible hooks, waiting. "And if it didn't want me to come, it wouldn't have opened the doorway." Her voice rang with confidence.

"You're wrong," I managed. But she wasn't looking at me; she was utterly entranced by the gate.

"Lana, listen! I don't know what you'll find if you go through that gate," Rives spoke fast, "but it sure as hell isn't paradise."

Lana glanced at Rives, a slight grin curving her lips. "It never was." And with that, she strode into the gate.

"Damn," Zane said. He stared after her, and I knew what would happen an instant before it did.

Zane. My lips refused to cooperate but I was already too late; Zane was leaping into the gate.

"Zane!" Rives shouted as he lunged toward him. His move took him within inches of the shimmering wall. He stood rock still, glittering light caressing his face as he stared at the gate where Zane vanished. Rives's mouth moved, but no sound came out.

"Rives?" I stepped forward—*it was so easy*—and reached to pull Rives back. The air became a mirror; I saw the reflection of Lana, then Zane. Then Paulo and another boy, a brilliant kaleidoscope of people, some I knew, some I didn't. Most I didn't.

The others faded and Talla filled the frame. Her clear blue eyes found mine.

Choose me, she whispered, her eyes pleading. She offered her hand. *Skye, choose me.*

In my ear, Rives's voice turned desperate. "Choose *me*, Skye. She's not real."

Come, Talla whispered.

The ache wasn't mine; the pain wasn't mine. It poured out of her, into me, through me; it filled me until it was all I could feel.

Time swirled in a circular rush. Images overlapped, spinning fast.

I was Lana jumping through the gate; I was the girl begging me to choose; I was Rives holding my hand; I was Rives holding me back; I was Rives yelling *Choose me.* I was inside the gate; I was outside the gate; I was reflected in the gate; I was lost in my own head. The girl's voice rang clear and true, cutting through the chaos like a crystal chime.

Choose me, the voice commanded.

Pushing Rives back, I launched myself into the gate, because in that moment, I had no choice.

I'm sorry, I thought, closing my eyes to block out Rives's shocked face. The heat seared my flesh and bones; the darkness closed over me, snarling in victory, cruel and controlling and frighteningly cold. It stopped my heart, encasing it in black ice; if the darkness pressed a single millimeter more, I would fracture. I would shatter into a million lifeless bits; I would become dust in the dark. In that moment, stripped bare at the darkness's mercy, I knew I'd made a crucial mistake: the darkness had won.

I was a fool, tricked by Nil.

I would never make it back.

CHAPTER 26

RIVES
SUMMER SOLSTICE, NOON

"No!"

I swung for Skye's arm, catching air; it slicked through my fingers like a ghost.

I'm sorry.

Skye's pain-filled thought lanced through my head, full of ache and regret and frightening desperation. The thought faded; the Talla inside the gate laughed. Her smile turned cruel, and superior.

Not Talla, I thought grimly.

The Talla I knew was gone.

And so was Skye.

I leaped toward the gate, but before I made it a meter, Thad wrenched me back.

"Don't do it, man," he warned.

"Let me go!" I ripped my arm from his.

"Li?" Charley stepped toward the gate, her eyes unblinking. Light bounced off her face in shimmering sets. "Is that you?"

As Thad spun toward Charley, I threw myself into the gate after Skye. I felt her essence—I felt her mind, her soul. I felt *her*.

I felt her fading.

"No!" I screamed.

My shout died as I choked on the heat. Black walls slammed down, then they closed in; I'd never felt so compressed—or so trapped. The darkness wanted me; it wanted Skye; it seethed with hunger and power on an incomprehensible level. But I also knew the darkness didn't want Skye half as much as I did.

She's mine, I snarled.

And then I focused on Skye, not the darkness. If I could take her pain, I would.

Abruptly the strange one-sided pressure slacked. I was falling, sucked inside the darkness like a shot. Like someone had pulled a cork, releasing pressure from one end, forcing me in one particular direction. In *Skye's* direction.

She's through, I thought with satisfaction.

And then the brutal pain hit.

Fire, pain, ice, more pain. More intense than before, more crushing, more cruel. Absolute sub-zero stealing every molecule of me.

And then I blacked out.

I opened my eyes to harsh black rock, familiar and foreign.

Blinking, I oriented myself in one long moment. No clothes, no surprise. A diamond-shaped eye watched me from the center of a simple sun boasting twelve distinct rays. Stark white sand filled the black lines. The air smelled of salt and sea. No smoke.

Skye lay beside me, eyes closed, still unconscious.

Or dead, came the cold thought.

"Skye?" I whispered. *This is not happening.*

An amused whisper sliced through the back of my head. *Of course it is.*

Skye didn't move. I gently pressed my fingers to her throat. Her skin was icy, but her heart still beat. Slow, but steady.

I took a deep breath and blinked against the brilliant sun and hell on Nil.

"Chief." Zane tossed me a pair of shorts. I caught them reflexively as he gently covered Skye with a cloth.

A meter away, the writhing gate flickered, then turned Nil black. Beside me, Skye twitched.

Thad fell out of the gate, barely missing me. As he touched the ground, the massive gate recoiled; it snapped back, collapsing on itself with an eerie hiss. And then it was gone. Closed.

And here we were.

On Nil.

With a gasp, Skye sat up, blinking. The chest cloth started to fall; she instinctively tugged it up, then wrapped it around her chest in a flash. Clearly Nil-autopilot survival mode was in full effect. As pale as death, she stared at Thad.

"No," she whispered. "This is wrong."

"Hell, yeah, this is wrong," Zane agreed. "It's twenty-seven kinds of wrong."

"No," Skye repeated. Her eyes never left Thad, who woke with a groan. Conscious and blinking, he stared at the empty air where the gate had hung. "It wasn't supposed to be you," she said. "It was supposed to be Charley. Charley should be here."

Thad's head whipped toward Skye, anger darkening his features. "What the hell, Skye? No, Charley should *not* be here. None of us should be here. And we *wouldn't* be here if we hadn't followed you to that damn island."

"It's not her fault." I managed to keep my voice level. "You know who to blame and it's not Skye."

Zane lobbed a pair of shorts over to Thad, who snatched them out of the air with a vengeance.

Skye hadn't moved.

"Skye?" I brushed a wild curl out of her face. "You okay?"

She looked at me as if seeing me for the first time—really seeing me. Relief flooded her face as she threw her arms around me. "Rives," she breathed, holding me tight. Emotion hit me in one massive wave: relief, love, hope, fear, and a dozen others, all raw, all pouring off Skye. "Thank you." Her whisper brushed my ear.

"For what?"

"For being there. For coming after me." Her voice was so small it threw me. "For a moment, the darkness won. And then I felt you." She held me tight, then, ever so gently, she placed her palm against my bare chest, over my heart. Classic Skye, bracing herself. Bracing *me*. "And I knew I wasn't lost."

"Never," I said. "We're a team, remember?"

She nodded. Lifting her eyes to mine, she looked miserable. "I didn't mean to take that gate, Rives, I swear. I'm sorry." *I wasn't strong enough,* came her thought.

"No apology needed. Nil is—" I stopped. *Determined? Hungry? Powerful?* Nothing fit, and now that I'd personally felt how much it wanted Skye, it was no wonder the island had tricked her into taking that gate. "Nil," I finished. "And you *are* strong enough, all right?"

Nodding, she exhaled slowly and pulled away, no longer trembling. With each breath, she called on that part of herself that survived Nil before, locking another chunk of Skye armor in place. A hint of color touched her cheeks. Not full Skye-fierce, but she'd get there.

She was okay.

For now, came the cold whisper.

I flinched.

Skye didn't notice; she was tying her skirt tight, moving methodically, already steeling herself against whatever lay ahead. "That gate was something else," she mused. "It's like the gates are harder to survive." The Skye I'd first met was back. Thoughtful, assessing, her short-lived panic gone. "Like the gates are changing too."

"Agreed," Zane said. "That gate hurt like an ugly mofo."

A few meters away, Thad stood rock still, every muscle wound tight, his eyes locked on Skye. "Skye, I need to know. What did you mean, it was supposed to be Charley? Did you two *plan* to come back?"

He obviously hadn't heard Skye's apology.

"Thad—" I started, but Skye pressed her hand against my heart again, this time to stop me from talking. She straightened her spine as she turned to Thad.

"No." She met his furious gaze straight on. "I promise you, I wasn't planning to come, and Charley wasn't either. But I couldn't turn away from that gate; it was more powerful than me. I totally didn't expect that. And when I stepped inside the gate, I felt how much it wanted me. To come, maybe even stay. In that darkness." She blinked. "And then just before I woke, I knew it wanted Charley. I could see her on the other side, and I could *feel* how much it wanted her, as much as it wanted me. Maybe it was all in my head—seeing her, feeling that want. But it felt real."

I didn't doubt for a second it was real.

"The island didn't like that Charley left Nil early." Skye spoke softly, still talking to Thad. "I don't know how I know that but I do. And when you came through that gate right now, the island got—" She paused, hunting for the right word. "Mad," she said finally. "I felt its surprise, and its fury." Skye shook her head slightly. "You surprised the island, threw it a curveball, I guess. Maybe it changed its mind but I don't think so. Otherwise, why would it be angry? And I'm certain that the island is not happy."

"Nil's never happy," Zane murmured.

Thad stared at Skye, like he was trying to process her words, or this jacked-up moment.

Skye stared right back. "I promise, Thad." Her steady voice radiated calm, all fear gone. The girl whose motto was *Think first, panic later* stood her ground. "Charley and I weren't planning to come. You have my word."

Tick.

Tock.

Abruptly, Thad sighed. His icy defense cracked. He ran his hand through his hair, breathing deeply. His eyes were closed tight, his face still a mask of fury, but it was no longer directed at Skye, at least not totally. "I'm just seriously pissed off."

Skye's smile was wan.

"For what it's worth, I don't think the island's too happy with you either."

"Good." His jaw was hard.

"Well, this has been fun," Lana said.

Hands on her hips, her expression was haughty. She glared at Skye. Paulo stood a few meters away, leaning against the black rock wall of the mountain, studying us. Not angry, just curious. Like he was either giving us space or trying to figure out what to do. Piles of clothes dotted the black rock. Small sets, freshly left. A stack of sandals sat near Paulo's feet.

He planned ahead, I thought.

Now I understood how Zane had scored clothes so quickly. Lana had obviously taken advantage of Paulo's consideration; she already wore an island skirt and chest wrap. He seemed to notice that detail at the same moment I did.

"You're welcome for the clothes, Lana." Paulo's voice made Lana's head snap to him.

"Paulo." His name was distasteful on her tongue. "I heard you took your brother's place."

Paulo smiled, his arms crossed but relaxed. "No, Lana. It was my place. My time. My journey, not his."

Lana raised an eyebrow, respect creeping across her face. She nodded. "I see that. So it is. Good luck with your journey, Paulo. Now it's time for mine."

"Wait." Paulo moved to stop her, his expression calm. "The island isn't what it once was. It's not what you were told. The island, it's cruel now." He paused. "I don't think it's a place you want to be alone."

A blast of burning air punctuated Paulo's words.

"Well, that's new." Zane pointed to a steam vent adjacent to the platform. "I guess Nil's just blowing off a little steam."

Lana snorted. "This is your group? Did you come to save them,

Paulo, or greet me? I'm fine, Paulo. I've waited to come for seventeen years. Let me go."

"Your choice, Lana." Paulo's expression stayed neutral, but his eyes were sad. Older. The last three months had inflicted invisible Nil scars. "I won't stop you. But here, I promise there is safety in numbers."

She laughed. "Nice try. But I'm fine. See you around the island."

And then she stalked off.

Only Zane watched her go.

"We okay?" I asked Thad quietly.

"Yeah." He sighed. "Man, I did not see this coming."

"That's Nil," I said crisply. Maybe Thad had his own blind spot too. Only his blind spot wasn't here; she was safe, back home.

My worst-case scenario was unfolding in front of me.

Paulo didn't look too happy either. "Why did you come back?" he asked Skye.

"Nil wouldn't let me go," she said.

"What does that mean?" Paulo frowned.

"Exactly how it sounds." She smiled. "And now here I am."

Paulo shook his head. "I wish you hadn't come."

That makes two of us, I thought. His troubled expression heightened my already elevated fear quotient. No one chose to come back to Nil, except of course, Skye. No doubt she was a first. She always did things her way, something I loved about her. But here, the thought wrecked me. Nil had its own agenda, and it didn't like to share. It liked to keep its prizes, its toys.

Which meant us.

But that part we knew. The rest of Nil's daily grind shifted like the wind. The island was unpredictable, an ever-changing variable, like us; I had yet to find the constant.

Maybe Skye's the constant now, came the unwelcome thought.

No, I thought savagely. Now Paulo was frowning at me.

I shrugged. I wasn't inviting Paulo into my head too. It was too damn crowded as it was.

Get yourself together, Rives, I thought. Daydreaming on Nil was a fast track to death, and it wouldn't help Skye, either. For her part, she didn't look like she needed a bit of help. Chin lifted, gaze sharp, she was slowly surveying the platform. I realized she was cataloging the items on the ground, taking care to keep anything useful, a smart-Skye move.

I missed my knife. Or rather, Thad's knife.

My hip felt dangerously bare.

Glancing around, I swept the platform for blades and came up empty. "Paulo, the knives that were here," I said. "Do you have them?"

"Not with me. I gathered everything and took it back to the City. Spears, knives, clothes." He shrugged. "Seemed a waste to leave it all behind, when it was really all anyone had."

I nodded, more than a little impressed, knowing that haul would have taken more than one trip.

Thad stepped forward and offered his hand. "I'm Thad."

Recognition flickered through Paulo's eyes as he shook Thad's hand. "Thad, as in after William and before Hiroto? On the Wall?"

"That's me." Thad nodded.

"Paulo." He shook his head. "And welcome back. I can't believe one person would come back, let alone four."

"I wasn't planning on it." Thad's voice still had an edge.

"No one was," I said. A point worth repeating, because I sensed Thad hadn't fully let Skye off the hook.

"Dude, I don't really even know what happened," Zane said. "I saw—" He broke off, staring at the steps where Lana disappeared.

"What?" Skye asked.

"Not what, who," Zane replied. He glanced at me. "I'd swear Lana turned around inside the gate and crooked her finger at me. It's crazy, because she won't give me the time of day now, but I'd swear she called me. And I couldn't say no." He turned slightly red. "Did any of you see Lana in the gate?"

"I saw someone else." *A ghost*, I thought. A cruel trick.

"Me too," Skye said quietly. "Only I saw a girl I've never met. Her name was Talla."

Thad sucked in his breath.

Skye glanced knowingly at him, then smiled wanly at Zane. "You're not the only one who sees dead people."

"Make that three of us." Thad rubbed his forehead. "I saw Li."

"Like Charley," I murmured, remembering Charley's question as she stepped toward the gate. "That makes six of us," I said. "Zane and Michael saw Sy; Skye and I saw Talla. And Thad and Charley saw Li. So six of us have seen people walking and talking even though we know those people died on Nil."

"It's like *The Walking Dead* without the zombie part," Zane said.

I shot Zane a sharp look. "The point is, Nil has some new tricks. New head games."

"Very true." Paulo nodded. Turning toward Skye, he drew something out of his satchel and offered it to her. I recognized it as her rock sling immediately.

"I've taken care of it, but it doesn't belong to me," he said. "If you want it, it's yours."

Smiling, she slid the weapon over her shoulder with an ease that was both reassuring and disturbing. "Now all I need is a rock."

He returned her smile, his caramel eyes light for a brief moment. "That I think you can find without me." His smile faded, his gaze still on Skye.

Her eyes had returned to the ground. To the sand-filled lines gouging the rock.

"Skye?" I stepped closer. "Do you see something?"

"No." She sighed. Striding forward, she scooped up a scrap of twine off the ground and tied back her hair with force. Her expression turned lethally calm.

"Now what?" Zane asked.

"Now we have three months," she said. "Three months to survive, three months to find others. Three months to figure out the last of Nil's secrets. The biggest one, the one we missed last time."

"Which is?" I asked.

"Which is how to end Nil once and for all."

CHAPTER
27

NIL
NOON

These humans were such fun. Completely predictable, until the moment when they acted inexplicably foolish, delightfully exposing their weaknesses and fears and vulnerabilities for the island to see.

The island would use each one toward its own purpose.

Acquiring the male, Thad, had been a delightful surprise, his bitterness extraordinarily refined, his fear palpable. He'd brushed the gate with his elbow, a careless mistake, and the island had been unable to resist. It had wanted the female, Charley, a female stolen from the island by her male. For a moment, the island had been abruptly furious. It had been tricked, denied Charley by her mate for a second time; it did not want them both: their connection was too strong, their bond too great. Individually they would be easier to break.

So the island had closed the gate. The biggest regret was the loss of the male, Michael; his strength had tempted the island, so much that the island had called him, a call made easier by the blood trail left by the male, Sy. Both Michael and Zane had worn Sy's blood like a marker, and it had used that marker to pull them back. The unpredictability of the humans frustrated the island immensely, and yet, this same *unpredictability brought the island such pleasure when it turned in the island's favor.*

Soon it would toy with the ones freshly called. It would use their weaknesses, prey on their fears.

But first, it would observe the ones denied. Noon cost the island, yet noon also cost those left behind. The pain of noon always proved entertaining, on both sides of the seam, a fact that had not escaped the island's notice.

Like now.

Charley stared at the black rock platform. It was empty, not counting an unhappy goat and a mewing snowy kitten. The white flowers littered around the platform mocked her. *They should be wilted,* she thought, staring at a handful of flowers where the gate had just been. It was so wrong that the flowers looked fresh, and alive. The blossoms were already dead; they just didn't realize it yet.

Reality rushed in like cold wind.

The gate was gone. Thad was gone.

And she was still here, denied the chance to help or choose for herself.

"What just happened?" Charley said, turning slowly to the boy beside her, whose name she couldn't remember. His eyes were locked on the place the gate had vanished. "Tell me that did not just happen. Please tell me this is a nightmare and I'll wake up any minute."

"It *is* a nightmare," he agreed, finally turning to her, "but a living one." His eyes were sympathetic. "Thad—he was your boyfriend, yes?"

Boyfriend, Charley thought. A weak word for how she felt about Thad. Soul mate, partner. A gift from Nil, now taken by Nil.

Abruptly she was blindingly furious.

"Yes," she said, her voice shockingly cold. "And I'm going to get him back."

Michael nodded. "This gate. It will reopen in three months. They will appear here"—he gestured around the rock—"in three months."

Three months, Charley thought.

Thad. She thought his name with all her might. *I love you. I believe in you. Be smart, be safe, be strong—and I'll see you in three months.* She couldn't bear to think of anything else. She also had the thought that if Skye could hear Nil *here*, maybe Thad could hear her *there*. It gave her small comfort. Stranger things had happened.

Charley lifted her chin. "Then let's get ready. But in the meantime, we need a way off this island. Our rowboat sank."

Michael nodded. "I have a canoe. Two, actually, because Zane had one too."

Figures, she thought. *I guess we got the canoes after all.*

"Time to go," she said, picking up the tiny kitten, her tone resolute. "We've got three months."

Tick tock.

Later she'd wonder if that thought was hers. But for now, it didn't matter.

The clock was definitely ticking.

Lana found the cave easily.

Her grandmother's directions had been clear. *Circle the mountain, trace the cliff. Look for the gap in the black rocks, the trailhead of a path. On the ledge, look for the giant ear.* She'd obeyed without hesitation, and now she was here: The cave mouth yawned a few meters away.

She moved toward the entrance, wasting no time. Here, time was not to be wasted; it was to be treasured. Used. Explored.

To explore within.

To invite the island in, as her grandmother had advised. And for Lana, it was all to begin at the Listening Cave, as it had begun for her grandmother, the one Lana herself was named for. Her grandmother, Alana, was one of the last seers to return from the island. Too many island women had not found the Sight in recent decades, or if they had, they had not returned. Lana's own aunt, Lina, had not returned, her fate a family mystery and secret wrapped in one.

Lana would be different. She knew it. She *felt* it.

Still, at the cave's entrance, she paused. She studied the mouth of the cave with a critical eye. Lana was loath to admit it to herself, but she was slightly unsettled by the ease with which she'd found it, yet at the same time, her success stoked her already glowing confidence. She could see how the cave would be easily overlooked, easily missed. An overhang shaded the mouth, rough and slanted. The actual opening faced east, opening toward the mountain, gaping as if to welcome lava in one big swallow. But no lava flowed this far; the lava that had carved this cave was long gone. Far to the north, lava still dropped into the sea with a silent hiss, but the molten river was too far away to be heard or seen; the clouds of steam in the distance were the only hint of heat at all.

There was no danger here, only safety.

Or so her aunt had promised.

Remembering Paulo's warning, Lana stepped into the cave with caution. As expected, the mouth opened to a surprisingly generous room on the left. Its ceiling sloped away, sloped *in*, a pocket crafted from lava or water or some other force of nature in the island's history. The small cavern matched her grandmother's description perfectly, except that the cavern wasn't bare.

Someone had been here recently.

A pile of coconuts and pineapple sat in a corner, beside a gourd and small coconut shell cup. Two stacks of cloth were folded neatly next to the fruit. A bag leaned against one stack. Nothing else was here, and no one besides Lana herself.

She was alone, as she had expected to be.

Relaxing, Lana moved around the cave, getting acquainted with her new home. She picked up the gourd, pleased to find it full, and sniffed.

No smell. She poured a bit into the cup, and dipped her finger in for a taste.

Water, she thought, pleased.

She drank it all, then set down the cup and gourd as she inspected the rest. The stacks of cloth were bedding, plus a bandana and two pairs of shorts. The bag contained knives. Mostly wood, but one was metal, an odd surprise.

Paulo had obviously taken pains to prepare this place for her. Considerate, but unnecessary, although the stash of knives could prove useful. Picking up the metal knife, she studied the blade with the same care she'd used to inspect the water gourd. Primitive, raw, and unabashedly metal, the knife seemed out of place. Rust coated the edges, adding to its aged look.

With a start, Lana realized the rust wasn't rust at all; it was dried blood.

"Put it down," a sharp voice behind her demanded.

Lana jerked her head up to find a girl pointing a matching metal blade at her heart. Luminous dark eyes set in a thin face regarded her coldly. A thick brown braid fell across the girl's shoulder. She matched Lana in dress and stance, only the girl radiated hostility.

"Now," the girl snapped. She flicked the knife once for emphasis.

Lana didn't move.

Still gripping the knife, she watched the girl carefully, surprise turning to outrage in her belly. This was *her* journey, *her* cave. *Her* time. Who was this girl to demand anything of her?

"Why?" Lana's voice stayed calm.

"Because I told you to." The girl's eyes remained fixed on Lana, like her knife.

Following some silent cue, two boys stepped from the shadowed entrance to flank the girl like lieutenants. Both were fit, with taut stomachs and lean muscles, but the similarities ended with their abs. One had dark hair, straight and sleek, capping light eyes and light skin that had recently turned tan. He wore a cocky smile like a prized accessory. The other boy had dark hair, dark skin, dark eyes, and no expression at all. He reminded Lana of a living shadow. He was, by far, the most alarming of the three.

"I said put it down," the girl repeated. Her icy tone warred with her lilting Spanish accent.

"I don't always do as I'm told," Lana said coolly.

A glimmer of respect flashed through the girl's eyes. "Neither do I," she said. She lowered her blade slightly.

Lana followed suit.

Abruptly the girl dropped her knife to her waist.

"Carmen," the girl said, still holding the knife. She tipped her head slightly toward the boy who was one step from blending into the shadows. "This is James," she said. "And this is Ace." Now Carmen pointed to the boy with the slick hair as his insolent grin broadened.

"Hi," Ace said. He winked.

Lana would've rolled her eyes or snorted but she didn't dare look away from the girl, or from James. Unlike Ace, James didn't acknowledge her. He had a predatory look about him that was deeply unnerving. No, not predatory. Piercing, as if he saw right through her.

"Lana," she said, fighting the urge to step back. She'd just realized that her back brushed the wall as it was; she was outnumbered, and trapped. In her own cave.

Her fury flared anew.

"So how long have you been staying here?" Lana bit back the words *in my cave.*

Carmen's eyes flicked to the side wall, where slashes marked the rock like graffiti.

"In this cave? Eighteen days," Carmen answered. "A few more on the island." She cocked her head, her eyes on Lana's. "And you?"

Tradition tied her tongue. Rives and Skye had warned her that the island had changed; Maaka too. He'd told her of the wild gates, warned her that she would not be alone. But she'd never anticipated that her own cave would feel so crowded, that she'd be trapped by bodies and weapons and the weight of a history she was forbidden to share. And the fact that it was all crashing in on her on her very first day was almost more than Lana could bear.

"I never asked for this," Lana murmured, her hand lowering another fraction.

"None of us did." Carmen's voice had lost its bite; something else had taken its place.

Pity? Lana wondered, her spine stiffening. It was unacceptable. No one need feel sorry for her, and they would not trap her either. Part of Lana knew she should tell Carmen and Ace and the mysterious James about the yearly time constraints and about the gates—all of them, even hers—but part of her knew that sharing her knowledge would bring her closer to them; they would become confidantes, and that cut directly against the very nature of this journey for her.

Let Maaka and Paulo get friendly with the haoles, she thought. *Not me.*

She walked up to Carmen, knife cradled in her hand. "You may be staying here," Lana said coldly, "but that does not make this cave yours. And this"—Lana raised the knife—"is mine. The rest of the island belongs to no one." With a calculating step, she moved toward Ace, away from Carmen and James. As she anticipated that he would, Ace slid to one side and Lana strode through the gap. She moved quickly, not knowing where she was going, her carefully orchestrated opening-day plan torn to bits within the first hour of landing.

"Let her go." Carmen's voice drifted behind her.

Lana didn't look back. At least she had the satisfaction of winning that hand. But she didn't doubt that she hadn't won the war. She knew without asking that she'd lost her cave, and that rankled her. She was homeless and aimless, not unlike how the *haoles* must have felt when they first arrived, a similarity that did not sit well. And a female *haole* with island knives and two bodyguards at her beck and call infuriated Lana on another level entirely.

No, this island was not a peaceful place to be.

Lana sighed. Know-it-all Rives was right, not that she would give him the satisfaction of telling him. And as for Paulo, who'd said she shouldn't be alone, the island no longer seemed like a place where she *could* be alone. Had he known that too?

Making her way around the ledge, she blinked. People were everywhere. In her cave, on her platform, behind her, in the air in front of her. She felt eyes everywhere, watching.

She sighed again. Seeking solitude, she had no idea where to turn to escape—from the people, not the island. But she was determined to try.

Carmen let Lana go.

She hated giving up the knife, but she knew that sometimes people must be allowed to feel as if they'd won until it was time to make the winning move, and Carmen wasn't done. After Lana disappeared, Carmen turned to James.

"She knows something," Carmen said slowly. "Something she's not telling us. Something she chose not to tell us."

"Like what?" Ace said. He faced the cave's exit with curiosity.

Idiot, she thought. She still couldn't accept that Ace was as dim as he seemed, but he'd yet to prove otherwise.

"I don't know," she said irritably. "But if it's important enough to hide, then it's important enough for us to find out." Her eyes were back on James. "I want to know who she meets up with, what she says. Where she goes. I want her followed." She nodded at James, who left without a word. He barely spoke, but in Carmen's mind, he was miles ahead of Ace in the brains and stealth departments. She'd met James when she was fleeing a leopard that he was tracking, and after a shared dinner of fruit and fish, they'd made a pact to look out for each other. Still, Carmen didn't entirely trust James or Ace, and they shouldn't trust her either.

In the end, she trusted only herself. Her instincts told her that Lana was hiding secrets. Secrets meant information, and Carmen excelled at encouraging people to share information they shouldn't. The key was finding the right angle, the right in, a weak spot.

Lana's weakness would be Carmen's gain.

It was just a matter of time.

CHAPTER 28

SKYE

I no longer heard Rives's dead ex-girlfriend in my head. It was almost worth being back on Nil.

Almost.

I'm back on Nil.

How do these things keep happening? It seemed as if my entire life revolved around Nil. I'd grown up with Nil as a family shadow, then I'd experienced Nil on paper, seeing it through my uncle's eyes, before experiencing the island firsthand through my own. I'd escaped, and then, lucky me, it was my turn to be haunted by Nil in the real world—and now I was back.

But as the curved steps left the platform behind, it became frighteningly clear that this Nil was not the same Nil I had left. We'd definitely left our mark.

Up ahead, black rock gave way to charred black ground. Green shoots were popping up like hope, but fire had wreaked havoc on a wide section of the once-vibrant swath of grasses. The lush trees at the far end were reduced to limbless black stalks; they lined the perimeter in eerie spikes, rising from the ground like brittle bones. No animals were in sight. It was as if someone had taken a vibrant landscape and cursed it with decay.

The field reeked of death.

"Skye?" Rives's hand slid into mine, warm and alive.

I'd stopped walking. I turned to find his eyes on me. Pure green, bright enough to hold the gray at bay.

"You still with me?" he asked, his voice steady. "In the now?"

I was so grateful he knew. That he didn't ask me if I was okay, because the answer was a firm *Hells, no.*

Dex died there. I am not okay. This is not okay.

"I'm not walking though the meadow," I said. "Or even close to it."

"Good call," Thad agreed. Beside me, his eyes swept the burned land, lingering on the far edge and sticking.

I followed Thad's gaze. A glint of gold defied the washed-out meadow. A second flash of light followed the first, popping into sight like a spark. The light moved, warm and alive—and furred. I squinted. At the far edge, two lionesses paced, their eyes fixed on us.

Abruptly, every cell in my body urged me to run; even the island breeze pushed me to *go.* To leave the meadow and devastation behind— right this very second.

I spun toward Rives, shocked to find him still staring at me. "We need to go. *Now.*"

Rives didn't move. A third lion raised his head, massive and way too alert.

"Rives!" I snapped my fingers in front of his face and he blinked. "Lions. Far end of the meadow."

He jerked his head to look, his face closing up as he saw the predators too.

Paulo and Zane were yards ahead now, still on the black mountain. Below us, the rock with the Bull's-eye carving winked in the sun. *I see you,* it seemed to say. Everything had eyes now; we were under a microscope, watched from all angles. The sun above, the sun on the platform, the carvings on the rock . . . the golden-furred beasts too close for comfort with hungry eyes and possibly empty bellies.

I pulled Rives's hand, using thoughts and feelings and touches to say what words couldn't; syllables tripped on my tongue, tangled up in fear and lions and *Nil*.

Thad followed quickly, moving as silently as me. We trekked in smooth sync across the rocks until we caught up with Paulo and Zane.

"Paulo," Rives growled, "did you see that? Lions at the meadow's far end?"

"I did." Without looking back, Paulo strode quickly, winding across the edge of the black rock, Zane by his side. "Stay above the grass," he added calmly, his pace brisk, one level shy of outright jogging. "Follow me."

He didn't need to ask us twice.

We stayed on the mountain, moving up, moving away, stumbling across the pitted black rock without pause until the meadow fell from sight, until lava greeted us. It crept like sludge, thick and black and laced with blood-red cracks, the steaming flow forcing us to change course and head down. Around us, the heat choked the air. Steam hissed as it fought for freedom, an eerie noise punctuating an already eerie moment.

Rives glanced behind us, again, his eyes roving, his shoulders tight. I didn't have to hear his thoughts to know what he was thinking. If the lions followed, we'd be trapped, penned by lava and a steep grade at our backs.

The five of us descended as swiftly as we could toward Mount Nil's base. No one spoke. Everyone screened the silence for sounds of pursuit.

To our left, the cliff narrowed. Lava dripped off the edge into the water below, sending massive cotton balls of steam into the air. Time passed, thick with anticipation, and then miraculously we reached the base without incident. I took a deep breath, my thigh muscles quivering from the descent, grateful to no longer have to fight the pull of gravity and the steep slope. Here the rock was just rock, solid and generally flat. Now that we'd left the slope behind, our pace quickened.

Ahead, the south cliffs loomed. Each step away from the mountain and the meadow brought a fraction of relief, as though distance meant safety, even though I knew safety on Nil was a relative term, and always changing. Still, the farther from the meadow we walked, the better I felt. Beside me, Rives still looked intense; he constantly glanced around, observing, calculating. Thad's face was blank, like he'd passed angry and just settled into shock. Zane and Paulo walked slightly ahead, their faces hidden.

The wafting breeze from the south carried a hint of salt. Soon the hiss of steam vanished altogether, and the air cooled.

An alarming sense of familiarity washed over me with the breeze. We were tracing the path my uncle Scott had walked on his first days, I realized; the weird coincidence didn't sit well. I felt manipulated. I had the strange sense that the island had driven us here, that the island had driven *me* here, to walk the path of my uncle, again. Only he hadn't encountered any lions, if his journal was accurate.

Technically you didn't encounter lions either, my mind clarified. They hadn't followed us, at least not yet. And my Nil sense told me they wouldn't.

A gift from Nil, or a warning? I wondered.

"Warning," Rives said, breaking the prolonged silence. "Something tells me Nil no longer gives gifts."

"Holy crap," Zane said, wiping sweat from his forehead as he dropped back to walk beside Rives. "Can we talk about that now? That was in*sane*. Nothing like a little mad cat welcome party to kick things off." His stride faltered as he stared ahead. "No way. That is not what I think it is." He whipped his eyes to Rives, then back ahead. "Do you see that, Chief? Is anyone *seeing* that?"

Thad shielded his eyes with one hand. "Is that—a *penguin*? Damn thing's *huge*."

"An emperor," Rives said. "The king of the penguin world."

"Unreal," Zane said. The penguin stood at the edge of the cliff like a giant bird statue.

"They *are* warm-blooded. And better than a polar bear," I added.

Zane pointed a finger at me. "Skye, we are not discussing bears. Of any kind."

"There is a brown bear here," Paulo offered. "Or at least, there was."

Zane's eyes went wide as he stared at Paulo. "So besides penguins and brown bears, what other fun creatures are camping out on Nil these days?"

"The question is, what isn't?" Paulo eyed Zane without fear. I studied Paulo, impressed. This Paulo was so different from the one I remembered. This Paulo was so calm, so assured, so much stronger mentally as well as physically. The panicked, defeated boy covered in monkey dung was gone. Even his limp had vanished.

"I've seen pumas, a jaguar, hippos, and rhinos, plus elephants and an ape," Paulo continued. "And the less deadly, like squirrels and rabbits, sheep and boar. I've even seen a camel, and a kangaroo. And of course, the lions and the penguin." He pointed ahead; the massive bird hadn't moved. I wondered if it was already dead but just hadn't fallen over yet.

"For months, I saw no people, just animals," Paulo said, his voice thoughtful. "One day it would be a goat, the next, a bear. One day something to feed me, the next, something to eat me. No rhyme or reason." He shrugged. "Then finally, people. But most of the animals that fall from wild gates now are predators. That I know. Nil is not a peaceful place to be."

"Nil never was peaceful." Rives's voice was quiet. "Not for us." He exhaled heavily, sweeping his eyes across our group. "We need a general plan. I'm thinking we head for the City and let you fill in the blanks as we go." He looked at Paulo. "Is that cool with you?"

Paulo nodded. He seemed content to let Rives take the lead.

"So, besides all of us, and Lana, who else is here?" Rives asked. He'd slid back into his Leader role like he'd never left; I wondered if he'd realized it himself.

"I can only answer what I know," Paulo replied. "In the City, there are six of us. I believe there are other people here too; I've seen signs. Hidden people." He smiled to himself. "But . . ." He paused, his expression troubled. "Like the animals, the feel of the island seems to have changed." He lapsed into silence.

"You can't leave us hanging like that, dude," Zane said. "What do you mean, the feel of the island has changed?"

Paulo shook his head. "I'll let you decide."

He glanced back toward the mountain.

"Are you worried about Lana?" I asked.

"Yes, and no," he said. "More no than yes." He smiled. "She *is* Maaka's cousin."

I wasn't sure whether that familial tie made her tougher than normal or just more stubborn—or neither. Regardless, Lana was nowhere in sight. For someone new to the island, she'd certainly disappeared quickly. I sensed she'd be as difficult to convince to leave as Maaka had been, perhaps more so. At least his time had been up. Lana's, on the other hand, was just beginning.

She hadn't even balked at the thought of Nil on fire.

"How bad was the fire?" I asked Paulo quietly. "When we left, everything was burning."

"Not everything," Paulo said. "The fire was contained to the meadow and the groves. But the fruit trees were decimated. A few mangoes survived, but not many. The deadleaf bushes have taken over."

"Nice." Thad shook his head.

"I salvaged what I could," Paulo said. "Let me know if you get hungry. I've got some dried fruit."

"Did you hear that?" Rives had stopped walking.

"What?" I craned around, listening. Thad and Zane had stopped too. Black rock sprawled in the distance, full of dips and holes and rises.

"Someone's yelling," Rives said. "Listen."

I cupped my ears to amplify whatever sound Rives had heard, straining to block out the crash of the waves.

A boy with dark spiky hair popped into sight, careening over a black rock rise as if he'd been shot from a cannon into the bright-blue Nil sky. He sprinted toward us. A light-brown strap crossed his chest, running from his hip to shoulder. He wielded a long wooden sword in one hand, brandishing it wildly; his other hand alternated between pumping and pointing at us. His lips moved, his mouth open wide, but the open air stole his shout.

"What's he saying?" Zane squinted against the bright light, a hand shielding his eyes.

"Not sure but if I had to guess—" Rives broke off as Paulo yelled, "Run!"

Three wolves burst over the rise behind the boy, stalking as a pack. Still a football field back from him, they were closing fast.

"Aw, no," Zane groaned as he took off at a sprint. Agony ripped across Rives's face for an instant before he glanced at me with fierce resolution. We were already running too.

"This way!" Paulo yelled, gesturing ahead. He pointed down the cliff line, straight toward the penguin. The boy raced over the rocks, catching up to us with remarkable speed.

The pack of wolves closed in too, snarling and growling and nasty-looking, the trio now thirty yards back at best. There was nowhere to go: We were trapped, again. The cliff's edge held us tight on one side, the frothing wolves on the other. We'd gone from lions to wolves in less than thirty minutes and we knocked on Nil's death door as if we'd never left.

We kept running.

The penguin startled, waddling away from the cliff with a jerk. His movement bought us precious time. The wolves' pace slacked a crucial bit; they seemed torn between us and the massive black-and-white animal—or thrown off guard. Perhaps they didn't know what to expect from a giant penguin either. *Are penguins aggressive? Do they attack?* Most animals do when afraid or hungry, and for all I knew, this penguin was both. Dad had never given me any literature on Antarctic animals, an unexpected gap in my survival education.

"Behind him!" Paulo yelled, pointing at the giant bird.

The six of us swerved behind the giant bird. He made a strange sound but didn't move.

Paulo dropped back. "Do you trust me?" he asked.

"Do we have a choice?" Thad muttered.

"Yes." I nodded.

"When I say jump, we jump!" Paulo pulled away again. "Don't stop running!" he yelled as he veered toward the edge.

"Off the cliff?" Zane asked, horrified.

The boy brandishing the sword had caught up to Paulo. His grave expression didn't waver, his eyes fixed ahead.

"Five meters!" Paulo shouted, sprinting ahead. And then he ran straight off the cliff and dropped out of sight. Without hesitation, the boy thrust his sword in the air, and with a cry, he leaped off the cliff after Paulo. He too disappeared into thin air.

"He didn't say jump," Zane hollered.

"Jump!" I yelled.

And with Rives beside me, I did.

CHAPTER
29

RIVES
94 DAYS UNTIL THE AUTUMNAL EQUINOX, AFTERNOON

Skye leaped into open air.

Of course I followed.

I threw myself off the cliff. No windmilling, no hesitation at all. Just a jump into the unknown—into the effing *air*—because the land route involved wolves.

Wolves.

We blasted through Nil sky, no gliders on our backs. Below me, frothing water churned, waiting like an answered prayer or watery grave, a fresh twist on the Nil crapshoot. The drop wasn't nearly as bad as I'd feared. I tried to breathe deep, to stretch my lungs, to stay chill, but my mind kept flashing back to the trio of wolves. *Wolves.*

Three more marks in the evil column of Nil.

My body twisted toward the cliff at my back, instinctively looking for fur, checking to see if the mutts followed. I caught the flash of a face—human, and surprised—and then I hit water, feet-first. The ocean closed over my head with a resounding roar.

Instantly, everything calmed. The light dimmed, all sound muffled; water enveloped me in a slick cocoon. Bubbles surrounded me, blocking my view, but I felt Skye nearby. She was close—and safe.

Damn if Paulo hadn't saved us all.

I kicked to the surface, thinking of Skye. Her face at the meadow had killed me. I knew she'd been thinking of Dex. She'd done so much for everyone, then Nil had reeled her back, trading her body for her sanity. I knew Skye had felt drawn to the Death Twin. Deep down, I'd feared all along that Nil would pull her back.

And still, the knowledge didn't help. Didn't matter. Didn't make a damn bit of difference. I'd been powerless to stop it, and now, here we were. Fully stuck at Nil's mercy, and the island never let us forget it.

Rivesssss . . . The hiss rode the waves, carried by the wind.

"Wolves," Thad said. I jerked toward his voice, surprised to find him treading water by my side. Trapped in my abyss of Nil hate, I hadn't noticed.

Not good.

"Nil has one hell of a twisted sense of humor." He spat out water. "You okay?"

"Yeah." I swam beside him, pushing Nil out of my head.

Look around, pay attention.

Skye was already climbing up onto the rocks. Paulo reached down, gripped her wrist, and hoisted her up. The black-haired boy with the badass sword and kamikaze attitude stood beside Paulo, his homemade katana peeking out over his shoulder, tucked in the strap secured across his chest. Zane stroked toward the group already out of the water, a few meters to my left.

Choosing my footing with care, I hauled myself out of the water and went straight to Skye. She was squeezing water out of her hair with one hand. My eyes met hers, finding enough steel for both of us. "Skye?" One word, a million questions.

She nodded. "Totally fine. You?" Her eyes searched mine.

"Yeah." My pat answer.

She nodded again, but her eyes were knowing, like she was privately calling bullshit on my answer but knew I needed to pretend it was all okay because maybe then it somehow would be. Like I hadn't almost had to watch her get mauled by a wolf pack.

Skye squeezed my hand.

Standing on her tiptoes, she whispered in my ear, "Think first, panic later." Then she grinned. "I'll let you know when it's time to panic."

"Deal." I slowly returned her smile. She was a force of nature, a force of Nil. A brave, clever girl, she'd nearly taken down an entire island in three months' time, and here she was set to do it again. She completely underestimated herself. Underestimated how tough and strong and bad-ass she really was.

But I didn't.

Watch out, Nil, I thought. *You brought us back, and you may have bit off a hell of a lot more than you can chew.*

I took pleasure in the fact that Nil had no answer.

With Skye's hand in mine, I surveyed the cliff. No one was there. No movement, no face. But I'd swear someone had been up there, as surprised to see me as I'd been to see him.

Or her.

"What is it?" Skye covered her eyes with her free hand, lifting her chin to look up.

"Nothing. I thought—I thought I saw someone as I fell, but maybe not."

"It may have been Lana." Paulo's gaze followed mine. "There's a cave here. Actually back there." He pointed. "The mouth blends in with the cliff, but if you know what to look for, you'll find it. It's always where we come when we arrive." He shrugged. "An island thing."

"An island thing, eh?" Thad's expression bordered on suspicious. "How many other *island things* are there? Ones you haven't shared?"

Paulo didn't flinch. "You know all I do. Maybe more, since you're with Skye." He smiled. "But you can ask me anything. If I know the answer, I'll tell you."

Thad nodded, obviously appeased.

"We should get going." Paulo studied the cliff base, surveying our route. It would be leapfrog, Nil-style, until we rounded the rocky bend.

"Hey, Chief." Zane nudged me, his voice a low whisper as he not very subtly jerked his head to the dark-haired kid shaking water out of one ear. "Don't you think we oughta give the rook the intro?"

"I'm not sure he's a rook," I said. "That katana didn't happen overnight."

"Good point," Zane said. He stepped closer to the kid, who eyed Zane with polite curiosity, feet planted a foot apart on the rock, lean arms crossed. His short black hair boasted the ghost of a mohawk. "I'm Zane," Zane said, offering his hand.

"Kenji," the boy responded with a nod.

"Good meeting you, man." Zane grinned. "Although this place is more whacked than ever. Sick katana," he added. Then Zane looked surprisingly businesslike. "So where'd you come from?" he asked. "The north side? Or the rain forest? And did you see anyone else?"

The boy looked perplexed.

Zane looked uncertain—of himself. "Maybe I should back up. Do you speak English?"

Annoyance flashed through Kenji's eyes.

"Yes, I speak English." The kid rolled his eyes slightly. "I'm from Sacramento, dude. This is a bokken, not a katana. And you're the first people I've seen."

Zane reddened. "Right on. I'm from Laguna," he offered, giving Kenji another wave. "So yeah. Welcome to Nil."

"Nil?" Kenji frowned.

"Nil." I nodded. "It's what some of us call this place, anyway."

I glanced at Thad, shooting him a clear *You want to take this?* look.

He tipped his head toward me. "Last time I checked, brother, you were the Leader, not me. Seems like this Nil belongs to you."

Or Paulo, I thought.

I turned to Paulo, expecting him to take the lead. His eyes were on the rocks ahead, like this discussion didn't matter. Like this *intro* didn't matter, only his footing. His aloofness brought Maaka to mind, a comparison that chafed.

"Other people have other names for it," I continued, stifling my irritation, "but regardless of the name, we're all here. An island that exists somewhere, but isn't on any map."

"Why are we here?" Kenji asked.

"It's the universal question, my man." Zane nodded. "Well put."

"I think he means why are we on Nil," Skye interjected drolly. "It's a great question, and I don't think there's just one answer, not anymore. But the simplest answer is a gate. A gate picked you up and brought you here, and a gate will take you home."

"Gate," Kenji repeated. "The hot air."

"Exactly," Zane said. "Portal. Gate. Blackout tube. A not-so-magical carnival ride."

Thad muttered something about island games that I ignored.

"Gates show up every day at noon," I said, cutting to the chase. "Somewhere on the island. And never the same place twice. But if you don't catch one soon, in three months, a big one will show up on the mountain, big enough to take us all back. So the short story is, you've got three months to survive. Do that and you're home."

"Different intro than before," Thad observed quietly, his blue eyes clear. "A survival countdown to a preplanned group exit. Not the same Nil, is it?"

"Not for any of us. Except maybe Paulo." For his part, he'd stalked a few meters ahead, leading the way, or maybe just keeping his distance.

Knowing Paulo, I'd bet on the latter.

"How do you know all this?" Kenji's voice stayed guarded.

"Firsthand experience." I smiled, hoping to put Kenji at ease. "How long have you been here, Kenji?"

"A little over a week. Closer to two, I think." He adjusted his bokken's harness. "I've been staying in the woods on the coast, exploring a little more every day. This is the farthest south I've ever come. And I haven't seen a single gate the whole time. Not one. But I've seen a crap ton of animals, and most aren't friendly, like the wolves." He glanced back at the cliff. "So how long have you been here?"

"Which time?" Thad asked dryly.

"What?" Kenji jerked his head toward Thad.

As a team, we filled him in as we picked our way along the cliff base. Thad and I did most of the talking, with Zane chiming in occasionally as the three of us caught Kenji up to speed. Skye had jogged up to walk with Paulo, and he hadn't moved away from her like I'd expected. *Friend or foe? Ally or loner?*

I hadn't figured this Paulo out.

We rounded the bend of South Beach, and the topography changed. Rocky, rough coast gave way to fine black sand; a beach sprawled wide. A bamboo thicket thrived far above the high-tide line, lush and large. A panda bear poked its head out, a piece of bamboo in its mouth.

"Oh, great," Zane said. "More bears. Yay."

We all veered closer to the water, giving the panda space. It seemed content, but no need to push it. Not on our Day 1, not when the animals already seemed restless.

As we passed the bear, Paulo dropped back to me. "Rives, thanks for welcoming Kenji. I never know exactly what to say, where to start. It's not as easy as you make it look. Believe me, I know." He smiled wryly. "It's your job, not mine." His smile widened, his eyes sincere.

I realized I'd read him completely wrong. He'd been listening, but not avoiding. He'd been giving me space he thought I needed.

Ally, I decided.

I shook my head. "It's your Nil now, Paulo."

"It was never mine. Or yours. It just is." He glanced up at the sun and frowned. Noon was long past. "We should keep moving. We need to be back at the City by nightfall, and we haven't even hit the Arches yet."

Picking up the pace, Paulo lapsed back into silence. Skye and I walked beside him, with Thad, Zane, and Kenji behind us. Two trios, one with a Nil veteran, the other with a Nil rookie; both groups rounded out with two second-timers.

Nil was all about the balance.

Around us, nothing chirped, nothing barked. Even the black sand shifting under our feet stayed silent, like the island was listening.

Had Nil always been this silent?

"I worried about you," Skye said abruptly. She was looking at Paulo. "After I left. Being here alone, the fire. The whole thing." She shook her head slightly—a classic Skye attempt to clear worries from her head, as if a quick shake would erase the images like a magical island Etch A Sketch.

If only it were that easy.

"How long were you alone?" she asked.

Paulo glanced around; he did that constantly as we walked. It reminded me of *me*.

"I don't think I was ever alone," he said finally. "Not really. Skye, I know you want to know what happened at that gate, on the day you left. The truth is, I'm not sure myself."

"It looked like you saw something. I was watching you, and you looked—" As Skye fought to find the right word, an image flashed through my head: Paulo, on the platform, a shadow passing across his face, darkness clouding his eyes from within. Skye's memory, not mine.

"Lost," she finished. "Not frightened, exactly, but it was as if you saw something. Something that changed your mind. Something that stopped you."

Paulo's expression was haunted. "That's just it, Skye, I didn't see anything. I remember you taking the gate, and then the gate was gone and I was alone. But I didn't see the gate close."

"So you blacked out?" A line creased the skin between her brows.

"No. I just don't remember. It's like that piece of memory is gone. Erased. Stolen. I don't know." He exhaled. "And it's happened again, maybe more than once since then. It's like I just zone out, and when I come back to myself, I haven't moved, but time has passed." He shook his head. "I can't explain it. It's like the island is stealing time."

"I don't like the sound of that," Skye said.

A crisp memory flashed. Me, in the Looking Glass Cavern, waiting to hear Talla's voice. Me, losing time. But it wasn't Talla I'd been hearing; it was Nil.

Merde.

And Paulo had lost time at *noon.*

"Nil's stealing time," I said slowly. "And not just any time, the most precious hour. Noon. That could be a serious problem."

I glanced at Skye. "Do you remember the day we found the platform, with Nikolai?" I hated taking her back to that moment, but I had no choice. "We all stared at the carving, for what felt like hours. No," I corrected myself out loud, "it *was* hours, but it felt like minutes. Do you remember that?"

She cocked her head. "I do. It was hours, but it felt like hours. I don't think we lost time that day, do you?"

Yes, I wanted to say, but her expression stopped me. Like she was trying to read me. I thought we'd lost time, but Skye didn't?

"I don't know," I admitted.

And that was the truth. I just didn't know what it meant.

"Chief." Zane's voice was low. "I think I see someone."

He pointed. At the high mark of the beach, where the black sand gave way to chunky rock, human feet pointed toward us, visible through a pair of black rocks. "Sleeping?" Zane asked. He squinted in the sun, trying to shade his eyes.

Permanently, I thought. The position seemed unnatural.

I jogged closer, and sure enough, a body lay half exposed to Nil air, a mix of flesh and bone partially sunken in a hollow. The eye sockets were creepily empty. *Look around, pay attention,* they crooned. *Death is everywhere, watching you.*

Got it, Nil.

Maybe I was finally learning after all.

Beside me, Thad swallowed repeatedly, looking with unblinking wide eyes between me and the body, then he turned and vomited on the sand. He choked as he stumbled a few steps away. "Need a minute," he managed, then gagged again.

"Take as many as you need." My eyes went to Skye, standing with Zane, Paulo, and Kenji a few meters away. "If you're willing, I could use a hand." My eyes back on Skye, I flicked my eyes toward Thad. *He needs you more than I do right now*, I thought. The words felt heavy in my head. Thad had buried too many people during his first Nil stay. To revisit those memories on his new Day 1 sucked for sure.

I know it did for me.

Skye nodded. As she turned toward Thad, the rest of us got to work.

Moving with care, the four of us carefully covered the exposed body in rock. Nil might not honor the dead, but we would. Still, the task was gruesome, given that decomposition on Nil moved slowly. We all breathed through our mouths, unwilling to risk a whiff of death.

Halfway through, Thad joined in. I didn't meet his eyes, didn't try to. He had to work through his Nil demons like anyone else, and we both knew it. Skye handed me rocks.

After the last rock was placed, I itched for my sack of white coral, to lay a cross or star or mark of some kind, something to say *Someone rests here*. But I had nothing. No coral, no mark. No clue who this person was, no insight into this person's identity or gender. Maybe he was a Buddhist, maybe a Christian. Maybe he had no faith at all. We'd never know; we'd never know him. Or her.

I stepped back, shaken by the rawness of this moment, knowing someone somewhere cared for this person. A person now covered forever in black Nil rock, a person who may or may not be on the Wall.

The Wall may not even exist anymore.

I realized my hands were shaking.

Clenching them into fists, I stepped back. Beside me, Kenji was pale. Skye's defiant-yet-horrified expression mirrored the one she'd worn after Archie had died.

Zane's face read shell-shocked. Thad looked sick, and shaken.

Too much, too soon, I thought. For all of us. Too raw a reminder of the death we'd seen on our last day here, of how little we knew. Of how much we existed at Nil's mercy, again.

"C'mon." Paulo jerked his head, then started walking away, by far the most composed of our group.

Taking Paulo's cue, we followed, everyone eager to get some distance from the gravesite. The sea breeze sounded like laughter.

The Nil silence had turned eerie.

Back on black sand, Thad gripped my arm. "Sorry about that back there." He looked at me. "I saw—" He broke off with a shake of his head, still staring at me. "Been a long time away, brother. I'd forgotten how much Nil likes to play head games." He squared his shoulders, his eyes as intense as I'd ever seen. Fully focused, fully clear. "Just know I've got your back. Skye's, too." He glanced ahead, to where she walked beside Paulo.

"Goes both ways, bro. No apologies needed."

He nodded.

Side by side, we crossed the last stretch of South Beach. Skye took point with Paulo; Kenji and Zane were next. Thad and I brought up the rear.

The Arches loomed up ahead.

"Rives." Thad's voice was measured.

"Yeah, bro?"

"Don't turn around, but I'm pretty sure we're being followed."

CHAPTER
30

The island watched the humans as they acclimated to the now, to the place the island had become. They had done well so far. So well, in fact, the island had chosen not to intervene.

Residual power still lingered from today's noon, but the island had consciously chosen to save it. To conserve it, to wait for the moment it would be needed most. For now, the island reveled in the fact that she was here, the one called Skye, the one the island needed beyond all others.

But she was not needed, yet.

For now, the island was content to wait, and to watch. It would act sparingly, until the pivotal moment arrived. Then it would fully engage; it would lean on the ones it needed most because there would be no other option left.

It ached for the pain to come, a price to be paid by all. For the island saw the future, the end already written.

If it could weep, it would have.

Calvin had never gone so long without a regimented workout or a home-cooked meal. Now he was hauling wood and hunting down food and sweating like he'd just finished a brutal two-a-day practice in an

Alabama summer, only there was no hot shower to follow or cool AC to chillax in later. His workout routine was completely shot. He woke up each day stiff and sore, and the so-called mattresses were crap. He missed the weight room, his teammates, his family, and he definitely missed his queen-sized bed. Sleeping outside had gotten old on night one. He'd never been a camper, and this whole island nightmare confirmed what he already knew: roughing it sucked.

"Watch your step," Davey warned.

Calvin froze, his arms full of wood. The City's edge loomed twenty yards out, the firepit a few yards more. But here, on the periphery, there were trees and shrubs and pockets of foliage and rocks where things could hide. He hadn't forgotten about the tiger.

"The bright-green bush on your left," Davey continued. "You do not want to touch it, trust me. Hafthor called these bushes deadleaf, and nothing with the word *dead* is good."

"Damn straight," Calvin said. Now that he looked, more of the same bright-green bushes curved around the City like a living half wall, with open spots cropping up here and there like doorless entryways. Or exits. He and Davey had left the City via the beachside route, so this side looked foreign.

"Deadleaf bushes." Calvin stared at the glossy green leaves, as bright as a green-apple Jolly Rancher. "What kind of place is this where even the plants can kill you? Like tigers aren't enough?"

"Right?" Davey nodded. He took as much care as Calvin to avoid the leaves as he passed. "Dangerous beauty, everywhere you look." He glanced ahead and gave a weird laugh. "Case in point," he mumbled.

By the firepit, Molly sat alone on the rocks. A small fire blazed, freshly made, no coals yet in sight. No Amara or Hafthor in sight, either. Calvin had to admit he was impressed. He had yet to be able to start a fire from scratch, but Molly? One quick session with Paulo on the fire bow and she'd started the fire, no problem. He felt certain she'd gotten this fire going too. Calvin secretly suspected Molly came from an outdoorsy family, because the girl had solid survival skills and no fear of the island or the outdoors.

The closer they got to the firepit, the more Davey withdrew. It was like watching a bulb dim.

Calvin set his pile of wood down and pain lanced across his palm.

"Dammit," he grumbled. Picking the largest black boulder of a set of three, he plopped down on a rock not far from the firepit.

"What's wrong?" Molly sat down beside him.

"Splinter." Calvin picked at his palm and winced.

"A splinter?" Davey raised an eyebrow as he dropped his load of firewood beside Calvin's. "Boo-bloody-hoo, big Cal. I've got a blister on my heel the size of Sydney. Not to mention a monster slice on my foot that won't heal." He glanced at the side of his foot, where bright-red droplets bloomed against an old scab. "Bloody thing stays bloody."

"Maybe you should be more careful where you step," Molly said, her voice saccharine sweet.

"I would've but I was too busy sweeping the rocks for animals with fangs." Davey shrugged. "Priorities and all that."

Molly tilted her chin up slightly. "Didn't see any, did you? Animals with fangs?"

"Not lately. But that's beside the point." Sitting down on Calvin's right, Davey rolled his shoulders, trying to loosen them up.

"Is it?" Molly turned to Calvin, who was attempting to pry out the speck of wood with his massive fingers and failing miserably. "Here." She offered her hand. "Let me take a look."

Calvin hesitated, then held out his hand.

Molly took Calvin's hand in hers, and with complete concentration, she worked the skin of his palm gently between her fingers. She didn't have much in the way of fingernails, but she had enough. "There!" she said, a note of triumph in her voice. She held up a tiny sliver of wood to show Calvin, then flicked the offending splinter away.

Brushing her hands on her thighs, she turned back to Davey. "I think it's quite important. That you didn't see any beasties with fangs. I'm starting to think the animals here don't want to mess with us."

Davey mumbled something unintelligible, his eyes glued to Molly's thighs.

She leaned forward and waved her fingers in front of his face. "Davey, focus!"

"I was." A smile pulled at Davey's mouth.

Calvin laughed, then froze. Something brown had just crept past his ankle. Peering at the ground, he squinted hard, then relaxed. *Damn.* This place wreaked havoc on his nerves.

"What?" Molly was peering at the ground. "I don't see anything."

"It's just a leaf. But I swore there was a spider." Calvin peered more closely at the ground.

"There are no spiders," Molly said cheerfully. "Or bugs, even."

"Really?" Davey looked curious. "How do you know?"

"Because I listened to Paulo when he told us about this place." Molly regarded Davey with undisguised annoyance, a look Calvin had grown accustomed to seeing on Molly's face whenever Davey was around. For his part, Davey seemed to enjoy baiting her. The weird thing was, when Davey wasn't around Molly, he was actually cool. A regular guy, pulling his weight, like earlier today when he and Calvin collected wood and passed the time talking about their families and home life and this freaky place. Davey had been laid-back and cool, no chip on his shoulder—but not now, not around Molly. Whatever the story was involving these two, Calvin sensed it went back before this island, maybe way back. And it wasn't done yet.

Neither was Molly.

She regarded Davey with an exasperated *You're an idiot* look.

"Paulo specifically said there were no bugs here. No bugs, no snakes." Molly scowled at Davey. "And no spiders."

Calvin had missed the no-spider speech too, but he kept that to himself.

"Right." Davey nodded. "No spiders. But"—he looked thoughtful, his tone as calm as Molly's—"there are tigers and hippos and an incredibly large lot of creatures that make spiders look tame."

It was Molly's turn to shrug.

Abruptly, Davey got up. "I'm going to see if Paulo's around yet. His mysterious excursion is quite the time suck."

He strode southeast, the direction Paulo had gone, toward the field full of flowers with the mountain in the background. Calvin wondered exactly how far he'd go.

When he glanced at Molly, she was watching Davey's back too.

"So what's the deal with you two?" Calvin asked.

"There is no deal," Molly said succinctly, pulling her eyes away from Davey and straightening her skirt. "There's just me, and then there's Davey. No deal."

"Uh-uh." Calvin shook his head at Molly. "You two have a history, big-time. I don't know what it's all about, but there is definitely a deal."

Molly sighed. She picked up a small black pebble and rolled it between her fingers as she spoke. "I grew up with Davey," she admitted. "I've known him forever. My older brother, JT, is Davey's best friend. Davey's always been around. Then, a few months ago Davey started dating my best friend, Lauren. And the night before I—we," she quickly amended, "landed here, I caught him with another girl." Her eyes glided back to Davey's retreating figure and she fell silent.

"And?" Calvin prompted.

"That's it." Molly shifted her shoulders dismissively. She turned away from Davey but not before Calvin saw the hurt flash through her eyes.

"Huh." Calvin thumbed his palm where the splinter had been. "I don't think so."

"You don't think what?" Molly frowned.

"I don't think that's it. But hey"—Calvin held up his hands—"I'm not saying I want to know. I'm just saying there's more to it, that's all."

Propping her chin in her hands, Molly glanced back at Davey. He stood, staring down toward the path Paulo had taken. "Maybe so." She cocked her head at Calvin. "But maybe not. I don't know." Molly closed her eyes. "It doesn't matter, not here anyway."

"I'm not sure here is any different," Calvin spoke slowly. "Maybe it matters more here, I don't know. Damn." He rubbed both of his hands over his head. "I'm just saying it doesn't matter any less. You get me?"

Molly smiled. "I get you."

A quiet moment passed as both watched Davey in the distance. He seemed busy watching something else.

"So back home, you camp a lot?" Calvin asked Molly conversationally.

"Never."

His jaw dropped. "For real? You use that fire bow like a pro. Plus, you don't seem a damn bit afraid of this place. Not the tigers, not the bugs. Not the dark. Nothing."

Molly smiled at Calvin. "Remember I come from Oz, a place with the most dangerous animals in the world. Deadly snails, spiders that would scare Freddy Krueger, and more venomous snakes than anywhere else, not to mention heaps of sharks and crocs and possibly killer koalas." She grinned. "I'm used to shaking out my boots before I put them on. But here? No snakes, no spiders, and the other animals are too big to hide in my boots, which I actually find reassuring. But . . ." Her smile faded. "I am afraid of this place, not because of the animals. I'm afraid of whatever brought us here, afraid of what we can't see."

Molly glanced toward the beach. Through the branches gently swaying in the breeze, bright-blue water glittered with bits of white and light. "I don't think anything here is exactly what it seems."

Suddenly Calvin found himself wishing for a spider. At least then he'd know what he was up against. Because Molly's words rang true. Something about this place gave him the creeps. Put his nerves on edge, and made him jumpy.

Time felt heavy here, expectant, like the calm before a storm.

As far as Calvin was concerned, tomorrow's noon couldn't come soon enough.

———

Trapped in chains not of its own making, the island simply watched.

And listened.

And learned.

The one called Calvin was wiser than he knew. Perhaps his fear would not best him after all. Then again, perhaps it would.

The island hoped for the former, and simply hoped.

Indeed, tomorrow's noon could not come soon enough.

CHAPTER
31

I glanced at Paulo as we walked, my old friend who, in many ways, was like a new friend. I had a million questions for him, but I didn't press.

I'd learned quite a bit during my first stay here.

I wondered what Paulo had learned. After all, he'd never left. He had the lean muscles and long hair and quiet confidence to show for it, not to mention a leg laced with healed scars, hard proof of time served. He was a Nil survivor and Nil veteran—the oldest veteran on the island, a seniority marked not by age but days spent.

Paulo didn't speak either. We walked in comfortable silence. As we left South Beach behind, Rives dropped back to chat with Thad.

Soon the Arches rose ahead, stunning and majestic. Massive rock formations, carved by the hands of invisible giants or Mother Nature herself, the Arches stretched toward the sky, curved and chunky and beautifully hollow. The black rock arches glistened with water at the base and winked matte black at the top, bathed in light from above.

Paulo broke the silence. "We took this route because I wanted to show you something at the Arches. It won't take long."

"You're kidding." Rives's incredulous voice came from slightly behind us; I hadn't heard him approach. "You said yourself we should get back by dark, and I think I've had enough Nil surprises for one day. Can't it wait?"

"I don't think it should. This place"—Paulo waved a hand—"is unpredictable. It could be gone tomorrow. Destroyed, altered. It's not a chance I want to take. It's nothing scary, I promise. But"—his eyes found me—"Skye needs to see it."

"Rives, it *is* the longest day of the year." I smiled. "We've got plenty of daylight left to see whatever this is."

Rives's tight expression didn't shift. His eyes remained on Paulo. "Exactly what is it that Skye needs to see?"

"Just wait," Paulo said, his tone encouraging. "See what unfolds."

His calm confidence reminded me slightly of Maaka, but where Maaka always spoke like a condescending Confucius, Paulo was kind, and patient. But he didn't elaborate on this mysterious detour.

Just wait, he'd said.

As much as it killed me, I did. I kept my questions to myself, wondering what the Arches could hold that I needed to see. And why me? Why single me out?

"This way," Paulo said. Following his lead, I climbed up, past the Man in the Maze. We walked to the smallest of the rock arches, the one farthest from the water's edge. Rives paused, waiting for the others to catch up, but his eyes stayed on me.

Behind the last arch, Paulo knelt. "Look." He pointed to the ground near the arch's base. A flat rock about the size of a dinner plate nestled against the base. Words graced the rock face, roughly cut into the surface.

Search.

Look inside.

Below the words, two smaller letters read *S. B.* All had a similar slant, as if carved by the same hand.

"Did you carve these words?" A powerful hope filled Paulo's eyes.

Shaking my head, I knelt beside him. With one finger, I traced the letters *S. B.* "These are my initials," I said, "and my uncle's." I glanced at Paulo. "Scott Bracken, the same uncle who met your aunt Rika."

He exhaled, relaxing. "I was right to bring you here today," he said with certainty. "I knew this was a clue. I'd thought perhaps you left it for me, but now I know your uncle left it for you."

How could there be a twenty-year-old clue? I wondered.

You have a twenty-year-old journal, my mind offered helpfully.

I read aloud. "'Look inside'? What does that even mean? I know they searched for gates, like us. But what does 'Look inside' mean? Look inside what? Ourselves? This rock?"

The rock didn't budge.

"I don't know," Paulo admitted. He regarded me carefully. "I didn't know you shared the same initials as your uncle, the one who knew my aunt. The one who told him about his destiny."

Your destiny wraps the island from beginning to end, Paulo's aunt had told my uncle.

But you didn't end it, my guilty conscience said. *You failed.*

Then, like the whisper of the wind, a gentle thought brushed the others away.

It is not over yet.

Rives stood near the Man in the Maze, his profile to me, deep in conversation with Thad. Neither boy looked my way.

I closed my eyes, hearing the echo of a thought that wasn't mine. Nil was everywhere: my past, my present, and maybe even still in my head. Or was that thought mine after all, whispered by my conscience? I couldn't sort it all out.

"Skye?"

I glanced up at Paulo.

"In the weeks after you left, I sat here a lot, alone, thinking. The day I found this carving, I was specifically thinking of *you.* It's like this carving was here, but I didn't see it right away. Granted, the carving is shallow, and dirt had blurred the letters, but still. I didn't see these letters until I was thinking about you. And now you're here. Again. It feels—weird. Like a coincidence but not really."

There are no coincidences on Nil. Johan's words haunted me.

The letters, my initials. My failure and my return.

"What did we miss?" I asked Paulo, desperate for understanding. "We *failed*, Paulo. The island wanted to die; I think it still does. It's why I'm here, why I'm back. I *feel* it. So what didn't we do last time? What didn't we see?"

"Skye, I've rewound that last day a million times, and I still have no answer. And since then? The island is—" He paused. "Different. Crueler. It's the best word I can think of. More vicious, more volatile. I'll see a rabbit one day, only to have a gate take it away before I can snare it. Then a camel falls out of the next gate, only to be eaten by a lion, and I don't even eat camels so it's like a warning: *You're next*." He shook his head. "There've been two earthquakes since you left. The first not so bad, but the second one opened steam vents on Mount Nil. The island is restless. I constantly *feel* a restlessness, and it isn't mine."

"Like the exhaustion wasn't mine," I said. Understanding crept close, then drifted away before I could grasp it.

"Looks like you found a little island graffiti." Rives's hands rested gently on my bare shoulders. "Your uncle's?"

"I think so." I stared at the rock, at the words etched in stone, letters looking back at me.

Search.

Look inside.

"He wrote in his journal that he heard the island telling him to search," I said slowly. Was my uncle to search, or was this word left for me? Was it a mission left for someone else, for *anyone* else? Was there a difference, and did it matter?

Did the island tell him to leave this mark?

I spun around, moving so fast I startled Rives. "The island told my uncle to search," I said. "But he didn't know what he was supposed to search *for*. Gates? Answers? Understanding? People?" A familiar sense of frustration washed through me. "We're back to square one, Rives. Sure, we know how to leave. We've got three months until our gate opens. But this time, we need to do more while we're here. We *have* to figure out how to end Nil. Or at least destroy all the gates." My voice reflected the urgent determination I felt.

Search.

Look inside.

"Maybe we aren't looking in the right places." My hands gripped Rives's forearms tight; my eyes stayed locked on his. "The problem is, we don't know what we're looking *for,* but we've got to figure it out because if we don't, then we're just resetting the clock, *again,* and the next group will be even worse off. This place is getting crueler, Paulo said so himself. Rives, we've got to search—"

He gently put a finger to my lips.

"We *will* search, Skye. We'll search this whole island. For people, for clues, for answers, and one epic island-ending solution. If it exists, we'll find it. But not today. Today we need to get to the City, meet the people already there, and get everyone up to speed. And then as a team, we'll make a plan, together. One step at a time. One *day* at a time. Okay?"

His green eyes were clear and bright, reassuring and ready—like Rives himself.

I nodded. "You're right. Totally right." I forced myself to take a slow breath. "Let's get a move on back to the City. But tomorrow, we start searching. For anything unexpected. For island clues. For what we missed the first time. Deal?"

"Deal." Rives smiled.

The breeze ruffled my hair, whispering like the girl in the dark, the one I couldn't see until I chose to look. But this whisper was everywhere.

So I'll look everywhere, I thought, lifting my chin. *Inside, outside, in every Nil nook and cranny. No stone will be left unturned.*

Switching subjects, Rives asked Paulo about the City, food stores, and a myriad of other daily details that seemed basic to survival, but I didn't add any questions of my own. I didn't just want to survive; I wanted *more.* I wanted escape and closure and an unequivocal end to it all. That was *my* focus, it always had been. I was already looking three months out, and I'd only been back for one day.

Less than a day, I reminded myself. *More like an afternoon.*

It felt like months, not hours. The exhaustion I'd experienced last time on Nil had roared back as if I'd never left. It had hit me the instant I'd come through the gate, initially making it hard to wake. Now fatigue swirled around me like a thick breeze pressing against my mind like the darkness of my dreams, but my constant fight with the darkness had served me well. Now I both acknowledged the fatigue and defied it, because I recognized it was Nil's weariness, not mine. There was an invisible line defining where I ended and Nil began, a line I recognized, a line I reinforced because my mind was *mine*.

I looked at Rives and felt the same. *Mine*, I thought.

I would protect all that was mine, with all that I had.

Concern flitted through Rives's eyes. "Skye?"

"Rives?" I countered, lifting my eyebrows.

A grin played at the corners of his mouth. "I know you've got it all under control, but for the record? I don't like you being last." He gestured ahead, to where everyone else waited.

"You never have. What makes today any different?"

Rives's jaw tightened. The flash of levity was gone. "Don't look, but I think we're being followed."

CHAPTER 32

"Followed?" Skye's body twitched as she fought the urge to look behind her. "By what?"

"Not what. Who. I think it's a person. Maybe Lana. Maybe more than one person. I don't know. My guess is that they're scared and keeping their distance until they figure us out. I just wanted you to know, okay?" I fought the urge to grab her and run, even though there was nowhere to go.

Eyes everywhere, I thought. Mine stayed wide open.

I kept my hands to myself. Instead, I winked. "Once your wingman, always your wingman."

Zane coughed. "Okay, lovebirds, let's get a move on before something decides to make us a snack. I'll feel better when we hit the City."

"Echo that." Thad nodded once then turned to me. "You've got the rear?" he asked, his eyes sharp. He was really warning *Watch your back*. He knew we were being followed too.

I nodded.

We climbed single-file down the south cliff, toward Black Bay. Narrower than South Beach, Black Bay lounged between two steep cliffs, like the ocean had scooped out a massive arc of rock, leaving a curved beach arching inward and lined with trees. At the heart of the bay, the scrub thickened. Trees gathered in awkward clumps, perfect places for things—both deadly and docile—to hide.

Without discussion, we hugged the water. In the fading afternoon light, coal-black sand glittered in the surf. Larger rocks littered the bay, visible through the clear water, their black tops repeatedly painted with froth. Black on black, the bay was a dark place, especially at night.

Thad strolled beside and slightly behind me. He kept glancing at the trees to our right.

For my part, I kept a close watch on our back. We hadn't lost our invisible shadow yet. I still felt him—or her.

My money was still on Lana.

"Thad's almost as observant as you," Skye said quietly, and sighed. "He's really struggling. He's been away from Nil for so long. I can't imagine what he's thinking right now."

"My guess is that he's thinking about Charley. He met her here. On this beach."

"I didn't know." Sympathy flashed through her eyes, and understanding.

I shrugged. "No way you would. Before your time." Skye knew so much about Nil, more than I did, that sometimes I forgot she didn't know everything. That there was a past here she didn't live, didn't read. Didn't know.

Up ahead, Paulo, Zane, and Kenji walked a few meters apart from one another, not talking. Everyone seemed lost in their own heads. Or maybe that was just me.

Nil air wrapped around us, cool and salty. Even our breath came at Nil's mercy.

Three months, I told myself. Ninety days.

Merde.

So much time, too much time. So much could happen in one day. It already had.

Look around. Pay attention.

All I could see was Skye; all I could *feel* was Skye. Beside me, in my head. In my soul. Talk about an epic blind spot. Shaking out my fists, I worked to control my breathing, knowing I needed to get my head clear or I'd get us both killed. Or miss something important that could help—or hurt—us later.

I wrenched my head back into Nil's game.

Skye was still watching Thad walk alone.

"I feel terrible that he's here," she said. "Even though I know it's not my fault, it feels like it is." She sighed. "And I think he's still upset with me."

"No, he's not. He's in shock. At being here, being back. But he'll get over it soon." I thought of his clear eyes back at the tube-side grave after he'd pulled himself together, and the way he now methodically swept the trees. "I think he already has."

"Really?" Relief mixed with curiosity in her tone. "How can you be so sure?"

"Because Charley's safe." This answer poured out without thinking.

Thad's worst-case scenario hadn't come to pass. But mine had. Skye was here, and I couldn't protect her. Nil had driven that lesson home, hard.

"It's going to be okay," she said confidently. She didn't have to read my mind to know my fear. "We'll make it."

Of course she believed that. She was as optimistic as her dad, but this was Nil we were talking about. Plus, this Nil was more cruel, more vicious; Paulo had said so himself. And it was this crueler Nil that had pulled her back.

I spun toward Skye, taking her hands in mine, needing her to listen.

"Look, Skye, I hate that you're here—"

"I know—" Skye started, but I kept talking as if she'd never spoken.

"—but you are. We are. And as much as I hate to admit it, I can't protect you, not here. Not against Nil. God knows I've tried, but I can't. So I'm only going to ask you once. Please don't do anything reckless, or alone. Think about things before you do them, okay? Come to me. We'll do this as a team. Seriously, don't do anything stupid."

"Like drink deadsleep tea?" She raised her eyebrows.

"That was different," I said flatly.

"Was it?"

"Yes."

She crossed her arms. "I promise I won't drink deadsleep tea if you won't."

Her fierce gaze held mine.

"I really do think it'll be okay," she said quietly.

"I know you do." My tone was flat. Beneath it roiled emotion too strong to let out. "I just hope you're right."

Leaving the black sand, we threaded through the trees, making for the shortcut through the cliff. A black slice marked the entrance, an opening dusted with diamonds and light.

I paused at the entrance. A shadow shifted on my right, at the edge of my peripheral vision. Tensing, I turned.

Nothing was there.

No one, no thing.

Still, the sense of being watched clung like a shadow. *Person, thing, or animal,* Thad had questioned me earlier. *Person,* my gut said. Animals wouldn't stalk this far. My gut also said that Lana had followed us after seeing us fly past her cave. Then again, it could be anyone behind us. But whoever they were, they were hesitant. Skeptical, maybe even suspicious. Probably a newbie, unsure of us and our motives.

Which basically were to stay alive.

I turned around and addressed the trees and open air.

"Lana, if that's you following us, it's cool. We're going to the City, a place where you're welcome to stay or just visit if you change your mind and want some company. But just so you know, there is no you and us, no dividing line. We're all islanders now. All just people, fighting to survive long enough to get home." I paused, hearing the bitterness in my own voice, feeling a Nil déjà vu from a similar argument with Maaka. "And if you're not Lana, if you're someone else following us, that's cool too. You're welcome in the City anytime. We have food, information, and a plan to get home, all of which we'll share with you. But word of warning: we don't appreciate raiders or thieves and we protect our own." I fought not to look at Skye.

"And stay away from the meadow," Skye added with extra sweetness. "Until the crescent moon rises over the heart of the island. Then we'll see you there."

That's my girl, I thought. A clever way to let whoever was watching know that she knew as much about the island as they did—if not more. A warning and a lifeline, wrapped in one.

"Come on." Skye grabbed my hand. "Everyone's already gone. Let's go meet Paulo's new friends."

CHAPTER 33

James had tracked the girl, Lana, easily. He'd watched her avoid certain plants with care; he'd done the same. He'd seen her pluck redfruit from a tree and eat it without fear; he'd followed suit. But she'd never heard him behind her, never sensed him, not once.

But the boy with an air of authority and blazing green eyes had nearly seen him, twice.

His brothers would be ashamed; they would laugh in his face. *You think you can track, Little J?* they would say. *You think you are ready to lead?* they would scoff. *You not ready, you just a boy. You need to be a man to lead.*

But he did not want to lead like his brothers back in Kenya. The thought of spending his days leading big-game hunts for rich Americans made him sick, even though it would make him money. He bled for the animals as they bled; their death gaze cut him to the quick. No, he had no interest in leading that. Killing did not a man make.

But leading did.

Perhaps that was why, when the green-eyed boy turned for the third time in his direction, James had nearly stepped from the tree's shadow, and when the boy spoke at the cave's edge, James had felt the boy was speaking to him, to his heart. He wondered if Lana had felt the same.

She'd stood still and listened too. And when she followed the group into the cavern a good hour later, James followed suit.

She'd led him to this group, and they had been more interesting than her by far.

He'd watched earlier as the boy led the group to bury dry bones, giving someone long dead a simple burial worthy of a bowed head, a show of respect. He couldn't help but respect that in kind. And the green-eyed boy was clearly in charge. All looked to him, all followed him. Even the blond one who called the green-eyed boy *brother*.

He'd heard little, but that word he'd heard as clearly as if it were spoken to him.

He knew he should turn back, go tell Carmen what he'd found, what he'd seen. But he wasn't sure he was done. She wanted information, and this group had it. The green-eyed boy had declared that truth himself.

Perhaps he was with the wrong group, James mused.

He would wait and see.

Davey surveyed the City perimeter for the third time in an hour. He'd swept all the way from the icy cove to the fish traps, and everything in between. He'd spent an inordinate amount of time strolling up and down the wooden wall full of names, wondering what happened to all those people. Some had checks or moons or some other sort of mark, but given the heaps of crosses sprinkled throughout, he couldn't help but assume that quite a few people had met their death here. It reminded Davey of the crude marks prisoners would make, something to scream *I was here*.

Creepy, he thought. He refused to add his name to the mix.

Still moving, he walked an invisible line along the City edge. Restless and worried, he couldn't sit still. Paulo had said the wild gates came every day at noon, and that a guaranteed gate would come in three months. The thought of sitting around twiddling his thumbs for three months drove him absolutely crazy. He'd go bloody insane collecting wood, cooking fish, and waiting for time to pass, not to mention constantly peering around for tigers. It was an island hell he'd never imagined.

But the night he'd spent curled against Molly on the beach hadn't been too terrible, even though he knew she'd felt differently. She'd even asked him to share her hut, if only because she didn't want to be alone. He'd do it again, every day, every night, even if it was a different kind of torture.

Where was Paulo?

Davey swept his eyes through the trees. What if Paulo didn't return?

We'd be completely screwed, he thought dismally. They were all banking on a mysterious mountain gate opening in three months' time, showing up in an equally mysterious mountain location known only to Paulo. And how were they to know exactly when three months passed? It wasn't as if they had a calendar handy. What if they miscounted? Davey constantly repeated the date to himself throughout each day, like exam material to be tested later. *Ten days*, he'd say when he woke. *Ten days*, as he ate. Ten days as he walked, ten days as he went to bed. And the next day he'd add another. Today was Day 11, but it was a poor system at best.

And how were they supposed to know when noon arrived? No watches, no clocks, no timepieces or sundials of any sort. *I guess we just hope to see a gate in time to catch it*, he thought.

But he hadn't seen one yet.

On the other hand, he'd seen a black panther, a wombat, a bison, and a bear, and that was just today.

Davey stood at the City's edge, pondering the ridiculousness of it all, when Paulo stepped out of the cliff, literally. Three more people followed, all boys about his age. Two had blond hair, with lanky, lean builds; both could pass for any of his surfing mates back in Melbourne. The taller, more muscular one looked like he'd just chewed nails; the shorter blond with shaggier hair seemed a bit strung out. Shadows bruised the skin under his eyes, dark enough that Davey wagered he partied harder than Davey did. The third boy had a straight spine and spiked black hair, with a lethal-looking sword slung on his back. *He'd likely hit it off with Amara*, he thought, *if she doesn't spear him first.*

Davey stood still, arms casually crossed simply because he had no pockets to stick them in, and watched.

The closer they got, the wearier they looked. Interestingly enough, they all seemed to know where they were going, which was straight toward him.

Another couple popped into sight from the cliff face, a couple who seemed to actually be a couple. They weren't touching, but something about the way they moved together screamed twosome. The girl had a mane of wild blond hair, a heart-shaped face, and a twine rope slung across her chest. The tall, dark-haired boy beside her walked with purpose and an air of power.

Actually the entire group walked with purpose, as if they owned the island.

"Paulo brings many." Hafthor's voice came from behind him. Davey looked up to see Hafthor's earnest expression. The Icelander always made Davey feel a bit stunted, which was new for Davey, who was accustomed to being the tallest on his football team.

"Five," Davey commented.

"Five we can see," Hafthor mused.

Davey fought the eye roll threatening to overtake him. *Hidden people*, he thought. It was as if Hafthor expected fairies to pop out at any moment. But this island seemed to call only people, and beasties. No fairies. And fairies didn't sound particularly frightening anyway.

A cold laugh rattled his skull; it drifted through his ears, from *inside his own head*, loud enough for him to twitch. It was one of those fleeting moments when Davey wavered and thought Hafthor might be onto something after all.

Paulo and his posse strode up to Davey.

"Welcome back," Davey said. "I'm guessing your trip went well?" He raised an eyebrow.

"Not exactly as I expected," Paulo said, "which, given this place, isn't surprising." *And yet*, Davey thought, *you still look surprised.*

"Davey, meet Zane, Kenji, and Thad." Each boy raised a hand in turn.

"And this is Rives, and Skye." The couple waved and said hello.

"Davey." He raised his hand, silently repeating their names, knowing he was missing something.

Hafthor stepped up beside him. He held two full nets teeming with fish, hefting them as if they weighed nothing. "I am Hafthor."

"Hafthor?" Zane's eyes widened. "Dude, you look like a full Thor."

Davey choked back a laugh as Hafthor raised his eyebrows.

"Where is everyone else?" Paulo asked.

"Molly's on the beach," Davey said, realizing one beat too late he'd answered about Molly's whereabouts first. "Calvin too. Amara is sharpening a wooden spear by the supply hut." He shrugged. "That's it."

"Small group," Thad commented.

"It *was* a clean slate," Rives said. Beside him, Skye's face paled.

Thad. Rives. Skye. Zane.

Davey snapped his fingers as recognition hit. "You lot were already here! Your names are on those planks, the ones stretching for meters." He cocked his head. "So where've you been?"

"Home," Rives said, his face unreadable. "And now we're back."

"What?" Cold rushed across Davey's skin, like the afternoon heat had been abruptly sucked from the air. "You went home? And now you're back? Bloody *hell. Why?*"

"Let's go to the City and we'll tell everyone at once." Rives walked as he spoke; the rest of the group followed. "Davey, I know you want info," Rives said, glancing behind me, then carefully screening the trees, "and you'll get it. But first we need food, some water, and to sit for a second without wolves or lions or anything else trying to make a meal out of us, all right?" Now he looked straight at Davey.

Davey nodded robotically.

Back in the City, his gaze went immediately to the wooden wall of names, some that now had faces. Rives. Thad. Skye. At least now he knew what a check meant: It meant someone had left. Someone had *survived*.

But why would anyone come back?

Darkness fell fast and thick, leaving Lana cold. A blanket of black wrapped the island tight, cloaking the trees in shadow and shrinking the world around her. Stars burst overhead, fiery ice in the sky, as clear and bright as she'd ever seen at home. A stone's throw away, a semicircle of thatched houses ringed an open center, a crackling fire burning at its heart. The girl with wild, curly golden hair who had tried to stop her this morning sat by the fire next to another girl, one whose face tilted toward the first girl, listening. From her vantage point through the trees, Lana could make out the blue streak in the second girl's dark hair; it caught the firelight like sapphire facets. The two talked animatedly, bodies as relaxed as their smiles, an easy camaraderie in the making. Longing welled inside Lana, and she stifled it immediately. She wasn't here to mingle and make friends, especially with *haoles*.

The wind shifted, and Lana's mouth watered. Too nervous to eat before she left this morning, all she'd had today was fruit. Something wrapped in green leaves sat nestled over the coals; it smelled delicious, hinting of mango and meat. Her grandmother's advice rang in her ears. *Make your own way; seek your own path. Each choice bears witness to who you will become.*

Turning away was one of the toughest things Lana had ever done.

She crept away, chilled and furious. She was hiding from a City built by her people, with huts left for her and others like her yet to come. The *haoles* were squatters, taking what was hers, just as the *haole* Carmen had hijacked her cave.

An animal howled in the distance, an eerie sound with a snarling echo too close for Lana's comfort. If only she were at the cave. That was the plan, and she was struggling to come up with another, a failing she placed squarely on the *haoles'* heads. She knew the City had been taken over by the *haoles*, yet now she'd have to hide among them for one night, until she could make her way to the next place her grandmother had advised.

Moving softly so as to alert no one of her presence, Lana crept forward, toward the most distant hut, the one farthest north. Slipping inside, Lana discovered an island bounty: clothes, twine, satchels, even sandals. And spears. Lots of spears. Clearly it was the cache where Paulo had gathered supplies.

A stack of cloth caught her eye. *Sheets*, she thought. An unnecessary island luxury, but since she was here, she might as well borrow them. After all, it was just one night.

As silent as the night, Lana removed the sheets from the shelf, spread one on the ground, and wrapped herself in the second. It was just enough to ward off the night chill.

She would sleep here, for one night, and then move on.

After all, this was just her beginning. She had nine months to go.

The island let her sleep. It kept the other humans away from her temporary resting place, through whispers and suggestions and cold pressure when needed, all read as their own. The female, Lana, had isolated herself well, wielding her own pride to push others away, and the island was more than happy to strengthen her self-imposed walls.

Isolation and pride always worked in the island's favor. The arrogant humans never understood until it was too late, their pride blinding them to the truth and keeping them in the dark.

Which was precisely where the island liked them best.

CHAPTER 34

SKYE

The ocean rumbled in the distance—the real thing, not my store-bought sleep machine. I'd woken more rested than I'd felt in weeks. For the first night in months, I'd gone eight hours without waking, my sleep dreamless and deep.

Nothing about Nil made sense.

Search.

The events of yesterday replayed in swift succession. Not unlike my first day here last December, yesterday was a strange déjà vu, only yesterday was a replay of my own experiences, not my uncle's. At times I'd felt like I'd never left.

Until we got to the City. Full of new faces, suddenly it seemed as though I'd been gone for longer than three months. Clustered around the firepit, Molly, Davey, Hafthor, Calvin, Kenji, and Amara had listened as we introduced ourselves and shared our history. Calvin had fidgeted while Hafthor sat with unnerving stillness; Davey's eyes had been calculating, Molly's more introspective. Kenji seemed remarkably calm. Amara sat alone.

Rives in his strong, quiet way had been the moderator, fielding questions, offering honest answers and reassuring everyone in the process.

Zane had turned in early after nearly falling asleep sitting up. One by one, people had peeled away from the fire and the conversation, to sleep or to murmur among themselves. Out of all the newcomers, I'd spent the most time with Molly, perhaps because she had the most questions. One careful query at a time, Molly had asked about my uncle's journal and my time here. She'd been fascinated by the Search system, the sheer volume of people who had come and gone, and the mysterious nature of the island itself.

"Boggling," she'd said, twisting the blue streak in her hair. "It seems like this place is all about searching, isn't it? For other people, for food. For the ugly beasties to watch out for. For a safe place to step or sleep or leave your bathers to dry, or for something you can't see. Something inside yourself to ensure your survival, for something you never needed before, maybe something you didn't even know you possessed. And now we're to search for a way to end the mayhem, too?" Her eyes had been keen. "I'm all for a challenge," she'd said slowly. "But I do wish we knew what to look for."

Me too, I'd thought. *Me too*.

I ached for something concrete, for something to guide me. Last time, the equinox gate had been my clue, my starting point, and I'd had my uncle's journal as a handbook. This time, I had nothing, just a burning desire to end this place once and for all.

Search.

The word echoed in the breeze; it thrummed in my blood. I gently moved Rives's hand from my hip to the bed, careful not to wake him, but I didn't dawdle.

If there was one thing I'd learned over the past few months, it was that Nil didn't like to be ignored.

I walked outside, breathing deeply. Cool air filled my lungs, crisp and clean. The firepit was cold, no torches in sight, lit or otherwise. I remembered that we'd used all the torches we had on our last day here, the last *time* we were here.

The ripples continue, I thought. We were living the Nil we thought we left behind, a Nil not built for the future.

To the north and east, greenish predawn light filtered through the leaves, casting shadows for the rising sun to burn away. One shadow moved.

Then it moved again.

Cloaked in the night's lingering gloom, a girl crept from the Shack and slipped into the dark sliver between two trees. She turned north, her thick hair swinging around her shoulders, then glanced back furtively and our eyes caught.

Lana.

She spun back around and strode away, her quick steps just shy of a run.

Does she really think she can lose me? I thought incredulously as I matched her pace. I'd spent three months on this island; so far she'd spent one day. She may be an islander but when it came to Nil, so was I.

Search, I thought.

Now I searched for one girl, one who might know something about this place I didn't. Something she knew based on her past.

Lana lengthened the space between us and I let her, because a few minutes into our stroll, I knew precisely where she was headed. Sure enough, the trees thinned, then stopped altogether. A gorgeous, clear pool of water filled the space, set into an alcove of rock as dark as slate. A black rock cliff speckled with emerald green rose into the sky, a perfect backdrop for the water falling down its side with a familiar roar.

At the Cove's edge, Lana spun around and shot me a haughty glare.

"What do you think you're doing?" she asked.

"Going for a morning walk," I said innocently. "What about you?"

"You're following me." Her eyes narrowed.

I sighed, already tired of the drama. "So what if I am. Does it matter?"

"Of course it does!" she snapped. "I. Just. Want. Privacy." Lana bit off the words.

"Funny that you slept in the City, then," I said sweetly.

"My cave was taken."

"*Your* cave?" I raised my eyebrows.

She waved her hand dismissively, like she'd already given away more than she wanted. "Why are you following me?" She held up her hands, showing open palms. "I didn't take anything from you, I swear on my life."

"I didn't think you did."

Lana crossed her arms, cocking her head at me. A long moment passed as Lana and I regarded each other without moving. The roar of the Cove's waterfall seemed louder in the lull.

"So." She drawled out the word, infusing that one syllable with as much disdain as she possibly could. *I'm busy*, it said. *I have more important things to do than stand here wasting time with you.* "What do you want?"

Lana's tone mimicked Maaka's detached annoyance perfectly, and it dispatched my last shard of patience. If anyone was wasting time, it was Lana. I wasn't here to replay the Maaka-Rives dynamic; it wasn't a cycle to be repeated. This entire Nil cycle wasn't to be repeated; that was why I was here. The equinox clock was ticking and I had a mission, one that went far beyond the two of us.

It took all my will not to snap.

"Lana, you know what I want." I forced myself to speak calmly. "I want this to stop, for your outdated island tradition to end. I want all the people here right now to get back home safely to the ones they love, and I want teens in both worlds to live without fear of Nil. I want to end this madness. The island must be stopped, Lana. Forever. *That* is what I want."

She stared at me, dark eyes calculating. "Bold," she finally said. "And rather egotistical, don't you think? Who gives you the right to decide that this place must end?"

"The island," I said unequivocally. "I told you once; I'll tell you again. I feel its exhaustion, its desperation. And it called me back. I don't understand what this place is, but I know it's more than just rocks and dirt. So much more. It's alive, Lana. Sentient. Knowing. It's something—otherworldly, possibly beyond my limited human grasp. But I do know this: the island is tired, Lana. And it wants our help."

She stared at me, lips pursed.

No response.

"You asked me what I wanted, and I told you." My tone stayed level. "Now I'll tell you what I want from you. I want you to choose to help us. I want you to think of anything you know that the island fears or wants, or that your history tells you is an island weakness or strength. I want you to think of any special rituals or places or times of day that have meaning or any other super secret island scoop that we don't know about. That we *wouldn't* know about. I want you to comb your mind and your past, and then I want you to share anything that might be important with me. I know your tradition tells you not to speak with us, with *haoles*, but I promise that's not so much a tradition as a prejudice." My eyes never left hers, but my tone softened. "I'm sorry that Americans dropped the bombs and altered your tradition; believe me, I wish that never happened. Desperately, I do. But it did, and now the wild gates are here to stay, along with the predators and unprepared teens they bring. You don't have to join the City, but know that you can. You also don't have to make friends, but know that you don't have to be alone, either. And of course you don't have to help us, but I really, really want you to. Because when that equinox gate opens in three months' time, we need all the help we can get, to make sure it never opens again."

There.

All my cards were on the table, and my hand was pretty darn good. Still, Lana wore her poker face well.

"You know what I want from you?" Lana quirked one brow.

"What?"

"Your name."

I was taken aback. *Had I never introduced myself? Not on the platform? Not today?*

"Skye," I said slowly. "My name is Skye."

Lana nodded. "Well, *Skye*, I'd say it's been nice to meet you, but . . ." She shrugged, her eyes turning cold. "It hasn't. I don't know you, or your friends, but all of you—and you especially—seem incredibly determined to tell me what to do, in the one place where, ironically, I'm supposed to choose for myself. You've spent time here already, more than me, obviously, and it seems you've figured out your path. Well, great for you. But your path doesn't have to be mine. Your *quest* doesn't have to be mine. I just got here, and you're already telling me when to leave, and what to do." She paused. "What I want is for you to leave. Me. Alone."

"If that's what you want, I will." I spoke quietly. "But I can't guarantee that the island will do the same."

"I'll find out, then, won't I?" she asked.

"I worry that you will." I feared that Lana might not like the island's attention. I glanced at the Cove, desperately wishing Lana would give up something before it was too late. "Maybe you'll find what you're looking for in the Looking Glass Cavern," I said, trying to be amicable. "Brace yourself, Lana, the water's icy." I pointed at the Cove.

She stared at me. "Point taken." Then she laughed, more dry than amused. "You act as if you know everything. About this place, about what is right. No wonder you can't find what you're looking for."

I stepped forward, a rush of anger heating my face. "I never claimed to know everything, Lana. Don't you see? I just told you I don't know enough, it's why I'm asking you for help!"

She shook her head. "You keep letting yourself think that, Skye. I hope the island gifts me with the Sight." Her look was scathing. "For I truly would love to know what the island has in store for you."

Without another word, Lana turned and walked into the pool. If the icy water stung, she didn't show it; she walked until the water touched her waist, and then without a backward glance, she dove.

This time I didn't follow.

I turned around and ran smack into Rives's chest. "Stalker," I said, looking up in surprise.

"Coincidence," he replied, his eyes twinkling.

Despite myself, I smiled.

"So things went well with Lana?" He crooked a knowing smile.

"Oh, I got tons of information. She's as forthcoming as Maaka."

"I figured." His gaze drifted to the Cove behind me. "Not planning to follow her to the cavern?"

"What's the point? She still believes the old island dogma, that this place is one of enlightenment rather than danger. It was like talking to a wall."

"Sounds like you rammed up against it."

He raised one eyebrow, his message clear: *You pushed, maybe too hard.* And he was right. I'd been as confrontational with her as I'd been with Paulo once, with the same terrible results. But this time, I had no regrets. Paulo hadn't been prepared for Nil; Lana had. She had secrets, I knew it. My worry was that maybe Lana didn't know the answers we needed, maybe even that she didn't know she *had* the answers.

Maybe she doesn't, whispered the falls.

Doesn't what? I wondered. *Know that she knows or know at all?*

"I don't know if you're talking to yourself right now or someone else," Rives said, his eyebrow arching higher. "If it's the latter, I'm not sure I want to know."

I opened my mouth to retort when, from far away, far *inside*, a scream split the air, human and terrified, muffled behind the falls.

Lana.

I grabbed Rives's hand. Together we dashed into the Cove, water splashing around our feet as we headed toward the waterfall. We jogged until we couldn't, then we swam hard and fast, the cold water feeding my own personal adrenaline rush as Lana's terrified scream echoed in my ears.

Together we burst into the vast air pocket behind the falls, side by side, our lungs burning, coming face-to-face with a lanky boy crouched on the damp rock ledge. The moment we surfaced he stumbled back in surprise. He held a sharpened four-prong spear in his right hand that he bobbled as he fell.

"You scared me, mon." The boy grabbed his heart, his eyes flicking to Rives and then me. Breaking into an easy grin, the boy laughed to himself. "About like I scared that girl, back in the cave." He jerked his head toward the passageway entrance. "Mon, I tell you, it is *dark* in that cave. Like night in the day." The boy's accent dripped off each word. Bahamian, if I wasn't mistaken.

Still smiling, the boy popped back to his feet, a lithe move worthy of a gymnast. "I'm Dominic. And you?"

"I'm Skye." I smiled.

"Rives." Beside me, Rives offered his hand.

Dominic pumped Rives's outstretched hand, then pointed to the cave with his spear. "You going in?" he asked, moving aside on the ledge.

"The girl you saw," I said, my tone urgent. "Is she okay?"

"Other than having a small heart attack?" Dominic's grin widened, then he waved his hand. "She'll be fine. We scared each other all the way to our roots, I tell you. And now? I see you, coming from the water like a living ghost. I see no one for days, and then? I see three people in three minutes." He shook his head incredulously.

Rives grinned. "Where are you from, Dominic?"

"Abaco, born and raised." He smiled again. "And you?"

"France. And Hawaii."

My teeth chattered, drawing Rives's attention. The water beneath the falls was so *cold*.

"Your lips are literally turning blue." He frowned. "We either need to check on Lana ASAP or go back. Your choice."

"I want to check on her," I said, climbing out of the water. Standing, I bounced on my toes, trying to get my blood pumping again. "Not to bother her, but just make sure she's okay."

Rives followed me out of the water.

"You can stay with Dominic and clue him in on Nil." I was already at the passageway entrance. "I'll only be a minute."

"You sure you don't want company?" Rives glanced at the cave opening.

I knew he wanted me to say yes, but I felt the need to do this alone. I wasn't sure what I was going to do exactly, but I felt drawn to Lana.

I wondered if this was how Rives had felt with Maaka.

"I'm good, Rives." I smiled to take the sting out of my words. "I'll be quick. I'll shout if I need you, but I really just need to make sure she's okay."

"Follow the arrows," he called to my back.

Darkness swallowed me in one giant gulp. I shivered, telling myself it was just because I was cold. I hugged the left side, where arrows pointed my way. I'd been here before, many times, but the chill of the passageway seemed to have worsened—like the darkness itself.

I passed the junction where the skeleton rested without a glance.

At the end of the passageway, I paused. Now I let the shadows cloak me, hoping to remain invisible. Sinking back into the darkness as much as I could, I leaned my head forward, looking for Lana.

She stood in the Looking Glass Cavern, her profile to me. She faced the pool, hands clenched into mad fists, shoulders shaking as tears full of anger and misery and lost expectations rolled down her cheeks; I knew this to be true because I could *feel* them. Not the tears, but the emotions: they coursed through the cavern like a roiling cloud—and then she turned toward me.

Anger and pain and hurt hit me like a physical wave, as fiery as the invisible heat of a gate, only with this wave, I didn't burn; I *felt*. I felt how much Lana *hurt*. I ducked back quickly, praying that she didn't see me. I knew she wouldn't want me to see her, not like that.

I already knew she didn't want anything from me at all—except to leave her be.

I should go back, I thought. *To Rives and Dominic*. But it felt wrong to leave Lana alone when she was so obviously upset. She was stuck here as much as I was, but unlike me, she had no support system at all.

She doesn't want you, I thought with a pang of regret. *Your pity or your help.*

I felt the truth of that in my bones.

I would honor Lana's wishes and let her be. Somehow I knew I'd see her again.

Turning back, I left her alone.

The darkness was only too happy to have me. The fatigue that constantly swirled around me pressed in, reveling in the dark, but the exhaustion was different now. Richer, filled with emotion. *The same emotion that was in the cavern*, I thought with a start.

Had I felt Lana's emotion, or the island's? Is there a connection?

Understanding brushed my mind, a thread to follow. As I reached further, I felt the line in my head, the stark barrier between Nil and me, the one I'd so carefully reinforced during my battles with the darkness before I'd ever set foot on Nil.

But I wondered. If I looked beyond the darkness *now*, when I was conscious and in a place so clearly connected to Nil, would I see Talla? Or would I see someone else? Some*thing* else?

Would I actually see Nil?

I'd barely had the thought when the darkness surged; it took all my will to stop it from pouring over the line. My back pressed against the rock as I held the line.

No.

My thought was fierce as I flew into mental motion, erecting more barriers, thickening the line dividing me from Nil. Walls rose higher in my head, built out of my sanity, as clear as glass but as hard as diamonds. I would not relinquish anything to Nil.

Nor would Nil give in to me. The blackness stayed black.

Darkness swirled outside my crystal walls, snarling and hungry; it pressed against the barrier like billowing black smoke, searching for a way in even as pinpricks of light punctuated the dark.

My barrier held. I could hold Nil at bay forever; I knew that now. I felt my own strength. A mental force, a show of will, on both sides of the glass.

The problem was, keeping Nil at bay took everything I had, and there was no energy left for walking. So I did the only thing I could.

I called for Rives.

CHAPTER
35

I stared at the cave where Skye had disappeared.

I wished I'd had a torch to give her, but I'd had nothing. No torch, no knife. All the metal blades had mysteriously vanished during our time away. All I'd had to offer was me—and she'd said no.

So I'd let her go. Just because Skye didn't need—or want—my backup, I'd never stop wanting to give it to her.

Merde.

It was going to be a long three months.

Dominic's voice broke into my musings. "Skye's a fiery one, yes?"

I rubbed my neck. "You have no idea."

Dominic laughed, a full rumble all the way from his gut. "My auntie says that women are the strong ones, that they hold all the power. I think she is right." He laughed again.

He shook his head, then his laughter ebbed like a retreating tide. His gaze turned earnest. "Hey, mon. I sit here with you, in this place"—he waved his pronged spear at the wall of water falling in front of us—"and I don't know what is happening. Where am I? Where are *we?*" Dominic cocked his head at me. "I keep thinking I'm in Atlantis, the lost city, but that city was underwater, and I'm on land. But it was a water light that took me, only it was on the sand. It makes no sense to me. No sense at all."

Dominic's story didn't make sense to me, either.

"Water light?" I frowned.

"You know the ones. Under the water, where the light appears and waits, a glowing wall in the water, and the sharks and the fish, they disappear into the light." He shrugged. "Some say it is mermaids come to claim the sea, some say it is the city of Atlantis reclaiming its own. I say it is an old wives' tale, but I tell you, I have seen a water light myself. I was only twelve years old, and I remember it like it was yesterday. And two weeks ago, a water light, it appeared on land. On the sand where I stood. It took me, mon. And now here I am."

Dominic's story caught me off guard.

A Nil memory rushed back.

Me, on the beach near Nil City, the sun blazing overhead. I'd just come out of the water, a desperate attempt to clear my head of Skye when I saw her. I always saw her. She'd waved me over, her face determined and defiant and full of fight. I'd walked to her, drawn like a magnet. Then her words set me on fire.

So I'm thinking there's a second gate, she'd told me, her words an excited rush, *a companion gate, a gate underwater on both ends that only transfers cold-blooded things. That* imprints *on cold-blooded things, like fish. It's the balance to our gate, the counterweight.* She'd paused, her steel-flecked eyes sparking with intelligence and passion. *Make sense?*

Hell, yeah, it makes sense, I thought, firmly back in the now. *The balance of it all. And living proof sits right here.*

Now the question was, how could we use this information to our advantage?

Skye would know, but she wasn't here.

"No," I told Dominic, who watched me expectantly. "It's not Atlantis. It's Nil."

Dominic cocked his head. "Never heard of it."

"You wouldn't have. But I promise you, it's very real."

I glanced back at the cave entrance. Darkness blinked at me, not unlike the darkness of Skye's dreams. No sign of Skye or anyone else. Just blackness that was far from flat.

Don't leave her alone.

Pouring in with the falls, the warning came in a rush.

"So what is Nil?" Dominic asked.

I scrambled to my feet, talking fast; I needed to find Skye, *now*. "Nil's an island. There's a City to the south, on the coast. If you get there before we get back, ask for Paulo. He'll fill you in." I ducked inside the passageway, turning back at the last second. "Sorry, Dominic. Skye needs me. Go to the City. I'll tell you everything I know. Or Paulo will."

Dominic nodded, then pointed with his lips toward the opening at my back. "Be safe in that dark place."

Rives.

Skye's call rang crisp and clear in my head, packed with an unmistakable *Come get me now* vibe. And then it was gone.

The echo of her whisper hadn't faded before I was running. I found Skye three-quarters of the way in. Her back pressed against the wall, she sat in a motionless crouch, head down, arms wrapped around her waist, feet flat on the ground, like she'd slid down the wall and stayed there.

"Skye?" I bent down beside her. "You okay?"

No answer, no response. Fear lanced through me like ice.

"Skye?" I touched her cheek. Her skin was cold.

"I have to get out of here." The words took a Herculean effort to get past her lips.

"Are you hurt?" I asked.

No answer, no response. She seemed trapped inside herself, held by the dark.

I didn't need a whisper in my head to tell me to get her the hell out.

I lifted Skye up and cradled her against my chest. I started back the way I'd come.

"No," she rasped. "Other way."

I turned back toward the Looking Glass Cavern and instantly her body melted against mine. I moved by rote, crouching as needed, thighs burning, wondering what happened to Skye in the few minutes we were apart. Was she hurt? Bitten? Attacked?

I stepped into the Looking Glass Cavern; the rush of light made me blink. At the same moment, Skye's entire body relaxed.

"Wow," she breathed, opening her eyes and stretching like a cat in a shaft of sunlight. "So that was weird." She smiled and actually yawned. *Yawned.* Like everything was totally fine, like she'd just taken a quick nap, like a minute ago she hadn't been almost paralytic, huddled in Nil's bowels. "I'm good. You can put me down now."

"You're good." I bit off the words as I gently set her on her feet. She stretched fully, her face relaxed. I stared at her, shocked at the quick 180. "A minute ago you couldn't lift a finger, Skye. Couldn't move at all. Weird doesn't cover it."

She stood on her tiptoes to kiss me full on the mouth. "I know. But I'm okay now."

"You're okay now," I repeated, stepping back to look her in the eye. "Well, I'm not. I heard you, here"—I pointed to my head—"and then I found you curled in a ball. *You couldn't move, Skye.* I had to carry you out of there, for God's sake. What happened?"

She sighed. "I saw Lana. She was here, and she was crying. She looked so alone."

I'd completely forgotten about Lana.

"And?" I prompted.

"It was weird." She drew out her words. "She'd already told me to leave her alone, but it felt wrong to leave her crying when she was so obviously upset. I stood there, inside the passageway, in the dark, not sure what to do." Skye swallowed. "She turned toward me and then—her anger and pain rushed at me; I can't explain it. I *felt* it, like a wave, and I knew in that moment she *wouldn't* talk to me. So I turned back. But inside the passageway, the darkness grew stronger. More—real. Like it drew power from the dark, from *itself*. It tried to cross the line, but I didn't let it." She actually looked triumphant.

"What line?" I asked, not following.

"The line between Nil and me." She said it matter-of-factly, as if it were obvious. "It's not something I can see, but can feel. After all those months of dreaming, I know exactly where it is and how to keep myself safe, in here." She tapped her head. "But back there, I thought maybe since I was awake, I could look into it to see the real Nil. But Nil doesn't want me to see." She shrugged, like it was no big deal. "I'm fine now. I called you and you came. I know my limits, Rives. I didn't anticipate the power in places belonging to Nil, and I know now that there are some things I'll never know. I let my guard down. I won't do it again."

I stared at Skye, stunned. She really believed what she was saying.

"Do you hear yourself? This is *twice*, Skye. Once yesterday, once today. Twice in two days that Nil got in your head."

"Once." Her steely eyes flashed. "Just once. Nil didn't get in my head today. Didn't you listen? *I kept Nil out.* It just took so much focus I couldn't move; that's why I called you. And you came." She smiled, then lifted her chin defiantly. "I'm stronger than Nil knows, Rives. Have some faith in me, okay?"

"I do have faith in you, *chérie*." I held her gaze tight. "You're the strongest person I know. I trust you, Skye, enough to follow you here, okay? But . . ." I paused, glancing around the cavern. "Nil's still an unknown."

And so is its strength, I thought. But I knew Nil was strong enough to reach into our world and lure Skye here, which spoke of a power beyond our understanding. *How could Skye defend herself against that?*

Feeling cold, I glanced at the wall behind Skye. It was packed with history and life. Carvings taunted me, etched by human hands. Hands belonging to people whose fate was written long ago. Had Nil crossed the line with all of them, gotten into their heads too? It had gotten into my head once, in this very place. Yesterday Nil had definitely gotten into Skye's head, deep enough to pull her back. And today? Maybe Nil hadn't gotten *into* her head, but it had messed with her mind, enough to incapacitate her.

I dreaded a third strike.

3-2-1-4.

Nil numbers, Nil nightmares, running the length of the cavern wall. Maybe three strikes on Nil didn't mean you were out; maybe they just meant you made it to second base. The next step, the next phase.

The middle.

Damn if I wasn't thinking like Maaka, but it was better than thinking we were almost done before we'd even started.

"Rives?" She pointed at the wall packed with primal graffiti. "Do you see something?"

Yes. No. I don't know.

A memory flashed; a thought struck. Me, standing here alone, listening for Talla. Fast-forward, take two. Me, standing on the platform with Skye, yearning for knowledge.

Merde.

Nil had already been in my head twice, deep enough for me to lose time.

I ripped my gaze away from the cavern wall to look at Skye. "That line you talked about? It can blur. And we don't want to be on the wrong side. I think maybe that's when we lose time. When Nil *steals* time." Suddenly I wanted to *go*, to get out of this sprawling cavern with its pool reflecting light back at me. Here we stood, spilling secrets in the belly of Nil.

"Let's go. But not through that passageway. We're taking the ocean route."

"Aye, aye, Captain." She winked. "Keep an eye out for buried treasure, will you? And by that, I mean clues."

"Always." But I didn't smile.

Look around. Pay attention.

Only now I looked with one eye, because the other stayed trained on Skye.

CHAPTER 36

The island watched the one called Lana, for she was watching too.

Her back to a rock, Lana sat on the white sand at the beach's edge, studying the black cliff that housed the Looking Glass Cavern. She'd seen Skye emerge from the ocean, the boy—the Leader—with her. At the water's edge, he'd wrapped her in his arms as if he couldn't bear to have any air between them. A surge of envy had flared inside her as they kissed, then Lana's anger resurfaced, dousing her inexplicable surge of jealousy. She didn't want to be kissed, not here, or be part of a twosome. She didn't need anyone else, *haole* or otherwise.

She did, however, want Skye and her band of friends to stop following her.

It made her furious that Skye had seen her crying in the cavern. A few minutes before her meltdown, she'd been shocked to run into a boy in the passageway. She'd been feeling her way along the wall, trailing her fingertips along the cold rock, and then, without warning, she'd touched a human hand. She wasn't a screamer, but she'd screamed then. She never even saw him, just heard his voice as he apologized, a deep voice vibrating with his own fright. She hadn't spoken, just ran around him, all the way to the cavern. Standing in front of the pool, her heartbeat had finally slowed, her own fright wearing off. And anger had followed. Why had her simple journey turned so complicated, so crowded? Her anger had driven her to tears, and then abruptly she'd felt she wasn't alone. And when she'd turned, there was Skye, an expression of pity and concern on her face before Skye ducked back into the shadows. It was unbearable.

So Lana had left.

She hadn't waited for Skye to barge out and annoy her; she was done with *haole* meddling. The problem was, now Lana wasn't sure where to go. In the span of two days, the *haoles* had driven her from her cave, the City, and then the Looking Glass Cavern, the three places she was to spend her first quarter on the island. *Reflection before Sight*, her grandmother had told her.

Lana sighed. Her grandmother had made everything sound so straightforward. But the reality was anything but. At least now she finally had the solitude she craved. She would embrace this moment for what it was.

White sand sprawled in both directions, crisp and calm, cooler than the hot sting of the charcoal sand to the south. In this quiet moment, the rising sun warmed her shoulders and the powerful waves crooned; they rolled into shore with whispers and promises of more to come.

Soft fur brushed her leg. Lana woke with a start, startled to find that she'd actually fallen asleep. A tabby kitten rubbed against her calf, mewing softly.

"Well, aren't you a pretty little thing," Lana said.

Smiling, she reached down and picked up the tabby, cradling the tiny body against her chest. The kitten purred, its body vibrating with happiness. The last wave retreated, leaving a stretch of silence in its wake, and the hair on the back of Lana's neck abruptly prickled.

An odd huffing noise sounded behind her, followed by a low growl. Tabby in hand, she turned, slowly. For the second time in one day, she screamed.

A massive brown bear stood on its hind legs, stretching to a height taller than her. It clacked its jaws, a terrifying sound. Ears back, the bear dropped to all fours as Lana stumbled backward, fully aware that the small boulder she'd slept against offered little in the way of defense, prolonging her life by seconds at most.

I'm dead, she thought. *It's over.*

What a pitiful end. She had no way to protect herself, nowhere to run. Time rushed backward and forward, a blur of memories and a well of regrets, the heartbeat of the kitten in her arms melding with the warm sand beneath her feet and hot sun overhead. Her world shrunk to the predator lurching toward her, its mouth open, teeth bared.

Her arms wrapped protectively around the kitten, Lana closed her eyes, willing the attack to end quickly.

The air in front of her thickened with heat and sound and the rush of hot breath. Liquid sprayed across her face, sticky and warm; something landed near her feet with a ground-shaking thud.

Her eyes flew open. The brown bear twitched at her feet, a dark body in a hollow of its own making. Crimson droplets stood out on the snow-white sand, ridiculously out of place. Paulo stood over the bear, bloody knife in hand, his torso and tattoos splattered with fresh blood.

"You killed it," Lana said, dumbstruck.

"Yes, I know." Paulo regarded her with a weary look, one she was accustomed to seeing only on elders. "And I wish I hadn't had to." Stepping back from the bear, he cleaned the blade on a nearby leaf as he spoke. "I've been tracking him for weeks. He's been hanging around the City. He steals from the firepit occasionally, and he's gotten bolder. I suspect he's just hungry and out of sorts. Was, I mean." Paulo glanced down at the silent bear with a pitying expression, then his head snapped up to look at her. Fire lit his eyes from within. "Let this be a wake-up call, Lana. My friends tried to warn you about this place. It's not the island of old. Honestly, you're lucky I was here, at this moment." He cocked his head. "But perhaps it wasn't luck. Perhaps it was meant to be. We're fast-forwarding to your middle, Lana. Whatever your plan was, it's shot. This bear is only part of it. You have to be smarter. You have to be alert at all times. There is no downtime, not here." His look turned scruti-nizing. "Unless you're ready to die. Cowering before a bear isn't wise. Looking large, fighting back—that at least gives you a chance. For a second there, I thought you gave up."

Lana bit back her retort, hating the truth she heard in Paulo's words.

"Two more things." Paulo's voice was disturbingly matter-of-fact. "First, you owe me. I actually don't want anything from you, but there's something we all need. So I ask this: regardless of what you choose to do in the coming weeks, if you're still alive in three months, meet me at the equinox gate. There is no doubt in my mind that we will all see the end that day."

"You're asking me to leave early," Lana said, her temper flaring. "To cut my journey short. To give up the chance for Sight. You ask too much." The edge in her voice matched the blade of Paulo's knife.

"Your life is worth less?" His voice was soft.

For the second time in minutes Lana held her tongue. She stared at Paulo, feeling her years of planning pop like a child's balloon.

"What's the second thing?" she demanded.

Paulo pointed at the sun. "Take note, Lana. This is what noon feels like on the island." With a wry smile, he stepped away, only to slowly turn back. "I'm going to get reinforcements to see what parts of the bear we can use. Feel free to hang out with the carcass until I get back, but I'd be careful if I were you. Other creatures will smell the blood. We might not be the only predators interested."

Lana felt her own blood drain from her cheeks.

"I'd guess bear hunting and cleaning wasn't part of your island train-ing. Mine either." Paulo's eyes were understanding. "Good luck on your own, Lana. You'll need it."

This time when he left, he didn't look back.

The one called Paulo kept walking.
The one called Lana let him go.

The island watched them both, waiting. Slowly inhaling. And then it breathed deeply, as it could only at this hour.

Noon.

Noon brought a surge of strength; it flowed through the island from both sides of the seam. The flash of energy burned bright; the island captured a fraction to keep. No more than a trickle, the bit of electria spilled into the island's reservoir, and so it would stay. In time, each bit conserved would be sufficient to give the island what it ached for: freedom.

The seam widened a fraction, and like a thread pulled taut, echoes of yesterday's pain drew the island directly to one it remembered. One it knew well, the one called Charley. Her pain mixed with determination and will, a powerful blend of human emotion so strong the island couldn't turn away, and for a timeless moment, it absorbed those feelings, plumbing their depths, noting their power. Yes, the island mused, perhaps the island could use her powerful connection with her mate to alter the fabric of the future.

Perhaps it could use her.

She already possessed the information she needed, if she chose to see.

The island waited to see if she would open her eyes.

"Dr. Bracken." Charley spoke slowly, her words measured. "We have to do something. I don't know what, but I can't just sit here for three months, waiting."

Skye's dad sighed. The lines on his forehead seemed to have deepened overnight.

"I understand what you're saying, Charley, I really do, but there's a limit to what we can accomplish from here. Simply put, we're here, and they're *there*. The best thing we can do is to be ready for when they return."

At least Skye's dad didn't say *if* they return.

Charley might have fully lost it then, because she *knew* Thad would return. Just like she knew that right at this moment, he was safe. She didn't know how, or why, but she knew that at this moment, his heart beat steady and strong and he wasn't in danger. *Well*, she amended to herself, *other than the fact that he's on Nil, which is an awfully dangerous place to be.* But he wasn't in imminent danger at this moment, of that Charley felt certain. Just like she felt certain she'd heard him moments ago.

Keep the faith, he'd told her.

And she would.

Thad, she thought with all her might, *I'm not giving up. Not on you, or Rives or Skye. Stay safe. I love you.*

Skye's dad regarded her quietly. "Charley, we need to call your parents. Let them know what's going on."

"I've already called them," she said briskly. *And they have no clue what's going on.* "I've told them we're traveling with Skye and Rives and you, and I gave them your cell phone number. But . . ." She paused. "They know nothing of Nil, and I'd like to keep it that way."

"I won't lie, Charley." The professor's voice was stern.

"I'm not asking you to. I'm just asking you to offer as little information as possible. I'm not on Nil; I'm on an island in Micronesia with you, exactly where we told them we would be. We're taking an extended summer vacation. It's educational, even. An archaeological expedition."

Skye's dad crossed his arms. "How so?"

"Because we're going to dig into Nil's past. We're going to talk to every islander we can find, we're going to scour that stupid Death Twin and its mate, and we're going to figure out how to help from our end. There must be a way. And if there is, we're going to find it. We're not going to waste one more minute." Charley sat ramrod straight, her golden eyes blazing. She held up Skye's uncle's journal. "And I think I know exactly where to start. Or rather, with whom." She stared at the professor with calculating eyes. "What do you know about a woman named Rika?"

As the professor's eyes widened, Charley smiled in triumph.

Thad, she thought fiercely, *stay safe. Stay strong. It's not over yet.*

By the Wall, Thad froze.

Behind him, the ocean's roar crashed through the trees. Around him, the breeze whispered and giggled and generally screwed with his head. But somehow, in the midst of it all, he'd have sworn he'd just heard Charley.

In his head.

He was furious. Classic Nil, playing tricks. Playing games with his head. Hell, Nil was messing around *in his head*. First it had flashed Rives's face on the body wedged in the rocks, now it was mimicking Charley. Thad clenched the knife in his hand so tightly his knuckles went white.

He closed his mind to everything but the here and now.

Charley's home, Charley's safe, he reminded himself. Nil loved playing head games, loved pulling the strings, only Nil rigged everything from the start, so Nil always won. But Thad knew that now, and it gave him an advantage.

So did the knowledge that he'd already won, once.

Nil says listen, the breeze crooned, its salty finger stroking his spine.

Not a chance. Thad's half smile turned cold. *I'm no longer playing.*

Time marched on. The seam narrowed, the surge of noon gone. The island had done all it could. The one called Charley knew whom to seek, but the one called Thad refused to listen, an unfortunate choice.

If his mind stayed closed, he would help no one, especially himself.

CHAPTER 37

SKYE

I sat beside Hafthor near the firepit. My legs were restless, like me. I needed to go. To *search*. Each moment sitting felt like a moment wasted.

Relax, Skye, I told myself. *Think first, act second.*

What I needed was a plan.

Which was exactly what I didn't have.

"Eat," Hafthor's command interrupted my musing. "You are too thin." He gestured to my fish wrap, which I'd barely nibbled.

I took a bite and Hafthor nodded, appeased. Since I'd returned from the Cove, I'd learned he came from a small village on the Icelandic coast, a fact that explained his prowess with all things fishing. He'd caught our lunch, cleaned it, and chopped the whole catch into individual fillets, and then with my help—although I had the sinking suspicion he hadn't needed help at all—we'd seasoned and cooked them over the fire. Throughout it all, he'd moved with the same calm demeanor: unruffled, methodical, yet no movement wasted. He ate the same way. So far he'd eaten three fish wraps to my one.

"Your tattoo is amazing." I gestured to his shoulder, where lines of crisp black ink stretched like arms. It looked like something I might find etched somewhere on Nil. "It looks like a rune."

"It's an Icelandic compass," he replied. "It's said to always lead the bearer the right way, even when the way is not known."

"Seems perfect for this place." Maybe I needed an Icelandic compass.

"Totally deep," Zane said, sitting down on my other side. He pointed at Hafthor's tattoo with his fish wrap. "Nil would approve."

"And that is a good thing?" Hafthor furrowed his blond brows.

"Tough to say." Zane shrugged, then took a hefty bite.

Paulo strode into camp, his hair and clothing wet as if he'd just left the Cove or the sea. His eyes sifted among the group eating lunch around the firepit and landed on Hafthor.

"I need some help with a bear," Paulo said.

"What kind?" Zane's expression was curious. "Panda or polar? Grizzly?"

"Dead," Paulo answered evenly.

Zane choked on his fish wrap. Molly passed over a coconut cup of water as Davey thumped Zane on the back.

Hafthor finished his lunch in two massive bites and gently set his cup down as he stood. "How far?" he asked Paulo. "And how big?"

"Above the Cove, on White Beach. And big. At least two hundred twenty kilograms, maybe more. I'm not even sure if it's full grown."

"I'd say it is now," Davey offered. "What?" Davey shrugged as Hafthor shot him a bland look. "I'm just saying the bloody thing isn't getting any bigger. Being dead and everything."

Rives stood beside Hafthor. "How can I help?"

"I'm not sure," Paulo admitted. "I don't know much about bears. But I figure we could use the pelt, right? And I figure at least some of it is edible. Seems like a terrible thing to waste." Emotion flashed across Paulo's face. "Otherwise it's just another death."

"Bears are edible, but the meat will taste different based on what the bear had been eating," Hafthor said. "Berries are good. A bear diet of fish, less so. The meat will taste of low tide, sat too long."

"Sounds delish," Zane mumbled. "Can't wait."

Hafthor turned to Paulo. "Is it a polar bear? If so, we must take care with the liver."

"*Hay-ell*, no." Calvin looked as if he might throw up on the spot. "Not happening. No way I'm eating bear liver."

"Wise choice." Hafthor nodded. "If it's a polar bear, the liver is toxic. Too much Vitamin A."

Calvin stared at Hafthor, his jaw dangling open.

"It's a brown bear," Paulo said. "And we'd better get a move on. It's getting ripe in the sun, and I don't want anything else to come calling from the stench."

Rives bent down and brushed a light kiss on my forehead, then after a brief discussion, left with Paulo, Zane, Hafthor, and Kenji. I hadn't seen Thad all morning. Same for Amara, although I doubted they were together.

I turned to Molly, Davey, and Calvin, an unofficial trio, feeling left behind although I hadn't even wanted to go, fighting the desperate need to do *something*—something not involving a bear. Lana was wrong. I didn't know everything; I barely knew anything. I had no idea *what* to do and that was the problem.

The ocean rumbled at my back, liquid whispers blending into one urgent plea: *search*.

How? I bit the inside of my cheek so hard it drew blood. At the same time, I realized Molly, Davey, and Calvin were all staring at me. Maybe the trio had seen something I hadn't.

"Listen, since the three of you have been here, have you seen anything unusual? I mean, unusual for this place?"

Three blank faces stared back at me.

"Like the labyrinths," I explained. "Like the Man in the Maze carving in the Arches."

Still blank.

"Okay, who wants to take a field trip?"

"Mind if I join you?" Thad asked as he appeared at my side. He carried a satchel over one shoulder.

"Sure. We're going to see the Man in the Maze." *And I'm going to look at my uncle's clue again.* This trip felt right. "Where've you been? On a field trip of your own?" I smiled, taking in his wet brow. He'd walked fast enough to sweat.

"Checking the crops. We've got a fraction of the taro we used to have." Thad sighed.

"Then it's a good thing we're only here for three months," I said.

Thad's eyes flicked to me. They were startlingly blue. "You're right, Skye. I need to stop thinking about indefinite survival. So whatever it is we need to do to wrap this up by then, let's do it."

"I'm trying, I promise."

He nodded, his eyes clear, his jaw set. I saw Thad in that moment, really *saw* him: the boy whom my friend loved with all her heart, the boy whom my own love trusted with his life, the boy who had once been Leader and still felt all the weight of the same. A boy who'd already done this once, escaped, and was back.

Because of me.

"I'm so sorry, Thad." My words tumbled out with force. "I didn't mean for this to happen, I swear."

"I know." His voice still lacked the vibrant warmth I'd grown accustomed to. He didn't meet my gaze, didn't even look at me as we started to walk. A heavy weight settled in my heart.

I wondered why he'd bothered to come along with us at all.

We were a quiet group walking to Black Bay. Instead of talking, I was looking. At every tree, every bit of island space, fully invested in my island investigation without a clue what I was looking for.

I'll know it when I see it, I told myself.

I hoped that was true. It didn't *feel* true; it didn't feel like anything at all.

Inside the Crystal Cavern, the air markedly cooled. My hand

reflexively went to my wrist, then my neck. Both still felt extraordinarily bare. When we'd arrived, I searched the platform for the raw diamond bracelet Rives had given to me last time we were on Nil; I'd hoped it would still be lying on the platform, where it had fallen when I'd leaped into the equinox gate. But I'd had no luck. My failure had bothered me more than it should.

I rubbed my bare wrist as I walked through the cavern. The trio followed slightly behind; they seemed content to let me lead. Awe lit their faces, but they never slowed. It gave me an appreciation for Rives, whom everyone looked to constantly for guidance and support, and made me grateful in a weird way that Thad was here, because I knew Rives relied on *him*.

Maybe that's why Thad's back, I thought. Another balance to Rives, one I couldn't give.

We exited the cavern into warm light. Black Bay glittered just past the trees. Coarse black sand glinted through the gaps like bits of obsidian.

A speck of silver glitter caught my eye.

I assumed the sparkle came from inside the cavern, sunlight bouncing off crystal. Then the shimmering speck exploded. In seconds, a glistening, iridescent gate hung fifteen feet away; it hovered a few inches off the ground and stretched well over our heads, a gorgeous mirror reflecting the five of us standing like stone.

One cue, every shining speck turned matte black.

"Run!" I yelled.

I grabbed the hand of the person closest to me, which happened to be Calvin. Pulling him deeper into the woods, soon he pulled me—*Oh my stars, Calvin runs fast,* I thought. Together with Molly, Davey, and Thad, the group of us crouched behind a knotty thicket: Calvin on my left, Thad on my right, Molly and Davey at my back. The soft ground felt spongy beneath my sandals.

"Animal," Thad murmured. Sure enough, a four-legged creature with hooves and a rack of antlers dropped out of the gate. With fur the color of apple cider and dotted with marshmallow spots, the animal twitched once, then lifted its head, nostrils flaring.

Just a deer, I thought, relaxing.

The gate collapsed and winked out. I started to stand but pressure on my shoulder stopped me. "Sit tight," Thad whispered. "Round two straight ahead."

I looked in time to see a second gate rise less than two yards away. Closer than the last—much closer, too close to run from—it quickly turned deadly black. Writhing and churning, the gate glittered like onyx in the canopied light. It was coldly beautiful, not unlike the darkness of my dreams: textured and layered and alluring, full of secrets and whispers.

I ached to touch it.

"Person," Thad said, breaking my trance. I snatched back my hand as a dark-haired boy tumbled onto the ground. Past the boy, the deer wobbled to its feet.

Something whizzed past my ear, missing the boy and deer by inches. A spear hit the ground and stuck.

"Jesus!" Calvin breathed. "Someone's trying to kill us."

"No." Amara stepped out of the woods. "If I was aiming for you, you'd be dead. I was trying for dinner." She pointed at the deer, which was bounding away. "I'm sick of fish."

"But you almost hit someone." I gawked at Amara, horrified at her willy-nilly spear throwing.

"No, I didn't." Amara's voice was cool. "You weren't even close."

"I was talking about her!" I pointed to an unfamiliar girl with a long dark braid, who stood by the edge of the woods, wearing City clothes and a look of pure hatred. Amara's spear lay at her feet.

Amara's eyes widened. "Oh my God. I didn't even see her."

Thad had moved up to the boy on the ground, who sat squinting and blinking, his chest rising and falling too rapidly to be good. Pulling a pair of shorts from his satchel, Thad squatted down beside the boy. "Hey, buddy." Thad's voice was calm and steady. "You breathing okay?"

The boy shook his head. His dark hair had frosted tips and, I suspected, a hefty dollop of gel, because sand, leaves, and even a twig looked glued to his head.

"Deep breaths, in and out," Thad said, his tone relaxed. "Just breathe. That's it. Slow and steady."

The boy stopped wheezing.

"Nice job. Okay, so, I've got a pair of shorts," Thad continued in the same calm tone. "Want to slide them on?"

The boy looked down and jerked, as if he'd just realized he was naked. His wheezing started again, worse than before.

"Yup, you're naked. The rest of us showed up naked too. But right now would be a good time to breathe. In and out," Thad said. "Breathe."

Breathing in time with Thad, the boy calmed down a noticeable measure. He slid on the shorts, his breathing still coming in alarming spurts.

"I'm Thad," Thad continued, as if this sort of thing happened every day, which, I realized, here it did. "And this is Skye, Calvin, Davey, and Molly. What's your name?"

"Chuck," the boy rasped. "Hashtag what happened?"

Thad didn't miss a beat.

"You're on an island called Nil. You came here through a gate, a portal. Same for us. But right now you just need to know you're going to be okay."

The boy stared at Thad. "Hashtag crazy. Hashtag creepy. Hashtag can't process this right now."

"Hashtag annoying," Davey grumbled.

"Out of curiosity," Thad said, "what date is it?"

"June twenty-second," the boy said.

Thad nodded. "Chuck, this is what we're gonna do. We're going to take a little tour, then we're going to go back to the City, and we'll fill you in as we go. Deal?"

Chuck nodded.

Behind me, Calvin jumped, bumping my arm as he stumbled back.

He hopped on one sandal-clad foot; clumps of dirt fell from the other as he shook out his bare foot and cursed. "That's a grave!" he yelled. "I just sank into a *grave!*"

He pointed to where he'd been crouched. The soft earth had shifted, revealing bones. His hand shook.

"Looks like the Reaper ate your thong," Davey observed.

"My *thong*?" Calvin asked, horrified.

"Your sandal." Molly looked puzzled. "Are you going to leave it?"

"Are you asking me to dig into a grave?" Calvin backed up another few feet. "Because I'm not touching a grave. No way." Still protesting, he backed into a tree and froze.

Thad walked over and clasped his shoulders.

"Look, it's creepy finding a grave, I know. Happened to me yesterday and I wigged out. But it's okay. It's not your grave, and it's not your funeral. The bones here won't hurt us, eh? It's the other stuff." Thad grimaced. "All I'm saying, try to relax. And keep your eyes wide open."

Chuck's wheezing had intensified again, drawing everyone's gaze.

"Breathe," Molly told him, smiling. "Maybe focus on the ocean?" she suggested. He nodded and turned toward the sea.

"Skye." Calvin's voice was low. "So, this grave. I'm guessing from what Thad said, it's not unusual for Nil?"

I shook my head. "Unfortunately, no."

"This place is one giant cemetery, isn't it?" Davey mused. Chuck's wheezing resumed.

"Not helping." Molly rolled her eyes.

"Just trying to figure out what's unusual," Davey said. "Other than you actually talking to me." He winked.

Molly scowled.

"What about that?" Davey pointed toward the beach. "Is that unusual? Because that's a helluva big fish."

"That's Dominic." I waved and smiled.

On the black sand ahead, Dominic held a massive fish. He waved back with his free hand. As we headed toward Dominic, I realized the girl with the braid was gone, just like the deer. Only the deer hadn't looked ready to kill us, and it hadn't taken Amara's spear.

CHAPTER 38

RIVES

"I don't think I can do this," Paulo said. He looked sick. "I can't gut this animal, I just can't."

"That makes two of us, Chief." Zane coughed, gagging. "It's like filleting Brother Bear. So wrong."

The bloody bear lay at our feet, waiting for the verdict. Bigger than I'd expected, the animal was a beast. Its claws were weapons as long as my forearm.

"I think the bear is best put to sea or buried," Hafthor said slowly. He stood over the bear, arms crossed as he studied the animal. "If you undercook the meat, you can become very sick. And to clean this bear is a project." He tilted his head at me. "I do not feel it is for us. Bears are revered in some cultures. I think we should be cautious. We should not butcher this bear."

"Why can't we just leave it here?" Paulo asked.

"We might have to," I said. "It weighs three hundred kilos, easily. I don't see how the five of us are going to lift that bear." I looked at Paulo, impressed. "And you brought it down alone."

Paulo shrugged. "It was distracted by Lana. I got lucky, I guess."

He looked more nauseated than lucky.

Hafthor started digging, hefting sand out with his bare hands. "We'll dig a grave next to the bear, and roll the body in. It feels right."

"Hafthor, let's find something to work as a shovel, okay?" Tools meant speed, and the faster we buried this bear, the sooner I got back to Skye. At least Thad was with her, a secret wingman.

I scoured the ground. Two flat rocks the size of my hand, a chunk of bark that used to wrap a tree, a half of a massive coconut shell later and we were in business. I passed out my tools and we got to work.

We'd no sooner started when a boy materialized from the trees; he held the other half of my coconut shell in his hand. I did a double-take, thinking it was Ahmad. But this kid was shorter, and Ahmad was long gone. He dropped to his knees beside me and began digging. "My name is James." He nodded at me, choosing his words carefully. "I heard you in the woods yesterday. I cannot say I will join your City, but I would like to hear your story."

My story, I thought.

"You got it," I said. "This is my second trip here, but I'll start with my first."

As we dug deep, the words rolled out. Me on Freedom Beach, me waking up on Nil. Meeting Li first, who gave me the intro; meeting Natalie second, who shared my birthday and sense of humor. Meeting Thad, the badass Leader and later, my closest friend. I spoke of Nil Nights and Nil nightmares, of year deadlines and friends slaughtered before their time. Me, meeting Talla. Me, burying her. Me, desperate to figure this place out. Burials, sunsets. Sunrises, departures. Fresh faces and fresh days. Thad left, I stayed.

The hole beneath us grew.

I talked of Maaka and secrets and island barriers that meant nothing, and then I spoke of Skye, who meant everything. Then I stopped talking, just thinking. Of how everything shifted with her, how *she* was the shift. In me, in Nil. I remembered memories passing between us, only for us. So much belonged only to me and Skye, and it would stay between us. Instead I skimmed the surface of Skye's time here last quarter: how her uncle's past changed that particular Nil present, and how we did our damnedest to end it all but Nil wouldn't let us. How Nil brought Skye back. Me, I was just along for the ride.

And I told them all of a ready-made gate in the wings, opening in three months to take us home.

I sat back on my heels. Below me stretched an empty hole, filled with my words. Covered in sweat, I felt lighter. Like that release had been a long time coming.

Hafthor spoke quietly. "I think we can roll the bear in now."

Together we heaved the bear's body into the pit. Working in reverse, we covered the bear with sand. The task went quickly with twelve hands at work and less space to fill.

When we were done, I turned to James. "Thanks for the help."

He nodded once, his eyes dark, and thoughtful.

"I don't know where you've been crashing, but you're welcome to come back to the City with us. No worries either way." I smiled.

He nodded. "I thank you for your welcome, and your honesty. And your story. There is something I must do, but I will see you soon."

He slipped away as soundlessly as he'd come.

"Well, that was whacked," Zane said.

"Really? Which part?" Paulo asked dryly.

"James's drop-in. A little afternoon grave digging. Chief's tale. Totally intense all around. But you know what's really whacked?"

Paulo raised his eyebrows.

"What wasn't said. The story's not done, dude." Zane waved his hand around. "We're here, and we don't want a repeat. So maybe Hafthor's onto something with his houses for the little people—"

"Hidden people," Hafthor corrected.

"—and respect for dead bears and his compass tattoo mojo, because you know what? I think there's so much here that we don't see. That we don't *know*. I'm not saying we go all Viking on Nil, I'm saying that we need to pull back. Seriously listen to what Nil's trying to tell us.

Maybe having our eyes open isn't enough, Chief. Maybe we need to listen, too. I used to dream of Sy but now I dream of Lana, like a little island voodoo's working in my head. And I swear to God, Chief, sometimes I think I hear the island talking to me, using Lana's voice. Maybe the island's telling us all different things, like giving us all one piece of the puzzle. Or maybe the island wants different things from all of us, I don't know." He paused to breathe. I'd never heard Zane sound so serious, or say so much.

"I'm just saying I think we need to look at it from a different angle. Like, don't look at Nil as a creepy island full of freaktastic creatures, look at it as a person. A living thing, with wants and needs. Hell, maybe if we look hard enough we'll find a little green guy at tiny controls running the show, like we're stuck in the universe on Orion's Belt, right?" Zane took in our faces and his eyes went wide. "Didn't any of you see *Men in Black*? No? Whatever." He waved his hand again, wildly this time. "I'm just saying, something's at work here, something bigger than us. Maybe not literally, maybe it really is a green guy the size of Hafthor's pinky. But more powerful. Look inside, right? Look *deep*. And maybe while we're looking, we need to be listening too. I don't know. I'm just saying we need to think outside the box." Zane exhaled, his mania ebbing. "All I'm saying is maybe we need to let Nil in a little to figure all this out. I'll stop now."

"I hear you, Zane," I said calmly. "And you've got a point. We need to be open to everything. But . . ." I thought of Skye crouched in the cavern, trapped in her own head by Nil. "I think we need to be careful about letting Nil into our heads. Don't let it get in too deep. Because I think that's how the island wins."

Maaka's words roared back.

The island's fire has touched you. It burns inside you. Do not let it consume you.

An epiphany struck, as clear as the Nil sky. *If we let Nil in, it consumes us because we're what it wants. Puppets for the puppet master.*

"And for the record?" I spoke quietly. "We know what it wants. It wants us."

I looked toward the mountain, the same peak framed by the Arches, hiding the platform still fresh in my head.

We want something too, I thought. *And it's completely at odds with you.*

Equal scales, the ultimate Nil balance.

Our deaths, Nil's life. Our lives, Nil's death.

What would be the deciding factor, the one that would tip the scales?

Or who? the breeze crooned.

My gut said I already knew the answer, I just didn't like it.

I never had.

Back in the City, Thad stood in front of the Wall, tracing names with his fingers.

"Where is everyone?" I asked. The City center was deserted, no one in sight. A huge fish lay roasting in the coals, scales on.

"If by everyone you mean Skye, she's on the beach, which is where everyone else is too." Thad's expression turned grave. "Got a rookie today. Chuck. Kid's fourteen, maybe fifteen, youngest one around these days. I think the kid's got asthma. Or panic attacks. Either way, I thought he might not make it past his opening minutes. But he did." His gaze flicked back to the Wall. "And the guy you met this morning. Dominic? He dropped off a fish. But he didn't stay."

"Why?"

"Said he'd catch you later. Had something to do."

Thad lapsed into silence, staring at the Wall. Staring at his name. Four letters and a check. A check that meant nothing at this moment. We were back, our clocks reset, only this time, the year deadline didn't have the same brutal feel. Now we had a ready-made gate on standby, three months out and counting.

Thad's gaze had drifted to the open stretch of Wall. A blank slate, raw and ready.

"You gonna put your name back up there?" I crossed my arms.

Thad shook his head. "You?"

"Nope." *Not a chance.* I had no plans to give Nil any more of me, not even my name.

"Been there, done that, eh?" Thad nodded. "Same."

I left him at the Wall, wishing I could shed the weight of the City as easily. New faces to know, new bodies to protect. New minds to shield. I felt stuck in a cruel cycle not of my own making, a human hamster stuck on a treadmill, going nowhere but in circles. For Nil's amusement, Nil's thrills.

"Rives." Skye's voice startled me. The rock in her sling dug into my hip as she kissed me, but I didn't care. I reveled in the fact that she was safe, so close I could wrap both arms around her. Protecting her here was impossible, but I didn't have a fighting chance when I couldn't see her.

She stepped away, her shoulders back and braced, her eyes flecked with iron.

"Rives, we need a plan. Right now the urge to get going, to *do* something, is so strong I can barely stand it. I want to go everywhere, only this time I don't know what I'm looking for—a clue, a place, or even a person." She shook her head. "It's making me crazy." She smiled. "Not really. I mean, it's *driving* me crazy, the inaction. The waiting. But last night Molly gave me an idea. She said this place is all about the searching. And she's right. So it made me think. Why not use the Search system we have, only instead of Searching for gates, we Search for clues? We start at the City and fan out from here, working each quadrant in a grid in teams like before, and hunt for anything that might be useful to stopping this place." Her face tilted toward mine with fiery hope. "What do you think?"

I think it sucks. I think it's a wild goose chase. I think it has a million ways it can go wrong and only one way it can go right.

The girl I'd bet could beat those odds stood before me. "I think it beats sitting around here, eating fish wraps and living the same nightmare, day in and day out. Maybe we'll win the Nil crapshoot after all."

She nodded. "Exactly. It starts tomorrow."

CHAPTER 39

NIL
TWILIGHT

James traced his steps back to the cave. As he expected, Carmen was waiting.

"So what did you find out?" Her dark almond-shaped eyes traveled his face, studying as always.

"That everyone else here knows much more than we do." James's tone stayed level. "There is a Leader in the City to the north. I've talked to him. We have one year to leave, or we die."

At this Carmen's brows shot up. "Really." Her lip curled. "They'll kill us?"

"Not they, the island. The island takes you at a year if you haven't left. Steals your blood and soul." He shrugged. "But in three months' time, a gate will open, and we can leave."

"Where?" Her word was as sharp as the fire-sharpened spear in her hand. "Where will this gate open?"

"On the mountain. That is all I know. But I want to know more." He watched Carmen, taking the measure of this tough girl he didn't trust but understood. "I came to tell you what I know, and tell you I am going back to that City. I might decide to stay there." James held Carmen's gaze. "But I will not steal from them, not anymore." He placed his fist over his heart. "That is the truth." Dropping his hand, he spoke from the heart, with a passion he didn't know he felt. "Carmen, we are not alone here, and I don't think it's wise to pretend we are. A City exists here for a reason, and there is an energy there. An urgency. I came back to honor my word, and tell you I am leaving."

Carmen didn't react. Coolly, she asked, "Did Lana stay in the City?"

He'd nearly forgotten about Lana. She wasn't important, not like the others.

"She spent last night." James wasn't sure why he declined to tell Carmen that Lana had gone north. All he knew was that he had no interest in getting in the middle of the two. "But the people in the City know more than she does, I am certain of that."

Carmen strode to the cave's exit. "Then by all means, let's go."

Carmen left the darkness of the cave, feeling a shift in power she didn't like at all. *A Leader in the City,* she thought, her curiosity piqued even as her blood boiled. One strong enough to make James choose the Leader over her. Not that she needed anyone; she didn't. But she didn't like feeling bested—or worse, insignificant.

And James had made her feel as though she mattered less than a pebble on the ground.

If anyone was worthless, it was Ace. He rarely had an original thought. Perhaps she could rid herself of Ace in the City as well. That thought made her smile. At least now she knew she would rid herself of all of them in three months. James's information had been unexpected, both in subject and source.

This Leader was someone she needed to meet.

Part of her was curious, to know all that he knew. Knowledge had given him an advantage, which was unacceptable. And part of her wanted to meet the man who felt comfortable in a city of ghosts, a city that reeked of death and loss and *blood.* But she would answer to no one, not here.

As twilight fell, she took the lead.

I freaking hate this place, Ace thought.

He leapfrogged across the craggy rocks, struggling to keep up with James and Carmen as they scaled the cliff. Why the hell they were heading out on this trip to the City at night was beyond him, but Carmen had been determined to go, *right now*. And it wasn't worth arguing with her about the timing.

He'd almost stayed behind, but being alone in the dark cave creeped him out more than a night walk.

He sighed.

Three months, he told himself. He was ready to jump ship *now*, not wait twelve more weeks. But it didn't look like he had a choice.

The breeze whispered, dry and thin, as if an invisible demon were slowly rubbing his hands together near Ace's ear. He shivered despite the warm air. Ace constantly heard whispers; they came over the water, in the grasses, through the cave. Sometimes he heard someone laughing, like someone was laughing at *him*. He'd look at Carmen, only to find her eyes elsewhere, not interested in him at all.

This place was making him crazy.

So was Carmen.

She stalked ahead with the same irritating hip-swaying swagger, like she owned the island and him too. Sure, she'd found the cave, but he'd found the edible greens and berries, thanks to all those years spent in his dad's kitchen. Being a fourth-generation Pericelli had kept him alive here, teaching him both what to eat and how to play. It was always about the game, he reasoned, and Carmen wasn't as cool a player as she thought she was.

Maybe he would stay in the City too, he thought, especially if that new chick Lana was there. Despite himself, he smiled.

He was valuable, he knew it.

He smiled again.

Carmen and James now walked a good forty yards ahead, with Carmen slightly in front. They'd already made it to the top of the rocky cliff, cutting the south corner as they made a direct line toward the City. The water tunnels sprawled ahead, slightly to the right. Clumps of scrub brush dotted the edge near the beach, growing more numerous to the north. Patches of tree loomed ahead too. In the fading light, a shape moved.

Ace stopped.

Is that a moose? he wondered. *Or a bull?* Bulls were dangerous, mean enough that some city in Spain made a profit off people trying to prove they had balls big enough to run with bulls. Moose, he wasn't sure about.

He squinted.

It was definitely a bull. And Carmen and James were looking the wrong way.

A favor, he thought smugly. *In the form of a warning. Then Carmen will owe me.*

Cupping his hands around his mouth, he shouted, "Carmen! James! Bull at two o'clock!" He waved his arms like he was directing a plane.

Carmen and James turned. James started yelling immediately, gesturing emphatically to Ace. "Run for the scrub brush!" He pointed to a large thicket of scrub brush to Ace's left. "Watch your right!"

Ace looked to his right and nearly wet his shorts. A rhino with a wickedly large horn bore down on him at breakneck speed. Now Ace ran. He dashed over the rocks, terrified, making for the thicket.

"Hide inside!" James shouted.

Ace dove into the brush. Brambles tore his skin as he plunged deeper into the thicket. His leg brushed something warm and soft. An instant later, something white and black clamped down on his leg. Fiery pain shot through Ace's thigh as the animal bit him again. With a scream, he backpedaled, punching at the animal in front of him, which somehow registered as a panda—one as startled as he was. Blood ran down Ace's leg as he fought his way back out of the thicket, his arms wild.

He turned and ran smack into the rhino.

The beast drove forward, tossing him through the air like a rag doll, its horn goring Ace's side with a pain that made the bite on his leg feel like a scratch. He landed on his back, felt something snap, and then Ace felt nothing at all.

James watched in horror as Ace twitched on the rocks. Why would he run out of the brush? If he'd stayed there, the rhino would've moved on and left him alone. The wind had shifted, blowing the human scent out to sea, and considering how poor a rhino's vision was, Ace was relatively safe. A tree would have been better, but the thicket would have been a strong alternative.

The rhino wandered away. It headed to the water and began to drink.

James turned to Carmen. "If the rhino charges at you—climb a tree. You will be safe." He doubted the rhino would charge again. Ace had startled the animal with his shouting and waving, and rhinos were vegetarian. Still, being cautious was always a wise choice, especially here. The bull was nowhere to be seen.

"Where are you going?" Carmen asked.

"To help Ace."

"You can't help him." The undertone said Leave him.

"Perhaps not." James didn't balk. "But I must see."

As he neared Ace, a giant panda peered at him from the thicket, skittish and startled, its mouth bloody. And he had driven Ace right into him.

He nearly retched right then.

Ace looked worse than James had imagined. His face and arms were lined with a crosshatch of fine scratches, same for his chest. Bite marks riddled one thigh, exposing bone; the other leg dangled at an odd angle, a gaping hole from his side weeping blood in a dark stream. The dry black rock sucked it up without a sound.

"Ace," James said gently.

Ace's eyes fluttered open. His mouth worked but no sound came out. James waited, not sure what to say. He barely knew Ace, didn't know if he believed in God or gods or nothing at all. He'd seen men killed by game animals before, but never a boy. God usually smiled on youth, or so he'd been told. So he'd always believed.

"—you." Ace's whisper was a rasp. Then the life left his eyes.

Beneath James's feet, the ground trembled.

James realized Ace had said *Thank you.*

The island drank in the rush of electria, the surge of power. This was the power it craved, electria in its purest form, not the bitter, diluted wisp leached from the furred beast earlier today. That had only served to taunt the island, tempting it, leading the island to now.

Now the island inhaled. The male, Ace, had served his purpose; if the fighter no longer needed him, expendable he would be. They all were expendable, and would be, each in their own time.

Time.

It gave and it took, and today it surprised, for the island did not foresee this male's death or the surge it would provide. But his abrupt swell of fear and pride mixed with the animals' own, a potent blend of panic ripe for manipulation. And ultimately, death.

The island reveled in its newfound strength.

It would not wait so long to take another.

If the opportunity came, the island would take it. Take and take and take, until there was nothing left but the island.

CHAPTER
40

SKYE
93 DAYS UNTIL THE AUTUMNAL EQUINOX, NIGHT

Finally, we had a plan. We'd leave at dawn. Rives, Paulo, Zane, and I would go on a Search for clues; Thad would stay behind, with the rest. Paulo seemed as eager to go as I was. Our destinies were still linked; I felt it.

Inside the Shack, I fingered the rope, debating whether to add it to my satchel.

"Rives." An unfamiliar silhouette appeared in the doorway.

"James!" Rives stuck out his hand, smiling. "Good to see you, bro."

"Thank you." James nodded, his expression intense. "I accept your hospitality, if your offer still stands."

"Of course," Rives said. "This City is yours, too."

James's eyes flicked around the Shack, landing on our satchels. "Taking a trip?" he inquired.

"More like a scavenger hunt," Rives said. He turned to me and said, "Skye, meet James. He helped with the bear burial today, which sounds as weird as it was. James, meet Skye."

"Hello, Skye." He lifted a hand in greeting, then glanced behind him. Rives stepped forward. "See something, James?"

"Nothing." James's voice was troubled. "We are alone."

Wrong, I thought, watching Rives stride outside to inspect the perimeter. *Not here.*

Darkness circled my mind; it was ever present, like the cloud of fatigue. Nil may have stopped haunting my dreams, but it hadn't stopped haunting *me*. Nil wanted to rest, forever, and it needed our help.

I'm trying, I thought, abruptly frustrated. *Give me something, won't you?*

The darkness in my head surged like a tsunami. I recoiled. My mental walls held, but my certainty shattered.

In that terrifying moment, I sensed Nil wanted something else entirely: something darker, something greater, something it coveted more than me or my help. Nil hungered for life on a scale beyond my comprehension.

Rives was talking to James outside the Shack. The rope shook in my hand.

Because I suddenly feared Nil was exactly as Thad always warned: a games master, a cruel croupier, and I was too blind—or naïve—to see it; I feared Nil was using me for its own horrible ends. And if I'd led my friends and my love back here only to watch them die, I'd never forgive myself.

Never.

•

CHAPTER
41

RIVES
83 DAYS UNTIL THE AUTUMNAL EQUINOX, MORNING

"We have to go back," I told Skye.

No edge, no bite. Just a matter-of-fact statement, like saying, *Hey, the breeze is gusting offshore and by the way, there's a koala by the cliff.*

She already knew. About the breeze, about the koala, about this trip turning out to be a total bust. It had been a complete waste of ten days.

A complete waste of *time*.

We'd crawled all over Quadrant Two, scanning and backtracking, using Charley's maps as our guide. We'd searched every damn millimeter, and had come up empty. There were the Arches, the cliffs of South Beach, the sands of Black Bay, the tubes, and the lava fields stretching out wide. We basically retraced our steps from our latest Day 1, and the only thing we'd found worth mentioning was a stand of mango trees that quenched our dry mouths and filled our empty guts.

Skye had grown more frustrated with each day that passed.

I don't know what we're looking for, she'd exclaimed, at least twice a day.

No one else did either. Except me. I knew what *I* was looking for. Animals. Predators. Anything that might look at us as a meal. So far we'd been lucky.

Too lucky.

We'd been beneficiaries of a deceptively docile status quo, one that could shift at any moment. *Would* shift, when Nil decided to play. Anticipating the worst, I'd spent the last ten days watching Skye's back and everyone else's, and the nights watching her sleep. Here, she slept without waking, without fear. Me, I slept like crap—when I slept at all. I dozed fitfully, Skye in my arms, my body on high alert. Not exactly rest. Then again, Nil was never meant to be a vacation.

As least not for us.

But maybe for the people lucky enough to crash here on their Day 1, like Paulo.

Skye hadn't answered me. She stood perfectly still, her eyes sweeping the inside of the cave. It was the same look she'd give a hotel room or hostel when we were traveling, making sure we'd left nothing behind. We'd spent last night here, in this cave near where we'd ditched the wolves a few weeks ago. Apparently all the islanders stayed in Cave Med on their Day 1. The rest of us only got the invite on round two.

"We're missing something," Skye said.

"Something here?" I frowned.

"No. I don't think so." She sighed. "This feels like a pit stop, just a place to sleep or hide. But something." She bit the inside of her cheek, her expression pensive. "This place is inside, but it's not where I'm supposed to look."

"There's a cave on the north shore," Paulo spoke up. "I've stayed there before. Maybe it has a clue?"

Skye nodded without enthusiasm. "Maybe. But if you've stayed there, then you already know it's nothing new." She sighed again. "We should get back to the City. If we leave now, we should be back by noon."

"You've got my vote to roll," Zane said. "Maybe noon will bring good news, like a mysterious benefactor has just shown up with a full spread of In-N-Out burgers, or better yet, Lana's chilling out in the City without a chip on her shoulder." He grinned as Paulo laughed. "Hey, a dude can hope. Noon is the best time on the island, right?"

"You know it." I returned Zane's grin. "But I think you've got a better shot at a burger benefactor than you do with Lana."

Zane grabbed his heart in mock hurt, then broke into a comical jog.

Skye didn't say a word as we left the cave. We walked in silence, climbed in silence. And when I tried to read her thoughts, I couldn't. Iron walls locked her mind out of reach. I couldn't care less, as long as her mental walls kept out Nil too.

Skye gasped.

"Hey." I stopped, and she did too. "What's going through your head, chérie?"

"You know how we came at noon?" Skye gripped my hand. "I just realized we'll leave at midnight. Or at least it means the next equinox gate will open at midnight. So while we came in the light, we'll leave in the dark." She let that gem of an announcement sink in.

"And Rives . . ." Her voice bled worry. "Darkness makes us vulnerable. It heightens our fears, and makes everything harder because our own eyes betray us in the dark. The night we leave, the darkness in here"—she tapped her head—"will have the edge." She bit the inside of her cheek. "I used to be so certain that the island wanted to die. But now—now I'm not so sure."

"Don't you still feel that fatigue?" I asked. "The island's exhaustion?"

"Yes, but I also feel the island's *want*. Sometimes I feel it wants to die, sometimes I'm not sure. Sometimes I feel that it wants to live, desperately. It's like the island is conflicted."

"I don't think Nil gets a choice." My voice was hard. "We're here. If we can end it, we will."

"That doesn't mean Nil won't fight," she said quietly. She lifted her eyes to mine, dread in their depths. "This whole destroy-the-island plan was a whole lot easier when I thought Nil was with us. If Nil's against us, this whole trip just got a lot tougher."

"Whoa there, space cowboy." Zane popped his head in between us. "I don't think Nil was ever with us, or not with us. It's just how you look at it, Skye. From what I can tell we've pretty much been on our own since Day One, and in the end, I think it'll play out the same way."

"How so?" I asked.

"We live as a group, we leave as a group. We almost did it once, and now we know to brace for Nil trying to mess with our heads. Or *in* our heads." He shrugged. "The island can't really touch us until a year, right? So we just watch out for dogs and cats and everything else that likes meat until we can work our group disappearing act in September."

Skye's face had gone white.

"Zane, that's it," she whispered. "That's what Nil wants."

"To get us home in time for Halloween?" He grinned.

"No. For us to die as a group." She looked at me, appalled. "Can you imagine how much power Nil would gain from all of us dying at once?"

My blood ran cold.

"Won't happen," I said quickly. "Zane's right. The island can't touch us until a year, and then it's still based on when each person arrived. The three hundred sixty-five days is person-specific. Only five of us came through that summer gate."

"Unless the island goes after us another way," Paulo said.

"How?" Zane frowned. "Wolves? Lions? Alien attack?"

"No." Paulo's voice was grave. "The Dead City. It has happened before."

"Dead City?" I echoed, just as Zane asked, "What happened? I mean, obviously something bad." Zane waved his hand. "The word *dead* was a dead giveaway."

"I don't know. I just know rumors. Remember, I wasn't supposed to come; it was my brother." Paulo raised his hands defensively. "He had the training, the history. All I know are bits and pieces."

"Well, give us whatever you've got," I said.

Paulo nodded. "This City—the one you call Nil City—we know it as the Silent City, because there were always empty houses and you would often be alone, in silence. The idea was that you would come and build a house to leave a legacy behind for those to come. A work project, also symbolic. The decision was made to stop building at ten. There were only one or two islanders here at any given time, and the empty houses represented both the past and the future. The general plan was to stay in the Listening Cave first, where we spent last night, with the rest of the time being spent in the Silent City or the Looking Glass Cavern. All places of reflection. But . . ." Paulo paused. "There are rumors of another city. One that was abandoned." He looked at me. "The Dead City."

"Where was it?" Skye asked.

"I don't know. Just like I don't know when it was abandoned, or why. But maybe Lana does."

"We need to know." Skye's tone was determined. "Or we might make the same mistakes, or meet the same fate. And I refuse to lose anyone else I care about." She kissed me fiercely, full Skye heat flooding her veins and mine. Then she dropped her hands into fists and spun around to Zane so fast that he stepped back. "I hope your long shot is hanging out by the fire. Because we need answers, and we need them now."

CHAPTER
42

NIL
LATE MORNING

The one called Zane stared at the one called Skye. He did not see the pieces she was putting together, just as she did not see the picture they formed. But she would, the island reasoned.

Because she was the one.

"Whoa," Zane said. "No offense, Skye, but when you go all Pamela Landy on us, it's way intense." She wore the same expression he'd seen the morning she'd killed the leopard with nothing but a rock sling, and damn if she wasn't a little scary.

Rives half smiled.

Skye narrowed her eyes as Zane raised his hands. "I'm not saying it's not effective. If that's what you're after," he added hastily, then mumbled, "Scary Pam."

Now Rives laughed.

"Who is Pamela Landy?" Paulo asked.

"*Bourne Supremacy?*" Zane's head whipped toward Paulo, who still wore the same interested, slightly blank expression. "*Bourne Ultimatum?* Nothing? What is wrong with you people? Total classics."

He shook his head, then he braced, struck by a stillness. No, a *thickness*, in the air, a potent anticipation and it wasn't his.

A fifth wheel, Zane thought.

He looked at Rives. "Chief," he said, "maybe it's because there's no bugs or frogs, and there's barely any birds, but it's always so quiet here." Zane's eyes darted from one end of the beach to the other before landing on the mountain and sticking. "It's like the island is listening. Or waiting. And not just for noon."

"I think it is," Skye said. "Both listening and waiting."

"Like us," Paulo said thoughtfully.

"Wrong," Rives growled. "This place is *nothing* like us."

He glared at the mountain.

For a long moment, no one spoke.

"Gate!" Skye cried. She thrust one finger toward the island's interior.

In the distance, a gate shimmered as it rose, framed by the blue Nil sky. It locked into place, then shot north, flying fast.

They watched the iridescent wall speed over Nil ground, until it vanished from sight.

"A single," Rives observed. "One and done."

"What a tease." Zane sighed. "We never had a chance."

"But would you have run?" Paulo asked quietly.

His question hung in the air, like noon.

The island had already turned away, toward the barrier between worlds. The seam had widened. Power coursed through the crease, flowing from there to here and back again. The seam could no longer be sealed, but it could be contained. It must be contained. But first, the island would look.

As always, it was drawn to her.

The other *her, the other one to leave early, yet with the same fire burning in her heart.*

This is it, Charley thought. *Rika's house.*

It had taken weeks of asking, cajoling, and downright begging, not to mention bribing; Dr. Bracken had lightened his wallet more than once in return for information regarding a woman named Rika. But still, nothing.

Until today.

At ten o'clock this morning, a boy who looked about eleven years old had shown up at their house. He'd knocked politely, and when Charley answered, he'd said, "I've come to take you to Rika." As if it was just that simple, as if Charley had an appointment scheduled and the appointed day had arrived, and that all their days and hours and minutes of asking were wasted because the appointed hour had yet to come.

Crazy, Charley had thought.

But she hadn't thought twice about going with him. She'd scrawled a quick note for Dr. Bracken and off she'd gone, following the young boy at a leisurely speed, each on their own bike. As soon as they'd arrived at this house, the boy had waved and biked on, never looking back until he'd turned from sight.

Now Charley stood alone, in front of a house she desperately hoped was Rika's.

Modest and quiet, an island cottage with a yard dotted with weeds and wildflowers stared back at her, as did the three white cats on the porch. The wooden house was painted salmon pink, the shutters a pale blue. Not threatening, just curious. Anyone could live here, anyone at all.

Leaving her bike, Charley walked up to the front door.

It opened before she could knock. A woman with big brown eyes highlighted in bright-gold eye shadow smiled wide, showing startlingly white teeth. Her long brown hair swirled down around her shoulders, broken up by one braid, no gray. Large beaded hoops swayed from her ears as she moved; so did her gauzy black dress. The two-dozen bracelets on her arms—bracelets of gold, bone, shell, leather, and more—rustled as she waved Charley in.

"Come in, child. I've been waiting for you."

"You have?" Charley asked. She stepped inside the house and looked around. Light streamed in through the open windows. A living room, bright and cheery, sat to the left. To the right, a small kitchen was tucked in the corner, clean and neat. "I didn't know I was coming to see you until a few minutes ago."

"I've been waiting for years. Of course, I thought it would be another, descended from another. But then"—she flicked her hand in the air—"it changed. And now it's you."

Charley didn't move. "What changed?"

Rika shrugged as if to say *Everything*. "The future. The present. You." She smiled, her dark eyes radiating power. "Let's do this properly, Charley. I'm Rika, and it's a pleasure to have you."

Charley nodded, fully aware that this moment wasn't hers. She hadn't offered her name, yet Rika knew it, a simple but effective way of saying *I know you. I know* more *than you.*

Point made, Charley thought as she stepped inside. There were a dozen ways Rika would know her name, Charley told herself. After all, Charley had been asking about Rika for weeks. Charley smiled. She would play the game too.

"Nice to meet you, Rika," she said. "Thank you for meeting with me." Rika's words swirled in her head like a sandstorm, chafing and raw. *I've been waiting for years. I thought it would be another.* "You expected Skye?" Charley cocked her head.

"No. Not now. Now I was expecting you."

But before, yes, Charley thought.

"Come." Rika waved Charley to the room to the left. "I have pineapple muffins."

A cheery yellow couch filled the space, along with three bright-orange chairs. Green plants and pots of pink flowers were tucked in odd spaces. It was a rainbow of color in one small room.

"Sit." Rika gestured. A tray of golden muffins and two small green bottles of Sprite sat on a square table in front of the couch.

An uncomfortable feeling bloomed in Charley's chest.

"How did you know I like Sprite?" she asked, hating the rise she heard in her voice.

Rika smiled. "I know many things, child. It's why you are here, no?"

Charley nodded. And she silently prayed she wouldn't be staying long. Rika made her less comfortable by the minute.

"Please." Rika waved toward the couch. "Relax."

As if I could, Charley thought. Still, she was a guest—*an invited, summoned guest*, she thought, and rudeness would not win her any favors or information.

Charley sat.

But she refused to waste another minute on idle chatter. Reaching into her bag, she found Skye's uncle's journal and grasped it tight. "You met Scott, who was my friend Skye's uncle. You met him on the island. When he came back, he wrote this." Charley waved the journal. "Skye read it, and then last December, she went through the winter gate on the solstice. And she returned in March. But—" Charley paused. Rika was staring at her with an unnerving curiosity, as if she already knew what Charley would say before the words ever left her mouth. Charley shook that feeling off and kept going. "A few weeks ago, the island lured her back. She took the summer gate and now she's stuck on the island."

Rika's smile developed slowly. "You don't believe that, do you?" she asked softly. "That she's stuck."

"Well, I know she's trapped until either a gate pops up at noon to take her back, or the equinox gate opens in September. So essentially, she's stuck."

"But not forever." Rika's voice was cool water running over hot stones.

"I hope not," Charley said.

A long pause passed between them. The ceiling fan whirred in the background, chopping the silence into slivers too sharp to touch. Charley waited, lips closed. Nil had taught her patience and an appreciation of time, and *timing*. The next words belonged to Rika.

A slight smile crossed Rika's face.

"So," she drawled, "tell me why you wanted to see me. Tell me why I am so important to you."

"Because you told Skye's uncle about his destiny, and how it wrapped the island from beginning to end. What does that mean? What did you see?"

"You want this information why? So you can help your friend?" Rika's dark eyes glittered with curiosity. "Or because you want to save your lover?"

"Both," Charley said without hesitation. "Helping one helps them all. I want to help them all get home safely and end this awful cycle once and for all." She leaned forward. "You saw something, about the island's end. You know what's going to happen, right? How can we help them?"

"Give me your hand," Rika instructed.

"What?" Charley asked, taken aback.

"Your hand. Please." With a flick of her hand, Rika gestured for Charley's.

Slowly Charley offered her right hand. Rika grabbed it, clutching it tightly as she inhaled. Without warning, Rika dropped Charley's hand as if she'd been burned.

"The answers you seek are already inside you," Rika said. "They lie here"—she tapped the journal—"and here"—now she brushed Charley's forehead. "And most certainly in here." She gently pressed her palm over Charley's heart, then withdrew it. "Now you know where to look, and where to tell your friends to search. Answers are not always pretty, or in pretty places. But they are always true." She closed her eyes again. "Let the past guide the future, Charley. Study it. Learn from it. And so it will be."

When Rika lifted her eyes to Charley, sadness engulfed the brown depths, rich and rolling and heartbreaking. "I weep for you, my child. And for all of them. If they ignore the past, they will repeat it, that I see. You, my child, you must look for what you don't see. And so must they."

Look for what you don't see.

It made no sense at all.

"That's my answer?" Charley asked, suddenly furious. She felt as though Rika was toying with her. If he were here, Thad would joke that Rika was in cahoots with Nil. But Thad wasn't here; he was on Nil, and this conversation wasn't funny at all. She was poised to leave with no more knowledge than when she came. "Look for what I don't see?"

Rika nodded. "It is one answer of many; there is always more than one answer to the same question, but only one is the truth. Only one will reveal the knowledge you seek."

Answers. Knowledge. Information.

They are not the same, Charley thought. And she'd been given nothing at all.

"Muffin? Sprite?" Rika offered politely.

"No, thank you." Charley's tone was strained. "I don't want a muffin or a Sprite. I don't want water or coffee or tea. I want you to tell me exactly how I can help my friends. Maybe you know this, too, but I can hear Thad. Not all the time, but sometimes. So I think he can hear me, too."

Rika's expression didn't change.

Charley continued speaking. "So if there's something that can help them, please tell me. I'm begging you."

"Begging doesn't become you." Rika's tongue sharpened, like her expression. "I never said it would be easy, or without work. You already have the answers you seek. Are you so lazy that you want me to spell it out for you, child? It doesn't work that way. The end is written, but the middle—that is up to you. And them."

Charley worked to ask another question but her mind spun in circles—jumping to the end, the middle, the coming equinox gate, and more; she constantly stifled her overwhelming fear of losing Thad, believing fiercely that they would win instead. She would accept nothing else.

"That's it, child." Rika nodded approvingly, her bone bracelets cracking together as she clasped her hands in her lap. "Fight. Don't give in to the fear or fear will win. It gives power to the dark places."

Rika's eyes dimmed and a single glistening tear ran down her cheek. "So much blood to come," she whispered. "The island will bleed, and people you love will be lost. That is the end you seek, child. Prepare yourself."

Jumping to her feet, Charley stumbled away from the couch. She had to get away *now*. She couldn't sit here another minute with this freaky woman who sent chills to her soul. "Thank you," she said, backing away. "For talking to me. I have to go."

"Of course you do," Rika rasped, her finger stroking her bracelets. "Remember what I said. Fight the fear. And prepare for the end you crave so badly."

Charley burst out into the open air, breathing like she'd just run a thirteen-mile race. Her heart pounded against her ribs; her chest was tight.

Behind her Rika called, "Child, don't forget a muffin!"

Pretending she didn't hear, Charley mounted her bike and took off the way she had come. Wind bit her hair as she pedaled; sweat ran down her back. She didn't stop. Not her legs pumping, or her mind racing.

You already have the answers you seek, Rika had said as she'd tapped the journal.

How is this possible? Charley thought. She knew the journal by heart; she'd read it so many times she could quote by rote, without error, any passage from any page. What could she possibly have missed?

Look for what you don't see.

Rika spoke in vague phrases that meant nothing to Charley. It was as if Rika talked in riddles.

Riddles, Charley thought, her mind following a trailing thread. A page of the journal flashed in her memory. Entry number thirteen. One line leaped out as if written in flames.

Mazes and men, caves and creatures, ruins and riddles, all wrapped up in an island bottle.

That's it, she thought, braking to a stop. Certainty halted her panic like the douse of a fire. *Thad needs to find the ruins and the riddle.* Maybe the ruins *were* the riddle, she mused. Or maybe they were just part of it.

Thad might know, if he could just hear her.

Thad. She thought his name fiercely, with as much intensity and love and clarity as she could muster. *Find the ruins, solve the riddle. Look for what you don't see.*

She repeated this thought until her head ached from the effort. Then she stopped altogether, and tried to listen. Nothing. No reply from Thad, nothing at all. But she didn't let that stop her from believing he had heard her.

Thad, I love you. I believe in you. Look for what you don't see.

She started biking again, slowly this time. Rika would tell her no more, of that Charley felt certain. But perhaps Maaka might be willing to talk about island riddles. It was worth a try. She had absolutely nothing to lose, not here anyway. But she had *everything* to lose there, and she wouldn't stop fighting to get her world back.

She glanced at her watch. It was noon on the dot. She closed her eyes and pictured the boy with sapphire eyes, the one she loved with every bit of her heart.

Thad, I love you. I believe in you. Look for what you don't see.

Thad.

On the beach, Thad sucked in a hard breath. His name echoed in his ears, a cruel taunt. It sounded so much like Charley he'd swear that if he spun around, he'd find himself looking into her golden eyes, close enough to touch. But Charley wasn't here. She was safe.

Nil was playing tricks again.

He closed his eyes, half wanting to hear the voice again, hating himself for even considering it was Charley.

Get out, he thought with a vengeance. *Go play in someone else's head.*

The whisper brushed his mind again, as warm as the noon Nil sun and just as fierce.

Thad, I love you. I believe in you. Look for what you don't see.

Thad's heart skipped in shock. It was *her* voice, *her* drawl, dripping through his head like honey; it stirred an ache in his soul that told him this was real. The voice *was* Charley, not Nil.

He'd bet his life on it.

The more he listened, the more he *heard*, the more Thad realized that was exactly the wager he would make.

Despite the hell of Nil around him, Thad smiled.

Nil still ran the tables, kept cards up her sleeve. But this time, he had a few of his own. One in particular, the ace of hearts, and his gut said the ace of hearts beat the ace of diamonds any damn day.

I guess I'm playing after all, he thought, jogging up the beach, toward the City.

In a few weeks, he'd find out who held the stronger hand.

CHAPTER 43

SKYE

83 DAYS UNTIL THE AUTUMNAL EQUINOX, AFTER NOON

Would you have run? Paulo had asked after that gate had vanished.

No, I'd thought. If anything, I would have run *away* from the gate. I had business to finish, ripples to stop. I eyed the mountain, picturing the platform in my mind, knowing our gate would rise in eighty-three days.

And then we would destroy it, if I could just figure out how.

Rives stood beside me on the black sand beach, his strong hand wrapping mine, our hearts and heads woven so tightly that we were one. The island had sealed our bond, branding a bit of each of our souls on the other, but the love we shared was ours and ours alone.

I could not lose Rives.

But the island wanted something, maybe some*one*. And now Zane had me thinking it wanted *everyone*.

The thought terrified me because it felt true.

An animal cry reached my ears, a predatory call that stole my full attention. An answering call replied to the first, louder. Possibly closer.

The three boys stared at the mountain, all oddly oblivious, all strangely still. Despite his hand in mine, Rives felt very far away.

"Rives," I hissed, tugging his hand.

He jerked his head toward me, his eyes clearing as he blinked. "How long have I been staring at the mountain?"

"Long enough. We need to go, *now*. Something's coming."

I slid my sling off my shoulder, rock in hand. On cue, a deer leaped from the bushes, its hooves gouging deep grooves in the black sand, slipping and slowing as it tried to gain traction.

"Zane. Paulo," Rives said sharply. Their heads snapped toward us, their eyes as clouded as his had been. "Let's move. A deer just showed up and something's chasing it. Keep your eyes open and minds to yourself, all right?"

As he raised his knife, two animals burst from the tree line. They moved sleekly, their coats a blurry mix of black and caramel, their teeth bared in feral snarls.

Hyenas, I thought. I was flanked by Rives and Paulo; I was caught between Dex and Jillian. The animals hit the sand in tandem, hunting the deer.

"Skye!" Rives jerked my hand, urging me to run. He held his knife out defensively; Paulo gripped his spear tight. Zane was unarmed and I wasn't much better off. I'd have to stop to aim.

The deer stumbled.

The animals pounced. They bit the deer repeatedly as it tried to escape; they nipped its legs, its hindquarters, its flanks, anything they could get their teeth on. I'd never seen hyenas attack so efficiently, and so brutally. I *hated* hyenas. I stood rooted to the sand.

"Not hyenas," Rives said as he pulled me along. Unwittingly, I'd slowed. "African wild dogs. They don't usually mess with people, but—" He left his sentence unfinished.

The deer may have survived Amara's spear, but it didn't last long with the dogs. The dogs feasted as we left them behind.

I realized I'd never been afraid, at least not for myself, but my fear for my friends had grown exponentially. I couldn't bear to lose anyone else I cared about—especially Rives. Especially since *I* was the reason he was even here. I would protect him at all costs from the greatest threat.

In that moment, *I* chose.

Rives must live, and Nil must die.

It was that simple.

CHAPTER 44

RIVES
83 DAYS UNTIL THE AUTUMNAL EQUINOX, AFTER NOON

We hit the City well after noon.

Maybe we'd misjudged, maybe we were tired. Maybe we were all trapped in our own heads, or working overtime trying to keep Nil *out*. Skye didn't have to tell me we'd lost time at Black Bay before the dog attack, time lost staring at Mount Nil like we were effing tourists with all day to waste. If Skye hadn't pulled me back, I'd still be there. Same for Zane and Paulo.

And since then, I'd felt abnormally drained. It occurred to me that Nil stole more than time when we checked out for a minute. It was like Nil stole a piece of *us*.

I passed the deadleaf barrier, eyes wide open, mind shut tight.

The City screamed ghost town, which in some ways it was. No Natalie, no Jillian. No Dex. Still, my mind played tricks. For an instant I thought I saw Dex crouched by the fire, his skin pasty white, hair dark and spiky with frosted tips, then my mind nudged—*Chuck*.

He crouched by the firepit, holding a stick, watching it burn. He didn't look up as I approached, his gaze riveted on the flames creeping toward his hand. It occurred to me he could use some supervision.

Thad stood at the far perimeter, his back to me.

No one else was around.

Thad turned as I approached. He broke into a relieved smile. "Good to see you, brother."

"Same. Everything okay here?" I braced for the answer.

"Yup. Just glad to lay eyes on your ugly mug." He grinned.

The knot in my stomach loosened. "Anything new?"

"A girl. Carmen. Quiet, pulls her weight. City's been quiet. How was Search?"

"Worthless." I paused. "So, besides Carmen, any other news?"

"Actually, yes." He slowly turned toward me, his bearing alert but calm. "I can't explain it, but I can hear Charley. I hear her talking to me, in here." He tapped his head.

Alarm bells rang in my head.

"Not a good sign, bro. That's Nil talking, not Charley."

He shook his head. "I don't think so. Last time I was here, I heard Nil. Calculating, cunning, cruel. I remember that voice; it's not one I could forget. This is different. I'm telling you, it's Charley."

I said nothing, letting my silence speak for me.

"The thing is . . . I only hear her at noon."

Damn.

I studied Thad, struck by the intensity of his gaze, and the newfound chill he was suddenly sporting.

"Maybe it is Charley," I said slowly. And the unspoken *Maybe not.* "Let me know if she tells you anything that can help get us off this rock."

Thad ran one hand through his hair as he spoke. "She told me to look for what I don't see."

"Well, that's helpful." Thad didn't flinch at my caustic tone. "Anything else?"

Thad shrugged. "She said she loved me and said something about a bottle."

"A bottle?"

"A bottle." Thad's face read completely serious.

"Like put a message in a bottle? Find the genie in the bottle? Don't play spin the bottle?" Davey had walked up from the beach. "As if we

251

could." He snorted then grinned at me. "Welcome back, mate. Glad to see you hale and hearty." He turned to Thad. "Did today's walkabout with Kenji and Chuck. No sign of anyone for at least one hundred meters in any direction, although Chuck talks so bloody much he probably annoyed everything and everyone within range. Hashtag chatty." He shook his head. "Hafthor, Calvin, and Molly didn't see anyone on the white beach to the north, either. And no one found a bloody thing on today's grid. Although big Cal swears he saw a silverback gorilla." He shrugged. "So he probably did."

"What about Carmen and James?" Thad crossed his arms.

Davey shrugged again. "Haven't seen them."

Thad turned to me. "While you four were gone in Quadrant Two, we did most of Quadrant Three. We'd go out in pairs or threes, working a set grid, going over the same spots on different days with different eyes. Didn't see anything new to me, with the exception of that cavern with the carvings. Except the animals." He exhaled. "Panthers, a wallaby, a jaguar, and a shit ton of hippos. We stopped at the mudflats, didn't go past to the hills." He looked with curiosity toward the Crystal Cavern. "That cave, the one behind the falls. It's something, eh? I could sit in there for hours."

"I don't recommend it," I said crisply. "Any sign of Lana?"

"None."

"We need to find her." Skye had walked up behind me, Paulo at her side. She turned to him as she spoke. "Where would she go?"

"I would say the Looking Glass Cavern, but—" He lifted his hands slightly. "I don't know."

Skye's face fell.

"What about Dominic?" I asked.

Thad looked blank.

"Big smile, thick Bahamian accent?"

Thad shook his head but Davey snapped his fingers and grinned. "That's it! Aquaman. He came by a week ago, asking for you. I told you went south. He left another giant fish with Hafthor and I haven't seen him since. But you know what was weird? He came up from the water and left the same way."

"Maybe it's safer there," Thad mused.

"I doubt it." *No place is safe here*, I thought. *Not the land, not the water.*

Not even our own heads.

Afternoon. Night. Dawn.

Noon.

Repeat.

Skye grew more agitated with each day that passed. She paced during the day, unable to sit still. To *keep* still.

The only time she stilled was in sleep, when she slept like the dead, a sickening thought.

Today was my fifteenth day back on Nil, and I'd woken before Skye, again.

On the beach, Calvin ran intervals, sprinting hard in the soft sand, his dark skin dripping with sweat as he pumped his arms and legs. I wondered if anyone had bothered to tell him the equinox gate was stationary.

Thad jogged up the minute he saw me.

"Does Calvin know the equinox gate doesn't move?" I asked. "No running required?"

"He knows. He does this every morning. The dude is seriously fast." He looked past me. "Is Skye up?"

"Not yet. Why?"

"Because Charley woke me up in the middle of the night. I think it was midnight."

"TMI, bro. Keep your dreams to yourself." I made light of Thad's words, unwilling to encourage the *I-hear-Charley* theme.

He ignored me. "She repeated the same thing over and over, like she was making sure I heard her. She said, 'Find the ruins, solve the riddle. Look for what you don't see.'"

"*Find the ruins?*" I frowned. "I don't know of any ruins. Or a riddle."

"Me either. We walked all over this damn island when we mapped it, and I don't remember seeing any ruins. But maybe Skye or Paulo know something we don't."

"What do I know?" Skye walked up to us, yawning.

"Ruins," I said, kissing her cheek. "Have you seen any here? Or know of any?"

She blinked. "No. Why?"

"Because Charley told Thad to find them. He thinks she's talking to him."

"She *is* talking to me," Thad said with conviction.

Skye's eyes cleared like she'd been doused with cold water. "What?"

"I usually hear her at noon," he told her, "but last night I heard her at midnight. She told me to 'find the ruins, solve the riddle.'"

"*Find the ruins, solve the riddle,*" Skye murmured. Then her eyes widened and she grabbed my arm. "Rives! I know what she's talking about! *Mazes and men, caves and creatures, ruins and riddles, all wrapped up in an island bottle.* My uncle wrote that in his journal!"

"So, that's the bottle Charley mentioned the other day." Thad nodded as if it all made sense.

I fought back a laugh.

"What else did she say?" Skye asked Thad. Her bright eyes told me she was all in.

"To look for what you don't see."

Paulo walked out from his hut and Skye practically pounced. "What do you know about the ruins?"

"Ruins?" His blank expression told me he was as clueless as the rest of us.

"Ruins. *Mazes and men, caves and creatures, ruins and riddles, all wrapped up in an island bottle,*" Skye repeated. "It's from my uncle's journal. The same uncle that met your aunt Rika."

"But it's his words." Paulo looked bewildered, like he was trying to find meaning in the mess.

Good luck, I thought.

Skye spun back to Thad. "Did Charley tell you anything else?" she asked hopefully, like Charley could feed us answers from the outside.

I wasn't convinced.

For all I knew, this riddle was Nil's newest *Ima mess with their heads* game. Nil was all about the fun and games, only the fun was all Nil's.

"That's it," Thad said. "You know as much as I do."

"Do you think the ruins are the Dead City?" Skye asked.

Paulo sighed. "I have no idea."

"We need Lana." Skye's voice dripped frustration. "And no one has seen her."

"Maybe he has," Paulo suggested, pointing.

Dominic was walking up the beach, holding a fish that required two hands to carry.

"Dominic!" I waved. "Long time no see."

"Same to you, mon." He grinned broadly. "Brought a grouper. Good eatin' here, enough for all of us."

Skye smiled. "Dominic, where have you been staying?"

"Around." He shrugged, still smiling, then set the fish down on the sand. "I sleep where the island calls me."

"Have you seen a girl? Long dark hair? Her name is Lana."

"I only see the people here. And a boy, on the other side. But the lion saw him too." Dominic sighed as he made a slicing motion across his throat. "I leave fish for the tiger, to keep him happy. But the lion . . ." Dominic shrugged. "No way to keep him happy." He made another slicing motion.

"Back to Lana." Skye's eyes were pleading. "Are you sure you haven't seen her? We can't find the ruins without her."

"The ruins?" Dominic raised his eyebrows. "The ones on the coast?"

"Which coast?" I asked.

"Due east. On the other side of the island. If you want, I will show you. But I'm telling you now, I won't go in that place. It's a living ghost town." He shivered.

Thad looked skeptical. "I can't believe Charley and I missed an entire *city* when we mapped the island."

"It doesn't feel like a city, mon." Dominic's expression was somber. "It feels like a grave."

"The Dead City," Skye breathed. She lifted her eyes to mine. "That's the answer. We need to go there, *now.*"

"Whoa there, island traveler." Zane walked up, rubbing sleep from his eyes. Salty and stiff, his blond hair stuck out in all directions. "Where are we going now?"

CHAPTER
45

*The fighter grew restless with the game. The island fueled her unrest,
stoked her anger. Hate was a powerful emotion and the island relished
hers; it would twist it for the island's own pleasure.*

It would twist her.

*In the end she would destroy the one with murder in her heart. The
fighter would serve the island's end, until the one who wished to harm
the island was no more.*

Then they both would bleed, and the island would savor every drop.

From her vantage point in the trees, Carmen studied the players
around the fire. Amara sat slightly away from the rest, rolling a small
knife through her fingers, listening to Skye talk with a remarkable lack
of expression on her face. *She's working hard to be intimidating,*
Carmen thought acidly as she glared at Amara. But she wasn't. She
couldn't even take down the deer and had nearly hit Carmen's foot
with her poor throw, a move that infuriated Carmen to no end.

The only one who annoyed Carmen more than Amara was the wiry
blonde, Skye. Carmen deeply resented how everyone treated her with
respect when she'd done nothing to earn it. She also resented how the
leader, Rives, looked at Skye as though she created air. It rankled Carmen

that this mouse of a girl turned the leader's head with the wave of one hand, that she meant so much to Rives he'd asked another boy, Thad, to watch over her when he left, as if she were a gem too precious to lose. This was a weakness for the leader, an obvious vulnerability making him less impressive in Carmen's eyes. But more than anything else, she resented the power that flowed from Skye, as if she were more important than anyone else—including Carmen. The more she watched Skye from the shadows, the more Carmen detested her.

Carmen had never liked being second place.

"Carmen." James spoke softly as he tapped her on the shoulder. He always took care not to startle her.

She turned. "Yes?"

James studied her, how fury flickered in her eyes like firelight. "Have you eaten?" he asked.

"Are you really here to make sure I had dinner?" Her tone matched her eyes.

"No. I am here to make sure you do not do anything that you might regret."

Her eyes flashed. "And who"—her voice was dangerously low—"are you to tell me what I should do?"

"Your friend. And as your friend, I am saying relax. This is not a competition."

"Isn't it?" She smiled in the feral way James had grown accustomed to. "Why do they get to decide what we do? How the days should be spent? How the resources should be used?"

"Because they know more than we do." James's tone was flat. "And they will help us live another day."

"I am the master of my own fate." Carmen lifted her chin.

" 'Invictus.' " James was not impressed. "As are we all. But they have been here before, and they know the way. I think it would be wise to listen and learn from them."

"Feel free to be their lackeys," Carmen snapped. "A trip to some ruins that hold nothing but death? Or stay and babysit that idiot Chuck? Have fun. I choose another path. I'm going to find Lana, the girl who knows more than anyone. Where is she, James?" Carmen's voice had grown dangerously soft. "I think she knows something. More than those fools. After all, she's not here, is she?"

James didn't respond. He didn't share Carmen's confidence in Lana. She had not seen what James had: Lana cowering on the beach, terrified of the bear; Lana creeping behind Rives and his friends. No, Lana was not a source of power.

But something on the island was.

Carmen bared her teeth in a smile. "Exactly. Good luck, James. I choose to make my own."

She stalked off. James watched her go, unsettled. He was wrong; they were not friends. And he wasn't certain they weren't now enemies.

CHAPTER
46

We'd split into two equal groups. Hafthor, James, Amara, Chuck, Paulo, Zane, and Kenji stayed behind, while Rives, Thad, Molly, Davey, Calvin, and I accompanied Dominic.

"Balance reigns," Rives had advised. *Nil truth number four*, I'd thought. I still hadn't figured all of them out. I was starting to worry that I never would. Nil remained so secretive, so mysterious. I'd been here almost a month, and I knew nothing more than when I'd arrived. Nothing important, anyway. Nothing that would help us end the Nil cycle once and for all.

It was all I thought about as we walked.

And Nil gave me plenty of time to think. Our trip had been strangely quiet. Maybe it was the coastal route, the open ocean that stayed on my left and the lack of predators by the sea. Even though it took longer, Dominic had insisted we travel along the coast; it was where he felt comfortable. Since the inland route presented its own hazards—mainly in the form of wildlife in unknown quantities and eating habits—everyone had agreed to the coastal plan without argument—except Carmen. She'd stalked off, choosing neither group. Secretly, I was relieved. She made me uncomfortable. I honestly felt like she hated me, although we'd barely spoken. Even her farewell of "Good luck" sounded more ominous than heartfelt, as if she were wishing me anything but.

That had been five dawns ago.

Find the ruins, solve the riddle. Look for what you don't see.

My head ached from *looking*. I constantly surveyed my surroundings from dawn to dusk, until all I saw were stars.

The first few nights we'd slept on the sand, under the open Nil sky. The north shore felt darker, angrier. Waves crashed against the rocks with lethal force; we'd nestled in the small pockets in the black cliff face, barely large enough to count as a cave. The third night we'd actually slept in a cave. It reminded me of the one on the southern coast, the one with the mouth shaped like an ear, the same cave Paulo told us all the islanders usually stayed in when they first arrived, only the cave on the north shore had a mouth shaped more like an eye. Creepy and cold, the entire feel fit the north shore perfectly. That was the only night I didn't sleep well.

Last night we'd been back on sand, and today was day five.

So far we'd made it all the way around the northern tip of the island and were heading south again, and slightly east. The island truly was shaped like a diamond, an irregular one, just as the carving on the Master Map Wall described. We were just below the rain forest, traipsing around rocky cliffs and making terrible time in my opinion. But no one else seemed rushed.

Probably because Dominic kept us well fed.

Each day he'd fished, and this morning he'd actually made conch salad. Honest-to-goodness seafood salad made from fresh conch, and it was surprisingly tasty—not slimy like I'd expected. He'd gone so far out into the ocean I'd lost sight of him, and then he'd come up with two giant conch, one in each hand. He repeated this trip twice, diving deep and swimming with ease. He'd broken the shells on the rocks, then, using the sharpest wooden blade we had, he'd filleted the fresh conch and sliced it thin. He added fresh lime juice and mango and a few other things I missed, then gestured to the pile. "Best conch salad you will ever eat. Back home, my cousin and I, we sell it for eleven dollars a bowl."

"And people pay that?" Davey had asked in disbelief.

"If they want it, they do." Dominic had grinned.

Who cares about conch salad? I wanted to scream.

That had been two hours ago. No longer smiling, Dominic had grown quiet. I realized he'd been stalling, delaying the inevitable—and the uncomfortable.

To our right, the green hillside was steep. Clouds swirled overhead, puffy but not threatening. Near the top, trees dripped ripe fruit, lush and thick, the start of Nil's rain forest. A large black cliff sat straight ahead.

"Around that bend." Dominic gestured ahead. "The ruins wait."

We rounded the cliff, the rocks fell away, and all of us drew a collective breath.

"The Dead City," Paulo murmured.

The remains of huts jutted from the ground on the hillside, their black rock foundations crumbled. All were partially hidden, with chunks already lost to the elements and the passage of time. I easily pictured thatched roofs, but they were long gone.

"This is as far as I go," Dominic said. "I will wait here for you when you have seen all you want to see."

The rest of us hiked over to the ruins. The layout mirrored Nil City to the west. There were ten huts, or had been ten huts, built in a half circle. There was even evidence of a firepit at the edge near the water. The Nil silence hung like a cloud, eerie and haunting. Even the wind blew without sound.

Something lingered here; it smelled of fear.

I shivered.

"How did Charley and I not see this?" Arms crossed, Thad looked dumbfounded.

"My guess? You weren't looking for it," Davey said. "It's like that YouTube clip where you're supposed to count only the red balls bouncing around between a group of guys on a basketball court. Balls are flying everywhere, white ones, blue ones, red ones; it's a bloody nightmare trying to keep track but you're determined to get it right. You're so busy looking for the red balls that you don't see the bloke in a gorilla suit run through the group." He shrugged. "So here? It could be a bloody island Stonehenge, but you weren't looking for it, and you were specifically looking for something else. So you didn't see it."

Davey's casual words seemed incredibly deep, like I should file them away to ponder later. Molly looked at him as if she'd never seen him before, her mouth slightly open in surprise.

She blinked and turned to me.

"Why would they leave?" Molly gestured to the abandoned houses. "Maybe a tsunami? Or natural disaster?"

"I don't know." But I desperately needed to; at the same time I wanted to leave myself. "Why leave a perfectly good city, where fruit is so close? And the stationary gate?"

"Don't forget. It's close to the meadow, too," Thad said. "Maybe the big animals drove them out."

"They didn't all leave." Rives pointed to the hut farthest south, where a skeleton lay fully intact.

Calvin stepped back and put his hands up. "All right, I'm done. You know in horror movies the black dude always bites it first. I'm going back with Dominic. Strength in numbers."

Rives walked closer to the skeleton, choosing his steps with care.

"Rives?" Now I saw a second skeleton a few feet away from the first.

Rives crouched by a large black boulder about three yards from the hut full of bones. An inscription covered the rock: *This place is not safe.*

" 'This place is not safe'?" Davey read aloud. "Is that a bloody joke? Of course this place isn't safe. Did they mean this city, or the island?"

"Does it matter?" Thad asked. "It's all the same. A death trap."

"I think it totally matters." I looked at him. "Is that the riddle? Is that what Charley wants us to solve?"

Thad shrugged. "No clue. At least we found the ruins."

I held back the urge to say *Big whoop*.

"Let's go find something worthwhile then." Rives's tone was firm. "I'd rather not stay any longer than we have to."

For the next hour, we marched all over the ruins. Other than the two skeletons and a large pile of rocks, there was nothing else. Nothing but the broken rock foundations of old huts, abandoned long ago.

Find the ruins, solve the riddle.

Look for what you don't see.

I saw nothing, found nothing, no insight or understanding at all. With each step, with each empty moment, I grew more disappointed. Water slid down my cheek like a tear, and for an instant I thought I'd actually started crying out of sheer frustration. Then I lifted my chin. Rain fell from the Nil sky, gentle and cool, as if Nil were weeping over our inability to *see*. Over *my* inability to understand what Nil's history meant for our future.

I closed my eyes.

Rain coated my skin, an island caress, but inside my head the darkness swirled close. It mocked my blindness, attracted by the desperation of my thoughts. It *liked* my suffering, I realized with a start; it relished my frustration.

It fed off my fear.

My *greatest* fear.

Suddenly I knew with frightening certainty that the darkness knew that if I lost Rives, I wouldn't survive; it knew the depth of pain that loss would bring. It relished that, too. More than relished, it *desired* it. Pain, and death. And power over me.

My lungs filled too fast; my breath caught.

I could not lose Rives.

"Skye?" Rives's warm breath in my ear startled me. "Is it time?"

My eyes flew open. "Time for what?"

"To panic. For the last hour, you've stomped all over the place like an angry bear, and now you're biting the inside of your cheek. So.

Time to panic?" His expression was light, a sign he was trying to lighten me, or at least my mood. But his green eyes were searching.

"Not time." I willed myself to relax. "I told you I'd let you know. And I wasn't stomping."

Rives smiled, that smile that made the world shrink to just him and me. "So what are you thinking about so seriously?"

"Everything." *You. Me. The island. What I need to do.*

He held my hand, pulled me close; my worries and fears spun so fast that they breached my mental barriers and poured into Rives's head. I knew it because I felt it; I felt *him*. I felt my mind touch his. For an instant I felt safe, and whole and *clear*; even the rain seemed to vanish.

Rives stiffened.

The world rushed back in, collapsing around me in invisible sheets. The rain, the weight, the darkness, the pressure.

"I can't lose you," I said, my voice thick with feeling.

He kissed me madly, desperately, a tangle of lips and heat and cool rain. With shaking hands, he pulled back and gently cupped my face, his green eyes like emerald fire as they searched mine with an unbridled intensity. "How can you lose me when I'm with you?" he asked hoarsely.

Rain streaked his cheeks and mine.

I reached up to catch the drops dripping from his lashes. "I don't trust Nil," I whispered, my heart aching.

Rives's eyes darkened. "I never have."

CHAPTER
47

I let go of Skye's chin.

I smiled. I breathed. I took her hand. As we left the Dead City and walked through a fading Nil rain, I pretended everything was okay.

Nothing was okay.

The darkness in her head had shocked me. Blown me away. The depth of it, the pure *want*. I felt it when her thoughts touched mine: there was a moment—a cold instant—when a surreal darkness flooded my mind, like when she'd shown me the darkness of her dreams, only *this* darkness was a hell of a lot more potent. A million times more tangible, more connected. More *alive*. Like for just that moment, Skye had cleared her head, expelling her thoughts and the darkness in one massive purge, dumping the whole mess into mine.

In that one second I saw everything so clearly: a crisp vision, seared into my brain with no room for misinterpretation. Skye, lifeless on black rock. Skye, claimed by Nil.

The darkness wanted her.

It wanted her *dead*.

Rivesssss . . .

Over the water, through the rain, I heard the papery hiss.

Be fearless . . .

I closed my eyes, working not to clench my fists. Working to breathe, which right now seemed like a monumental task. It's easy to be fearless when you have nothing to lose.

Me, I had everything.

I'd never been more scared in my life.

CHAPTER
48

The one called Rives had weakened.

The island knew there was a strong possibility he would break. He believed he had nearly broken while he was here before, but he was wrong. If anything, he had fought a fracture there. But those cracks were minuscule compared to the fissure that was coming. The island hurt for him, for the pain to come. Pain the island itself must deliver.

The island regretted the pain to come, but it did not regret its choice. It only regretted that there was no choice.

And so it would be.

The pain in his head forced the island to turn away, to turn elsewhere. It turned to one far less powerful, one who was still lost.

Lana huddled in the trees, watching Zane paddle out. Yearning rolled over her as powerful as the towering wave he'd just ridden. A giant blue beauty, Zane had carved it with admirable precision, his board one with the wave, never pressing, his stance relaxed and powerful, bliss on his face.

She wanted that. Not Zane, that was ridiculous. No, she wanted the freedom of the water, a place she knew like the back of her hand. She'd been island raised and island bred, and even though this wasn't *her* island, she knew the water, and it called to her. It called her *here*.

First she'd guiltily raided the storage hut for food, finding salted fish and mounds of guava; she'd been so hungry she'd forced herself to slow down so she didn't get sick. Then she'd huddled in the trees, watching.

"So *this* is your grand plan? Hiding in the bushes?"

Lana turned. A girl stood behind her, hips cocked, thick dark braid, angry eyes. Proud stance. *Carmen*, Lana remembered. The girl from *her* cave.

"Hello, Carmen." Lana's voice was smooth, giving no hint of anything but control. "Enjoying your island vacation?"

"Here you are, in the shrubs. Watching *them*. And yet you haven't joined them. Why?" The girl's eyes blazed with a hunger Lana didn't like.

"Why should I tell you?" Lana's tone stayed controlled.

"Because I asked."

Lana smiled, enjoying the flare of fire in Carmen's eyes. She smiled wider. "I have a different path. It might lead here"—she pointed toward the beach, where the heady waves rolled into shore—"or not." She shrugged. "But I won't be bullied into a choice." She stared at Carmen.

A long moment passed.

Then Carmen nodded. "So the escape gate. It comes in three months?"

"A little less now," Lana said. *Did everyone know the island's secrets?* she thought. *Apparently yes.* Suddenly the weight of all the secrets exhausted her. What was the point? She'd been hiding out in caves on the north shore, half starving and totally miserable, until the latest group of people had driven her away, people led by Paulo on a mission that she hadn't bothered to care about. She was finally listening.

She'd reflected enough.

She looked at Carmen. "In less than three months' time, that gate will open. On the mountain, past the meadow, when the crescent moon is high. If you're there, it will take you home. Or . . ." She paused. "You can take a rogue gate, a wild one, anytime. They come at noon. Which," Lana said with a wave of her hand, "is now." The sun was high, the wind still blowing offshore. The waves ramped into perfect blue lines, begging her to ride them. On the far side of the island, gray dusted the sky, a hint of rain. But here, the sky was clear.

Like the water.

Like her path.

Screw it, she thought. She stood. She leveled her eyes on Carmen. "Good luck, Carmen. I hope you find your way. Now if you'll excuse me, I have a wave to catch."

Lana turned and didn't look back. Leaving her hiding spot and Carmen behind her, Lana strode to the storage hut, feeling lighter with each step, and picked the smallest surfboard propped against the hut's side. She ran her hands over the smooth wood, history rippling beneath her fingers. With a smile for no one but herself, she tucked the board tight to her hip. Carved by her ancestors' hands, this was one island tradition she would embrace with all she had.

She walked to the water, waded until the waves hit her thighs, and then slid onto the board, paddling with power, feeling more confident than she had in weeks. She pulled up beside Zane, who sat reading the horizon. He looked over and did a double take. "Lana?"

She cocked her head, her joy at being out on the water making her giddy. "Now would you like to see how to really ride a wave?"

The island watched the one called Carmen with concern. It had taken an unacceptable amount of the island's remaining strength to alter the path of Carmen's blade. Responding to a calculated dose of pressure, the knife had sailed wide, barely missing the one called Lana's back. Intent on the water, the one called Lana had not seen it, had not felt it; she had no inkling that her fate had nearly been altered by a hate-driven hand.

The one called Lana had walked on, unharmed.

The one called Carmen had shaken with fury.

The blade's error had stoked her anger, an unfortunate effect of the

270

island's interference, but the one called Lana's choice to engage with others had already been seen, and she had a role to play. Her death was not written yet.

But alteration of the knife's trajectory had cost the island in many ways; it had sapped its reserves beyond acceptable levels. The island had no strength left to guide today's noon. So when a frightening beast with blood dripping from its jaws arrived through the gate and ambled toward the human City, the island simply watched. And hoped that the humans still had strength to run.

Days passed.

Time passed.

The island was accustomed to the passage of time; time gave and time took, because time always was. But now, time bled like an island wound. The one called Skye felt the loss as keenly as the island.

The island shared her agitation, and her mounting frustration. The one called Thad had given her the clues, yet she did not see. The monumental blindness of this species baffled the island; it hindered their ability to learn and grow and transform. Even once Sight was bestowed, understanding did not necessarily follow, as if the blindness continued by choice, a completely illogical course of action. But the island believed that if given the opportunity, she would understand; she would not turn a blind eye to the present, or the future.

But first, she must open her eyes. If she could not open them on her own, the island would assist her.

Time would wait for no one, and the island could no longer wait for her.

She must look, now.

CHAPTER 49

SKYE
42 DAYS UNTIL THE AUTUMNAL EQUINOX, MORNING

Skye. The girl who wasn't really a girl at all crooned in my ear. *Look for what you don't see.*

I'm trying, I wanted to snap. I was trying so hard I thought I might combust internally from the pressure building inside myself. I had no idea what befell the people lying still in the Dead City, and no clue how to save my friends and end Nil's deadly cycle. Frustration didn't cover how I felt right this minute.

At the water's edge, froth wrapped my ankles and tickled my toes, begging me to play; the sun kissed my shoulders, warm and soothing, an invitation to relax. But deep inside me, something shifted, something untouched by what was happening around me.

Look.

As if I looked through the eyes of a stranger, I took in the entire scene before my eyes. One click of a frame, then two.

Rives and Thad carried their boards up the beach, laughing and smiling over a joke I couldn't hear; closer to me, Lana squeezed water from her hair, her eyes closed, her expression content. To my right, Hafthor stood near Kenji, inspecting Kenji's last bokken creation with approval; Chuck sat alone, rocking slightly as he played with fire. On my left, Davey strolled along the beach, away from me, cane pole in hand.

Molly was talking to Calvin; Amara was talking to no one. Carmen stared at the sun. Paulo stared at her.

Everyone moved slowly, unhurried, playing into the island feel. It could have been any day, any beach, anywhere.

But we weren't on just any beach, just any island—we were on Nil, and the entire scene was a mirage.

Something inside me snapped.

We had no time to waste, no time to play. We had six weeks left to figure this whole end-the-island thing out. I seethed with frustration; it welled inside me, building without end. I wanted to scream, to run around and shake everyone and yell, *Wake up! Wake up!*

"Skye?"

"What?" I spun around and came face to face with Zane. His eyes widened, his grip on his surfboard tightened.

"Hey, sorry. I was just thinking."

"It looked like you were surfing." My words practically cut my own tongue with their edge. Part of me felt terrible for being so rude to Zane, but my frustration bubbled over. "Sorry for snapping," I snapped again. Then I gave up. "What?"

He shook his head. "Listen, when we went to Quadrant Two on our magical mystery hunt, you said we were missing something, remember?"

"I remember." *It's all I think about.*

"I know what we're missing. Gates. Specifically, outbounds. When you went on your trip to the Dead City, did you see any?"

I thought back. Had I seen any on our trips to the ruins? I hadn't, but then again I hadn't been looking for one, either.

Davey's words echoed through my head. *You weren't looking for it, and you were specifically looking for something else. So you didn't see it.*

"No," I admitted, my tone slightly less acidic. "But I wasn't looking for any, either." I'd already decided the wild ones weren't for me.

He nodded. "Well, I've been looking, and I haven't seen one. So." He paused, his expression incredibly serious for Zane. "If Nil's not sending us gates, then we're all waiting for the golden equinox ticket, right? What if it's a no-show, Skye? What if the island's losing the ability to bring gates? Or, what if it's waiting to take us down a group, like the Dead City? I'm starting to think you might be onto something." Zane glanced at Mount Nil. "Hafthor says he feels tremors constantly, like the ground is restless. Says they're worse by the mountain, but he feels them here, too."

"Really?" *Were there more steam vents than before?* I wondered. *Was magma building, like fire within, and here we were, trapped like the poor souls in Pompeii?* I studied the mountain. From here, the mountaintop hid in the clouds; the west slope gleamed bright green in the sun. A wash of red flashed near the clouds, then vanished. I squinted, blinking. My eyes were playing tricks. "I haven't felt any tremors," I said, as if my declaration might make it true.

Zane waved off my words. "The point is, what if the volcano erupts or a quake happens and the island takes us all at once?"

"I don't know. But I don't think we can worry about the what-ifs. I think we have to worry about the now." I wasn't sure if I was talking to Zane, or myself, or both. "And right now, we need to figure out what we're missing other than gates."

On the beach, Lana was gone. Davey was nearly out of sight. Rives now walked toward me, eating a mango; Thad talked with Paulo. The water had nearly reached the high-tide mark, but not quite. Part of my brain processed the slight shift in people and places, taking note out of habit; the rest of my mind screamed, *None of it matters because you can see it.*

Wild splashing caught my attention. Dominic surfaced, breathing hard. He raised his empty spear and grinned.

"That was a big one, Skye. Too big for me."

"A fish too big for you, Aquaman?" Zane grinned. "I don't believe it."

Dominic laughed. "I telling you, mon, that fish was *huge*. Twenty feet at least, maybe more, the kind of fish that might eat me. The minute it popped out of the water light, I was gone. No need to wait for it to wake up."

"Water light?" I frowned.

He nodded. "I see many here, in the water." Seeing my blank expression, he continued. "The light holes. You know the ones, under the water, where the light appears and glows, and the sharks and the fish, they disappear into the light. I see many here. Sometimes, I see the light turn dark and spit out fish." He grinned. "Yesterday I saw it deliver a stingray. Today, a tiger shark. Who knows what tomorrow will bring?"

"Amen, brother." Zane nodded.

Dominic's casual revelation sunk in. "Gates in the water exist," I said slowly. "You've seen them. And they bring cold-blooded things. And you're mostly seeing outbounds, the opposite of the land gates." *Because they're linked*, I thought. I'd suspected underwater gates existed; now I knew. *The yin and the yang. The balance of it all.*

Balance reigns, Rives had told me more than once. *It's Nil truth number four.*

I closed my eyes again, desperate to *see*.

Land gates, water lights.

Nil City, full of people; the Dead City full of ghosts. Twin cities, on opposite coasts.

Four labyrinths, four quadrants, equally spaced like the points on a compass.

Four numbers, two sets of two. Both pairs equaling five, adding to a perfect ten.

The cave of South Beach, shaped like an ear; the cave on the north shore, shaped like an eye.

One mountain.

One Looking Glass Cavern.

They were not a match.

My eyes flew open, finding Rives. "They don't match," I exclaimed. "The mountain and the Looking Glass Cavern! The mountain's balance might be us, or maybe it just represents the island. I'm not sure it *needs* a match, because it houses the platform, and the platform's mate would be underwater, right? Or back on the Death Twin. Either way, it's not the Looking Glass Cavern. Which means, the Looking Glass Cavern should have a match, a balance, on the opposite side of the island. That's what we need to look for." I smiled triumphantly. "We need to find the Looking Glass Cavern's island match."

Rives hadn't moved. "Why?"

"Because it's important! Balance reigns, remember? It's what we don't see, and we have to look for it!"

Rives didn't look convinced. "To draw a direct line from the Looking Glass Cavern across the island puts its complement on the east coast, below the ruins." He paused. "Directly below the meadow." He crossed his arms. "We can't take the coastal route to the south, because it's blocked by lava. The northern coastal route will take us about a week, right?"

I shook my head. "I say we go direct."

"Skye—"

"I know what I'm asking." *We'll have to go through the meadow.* But the thought didn't worry me like it did Rives, because I felt certain that if the island wanted me there, it would protect me, too. "I think something's there, something important. I'm not asking anyone to come with me this time," I added.

Rives's jaw ticked. "You know you don't have to ask. Of course I'm going with you. Let's just think about it for a few days, okay?"

"We don't have a few days! The clock is ticking, literally. We've been here for forty-four days, Rives. Forty-four days! And we've found nada. Zip. Zilch."

"Nil," Zane added.

I ignored him as I stared at Rives, my eyes pleading with him to understand. "If I sit around and do nothing," I said quietly, "I'm going to go crazy."

"Why don't we ask Paulo if he knows of anything on the other coast?" Rives said. "Or Lana? Or both?"

"Fine." I started up the beach. But I didn't say I wouldn't go.

CHAPTER 50

RIVES

Merde.

Skye's think-first, panic-never mode was in full effect. As much as I hated to admit it, her decisions were never impulsive, even though they looked that way on the surface. She was cerebral, almost to a fault. But she tended to ignore dangers right in front of her face, or rationalize them away.

Like now.

A trip through the meadow?

Suicide.

The image I'd seen at the ruins flashed through my head. Skye lying on black rock, eyes closed forever, claimed by the darkness. Nil wanted her *dead.*

How could she not see it?

Skye was already walking away, toward where Paulo stood beside Thad. The two talked in low tones that Skye obliterated without introduction.

"Paulo. I have a question. Do you know of a cave or cavern on the far side of the island? Like if I drew a line from the Looking Glass Cavern across the island, what would I hit?"

"Other than the meadow?" Paulo thought for a moment. "Nothing."

"Are you sure?" Skye lifted her chin but I felt her rush of disappointment.

"Positive. As far as I know, there's nothing on that side of the island but the platform. And the mountain, of course."

Skye fell silent.

Skye turned to me, her eyes full of determination. I knew that look. It said I may as well start packing.

"Rives, I have to go," she said, her tone adamant. "To rule it out. Just because Paulo doesn't know of it or we haven't seen it doesn't mean it's not there." She paused. "And we actually don't need to go direct. We can skirt the base of the mountain and drop down below the platform to the coast, rather than going through the meadow." She cocked her head at me. "Deal?"

"Deal." *As in package. As in two for one. As in if you're going to risk your life, I'm going to be right there with you.*

She smiled as she rolled her eyes. "No need to be so melodramatic. It's just another hike. No big deal."

"Right. I'll be sure to file away the wolves and the tigers and the hyenas in the *no big deal* column of Nil." I shot her a pointed look.

"I will come and feed the tigers," Dominic said soberly.

"You *want* to be a tiger treat?" Zane looked confounded.

"I am not the treat, but the fish I catch are. I toss fish into the meadow to keep the big cats happy. So far, so good." Dominic smiled.

"So crazy," Thad murmured.

"Amen, brother," Zane agreed, his eyes wide on Dominic.

Thad turned to Skye. His gaze was wary. "So when do we leave?"

"Tomorrow." Skye spoke the word with finality. "We leave at dawn. We only have six weeks until the equinox gate and we don't have a minute to waste." She glanced around. "Has anyone seen Lana?"

Paulo pointed up the beach, toward the trees. Skye strode off, her steps full of purpose.

"Scary Pam," Zane mumbled.

Paulo watched Skye go, his arms crossed, lips closed tight. Normally calm, he looked worried. *No*, I corrected myself. He looked disturbed.

"What's running through your head, Paulo?" I asked. "And does it have to do with Skye, or Lana?"

"Both." He sighed. "I don't think this trip will be as easy as Skye thinks. It's one thing to travel the island for clues; it's another to go to the mountain—the heart of the island." He shook his head. "The island didn't like that we tried to leave as a group last time, that we tried to cut off its lifeline. I know that in my soul, just as I know noon is close. And while the animals have left us alone in the City lately, Nil's paying full attention. Maybe it's trying to lull us into complacency; I don't know. But I don't think that equinox departure will be smooth, or this trip. And if this trip is easy, that worries me even more." His voice grew quiet. "I worry the island is biding its time."

Damn, I thought. Paulo had a solid point. Every move Nil made here was calculated. Point, counterpoint. Pawn, king. It had been quiet in the City, too quiet.

What the hell was Nil up to?

"Whoa," Zane said. He'd paled under his tan. "Talk about a downer. Not exactly the pre-trip pep talk, dude. I'm thinking you could cross motivational speaker off your career list. No offense," he added hastily.

"None taken." Paulo grinned but his eyes remained troubled. "Go team. Better?"

"Totally. I really felt that, here." Zane thumped his chest.

Paulo laughed, then looked away toward Carmen. His grin vanished. And then the breeze stilled.

CHAPTER 51

NIL
NOON

The group conferred among themselves, consumed with plotting and planning and other meaningless minutiae. Intent on searching for answers they would never find, the humans had grown rather boring.

Yes, the island mused, it was time for some fun.

After all, it was noon.

It was the best hour to bleed.

Paulo glanced at Carmen. She smiled, feigning politeness, but before her bland mask slipped into place, he glimpsed the hate on her face. He didn't trust her. He didn't care for her much either. She played the part of a team player, but not well. Paulo didn't understand why she bothered to pretend at all.

People only pretended when they had something to hide. He watched her, carefully, waiting for a slip.

The air stilled, as if the very breeze itself had been inhaled.

Rives noticed the lull at the same moment Paulo did.

"Gate at one o'clock," Rives said abruptly. "Mid-beach."

Paulo spun to look. Above the sand, a gate stretched to its full height and locked into place, then an eerie, utterly still moment passed before it began to roll. The wild gates still unsettled Paulo; thinner than the solstice gate, the wild gates writhed and glittered and *moved*, shifting as if they were alive, like heat-seeking missiles.

Out of the corner of his eye, Paulo saw Amara take off toward the gate, spear in hand, feet flying, face set. One second later, Carmen gave chase, a few meters behind.

"Carmen, stop!" Paulo yelled, jumping toward Carmen and waving his arms. "Let her take it!"

The gate writhed and glittered over the sand.

Come, it whispered gleefully. *Run.*

Fine, Paulo thought. *I'll run. But not for the gate.*

Amara closed the gap to the gate; so did Carmen. Cutting diagonally, Paulo tackled Carmen just as Amara leaped into the gate. Amara flickered inside the iridescent light, her face shifting from fight to relief. The gate winked out; Amara's spear lay on the sand. Carmen spun toward Paulo, her scowl furious. "How dare you! That was *mine!*"

"No, it wasn't," Paulo said, his voice rising. "The gate would've killed you."

"I would have made it *first*," she spat.

"Feel free to try again," Rives said courteously. "It's a double. Gate number two just dropped in." He pointed. The second gate glittered at the tree line as it locked into place.

Carmen scrambled to her feet and took off running. Near the trees, only a few meters from the gate, Lana stumbled backward, away from the gate, a tiny kitten in her arms. With a muffled squeak, the tabby clawed its way free. It streaked toward the gate as Lana's jaw dropped.

"Kitten's gonna win," Zane murmured.

Carmen realized it too. With a frustrated scream, she hurled her blade at the iridescent wall as the kitten crossed the rippling edge. The kitten shimmered; Carmen's aim was true. The blade would pierce the animal's heart.

White light flared like a firecracker.

The knife shot back with lethal force, slashing Carmen's bicep, leaving a shiny ruby line in its wake. She shrieked; the blade fell. Blood dripped onto the sand, thick and red.

"A third?" Thad's eyes swept the beach, his bearing tense and alert.

"Don't think so," Rives said. "The breeze is back." He strolled up to Carmen and plucked the knife out of the sand.

"That's mine!" she snapped.

"Actually it's not. At least, not anymore." He handed her a strip of cloth. "For your arm."

She took it, reluctantly.

"Listen, Carmen, we all want to bail. But you could've killed yourself or someone else with your little knife trick." He raised the knife. "I'll be keeping this. And if I were you, I'd think twice before racing after every gate you see."

"I'm not you." Her words were cold.

"Obviously." Rives's cordial expression did not match his eyes. "One more thing. I don't care what you do, or where you go. But, I'd appreciate it if you didn't kill anyone. It makes Nil too happy."

Lana watched Carmen stalk off. In her wake, blood dotted the sand like paint, like the bear's blood to the north.

Lana shivered.

Her arms felt empty. She missed her kitten. She'd been taking care of him ever since the bear attack, and she couldn't imagine what possessed her tabby to jump from the safety of her arms into a wild gate. Somehow it felt like a message. A reminder, a three-prong warning.

Wake up, it said. *Nothing is permanent.*

Don't get attached.

Too late, she thought.

She wasn't sure if she was thinking about the kitten or something else. Someone else.

At least Carmen hadn't killed the poor kitten. That girl was crazy.

Skye walked up the beach, closing the distance between them, but Skye's eyes were trained on the mountain. It occurred to Lana that Skye looked tired, but more striking was the fact that Skye was *alone*. Normally she had someone with her. Lana couldn't figure out why Skye drew so many people to her, how she had so many *friends*. Her extreme nosiness and insistence on meddling was an incredible turnoff as far as Lana was concerned. Skye turned her gaze to Lana as she approached.

"Are you okay?" Skye asked.

"I should be asking you that. You look—" Lana cocked her head at Skye. "Stressed."

"I *am* stressed, Lana. And you know why. We're running out of time to figure this place out. We're going back toward the mountain tomorrow, to search the east coast. The southeast coast." Skye's sigh was heavy. "We're going to look for the balance to the Looking Glass Cavern. Unfortunately Paulo doesn't know a thing about it."

"He wouldn't know." Lana's tone dripped ice. "Obviously."

Skye looked lost.

"Because he's a boy," Lana said with exasperation.

"So?" Skye frowned.

She is so slow, Lana thought. No wonder she found nothing.

"So," Lana said as if talking to a child, "the island only gifts Sight to women."

"So Paulo hasn't seen where the place is." Skye cocked her head. "But you have? Where is it?"

Lana lifted her chin. "Reflection before Sight, Skye. The island will call you to the Pool of Sight if you're ready, if you're to know. If the island doesn't call . . ." Lana shrugged.

"So, you know where this place is but you won't tell me." Skye's eyes sparked with anger.

"I have not been called yet; maybe I never will be." Lana's bored expression turned defiant. "But for this journey, you're on your own."

And so am I, Lana thought, turning away.

Molly had watched the entire scene with Carmen unfold. As Rives strode away from Carmen, Molly turned to Calvin.

"You would have beaten Amara to that gate," she said. "You're so fast. Why didn't you go for it?"

He rubbed his head. "Paulo says those running gates dump you anywhere. I could end up in Antarctica, you know?" He shrugged. "Seems like it's better to wait six weeks for a sure thing than take a wild card early."

"I'm not convinced there is such a thing as a sure thing." She spoke slowly. Thoughtfully. "Not here, not anywhere."

"So you think I should've run for it?" Calvin asked, frowning.

"No." Her voice was certain. "I think you did the right thing. But I think if you had felt the right thing to do was run, then the answer would be different."

"She is right," Hafthor interjected. "You must listen to the voice inside. You must go when the time is right." He shook his head slightly. "When it is *your time*." He gestured to Carmen's retreating back. "Today was not her time, but almost."

Hafthor nodded. Without another word, he walked away.

"Damn," Calvin said in the silence that followed. "That was intense."

Privately, Molly agreed. An uneasy sensation grew in the pit of her stomach as she watched Hafthor kneel on the sand.

Had Hafthor been talking about escape, or death?

On the beach, Carmen's blood splattered the sand, a macabre Pollock-esque rendering of the scene moments before. As he neared the blood, Hafthor felt the ground shiver. He knelt, overcome by a profound awareness.

The hidden people are not happy, he thought, and they grew more unhappy by the minute.

He felt as though he were a trespasser, even though he'd never chosen to come. He felt unwanted. And yet he also felt highly *desired*, in a way that made his blood run colder than winter in Iceland.

He glanced toward the mountain. *Perhaps I should make an offering*, he thought. *Something to appease the hidden people.*

He glanced back at the sand. Carmen's blood was gone. Absorbed by the sand, by the island, as if the blood had never spilled in the first place. The white sand glittered as pure as the fresh chill down his spine.

Offering already accepted, Hafthor realized. *Or taken.*

The thought did not sit well. Neither did the ones that followed, but those thoughts, those *orders*, he would not ignore.

He'd been summoned.

The island devoured each emotion, greedy for more. It reveled in the frustration and worry, the anger and the pain.

But more than anything else, the island reveled in the fighter's blood. It had expected the male's blood, the one who had stayed before: Paulo. But he had misunderstood the island's call. The island was certain the fighter would have bested him with a blade to the heart, spilling first his blood and later, his electria. But these humans were unpredictable. Volatile, and in their own human way, unique.

Still, they all bled.

And soon enough, they all would.

CHAPTER
52

SKYE
41 DAYS UNTIL THE AUTUMNAL EQUINOX, BREAKING DAWN

Zane prowled around the City. He was more restless than I was, which said something considering I'd woken well before dawn and had been dying to leave ever since. And Zane wasn't the one leaving—that was me.

He stopped me on his third pass. "Skye, have you seen Lana? I can't find her."

"I haven't. But I don't think she was planning on coming, do you?"

"No. But I've surfed with her at dawn every day for almost three weeks, just me and her. I just thought—" He stopped. "I don't know. That she would've at least waited to say good-bye or something."

I frowned. "Why? Where are you going?"

"I wasn't talking about me. I was talking about Lana. She's gone."

"*Gone?*"

He nodded. He ran his hands through his messy bleached hair, perpetually stiff with salt. Eyes closed, he gave the whisper of a laugh. "Want to hear something crazy? I don't know if I like her because *I* like her or because Nil's screwing with my head. Seriously *in* my head. I mean, do I like her because she's the most badass surfing Betty I've ever ridden a wave with, and because together we're riding swells that make my hometown waves look like a kiddie pool? And she's smart and funny when she's not trying to be some version of a Maaka island mystic? Or do I like her because I dream about her, because this place won't let me stop thinking about her?" He looked at me as if he needed an answer and hoped I might have one tucked in my satchel. "I don't know, Skye. It's so messed up. Which Lana is the one I know?"

"Maybe they both are." I smiled, hopefully reassuringly. "Maybe they're not so different. Trust your head, but most of all, trust your heart." *Because the island doesn't have one,* I thought.

Or does it?

As we left with first light, I thought of all that Zane didn't say. That he suspected he and Lana were *more*—and that somehow he knew her absence meant more too.

Lana's gone, I thought.

I felt the truth of it, that she'd left the City. Maybe permanently.

I couldn't help but wonder if she'd received the call she'd been waiting for. Me, I was traipsing off uninvited, and I wasn't crashing the Nil party alone. I had Rives, Thad, Davey, Hafthor, Molly, Paulo, and Kenji. Hafthor had switched with Calvin at the last minute, sticking close to Paulo with the most serious of bearings. This time we didn't have even numbers, but then again, it wasn't really my choice to turn people away. And part of me thought the more eyes the better. Maybe someone else would see what I couldn't.

Yesterday Dominic had volunteered to come, even though I knew he had serious reservations about walking inland. I wasn't sure if he'd changed his mind about joining us after all, because when it was time to leave, he was as absent as Lana.

Look, Skye.

Look for what you don't see.

Every step, every minute, I heard the whisper, felt the pull. I never *stopped* looking as we walked.

We passed quickly through the Flower Field, where color patterns shifted with the breeze, and onto the ancient lava flow to the south, where cracks fissured the gray ground like a deadly web. To the north, red gleamed, another lava flow, newer yet still older than I could possibly guess; it tinted the sky rust. The cliffs of the southern shore guarded the side on our right, a dusting of black that ended in Nil sky; beyond them the ocean boomed with reassuring constancy.

Look, crooned the breeze.

Look for what you don't see.

"I don't see any animals, Rives," I said slowly. It was early afternoon. "Not even small ones. Not even a mouse."

"No people either," Rives observed.

"It's like the island is helping us," I said.

"Or herding us." His voice was grim.

"I pick the former," I said, smiling.

"I know you do." His jaw stayed tight. His eyes never rested as he swept our surroundings, like me. But I wasn't sure we were looking for—or seeing—the same things.

Another step, another hour, one rolling into the next. The sun grew warmer, and stronger. One by one we all wrapped our shoulders and heads with cloth to ward off a major burn. The gentle breeze stayed steady, blowing from the south; nothing changed but the scenery. Boulders shifted and changed, morphing in size and shape from one mile to the next, clumps of scrub brush crouched without moving. There were no animals, gates, or people. The lack of life was eerie, even for Nil.

The rusty red to our left faded; the black lava field around us gave way to tangled thickets and tall grass. Green shoots filled the meadow, hope rising from the ashes.

"Tiger," Kenji said abruptly, pointing with his bokken. At the far end of the meadow, the massive striped cat stood as still as death, facing us.

Davey swore. He turned to me and Rives. "Now what? Go back?"

"I think we're okay," I said.

"You think?" Davey raised his brows. "Bloody big risk to take on a hunch, Skye."

"Woman's intuition," Molly interjected with a wink. "And experience." She turned to me. Her levity faded. "This is the same tiger that let you go last time, right?"

I looked back at the tiger. *Was* this the same one?

For one long moment, I swear he looked at me. Just *me*, his big golden eyes somber and keen, as if he knew all there was to know, as if he were wishing for me to see.

Then the moment passed.

He swung his head toward the coast and snatched something out of the air.

"Bloody *hell*. Did you see that?" Davey gaped. "That big kitty just grabbed a fish out of the air."

Hafthor squinted. "A grouper." He nodded, as if the airborne fish snack was unsurprising. "Dominic is here."

The tiger lay down with his catch, literally.

"Let's go." I spoke with confidence I felt. "Hug the mountain, and we'll be fine."

"It feels right," Hafthor said quietly. "Here, the hidden people are not unhappy."

"And that worries me," Rives said as he looked around.

Single file, we circled the mountain, keeping the slope on our right. The tiger watched us as he ate his lunch.

We passed the rock bearing the Bull's-eye carving and kept walking, hugging the mountain, working our way around to the steps leading up to the platform. Creeping up the mountain, the steps angled away, angled *back*, toward the platform just out of sight.

I walked past the steps to the coastline's edge and peered down. On a line directly across from the base of the steps that led to the platform, another pair of steps curved down. Camouflaged among black rock, the subtle path was easy to miss, especially if you weren't looking.

But I was, now.

And every instinct I had told me that these steps led to more than another Nil beach. Excitement flooded my veins as I spun around to face Rives, smiling like the crazy girl I wasn't.

"Isn't this cool? These steps have to lead somewhere important. After all, the matching set leads to the platform, right?"

I started down but Rives pulled me back. "Hang on a sec," he said. He peered over the cliff's edge, his expression flickering between anxiety and dread.

"You worry too much," I teased. I squeezed Rives's hand, willing him to feel the rightness of the moment, knowing he would *if he just stopped worrying*. "Trust me; we're where we're supposed to be; I *feel* it." I stood on my tiptoes and kissed him fiercely. And then I pulled back.

"I love you," I said, placing my hand on his heart for one steady beat. "Now let's go!"

I was first down the steps, Rives and Molly just behind me.

"Oh," Molly breathed. "It's gorgeous."

It was. At the bottom of the cliff, I stared in wonder. Chunky rocks glistened like black jewels jutting above the water, covered in spray from crashing waves. To the left, clustered into a long oval shape, the rocks formed an open-air swimming pool, completely enclosed. The breeze blew, wafting a hint of sulfur.

"I know this place!" Paulo snapped his fingers. "The hot springs. My brother told me about it. This pool is heated by the volcano, so it's warm."

"Warm or hot?" Hafthor frowned.

"Warm."

Behind the pool, a long ledge ran along the cliff's base, like a knee wall; it disappeared around the corner of the bay, curving out of sight. Near the far end, a hole gaped at us, the opening of something.

Look.

I started over, walking along the ledge. Rives grabbed my arm from behind. "Skye, *stop*. Look at the entrance." He gestured ahead. "Dead animals. And bones. Something's already in there, something that might still be hungry. Maybe that's where all the small animals went." He shot me a pointed look.

I squinted at the opening, and sure enough, Rives was right. Bleached bones lay scattered around the entrance, along with a freshly killed raccoon. I was desperate to *know*, but I didn't want a run-in with a predator, either.

No other caves were in sight.

"There must be another cave," I said stubbornly. "There has to be."

"Maybe. Maybe not." He looked north. "I'll scout out around the corner." He glanced at Thad, who nodded, then Rives raised an eyebrow at me. "Stay clear of that cave, okay?" And the unspoken: *Don't do anything stupid.*

"Stop telling me what to do," I said irritably. "And for the record, I don't have a death wish." I glared at him.

He smiled. "I know." His eyes grew flinty. "But Nil does."

"That's a good thing. We want Nil to die, remember?" I waved my hand. "Go. Be careful."

After giving me a long look, Rives went, with Thad and Paulo by his side. Hafthor, Molly, and Davey waded into the pool.

I slid into the water, using the time alone to think. Warm water wrapped me in comfort, too deep to stand. Hanging on to the ledge, I relaxed, listening to Molly laugh and Davey crack jokes, wondering where Dominic was and why Hafthor was so silent.

Look for what you don't see.

It's under the water, I thought suddenly. *Just like the Looking Glass Cavern.*

I slipped under the surface.

I swam forward, passing the legs of Hafthor and Molly and Davey in the clear water as I felt along the edge, swimming south, leaving the cave with dead bones at the entrance behind. Up ahead, with a gap as wide as a car, an opening in the rocks beckoned.

Come.

I was being called.

With a deep breath, I swam into the hole, feeling my way with my hands and pulling myself along. I surfaced into a small cavern, in the midst of a pool the size of a hot tub. Light leaked from an opening on the far side. Molly popped up beside me and tapped me on the shoulder.

"You're mental, you know that?" She grinned.

I laughed. "Not a bit."

Slowly, my eyes adjusted to the dim light.

"Isn't that the same carving that's in that other cave?" Molly said. "The Looking Glass one?" She pointed to the wall, where a single carving watched us: a large eye, five feet across at least, etched inside a diamond. No other carvings were in sight. This cave was significantly smaller than the one housing the Looking Glass pool on the other side of the island, but still had one striking similarity: a passageway, curving inland, curving back, toward the mountain—just past the carving of the eye. It was the source of the light.

"I'm going in," I told Molly, climbing out of the water and peeking into the passageway. At its end, light beckoned.

Molly followed.

"For the record, this might be a bad idea," she said.

"For the record, so noted." I couldn't stop smiling. It didn't feel like a bad idea; it felt like the most perfect idea in the world, the natural thing to do. The *right* thing to do.

I felt the rightness of this moment in the very essence of me.

We made it through the passageway quickly. Now we stood inside another cavern, one with a pool of water bigger than the last; it matched the size and shape of the pool in the Looking Glass Cavern exactly. It too had a skylight, just like the Looking Glass Cavern, but no water poured into the cavern from the hole, only light.

This cavern *radiated* light.

"This is it," I whispered reverently.

The water's surface shimmered like mercury glass, infused with light, not unlike the iridescence of a gate—but richer. Deeper. Like it could birth a gate, like it held *life*.

Color rippled beneath the water's surface, shifting into silver and then disappearing altogether. The water turned clear and pure, then another hint of color would sparkle. Silver flashed. Colors and light and metal swirled and vanished; the water glittered like a diamond.

I was utterly bewitched.

"What is this place?" Molly asked. She was looking at the walls surrounding the pool. They were pristine, not a carving in sight. If human hands had touched them, they'd left no sign.

"I don't know." I crouched, mesmerized by the liquid light. I had the urge to touch the pool, like I'd wanted to stroke the captivating onyx of the incoming gate near Black Bay. The water rippled inches from my hand, like a diamond pulse.

Skye. Whispers in my head crooned like warm silk, begging, wanting.

Look.

See.

I held my hand over the water. In response, the water's surface brightened, the colors beneath rippling and twinkling and shifting faster. More flashes of silver, more light.

Yessss, it seemed to say. *Touch.*

"Skye, I don't think you should touch it." Molly's voice was worried.

"It's okay." Molly didn't understand, not like I did. I *had* to touch it. I had to *see.*

I gently touched the water with one finger. It felt more thick than wet. Before I could blink, my entire hand was sucked beneath the surface.

My mind exploded into a fireball of color and light and sound.

Me, crouched by the pool, aching to see; Molly, reaching for me, her eyes wide in fear. Rives, spinning around, his face draining of color.

More.

Thad, watching Rives stumble, dread squeezing Thad's lungs; Paulo, shouting for me, the sea stealing his words. Hafthor, leaving the water, certainty in his steps; Davey, searching for Molly, fear in his heart. Lana, facing the mountain, shock on her face; Carmen, glaring at the meadow, hate in her heart. A boy named Dai, curled on the sand, sick with fever.

More.

Charley, begging Rika, Uncle Scott's journal in her hands. My dad, closing his eyes, lifting up prayers.

More.

Davey, staring at Molly, aching for her. Charley, touching Thad's scar, aching for him. Rives, smiling at me, aching for us.

Zane, surfing beside Lana, riding sheer hope.

Jillian, clinging to Rives, tears in her eyes.

A boy with hair like fire, bleeding on the sand.

A girl with hair like obsidian, collapsing on the rocks.

Charley, falling into a gate, a scream on her lips.

Thad, his torso dark with blood, a cheetah on his shoulders.

A girl with strawberry-blond hair, setting a boy's broken arm.

A boy with dark hair, staring at his reflection.

A boy with a shell necklace, sleeping forever.

Images played and time blurred, running backward, forward, sometimes horizontally.

And then everything stopped.

It was the beginning.

The choice, and the chosen. The island unfolded, the bloom of a new bud. The first gate rose, blossoming like a flower on the first day of spring.

There was the prince, regal and brave, striding through the first gate, curiosity and hope in his heart, a snow-white cat following one heartbeat later. The gate closed; the interval chosen. There was the prince, standing tall, marveling at the island's beauty and peace, his strength and respect for the earth flowing to the island and leaving a mark. There was the princess, waiting outside, head held high despite the fear in her heart, demonstrating a different kind of strength.

A new time, a new gate. The prince and princess together again, revealing the unbreakable power of a pair.

I saw it all and felt the same. One after another, the island's memories became mine, trapped in my head for me to see and understand and *feel*. Every word spoken, every thought, every choice made. Every victory, every defeat.

Every life.

Every death.

More, the island whispered.

CHAPTER 53

RIVES
41 DAYS UNTIL THE AUTUMNAL EQUINOX, NEAR TWILIGHT

Pain ripped through me, cutting and visceral; it sliced so deep it stole my breath and I stumbled. Only the brutal pain wasn't mine—it was Skye's.

Something terrible was happening.

She never promised.

"Skye!" I screamed.

And then I ran.

CHAPTER 54

NIL
TWILIGHT

The one called Skye hovered at the breaking point.

For a whisper of time, the island hesitated, unsure how much she could handle. To shatter her mind would be excruciating and wasteful, yet without the cruelest memory of all, the rest would be worthless. She would not understand, she would not see.

Either way, there would be a cost. The island understood that, and if she survived, she would come to understand that too.

The island had no choice left.

It would borrow from the humans, borrow the emotion they called hope. It would hope the one called Skye was as strong as the island believed her to be, that her mind would not break.

For the first time, the island opened itself fully to a human: it let the one called Skye see.

Everything.

CHAPTER 55

SKYE

41 DAYS UNTIL THE AUTUMNAL EQUINOX, TWILIGHT

The protective boundaries of my mind shattered. Crystal walls imploded, fragile after all; shards rained down like ice, cold and cutting and slicing through every cell of me. Darkness poured in, unrestricted.

Unrestrained.

The pain was excruciating, as it would have been. Was. Is.

And in that moment, I understood.

I understood *everything*.

Too much.

CHAPTER 56

RIVES

Skye!

Nothing.

No response, not even a whisper. I couldn't hear her. Couldn't feel her. My mind filled with worst-case scenarios, raging out of control. Only my legs worked properly. Pumping, scrambling, running, doing whatever it took to get back to her.

I whipped around the cliff's corner and nearly knocked Davey down. "Where are they?" I grabbed his shoulders. "Where's Skye?"

"I was coming to get you. Follow me."

He stepped off the ledge and switched to freestyle, kicking hard. I followed. Beneath the water, he pointed to an opening in the rocks, one similar to the oceanside exit of the Looking Glass Cavern.

I hurtled through the underwater passage. When I surfaced into clear air, I heard my name.

"Rives!" Molly's shout was an echo. It bounced around, ricocheting off rock. "In here!"

In here. In here. In here.

"Rives!" she shouted again. Fear laced her shout, reminiscent of another shout before: Miya's. A lifetime ago, lived by a different Rives.

Molly's shout faded. I scrambled out of the water and into the dank opening, following the echo and the light. When I burst into the widening space—another cavern, bigger, full of light—Molly lifted her tear-stained face to me. Skye lay in Molly's arms, eyes closed, head and body still.

I dropped to Skye's side. Her skin burned hot, like she had a fever.

Gently, I brushed Skye's cheek with my thumb. "Skye?" I whispered, my chest tight.

Nothing.

I looked up at Molly. "What happened?"

"Skye found this place, and I followed her. First the cavern with the eye, then this one. There was water. She touched it, and it sucked her entire arm in, up to her elbow. The water lit up like liquid sunlight, like it was happy. I *felt* it was happy, ecstatic even. But Skye's face went white. I pulled her out as fast as I could. Rives . . ." She swallowed. "Skye only put her hand in the pool for a moment, I promise. Maybe five seconds at the most. But she hasn't moved since." Molly glanced around. "And the pool disappeared."

"Disappeared," I repeated.

Molly nodded. "It seeped into the ground, like it was never here." She pointed across the cavern. The bottom was bone dry.

No evidence left of Nil's poison, just the victim.

Skye.

We were trapped inside Nil ground.

I lifted Skye from Molly's arms into mine. "I'm going to stay here with her until she wakes up." *If she wakes up*, came the cruel whisper.

Molly was still looking at me. I said, "She can't swim out when she's unconscious. Tell Thad, okay?"

Molly nodded, and left.

Skye didn't move, other than breathing.

Mine. Mine. Mine, whispered the breeze.

No, I thought fiercely. She was in *my* arms, in *my* soul. But Skye belonged to no one: not me, and definitely not Nil. Her will and spirit were hers alone.

Thad showed up, breathing hard. His eyes went directly to Skye. "How's she doing?"

"Not good. I think she might have a fever."

I felt so helpless. Didn't know what the hell was wrong, didn't know how to help.

Thad sat down and leaned his back against the wall, getting comfortable, like he planned to stay awhile.

"You don't have to stay," I told him.

"I know." He closed his eyes.

A long minute passed.

"Thanks," I said.

"Not necessary, brother," Thad said. "We're getting out of this together. All of us."

Inside the cavern, night fell. Time passed. Skye didn't stir. The light faded completely and the noise in my head grew.

Rivessssss . . .

She's mine, snarled the darkness. *I've touched her. Felt her. Claimed her.*

No, I lashed out. Lashed *back. She is* not *yours, and she never will be. Too late.*

The two words echoed in my head. Laughter followed, smug and satisfied; it bounced off cerebral walls, burying deep.

Hour after hour, taunt after taunt.

Skye didn't wake.

Dawn broke, shooting light into the cavern. Skye lay as still as death, her skin still hot. Thad looked like he'd pulled an all-nighter, like me. My mouth was dry. My head, bruised.

"Thad, we have to get her out of here. Now."

"No argument there, brother. Just tell me how."

CHAPTER 57

NIL
DAWN

Toying with the male, Rives, had been exceptionally fun. He was so vulnerable, so emotive, his greatest weakness easily read and just as easily manipulated. The island had baited him until he stopped responding, forcing the island to look elsewhere for fun.

Taunting the male, Thad, had been less rewarding. His link with his mate buffered his mind; there were few cracks, no fissures. No open window for fear to pass through.

And the female, Skye, had refused to play at all. The link to her mate fractured, her mind had shut down, gone blank.

Unsatisfying, the island thought. And unproductive.

Perhaps that was why when the male, Hafthor, called to the trio through a sliver of rock, the island cared little if they heard or answered. The island had lost interest in entertainment; instead it sought power. It needed the latter to have the former.

Power first, it decided.

The island turned toward the male, Dai, hovering as he clung to life. The island quivered, anticipating the final slip, the one that would mark him as the island's forever.

CHAPTER 58

SKYE

40 DAYS UNTIL THE AUTUMNAL EQUINOX, DAWN

Everything felt raw: my head, my limbs, my heart. Every cell in my body *ached*.

It took a monumental effort to open my eyes. Around me, ghosts moved and swirled, their stories now mine, etched on my brain for life. Rives stared at me, as real as the ghosts, as if I'd conjured him up too.

"Skye." His eyes burned too bright. "Are you hurt?"

Hurt, I thought. Such an insignificant word. *Hurt* couldn't begin to describe what had happened to me; *hurt* barely brushed the surface. My brain had been turned inside out and set on fire; my body, too.

"I'm so tired." My voice sounded different. Thin, and distant. Hollow.

The light in the cavern dimmed.

"Hello?" Hafthor's voice rang down from above.

"Down here!" Rives called.

Hafthor's face filled the skylight, completely blocking the light. "I found this opening. I think I can enlarge it, and you can lift Skye up through the hole to me. Stand back."

Rives shielded me with his body, the warmth of his chest pressing close. Blistering fear and want seared through me with his touch.

Too much.

I closed my eyes. Around us, pebbles fell like rain; I felt the shower of dirt and rock as Hafthor pounded away at the rock above. *Stop*, I wanted to say. This place was sacred, a place that should not be disturbed. And yet, it also felt right. The radiance I'd felt before was gone; something had shifted.

It *hurt* to be awake.

I woke hours later in Hafthor's arms. We were moving through the grayed lava field, under a scorching Nil sky. The light stung my eyes, making me shut them as quickly as I'd opened them.

Around me, everyone was talking about *me*.

She's burning up.

Is she in a coma?

What did the water do to her?

It wasn't water; it was something else.

Eyes closed, I let it all sink in. Now wasn't the time to wake or talk. I couldn't begin to discuss what happened until I'd sorted through it myself. I retreated, into myself; I sifted through one memory at a time, knowing it was too much to absorb at once. It was still too much. Minutes and moments played and shifted, bits of the past seeking traction in the present.

Time passed, my mind a mess, my mental walls in shambles, unable to be rebuilt. It didn't matter; the barriers were no longer necessary. There was no need to keep out what had already poured in.

I retreated deeper, away from the past, away from the present. Away from *me*. I found a place deep inside me, untouched by Nil. No color, no sound, just pure white walls. Impenetrable.

Mine.

In that quiet moment, in my private room of clean white walls empty of all but me, I breathed. I rested. And then everything clicked.

The past and present merged into one; the depth and breadth of clarity was stunning. This moment, this *now*, was yesterday's future.

And I needed to see tomorrow.

Flinging open the door, I stepped outside my private room. The whiteness fell away; memories roared back. Around me broken pieces tumbled together, the past reforming into a portrait of the future. The lines vanished; the pieces became one.

One future. Two paths.

I saw the path less taken.

In that clear moment, I knew exactly what to do, what had to be done.

CHAPTER
59

Hafthor carried Skye the entire way back.

I protested, but Hafthor refused to relent. "I am to do this," he'd said in a calm but unshakable tone. "The island told me. It is what she needs."

More like what the island wants, I thought bitterly. *Keeping us apart, creating distance between us.*

Nil was plotting and planning and using us all.

My fists ached from clenching them. I shook them out, watching Skye's head lie motionless against Hafthor's chest. At least the guy was a beast, Iceland's version of Captain America. I knew he wouldn't drop her, I just wanted to be the one holding her.

Our trip back was as uneventful as our trip out. I catalogued a horse, a buffalo, a lemur, and a giraffe. Skye would've caught the irony, but her eyes were shut tight.

Back in the City, Hafthor put Skye in her bed. I sat with her, holding her hand. She looked smaller somehow, tucked under a sheet.

Please wake up.

Her color actually looked decent, but her skin still ran hot. And her mind was untouchable. No more dark wall, just—nothing.

Our link was gone.

Thad and Molly checked on us throughout the night. I dozed off and on, sleeping only because I'd been awake the entire night before. At least here in the City, Nil let me sleep. No whispers, no taunts.

I hoped it wasn't messing with Skye's head. *In* Skye's head.

I feared it already had.

Nil stealing time, Nil stealing lives.

Nil was a cruel thief, taking without remorse. Taking without any thought or regard for others, its pleasure its sole focus.

Nil's selfish, I realized abruptly.

Knowledge was power. The question was, how could I use that revelation to beat it?

Zane and Molly came in the next morning with water.

"Chief, you need some fluids. And some food. And no doubt a bathroom break."

"I'll stay with her while you scoot out for a bit," Molly added.

I was back in less than ten minutes.

"No breakfast?" Zane asked, eyeing my empty hands.

"Not hungry," I said. I sat down beside Skye. Her eyes were still closed, her breath even, her skin hot. I gently wove my fingers back through hers. Skye didn't move.

"Unreal," Zane said, staring at Skye. "Thad filled me in. Said Skye and Molly here found a super special secret cavern. Then Skye touched the liquid RoboCop, it zapped her, and she's pretty much been like this ever since."

"Not sure about the RoboCop part, but the rest is about it." Molly nodded.

"Did you ever see Lana?" Zane's eyes were hopeful.

"No Lana, no Carmen. No one else. And we learned absolutely nothing."

"You're wrong." Skye's quiet voice made everyone's eyes jerk toward her. She dropped my hand as she sat up slowly, her blond hair Skye-wild, her chin Skye-fierce. But something in her eyes unsettled me. Something foreign. It kept me from wrapping her in my arms.

"How are you feeling?" I asked, fighting the urge to pull her close. I studied her face and body movements for the answer.

"I'm okay." She smiled. The half-moons under her eyes were back, subtle but real. "But there's something I need to tell everyone at once."

She swung her legs over the edge of the bed and stood, then walked outside the hut without looking back. Zane and Molly exchanged a worried glance. Skye took a seat by the firepit, on the largest boulder of a group of three, as everyone gathered around her. I sat beside her, but the island sat between us.

She lifted her chin. "A few minutes ago, I told Rives he was wrong, that we didn't return with nothing. I learned *everything*." She paused, her eyes sweeping across each of us in turn, an eerie glance totally unlike Skye. "When I touched the pool, the island showed me its history, including the stories of all the people who came before." Skye blinked slowly, like she was walling off memories, but her calm expression never changed. "The island was good. Benevolent, at least at first. No"—she shook her head slightly—"that's not right. At first it was just existing. Drifting. It found this place—this *layer* of space, a fragment that mirrors our world—and it paused. It waited. It wasn't good or bad, it just *was*. The first gate opened, drawn by the prince. He taught the island strength and kindness, and then the princess—the next one through the gate, who had waited for him—she taught the island about hope and a different kind of strength. Through that pair, the island discovered depth of love and the incredible power of it, and the power inherent in the balance of the two. Knowledge went both ways."

She exhaled, twisting her hands in her lap.

"It still does." Her voice was quiet. "We have taught the island things. Good things and terrible things. We taught the island about strength and kindness and love, and we taught the island about cruelty and power and pain. And when we unleashed the atomic bombs on that solstice day, we caused the island pain on an incomprehensible level and scope. Unbearable pain, as if the island were burning alive. And in that moment, when the pain became too much, something splintered." She flinched. "Maybe to protect itself, maybe it just happened. But after that, the dark side of Nil grew. And it's been growing ever since."

Zane whistled between his teeth. "So the island's crazy? Literally? Like we're stuck on Sybil?"

Skye took Zane's question seriously because he actually wasn't joking.

"Maybe. I don't know whether the bombs—the *pain*—caused a separate personality to develop in response, or whether the pain supercharged the dark side of Nil, like a boost of nitro. But . . ." She looked thoughtful, enough like Skye to almost make me relax. "I think both sides were there all along. The good and the bad, the dark and the light. But now, the dark side has grown so powerful, it's choking out the light. It feels like we infected the island. Like the bombs caused a disease that can't be cured—and it's getting worse.

"Either way," she continued, "whether it's a cancer growing from within, or whether it's a dark personality taking over, the result is the same: it's getting stronger by the day. It's feeding on us, and it's darker than any of you know." She shuddered. "But that's not the worst part."

"Really? What's worse than this?" Fear sharpened my words. Because *Skye* looked ill again. More—empty.

"The good side's dying," Skye said quietly. Her voice was scary calm, almost clinical. "That's why it wanted me back. To show me the past, so I could understand. The good side has been fighting to keep the dark at bay, and it's losing. It's so weak. It used to help the people who came, guiding them, keeping them safe as they found their own strength. But now, it can barely help. And the weaker the light side gets, the stronger the pull the dark side has into our world. Soon the light side will disappear, for good. And if the dark side wins? It will reach into our world without restraint. Without a barrier, without a consequence. The seam between worlds has weakened too; the good side has been guarding it. If the seam collapses, the consequences will be disastrous."

Everyone was silent.

Firelight bounced off her eyes, but the steel flecks glittered rather than sparked, as if they'd cooled. Despite the heat raging in her skin, some of Skye's fire was gone.

What did Nil do to her?

Nil's light side had shown her the past, but Nil's dark side had snuck in too. Maybe Trojan horse—style; maybe it had just barreled straight in. Either way, despite the split, it was all Nil. *Both* sides wanted her, for different reasons. And I knew full well that the dark side wanted to keep her.

She's mine, it had snarled. *I've already claimed her.*

No, I thought viciously. *Not as long as I'm alive.*

I reached for her hand, and to my relief, she let me hold it.

"And by disastrous, you mean—" Davey broke off.

"I saw the past, not the future," Skye said quietly. "The past simply predicts the future. So while I can't say *precisely* what will happen, I know it will be terrible. If the seam collapses, Nil will bleed into our world and affect it. Permanently. Our world will become Nil's; I think it will become the new Nil. The dark side of Nil, that is. And there will be no light side left to balance it."

"And no way to escape," I said.

"Exactly." Skye nodded.

Another loaded moment of silence followed. The pop of the fire echoed in the stillness like a warning.

"We have to stop it." Paulo's voice was resolute.

Skye nodded again.

"But how?"

"The key was in the Dead City." She cocked her head toward the woods, as if listening, then she looked directly at me. "We have to blow up the island."

CHAPTER
60

The one called Rives understood the island like no other.

He understood that the island was truly one with two faces, with dueling agendas fighting for supremacy. Without his mate voicing the words, deep within himself he already knew the end was written, and he knew the end.

He simply refused to see it.

Perhaps it was a human trait, or perhaps the flaw was personal to the one called Rives.

Perhaps he thought he could change it.

Perhaps he understood he couldn't. Either way, his mind was closed, an unfortunate development. If the one called Rives refused to see, perhaps the one called Lana could benefit from Skye's Sight, or at least learn from it.

The one called Lana certainly knew how to listen.

Lana eavesdropped from behind a cluster of trees. She pressed her homemade amplifier, crafted from a large taro leaf, to her ear.

She had beaten the group to the cliff housing the Pool of Sight, but had waited to enter; Lana hadn't really believed that Skye would find it. She hadn't believed the island would actually call Skye to the Pool, a girl so opinionated and intrusive, and she'd been shocked when the island had gifted Skye with Sight. More shocking still was the fact that Skye had *touched* the Pool. Skye shouldn't have been *able* to touch the Pool; Lana's grandmother had claimed the Pool *couldn't* be touched.

Stretch your hand over the water, her grandmother had advised, *palm down. The water will respond if it approves, and you will feel the Sight rise like liquid air, invisible and warm; it will flow over you, over your mind. You won't touch the water. Indeed, you can't; the water won't allow it, but don't worry, child, touch isn't necessary. If it deems you worthy, the Pool will impart the Sight, which is knowledge of the future. A true gift, given to a chosen few.*

Not me, she thought dismally. *Not now.*

When Lana had entered the cavern, the Pool was gone. Only a dry cave bed remained. Looking at the depression littered with pebbles and chunks of rock, Lana would have wondered if the sacred Pool had ever really existed, but a clear image had coursed through her head: Skye, kneeling beside the Pool, her arm immersed to her elbow.

Skye *had* touched the Pool, just as she'd told the others. Lana knew it to be true; she'd seen it in her mind as clearly as if she'd been there. And Skye had ruined it, just as she knew Skye's friends had ruined the skylight. The cavern ceiling was destroyed, the floor riddled with rocks and chunks of earth.

Would the haoles *ever cease their destructive ways?*

And why had Skye's Sight run in reverse?

Lana wrenched her thoughts back to the group. Skye had paused, tilting her head toward Lana's hiding spot as if she knew Lana was there. A long moment passed, during which Lana was certain Skye would call her out.

But she didn't.

Skye resumed speaking to Rives, as if Lana's presence was unsurprising, or unimportant.

"We have to blow up the island," Skye said calmly.

Lana's mouth fell open in shock. She strode out from the shrubs like a wild beast. "Will you ever stop destroying things?" she exclaimed. She waved her hand. "First the bombs, then the cavern. Now you want to blow up the entire island? What is *wrong* with your people?"

"Back to your people and ours, are we?" Rives's voice was cold.

Skye's expression didn't change.

"Lana." Skye spoke with calm certainty. "The island seeks its own death. Did you not just hear what I shared with the group? That the light side is *dying*, Lana? But the dark side isn't?"

"I heard you," Lana admitted. "But I'm not convinced."

Skye regarded her carefully, then nodded. "I understand." Skye turned to Rives. "Give me a second, okay?" She squeezed his arm, then looked away, but not before Lana caught the acute flash of pain in Skye's eyes, so startling that Lana nearly felt it herself.

What was that? she wondered. Lana was so taken aback that she stood rock still as Skye approached; she actually forgot to move.

"Can I talk to you a minute?" Skye asked softly. "Alone? Maybe at your hiding spot?" Skye's knowing smile was wry.

"Sure."

The two walked away from the group, which started muttering immediately, their words blending into a background noise competing with the ocean.

"Lana." Skye rubbed her temples. "I know you don't care for non-islanders in general, and me specifically. I get it. But listen. I saw . . ." She paused for a moment. "Everything. I know about your aunt, Lina."

Lana jerked in surprise. Skye kept speaking as if nothing had happened.

"I know she ignored the island's call, and that she never received the gift of Sight. I know she'd fallen in love with a boy from Turkey, and that she didn't want to leave him to go to the Pool of Sight, that it was a long journey from where she was, and I know she was scared. I'm not judging, Lana, I'm just telling you what I know. But I also know that if she'd received the gift of Sight, she would have known that the rockslide

314

at the north shore was coming, and two people would've been saved, one being the boy she loved. And I know that she would've known better than to take the wild gate that she did. It opened on the other end, in the middle of a major highway. I know that if she'd received the gift of Sight, she would have survived." Her voice was a whisper. "But she didn't." Skye closed her eyes, her voice a remote whisper. "The island doesn't like to be ignored."

She opened her eyes again. "And the other night, the island called you, but you didn't come in time. You waited to see what we would do. And now you don't have the gift." Skye's tone turned frustrated. "You were supposed to help me. I would see the past; you would see the future. The island only had energy left to bequeath Sight once more, in one episode." She sighed, then lifted her tired gaze to Lana.

"Weeks ago, I told you that you didn't have to do this alone. But now, I do. I have to convince everyone the past is real, and can't be repeated. Time is running out. If you heard me talk, you know I didn't just see your aunt's history, I saw *all* the history. Of the island, of every single person who ever came through a gate, and I felt the suffering. Like it was my own." She swallowed. "And that's just a taste of the island's potential to inflict pain and sorrow. If it creeps into our world, its power will grow exponentially and the damage will be catastrophic. We can't let that happen. We have to end it." Skye's tone had grown so calm, so detached, Lana had the strange urge to shake her. "Make no mistake, Lana, this world as we know it"—Skye waved a lethargic hand around—"will end at the equinox, one way or the other. This chapter of Nil is over. Either we end it, or it ends us, and not just us, but our world as we know it back home. It's a living threat, Lana, but we have the ability to stop it. Right now. So I choose the former. Blow up the island and leave as one." Skye's firm gaze held Lana rooted to the ground. "All I ask is that if you won't join us, please don't stand against us."

Lana said nothing, still processing all that Skye had said.

"The choice is yours." Now the shadow of a smile crossed Skye's face.

"I told Paulo that once." Her gaze stilled completely on Lana, her voice fading like her smile. "Lana, you don't have to like me, or talk to me. But I know you can talk to Paulo, or Zane. Talk to someone, even yourself. Know there is power in whatever choice you make."

Skye started to walk away.

"Skye." Lana spoke quietly.

Skye turned back.

"Why you?" Lana asked.

"Why *not* me?" Skye raised her eyebrows, amused. "But for the record, it could have been you. I guess I just got lucky. Or perhaps the island saw something in us we didn't see in ourselves." She shrugged. "I guess we'll find out." Sadness swirled in her eyes, so profound and moving that Lana's own breath hitched in her chest. "I'm sorry about your aunt." Skye's whisper rippled with pain. "You look like her, you know."

Skye turned away again; Lana stood rooted to the leaf-strewn ground.

Make your own way, her grandmother had told her. *Do not repeat the past.*

Perhaps, Lana considered, as Skye walked away, perhaps she'd misunderstood her grandmother's words entirely.

As Lana watched, Skye took her seat with the group around the firepit. Everyone's voices died at once. Rives stared at her as if she might break; Thad looked pensive. The morning light crept through the trees, painting some faces with golden light, casting others in shadow. All eyes were trained on Skye, including Lana's.

It was as if the entire world were holding its breath.

Something was unfolding right before her eyes. A shift was taking place, right here, right now. Just as Lana knew that she was to stride through that solstice gate last June into the island unknown, Lana understood that this moment was pivotal—that she would either embrace the shift, or stand on the sidelines forever.

Lana, whispered the breeze. *Choose.*

Without hesitation, she walked forward and sat in the only space available: next to Zane.

Davey watched Lana the loner stroll back into camp and plop down next to Zane as if she'd never left. Zane's eyes widened and Davey didn't miss the slight lift of his shoulders. The girl messed with Zane in every which way.

Zane cocked his head at her. "Do I know you? Because you kinda look like this girl I knew; her name's Lana? Dark hair, surfs like a champ? Likes to bail without saying good-bye?"

Lana rolled her eyes.

"And she has a serious attitude." Zane grinned.

"This is lovely," Davey said, breaking into the Zane-Lana dynamic. "Truly touching. But can we get back to the blow-up-the-island plan? And by plan, I mean idea that sounds epically dangerous and not exactly possible. Unless I missed something, there aren't any explosives stashed in the Shack."

"We were *all* missing something," Skye said quietly. "Something invisible, something volatile. The island told me to *look inside*. Well, inside the island is an odorless gas. You can't see it, or smell it. It killed the animals by that cave, and it killed the people in the Dead City while they slept. I saw it happen." She twitched reflexively.

"Makes sense," Thad mused. " 'Look for what you don't see.' "

Paulo was nodding. Rives stayed silent, arms crossed, eyes locked on Skye. Davey guessed that more was going on behind Rives's green eyes than his blank expression revealed. He sat too still, like a coiled spring. Ever since Skye had been lifted out of that pit, Rives reminded Davey of a caged tiger, pacing and waiting and always on edge.

"We couldn't see any evidence of an attack; it was like they died by magic," Skye continued in the same aloof tone. "But it wasn't magic. There was a vent, and gas seeped into the Dead City; eventually an earthquake readjusted the rocks and sealed it from within. The gas pocket runs along

317

the mountain, underground. So if we ignite the gas, the volcano might erupt. At a minimum, the mountain and the platform will be destroyed. We need to light it the night of the equinox gate."

"And you want to be the one who does it." Rives's words cut the air like a hot blade. His face had gone white. "Skye, you'll *die.*"

Skye shook her head. "No. I think we can detonate it remotely, if we can just figure out a fuse. I don't think anyone needs to stay back to light it. That's the worst-case scenario."

Rives didn't look convinced.

"Hashtag fuse. Hashtag flammable. Hashtag remote burn. Hashtag string," Chuck mumbled to himself. He rocked slightly as he talked.

"This idea is way intense," Zane said.

"Hashtag agreed," Davey mumbled.

"Stop it," Molly hissed in Davey's ear. He almost dropped another *hashtag* just to get Molly to lean close again, but he didn't. Chuck wasn't a bad guy, just quirky.

"I think we can do it." Skye's cool tone radiated confidence.

"Really?" Rives asked. "How?"

"Fat lighter," Chuck said abruptly. "We need fat lighter. Dry out twine, rub it with pine sap. Make a sticky fuse. Light one end and *boom.*" He made a large hand motion.

Davey's jaw dropped slightly. Chuck sounded certain, actually convincing.

"Where's the hashtag?" Davey whispered in Molly's ear. Molly poked him. He grabbed her hand. Sparks flew between them. His eyes caught hers, full of heat; Molly dropped his hand like she'd been burned.

No one was looking at them.

"Are there pine trees here?" Thad asked Chuck.

"Yes," Skye and Chuck said together.

Skye nodded. "It sounds like exactly what we need. The only other thing—or person, rather—we need is someone who is fast. Because after they light it, they're going to have to run to the gate. Any volunteers?"

"I guess that's me," Calvin said.

"You don't have to do it, big Cal," Davey said quickly, his head still reeling from Molly. "We can draw straws."

"Yeah, I do." Calvin nodded. Then, unexpectedly, he grinned. "Nobody's faster than me. Hell, now I get to race fire."

Or death, Davey thought worriedly.

Smiling, Molly squeezed Calvin's hand, then blanched.

"Molly, what's wrong?" Davey asked.

"Nothing." Molly tucked her hands tight into her lap. "Just thinking about that plan." She looked up at Calvin. "You are fast, Calvin," she said solemnly. "There is no one faster than you."

"Looks like we have a plan, people." Zane smiled broadly. "Operation Detonation is a go."

CHAPTER
61

SKYE

"Skye." Rives gently took one of my hands in his. "Look at me, please."

I did.

"I don't know what's wrong or how I can help. You're fading away right in front of my eyes, like when we were back home, but here it's worse. Skye—" His voice cracked. "Let me in, let me *help*. Talk to me, Skye. Please don't shut me out."

But I already had. I'd had to, because Rives was the one person who could break me completely.

"I love you, too. More than you know." I closed my eyes and climbed inside my tiny room of pure white walls. The door closed; I was completely alone. Less hurt, less feeling. Less *me*. But at least here I could breathe. Exhaling slowly, I opened my eyes to Rives's pain-filled ones, knowing mine looked blank. "But right now this is about more than us. Trust me to know what the right thing to do is, okay? Trust me to do the right thing."

"For us?" He barely breathed.

"For everyone."

"That's what I'm afraid of." The light left Rives's eyes.

For a moment, time stopped. Seconds fell, untouched, vanishing into the gulf growing between us.

"Rives!" Paulo's shout restarted the clock. "Got a minute?"

Rives dropped my hand, kissed my forehead, and left me sitting alone in the midst of a crowd. I walked to the ocean, drifting slightly north to a pile of black rocks that jutted out. Climbing onto the biggest one, I sat down.

I'd seen too much.

Too many hopes and dreams, too many loves lost, too many hearts broken and minds shattered. I'd seen beauty on a grand scale, and ugly on a microscopic one; I'd observed cruelty and kindness and courage and cowardice. I'd seen every visitor to Nil through Nil's eyes; I'd witnessed each visitor's journey. And I'd felt what Nil felt, mirroring us.

I'd felt the island's growth and change and horror and more.

I'd understood its evolution.

It. Was. Too. Much.

But I couldn't go back, and I couldn't stop *knowing*. New pathways had been forged, new memories seared permanently into place. I was the ultimate accidental voyeur, and I could hardly bear it. I'd never felt so insignificant in my own head—or so overwhelmed.

I dropped my head into my hands.

"Skye?" Thad touched my shoulder like the wind. "Are you okay?"

Not even close.

"No," I said slowly, "I'm not okay. I thought it would get better. That the memories would fade. That the *pain* would fade." I looked at Thad. "But it hasn't. And I don't think it ever will."

Thad was silent at first.

"Rives is worried about you," he said finally.

He should be, I thought.

"I don't know what you're thinking," Thad continued, "but if you need an ear, you can talk to me. I know Charley would be a better listener, but I don't totally suck." His slight grin was crooked.

"Thanks." I looked at him, seeing everything so clearly. "I know you still haven't forgiven me for being here. I understand why. But you truly have my word that I didn't mean for you or Charley or Rives to come back, or me either. But that doesn't mean it wasn't meant to be."

Thad regarded me quietly.

"You need to get Nil out of your head, Skye. Don't listen to it. You're stronger than Nil. Block it out."

"I wish I could," I whispered. Thad couldn't understand, because he hadn't *seen*; he hadn't *felt*. Not like me. But I could show him one tiny drop of the ocean of memories swimming in my head.

Slowly, deliberately, taking care with each syllable and line, I recited words that weren't mine, each one brimming with the pain and desperation and hope saturating the memory behind it:

a cruel joke
a twist of fate
to meet you when it's almost too late
my days are numbered
my clock is ticking
shattered hopes are wounds I'm licking
you only live once
I get it now
I've lost my heart don't even know how
take it break it
don't want it back
I'm bleeding out the odds are stacked
for you I'd run
for you I'd die
c'mon Nil
just one more try

I fell silent.

Thad stared at me, stunned. "How could you know that? I wrote those lyrics in my head on my last night here while Charley was sleeping. I never told her, never wrote them down. *How could you know that?*"

"Like I said, I know everything. Saw everything." My tone had grown detached. When someone else's memories spilled, there was little room left for me. "It's all here." I tapped my head. "But the memories aren't mine anymore, Thad. And it's not just the memories; it's the emotion they bring. I can't shut it off. Can't shut it *out*." *Not without shutting out me.*

Thad still looked stunned, and slightly skeptical.

"One more?" I asked. Without waiting, I recited Thad's own words, desperate to get them out of my head.

barrel pointed
at my head
noon tells me
you want me dead
go on do it
squeeze the trigger
whispers
laughs
they're getting bigger
drop the gun
throw it down
I hate you
I own you
I'm your clown
hold up lash out
sling it back
run it
time it
I bet on black—

"Stop." Thad's voice was hoarse as he cut me off. "I get it." His expression had shifted to understanding and, if I wasn't mistaken, fear. "That's a lot of information."

"You have no idea." My tone was matter-of-fact. *How can I feel both hollow and saturated to the point of bursting?* I couldn't bear to be in my own head.

A moment passed where the only noise was the crash of waves.

"I didn't even know you played the guitar," I said quietly. It seemed important, now.

"I do," Thad said absently. He turned to me, all traces of resentment gone.

"Can I do anything?" he asked.

"Actually, yes. Do you remember how, on your Day Three Hundred Sixty-four last time, you asked Rives to have Charley's back if your last day didn't work out like you hoped?"

Thad's expression was wary. "Yeah?"

"I want you to have Rives's back. If the last day works out like I think it will, he'll need you. And you have to make sure he takes the equinox gate—before me."

"Skye, no." Thad's eyes widened in shocked comprehension. "Don't do this."

"I don't have a choice. I'm the only one who can do what has to be done. Promise me, Thad. Promise me you'll have Rives's back. Promise me you'll make sure he lets me go."

Thad understood that I was talking about more than the gate. He shook his head, over and over. "Please, Skye. Please don't do this. It'll kill him."

"No, it won't. It'll save him. Promise me, Thad."

"I promise." His voice was dull.

"One more thing." An image of Dai's trembling figure flashed through my head, and I felt terrible that I hadn't made him a priority before. "There's a boy on the sand of South Beach and he's fighting a fever. We need to send someone to help him before it's too late."

Thad stood. "I don't know how much we can do for him."

"We can make sure he doesn't die with only Nil for company," I whispered. "We're better than that."

"Okay, Nil slayer." Thad's tone was heavy. "I'm on it."

CHAPTER
62

RIVES

37 DAYS UNTIL THE AUTUMNAL EQUINOX, MID-MORNING

Something was wrong.

Epically wrong.

Something invasive and invisible had shifted in *this* world, and it threatened to obliterate *my* world. But it wasn't over. Another shift was coming, I just didn't know when. All I knew was that it was Nil-related and Skye-centered.

She had disappeared while Paulo organized a fresh team to gather heart pine and twine for Chuck to craft into an island fuse. Thad had vanished too. Somehow I wasn't surprised to find the two together, sitting on the rocks at the beach. A memory flashed: me giving Skye a bracelet on these same black rocks, her birthday wishes written in the sand.

Now her back was to me, a sign that spoke volumes.

Thad stood as I approached.

"Care for some company?" I asked.

Thad turned around, gesturing to the now-empty space beside Skye. He swallowed. "All yours, brother. I'm heading to South Beach. I'll catch you later, eh?"

I nodded, but my eyes locked on Skye. She faced the water, sitting too still for my liking. "What's going on?" I said as I sat down. "And please don't tell me nothing. I'm not stupid, Skye. Or blind. And I'm going out of my mind with worry."

"I know." Her words were soft. She turned toward me, her hands wrapped around her knees. "Do you remember what Maaka told you on the platform?" Skye's eyes were dark. Packed with emotion, yet unnervingly distant.

"He told me lots of things. Which one?" I said.

"About the fire. He specifically told you not to bring fire into the gate."

Remember what I told you, Maaka had warned me, the day before we took this trip. Had he known I'd be having this convo, right here, right now?

I wrenched myself back to the present.

"And?" I raised an eyebrow.

"We need to bring fire into the equinox gate," Skye said unequivocally. "That's the second part of the equinox equation. We blow up the island from within by lighting the gas-filled cavern, and then we take fire into the gate."

"We," I repeated. Something tilted beneath me, cold and real. "You and me?"

She shook her head. Sadness flickered in her eyes, tempering the steel. "Not you," she said quietly. "Me. This time I'm last."

"No way." I was on my feet. "Who knows what would happen! The gate could implode. It could *kill* you, Skye. Maaka specifically said *not* to do it."

She nodded, her face too calm. "I know. Because he wanted to save you."

The vision of Skye dead on Nil rock flashed through my head. Skye sat before me, eyes blank, voice hollow. I started to shake. "What are you saying, Skye? That you *want* to die? That you don't *care* if you die?"

She blinked slowly. "I'm saying that I know what I'm doing. That I'm doing what needs to be done. I should have been the last one through last time. This time, it *has* to be me. There is no other option."

"Of course there is!" I exploded. "There are always options. Choices." *Choose me*, my heart begged.

Her expression didn't change.

"You're telling me you're willing to die. For Nil."

"Not for Nil, for everyone else." Skye's voice was soft.

"Not for me." My voice broke. "I want you to *live*."

Skye said nothing.

"This isn't you talking," I said abruptly. "It's Nil. Nil did something to you when you touched that water and you're not thinking clearly. This isn't your choice!"

Anger and hurt flashed in Skye's eyes, setting them on fire for one brilliant instant; in that moment, I recognized *my* Skye. "Of course Nil did something to me when I touched that water!" she snapped. "I saw everything! Every escape, every death. Every thought, every hope, every fear. *Every moment of suffering.* And if I have the chance to stop it from repeating, I have to do it. Don't you see that?"

I swept her into my arms and held her tight. "Yes and no. I see how you're driven to end it more than ever, but I don't see why you have to be the last one through. I won't lose you, Skye."

Too late, cackled the wind.

Skye didn't return my embrace. Didn't respond. I held her at arm's length, searching her eyes for the flash of fire I'd seen seconds before. It was gone. But my Skye was still in there, trapped.

"I'll find another way," I vowed. "I refuse to lose you to this place. I refuse to lose you at all. You're my best friend. Remember our plans? Our future? You, the travel writer, and me, the photojournalist? That's us. You and me. Seeing the whole world together, not just this hellhole." My eyes scoured her face, her eyes, the set of her shoulders, hunting for any trace of Skye.

Nothing.

"We'll figure out another way," I said, desperate to break back through to her. "I can't imagine life without you, and I don't want to. I won't let Nil win."

A single glistening tear trailed down Skye's face.

"It already has," she finally whispered.

CHAPTER
63

The female, Skye, must die. She should've broken before, many times before, many times over. Her resilience had become highly irritating.

Enough, the island decided.

The fighter had been prepared; her heart transformed. She was the perfect one to eliminate Skye, when the time was right. The darkness of night would provide perfect cover for a precisely thrown blade. Or better yet, perhaps the fighter would let Skye burn, a fitting end. The means didn't matter, just the end, and the fighter would use whatever means necessary to bring Skye to an overdue end.

A surge of power and might coursed through the island at the thought. The island seethed with the need for power, and power they would bring. Power they would bleed, all of them.

They all would burn, all perish. Every last one of them. Their grand plan would fail.

And it would be glorious.

Carmen had watched and listened as the fools in the City bought into Skye's destructive plan. The only part that Carmen personally accepted was the leave-at-midnight agenda; the rest she ignored. But, she'd thought as she listened, *Skye's clearly insane. An unstable,* unpredictable individual who actually believed that she was called to destroy the island.

Yes, Carmen mused, *Skye must be stopped.*

Skye could not be allowed to carry out her plan. In fact, she must not be able to leave or to live, because she might try to return for a third time. She was just that crazy.

It's why I'm here, Carmen realized with a jolt. She, Carmen Medina, had been brought here to save this place.

And so she would.

She would act when the time was right. The sense of purpose filled her with such a rush of pleasure that she smiled, baring her teeth in a frightening grin.

While the City made their plans, so would she.

Near the Wall, Molly sat on a rock, studying her hands as though they belonged to someone else. There were the same broken nails, same torn cuticles, and the same starburst scar near her left thumb from when she'd burned her hand on a sparkler.

They were her hands.

But somehow, they were inexplicably, completely different. These hands held power—or took it, she wasn't quite sure which one was true. But something had happened to her in that cavern the other day—something odd. When she'd pulled Skye from that pool, she'd felt a rush of warmth pass from her head to her toes, as if someone had cracked an invisible egg on her head and let it drip down, covering her completely before vanishing altogether. At the time she thought nothing of it, thought perhaps it was a rush of panic or adrenaline or something equally necessary giving her the strength to pull Skye free of that wretched water. But now she wasn't so certain. Since then, she'd seen things. Things she didn't want to see.

Each time she touched someone, she got flashes of them. Of their *future*. Not the whole picture but a glimpse: snapshots of decisions made, actions taken, feelings expressed, all fragments of moments to come, leaving it to Molly to piece together the details.

And the image she'd gotten from Davey the other morning brought heat to Molly's cheeks just thinking about it.

As if she'd thought him into appearing, Davey sat beside her. "Are your hands okay?" he asked. "You've been looking at them for a good hour."

"They're fine." Molly turned her eyes to Davey. She thought of how he brought her a cup of water each night without being asked and left it beside her bed. She thought of how he comforted Rives with a hand on his shoulder and water in his eyes, and how he buried a boy Molly had never seen, working beside James and Thad without question, without break, emotion twisting his face and her heart as he dug in the sand, his dark hair matted with sweat. The latter images were from the future, eerie glimpses of events to come.

Davey's eyes stayed on her hands, as if he were inspecting them himself.

"Did you cheat on Lauren?" she asked abruptly. *Where did that come from?* she wondered.

"No, I didn't. I swear on my life." He still looked at her hands. "I'd actually broken up with Lauren, or maybe she broke up with me, the night before we came here. We both knew it wasn't working. My heart wasn't in it."

"So, Emma? Was she your rebound?" Molly's voice was colder than she liked.

Davey snorted. "Hardly. Emma was trying to prove a point."

Molly raised her brows. "With her lips?"

Davey glanced back at the sea, his dark hair falling into his eyes. *He needs a haircut*, she thought. As if that mattered.

She sighed. Her mind was all over the place.

Not Davey's. His was clearly still on that night.

"She accused me of being in love with someone else," Davey said quietly. "She kissed me, daring me to prove her wrong. I didn't kiss her back." He shrugged. "You didn't see what you thought you saw."

I see more than you could imagine, Molly thought.

"Are you?" she said, feeling her world spin. "In love with someone else?"

"Completely." Davey's gaze was back on her hands. Something crackled in the space between them. Syllables flush with power hung in the air, waiting to form words that could change everything. Or nothing.

Molly let them float away, unacknowledged. The weight was too much, the shift too fast.

Abruptly Molly changed the subject. "Davey." She twirled her blue streak of hair around one finger. "Something happened to me in that cavern when I was with Skye. I didn't touch the water, at least I don't think so. But something happened. Ever since then, when I touch someone, I see their future. Not the whole thing, just glimpses here, on the island. Like parts of a puzzle that I have to put together."

"Like Skye in reverse," he said, frowning.

Molly nodded.

Worry shaded his blue-gray eyes as he studied her. "You doing okay?"

"Yes. Maybe. I don't know." She twirled her hair relentlessly. "I'm just not sure what to do with it, or how it can help Skye, and us."

Davey's eyes held hers. "I'd hug you but I'm scared to touch you." His slight grin didn't dent the concern in his eyes.

"You should be," she joked.

"Now you sound like your brother." A wry smile twisted his mouth. He looked away, toward the water.

His profile was striking; no wonder Lauren had fallen for him. Messy dark hair, great cheekbones, full lips. His long lashes curled slightly at the tips, something she'd never noticed before. They'd never sat, just the two of them, without one of her brothers or a friend or someone, until they'd come to Nil.

She'd never thought about how strange that was until now.

"When I grabbed your hand the other morning." Davey spoke slowly, like each word had been carefully considered before being approved. "I felt something. You did too, right?"

She nodded.

"So you—saw something?"

She nodded again.

"What was it?" His graphite-colored eyes roamed her face. "What did you see?"

"Different things. You comforting Rives, you on the beach with Thad and James." *You kissing me fiercely, me kissing you back.* She turned away so he couldn't see her face, which had grown hot again.

His gaze was back on her hands. "I remember when you got that scar," he said quietly. He reached out to touch her left thumb then jerked his hand back at the last minute. "JT was chasing you around with a sparkler, and I was so worried he'd hurt you that I tackled him. And when he fell, you came running and the sparkler flew from his hand and hit yours anyway. I hated that you got hurt."

He looked up, his eyes pained. "It's you, Molly. It's always been you."

Her jaw dropped as her entire world fell apart and came back together again.

"Why did you always let me think you were a jerk?" she asked, dumbfounded.

Davey half smiled. "Why didn't you ever see the real me?"

"Davey!" Thad called from just up the beach. "Can I borrow you? We need to take a trip to South Beach."

Without turning, Molly knew James stood silently beside Thad, waiting. And she knew what they would find. She nearly threw up, nearly asked Davey to stay. There was so much left unsaid. His words lingered, a question needing an answer.

Instead, she looked at Thad.

"Bring a shovel," she said, her voice raw with empathy. "You'll need it."

CHAPTER 64

SKYE
23 DAYS UNTIL THE AUTUMNAL EQUINOX, MORNING

I missed Rives terribly. Part of me was gone. I'd ripped it out myself, trying to protect us both. Since Nil had emptied its memories in my head, I avoided Rives as a matter of course; it was just too much.

Better for Rives to get used to life without me, I reasoned. Because my end was written; there was no other choice. I didn't need the Sight to know that. The future I desperately wanted with him was never going to happen. And because of that, being around Rives brought more pain than I could handle. His strong presence, his familiar touch, his knowing gaze that set me on fire—all were a stark reminder of what I'd already lost.

Now I sat alone at the edge of White Beach, trying not to think. Near the trees, a giraffe munched on a branch. He looked so content, so at home, probably because he'd never leave.

Like me.

A few yards from the giraffe, the leaves rustled. The giraffe stopped its chewing, ears pricked.

Black fur gleamed in the sun, muscles rippling. The green shifted, revealing paws and whiskers and eyes like slits. A panther, powerful and predatory.

He crouched ten yards away, at most.

I sat motionless, hoping the giraffe would pull out a kick or some other survival trick in its giraffe arsenal of defense.

The panther slunk forward, eyes glittering; the giraffe turned toward the cat. In one fluid move, the panther brought down the small giraffe in a clean kill. I watched it happen as if it were a movie. I knew the island would protect me, because it needed me.

Curling into a ball, I covered my ears with my hands until the giraffe fell silent, its death cries blending with those in my head.

"Skye." Molly's gentle touch on my shoulder brought me back. "Are you okay?"

I opened my eyes. Molly knelt beside me. "Skye?" she repeated. She gently wiped tears from my cheeks.

I blinked. "Yes?"

"We've been looking for you. Rives is beside himself. He went to the Arches thinking that you might be there. I know you're struggling with—" She paused, her voice softening. "The weight of knowledge," she finished. "I can't imagine how difficult this is for you. But running away isn't the answer."

"I wasn't running away." *Was I?*

The panther was gone. The giraffe's carcass lay on the sand, partially obscured by the trees.

"Okay," Molly said calmly, "you weren't running away. But disappearing without telling anyone where you're going isn't good. We should get back. There's a panther in the area, and some wild dogs too. It's safer in the City. I don't like you being here alone."

I had a flash of Dai on the beach, alone. He'd died, alone. Somehow I knew my hunch was true.

"They buried Dai, didn't they?" I looked at her. "Davey and Thad. And James. They buried him at South Beach."

Molly nodded.

"Do you know why he had a fever?" I didn't wait for her to answer. "Because he cut his leg on the rocks when he fell out of the gate, and the cut got infected. He never had a chance."

I looked back at the ocean. "No one arrives sick. Did you know that? The island doesn't transfer bacteria or viruses, just the DNA in its pure form. And the island prefers Americans, because we're the ones who dropped the bombs. Pain for pain. The wild gates are drawn to us." I closed my eyes. *Too much. I know too much.* I was a walking Nil encyclopedia.

"Okay," Molly said again. "Good to know."

"Is it?" I asked. I wasn't certain.

We ran into Chuck and Davey halfway down the beach, heading north.

"Good morning, ladies." Davey grinned. "The Chuckster and I are guava hunting."

"There's a panther up there," I said, realizing I'd forgotten to tell Molly. "It just got a giraffe so I don't think it's hungry, but just wanted to let you know."

Davey did a quick 180. He'd no sooner spun when the breeze stalled. Twenty yards out, a gate shot into the air, glittering in the noon sun.

It would roll north in seconds.

"Chuck, go," Molly said, her quiet voice commanding. "You've done what you came to do." Then she grabbed my hand and Davey's. "Run!"

We ran. Out of the gate's way, as Chuck sprinted straight for it.

And then he was gone.

We had twenty-three days left.

CHAPTER 65

Skye had shut me out.

She didn't ignore me, or fight with me. In some twisted way, that might have been preferable. At least then I'd know she cared. She treated me like a casual acquaintance, not someone she loved. Not someone who would walk through hell for her, and already had.

My grip tightened on my board. I ached to get out on the water; it was the only place my fury didn't rage these days. I hated touching Nil ground. Part of me envied Chuck, who'd caught a gate, a ticket out. The rest of me wanted to stay, to beat Nil senseless, to see it burn.

I hated this place.

Thad was moving faster than me this morning. He already stood at the water's edge, back to me, board tucked under his arm, gauging the swells. Or maybe he was gearing up, bracing himself against the water's chill. No wet suits here, and if you stayed in the water long enough, the cold crept in.

Classic Nil.

"Thad," I called.

At the sound of his name, he turned and gave me an easy nod. "What's up, brother?"

"You still talking to Charley?"

"Absolutely." He smiled. A chill smile, the lucky bastard.

"Well, the next time you talk to her, ask her what the hell I'm supposed to do to save Skye." I wasn't kidding. I was grasping at straws, but it was all I had left. "I can't accept it, Thad. She's set on being last, on carrying a torch into the stationary gate. Nil's gotten in her head. But it's not her choice, it's Nil's."

"I'll ask Charley. But it won't matter." Thad gripped my shoulder. "Rives, Skye knows what she's asking." His voice was heavy. "She's asking you to let her go."

I threw Thad's hand off. "You don't get to tell me that," I snapped. "You've got Charley back home, waiting for you. I'm losing Skye, Thad, I'm *losing* her. Forever. And you're asking me to let her go. To say it's okay. I can't do that. I *won't*."

"It's what she wants." Thad's voice was quiet.

"Wrong. It's what Nil wants," I said bitterly.

Now it was Skye standing on the edge of a cliff; Skye, ready to fall. And Thad was asking me to stand back and do nothing. Let her fall, let her go.

Let her *die*.

"You don't know what Skye wants." My tone ran cold. *You don't know* her.

Thad didn't react. "I do. I've talked to her, Rives, every day. I've listened to what you don't want to hear. She can't take it." He pointed to his head. "It's too much. The island changed her, and she can't go back. She can't rewind the clock, can't reset. Can't get all she knows—and *feels*—out of her head." He swallowed. "Molly saw it. It's the only way."

"Like hell it is." My voice was a growl. "I didn't come back here to lose her. I came back to save her. Wait—" I paused. "What do you mean, Molly saw it?"

"You know how Skye saw the past? All of it?"

I nodded.

"Well, Molly sees the future. Totally whacked, but ever since she was in that cavern with Skye, she gets flashes of the future when she touches people. Like Ramia did. And Molly saw Skye walk through the gate holding a torch. She saw it, Rives. I wish it were different." His eyes were pained.

"So what if Molly gets a flash? It's an image Nil stuck in her head. The island's playing games, Thad. You know how it is. And even if somehow Molly got a flash of the future, she's not getting the full picture. It's not over. Not by a long shot."

I spun around, done with Thad. Done with this whole Nil mess. In that moment, the twin columns of Nil melded completely into one: cruel.

Thad had been right about Nil.

But he was dead wrong about Skye.

I strode back to the Shack, my dawn plans shredded. All I wanted to do was talk to Skye. Beg her if need be, make her see that sacrificing herself wasn't necessary. I had to convince her, rationalize with her, get her to see that she wasn't thinking clearly, that Nil had camped out in her head. That somehow there must be another way.

Back in the City, I headed for our hut. I was so deep in my head I didn't realize anyone was inside until I got close. Skye's voice stopped me short.

"So they're pieces of the future," Skye was saying.

"Yes, different images every time, every touch. But—" Molly paused. "Not with you. It's weird. When I touch you, I get only one picture, every time. The *same* picture, as clear as day. You walking into the gate with a lit torch, a fireball exploding in darkness, and then nothing. Just black. But the black—" Molly shuddered. "It's intense."

I stood in the entrance. Neither girl noticed me. Sitting on opposite beds, they were fully focused on each other.

"After the black, do you see anything?" Skye asked. The hope in her voice buoyed me, the first positive sign in weeks.

"No." Molly shook her head. "The vision is over."

Skye smiled, with a satisfied look that shocked me.

"It means nothing." My voice ripped through the hut, hot and desperate, making both girls look up. "Skye." I looked only at her. "This is what Nil wants. It's what Nil has *always* wanted. You. Dead." My tone went flat. "Please don't do this. It's Nil talking, not you."

Skye sighed. The pity in her eyes took me aback. "Rives, I know what Nil wants, and what it needs. Yes, Nil is in my head, in *me*. I won't deny it. But I'm here too." Her eyes sparked. "And it's *my* choice to go last and end this thing once and for all. It's what I was brought here to do." Her voice carried the same resolute tone as when she said she was going to the Death Twin weeks ago; it made me sick. She studied me, from a place much farther away than just a few meters.

"It's my choice, Rives," she said quietly, her eyes on mine, her tone Skye-fierce and deeply sad. "Nil can't die if I live. I *will* be last. You have to let me go. If you love me, you'll let me go. This is why I'm here," she whispered. Then she closed her eyes. "I'm sorry."

I'm sorry.

Somehow we'd moved past excuses to apologies when I was still fighting for a chance, as if the discussion were over.

It is, I realized.

She'd made her choice, and it didn't include me.

My heart froze. Shattered, then flatlined.

I turned away first.

CHAPTER 66

The island left the humans alone.

Their pain was too much; there was no reprieve.

Instead, the island focused on the four-legged creatures; it wielded its dwindling power in bursts, perfectly timed, purging the island of beasts, especially those that preferred meat. If the humans failed, if she failed—the one called Skye—then the island would be helpless to guide or sustain human life in the eons to come. The beasts here would be the least of their worries, but for now, the island wished to preserve as much human life as possible with the end drawing near.

In three weeks, the crescent moon would rise.

The end was written.

Noon arrived, powerful and alluring, and with the island's help, a cat departed. His stay had been short, which was just as well. Still, three similar cats remained, all with glossy golden coats, one with a thick mane. They could be a problem.

The seam rippled with power surging from both sides.

It widened, and the island couldn't resist the call to look. To see the world beyond the seam, fascinating and raw, full of electria pulsing and flowing, in ribbons crisscrossing like light.

But as usual, the island's gaze was drawn to her, the other powerful *female, the one beyond the seam. Her bond to her mate drew the island like the brightest of lights, and for a moment in time, the island paused, caught by the glow. Yes, the island thought. It would give her the chance for knowledge, and it would be up to her to pass it on.*

Charley marched back up the steps to Rika's house and rapped hard on the door.

Maaka had vanished. If he *was* still on the island, no one would tell her. No one would tell her *anything*. In fact, lately she suspected people were outright avoiding her.

But Rika, she knew things. Rika's parting words gnawed at her heart.

The island will bleed, and people you love will be lost. That is the end you seek, child. Prepare yourself.

How can I prepare myself for? For the unknown? Charley wondered. She needed to *know*.

She lifted her hand to knock again.

The door flew open. Rika stood in the doorway, a slight smile on her face. "Come back for the pineapple muffins, did you, Charley?"

Charley found herself nodding. "Yes." *Among other things.*

"Then by all means, come in."

Charley walked in, absorbing the same bursts of color in the house, coupled with the same eerie feel of knowledge and truth. But this time Charley was prepared. She didn't even flinch at the tray of muffins and cold bottles of Sprite waiting on the table.

"Please. Sit." Rika gestured.

Charley sat. Slowly she opened the soda, took a sip, and smiled.

"Rika, thank you for having me, especially since I showed up unannounced."

Rika tipped her head.

It's a game, Charley thought. They'd both known she was coming. Charley cut to the heart of the matter; she had no time to play.

"You said people I love will be lost. What can I do to prevent it?"

"Nothing. They are *there*, you are *here*. If they are lost, they must find their own way. They must find themselves."

Lost, not dead, Charley thought.

"So they can be found, right?" Charley had the sense they were talking in circles.

"Some," Rika said. "Not all. Three will be lost forever."

"Not Thad," Charley said. "Please tell me Thad is not one of the three."

Rika stayed silent.

Charley's temper flared. "You can't tell me, or *won't*?"

Rika studied her. "A bit of both. The end is written, but the middle shapes it."

"So basically you know nothing," Charley snapped.

Rika's eyes held pity. "You are so young, as they all are. I know the island will keep three. Which three, well, that may change."

Charley closed her eyes. "There is so much I don't understand." Her voice ached with frustration. "I want to find something *here* to help them *there*."

"Tell your friend to look, my child. Then she'll find what she's looking for, right, my child?" Rika's half smile was sharp.

Charley gaped. Those were her words, spoken months ago. *My nana likes to say that you'll find what you're looking for*, she'd told Natalie. And somehow Rika *knew*.

Rika nodded in approval. "Your friend already has the answers she seeks; the riddle's answer lies within. The end is written, but not the future. I will say no more. You can come back, anytime, for my muffins or my company. But I have no more wisdom to offer, no more insight to share. You already have the answers you seek, child, every last one. You know you do."

She cocked her head at Charley. "Take heart, my child. All is not lost." She flicked her hand. "Now go. You have somewhere to be."

"I do?"

"It is noon, my child. There is always somewhere to be at noon. Or not to be," she added.

So true, Charley thought. She left, thinking of Thad, praying that he could hear her.

All is not lost, she thought fiercely. *Tell Skye that she has the answers. Tell her to look inside, that the riddle's answer lies within. And tell her the end is written, but not the future. I love you.*

As she ran down the steps, she knew she would not come back.

The seam narrowed, the island retreated.

In three weeks, all here would be lost. Time would declare a victor, as always.

It would be all that survived.

CHAPTER 67

Rives won't talk to me, or look at me. He believes I chose Nil over him. *How can he not see that I have no choice?*

I wish he could remember his own words. *I think maybe Nil is your destiny, so how can accepting your destiny be selfish?* he asked me the last time we were here. A different hour, a different Nil, but his words still rang true.

How could he forget? How has he lost sight of me?

My entire life has revolved around Nil, even when I didn't know the island existed. My destiny is to end this place, to end *with* this place.

To die. Here.

I don't have a choice.

Nil does have a heart; I know that now. It's black. Diseased. The darkness I've been seeing is the essence of Nil; it's cold and dark and cruel and dead. I see it now as never before. I'm the only one who can defeat it, because I'm the only one who truly understands it. Nil's heart beats with stolen life, powerful and sickening. It must be stopped.

And somehow, we're connected.

We both live, we both die.

It was Nil's plan all along.

If I had my journal, this is what I would write. Instead I write in my head, letting the words flow in my private room, spilling ink the color of Nil's heart on every white wall, erasing the lines each day and starting again. Pouring it all out, in my head.

I have seven days left.

I will make it.

I will write Nil's end.

My name is Skye Bracken and this is my destiny.

CHAPTER 68

I worked on autopilot.

For the past three weeks, I'd gone through the motions. I'd hunted with Thad and brought back rabbits and a small boar. I'd tracked a rhino with James, where he was the master and I was the student, just to know where the hell the animal had settled. The answer: nowhere close to us. I'd scavenged with Paulo and stripped plants to make twine. I'd worked with Kenji and Hafthor to coat the twine with sap to amp up the flammability for the island fuse, a tedious process that couldn't be rushed. I'd gathered candlenut fruit and made torches, knowing we needed them to light our way on the last night, wondering with every move whether the torch I crafted would be the one to kill Skye.

If our plan worked, the island would die.

So would Skye.

"Rives." Thad's voice broke into my brooding.

I sat on the sand, near the beachside pit lined in hot rocks, where the boar would be cooked by nightfall. I cared little. My appetite was nonexistent, like my future.

Sensing Thad waiting, I turned.

"Molly says there's a boy who just showed up on Black Bay," he said.

"Unlucky dude caught the late gate in, I guess. Want to go with me to greet him?"

"Not really."

"Is that a yes or a no?" Thad waited patiently.

"A yes, I guess."

We walked in silence. I was still pissed at Thad. He'd taken Skye's side. They talked constantly, at all hours.

Skye and I barely spoke at all.

"Skye could use your support, you know." Thad's voice was quiet.

"Support her suicide? Are you insane?" Thad still had Charley, waiting back home and sending him mental love notes. I was making torches to send the girl I loved to her death.

I fought the urge to punch him. I glared so hard he stepped back and raised his hands.

"I'm saying support *her*. Right here, right now. While you can. You've shut her out, Rives, right when she needs you most."

"Right." Bitterness dripped through my words like acid. "*She* shut *me* out, Thad. It's her choice. Her decision. Half the time she sleeps on the beach."

"Only because you won't talk to her."

Silence fell. The Crystal Cavern glittered, full of Nil ice.

When we broke back into the open air, I turned to Thad. "You have no idea how I feel," I said, my anger barely restrained. "None. So, please"—I clenched my fists—"don't tell me what to do, all right?"

Thad ran his hand through his hair with a sigh. "You're right. I don't know how you feel. But I do have a clue how Skye feels, and right now she needs you, even if she doesn't say it. Or *can't* say it. I'm your wingman, but you're hers."

Not anymore, I thought.

"Just think about it, okay?" he said.

"Trust me, it's all I think about," I snapped.

Thad looked toward the beach. "Two more things. First, tonight's Nil

Night. Skye insisted. For morale and good luck for our trip tomorrow. Her words."

Good luck. Right. I almost snorted.

"And the second thing?"

"Charley told me that we'll find what we're looking for."

"What the hell does that mean?" I asked.

"I think—and I can't believe I'm saying this—that it's something to do with the light and the dark. Like if we look for the dark, that's what we'll find. Or if we look for the light, we'll find that, eh?"

"She's wrong." My voice was flat. "It's all the same. The light, the dark, it's all Nil. All I've been looking for is another way. Another plan, another solution—one that doesn't involve Skye torching Nil and taking herself down in the process. I've got three days left to find it, Thad. Seventy-two hours. That's it. And then I need to convince Skye to go with Plan B, and I have no Plan B. That's what *I'm* looking for. So why can't I find it?"

Thad crossed his arms. "Charley told me that Skye needs to look inside. That Skye already knows the answer to the riddle, that the answer lies within."

"What riddle? This whole place is a riddle." I shook out my hands because they'd lost all feeling. Thad stayed silent.

"Did Charley give you anything else? Anything that can help? Something concrete?"

"Well . . ." Thad looked uncomfortable. "She also said, 'All is not lost, yet.'"

"Obviously. Because Skye's still alive." I turned away, wound tighter than Mount Nil and just as ready to blow. "Let's go find the rookie and get this done." And by *this*, I meant Nil. It was a nightmare from which I couldn't wake.

The rookie sat huddled on the black sand, blinking. Judging by the marks in the sand, the kid hadn't moved far from his landing spot.

I knelt beside him. "Hey, buddy, I'm Rives. What's your name?"

He jerked to look at me. "Garrett." His dark eyes were wide with fear.

"Well, Garrett, today's your lucky day. You ended up on Nil, an island that shouldn't exist. But the good news is, in four days you get to leave, so it's a short visit for you. Key thing is to stay alive." I smiled, hoping it looked warmer than it felt. "Want some clothes?"

Hafthor, Paulo, and Zane were eating pineapple when Thad and I walked up and introduced Garrett.

Garrett looked up at Hafthor. "Half a Thor?" he asked, a quizzical expression on his face.

Hafthor held up both hands and nodded. "No hammer."

"Oh my God, did you just make a funny?" Zane burst out laughing. He cupped his hands around his mouth. "It's official, guys. The end is near. Hafthor's making jokes." He high-fived Hathor and something inside me snapped.

I swung at Zane but Thad stepped in front of me. "Take a walk, Rives," he said quietly. "Go cool off."

I strode away, then broke into a run.

Rivesssss, hissed the sea. *I won. She's mine. And I own you, too.*

Like hell you do, I thought.

I still was desperate for a Plan B. Because if Skye had the answers, she sure wasn't sharing them with me.

Maybe there is no Plan B.

Cruel laughter echoed in my head, followed by a cold thought: *You're finally learning, Rives.*

CHAPTER 69

Let them plot, let them plan, the island thought with pleasure. The island took in this group's shape, took its measure. With a few measly exceptions, this entire lot was under the island's thumb. It made for a perfect picture of the island's now. No other human would be called, and no one would leave, not for the next three days.

And in three days, the carnage would be glorious.

In three days, the crescent moon would rise. In three days, all the humans here would perish. For the island had plans of its own, and these humans were no match.

But for now, the island rested. Waited. Prepared.

It inhaled deeply, reveling in the sweet scent of fear and the unprecedented surge of electria to come.

Molly tensed.

"Did you feel that?" she whispered to Davey.

"What?" He rubbed his eyes.

"A rumble. Like a laugh. I don't know." Molly sat wide awake, cross-legged on her bed. "It was weird." She gave a little laugh. "This whole place—this whole *thing*—is weird. My life has turned weird."

Davey got up to sit beside her. She was all shadows and angles and bare legs, her hair as wild as the island now, her blue streak swallowed by the night.

"It's all weird," he agreed. "But there is no one stronger than you, Molly. No one. You can handle anything this place throws at you, and then some. Okay?"

She tilted her face toward his. Her gaze swept over his eyes, his cheekbones, his lips, all in a slow, liquid way that set his blood on fire. "If it was always me," she whispered, "why didn't you say anything?"

"Because JT told me he'd kill me if I ever touched you. Big-brother bro code and all that. And you told Lauren that you thought of me like a brother."

"I lied," she said, her voice husky. "And JT isn't here."

Davey leaned forward, but stopped short of her lips. This moment was everything. "I wouldn't care if he were," Davey whispered. He reached up to brush her jaw with his thumb. "If he were, I'd tell him the truth. That I'm so in love with you it would be worth any punch he could throw, and I was a bloody fool for not telling you sooner."

With that, she kissed him. Fiercely, deeply, without holding back, as if this one kiss had to make up for years of waiting.

It is everything, Davey realized. The chance to be with Molly, back in Oz, away from here.

And he'd bloody well fight for it.

CHAPTER
70

SKYE
3 DAYS UNTIL THE AUTUMNAL EQUINOX, DAWN

Dawn opened like a million other Nil dawns before. Only this dawn ushered in the final countdown.

Nil's own clock was ticking—and so was mine.

I'd never been so tired. Nil's exhaustion and mine were woven together so tightly I couldn't tell where mine ended and Nil's began. I fervently hoped that in the end I had the strength to do what had to be done, and that Nil didn't pull a trick with me like it had with Paulo, or like it had done with me that first morning in the Looking Glass Cavern.

It felt incredibly good just to sit. It took all I had not to close my eyes.

Beside me, on another fire-warmed rock, Thad sat, arms crossed as he studied the group gathered around the firepit. Paulo's expression matched Thad's: intense and focused. Talking to Lana, Zane was smiling, perpetually happy as always; Lana, on the other hand, seemed pensive. Molly sat on my other side, eating pineapple, her legs almost touching Calvin's. He spoke quietly as she listened and nodded. Davey, Hafthor, and Kenji stood without talking, a trio more sleepy than stoic. Garrett seemed alone even though he sat on Thad's other side. Dominic leaned against a tree, trident spear in hand. Catching me eyeing him, he winked.

I smiled back. I took it all in, then my eyes found Rives, and stayed.

My beautiful Rives. He stood brooding by the Wall, fingering the blade on his hip. If anyone had Nil in his head it was him. I wanted to shake him, to yell at him, to ask him to come back.

But he'd made his choice too. He'd chosen to see the worst in my choice, and in me.

We had nothing left but memories.

Rives strode over to Thad. He never looked my way. "Let's go over the plan one last time."

Thad nodded.

Rives faced the group. "Okay, people, listen up. Quick recap before we set out. Molly hasn't seen anyone new other than Garrett, and as of today, there won't be any wild gates for the next three days. So we think Garrett is our last rookie, and hopefully the last ever."

Garrett gave a halfhearted wave, his expression still slightly bewildered.

"But we need to make sure. To be certain that we've found all new-comers, we're going to sweep the island in teams and meet at the mountain in three days. Departure time is midnight, but we should be at the platform and ready by noon, just to be safe. We also need to find Carmen and warn her if we can. Skye, Zane, and Paulo did this last time, so they know the drill. Same for me. Stick with your group. Everyone has a whistle, in case you get separated or need help. Two quick blasts means *I'm here*, and two quick blasts back is the reply. Three quick blasts means danger, and you can switch it into an SOS for help. Three short, three long, three short. Everyone clear?"

Rives paused as heads nodded.

"Paulo, James, and Kenji will go northeast, sweeping the interior. Steer clear of the mudflats. Molly, Davey, and Dominic will go due north, sweeping the coast and northwest corner. Lana, Zane, Garrett, and Thad will go south, taking the coast and southeast corner. Skye, Hafthor, Calvin, and I will head straight to the mountain, covering the south-western interior as we go. Everyone has a quadrant, don't mess around. Just sweep for people. We don't want to leave anyone behind." His jaw muscles tensed. "Hafthor will carry the fuse. The rest of us will carry torches, extra twine, and food. Our goal is to meet up at the platform by noon in three days' time. Our team will get there first, lay the fuse line, and start lining Calvin's route with torches to help him see. I know he'll have his own, but the more light the better. At midnight, we'll all be in place, all torches lit. When the gate starts to rise, we all blow our whistles, and that will tell Calvin to light the fuse and run. He'll have less than two hundred meters to cover in just over a minute, so he can make it to the gate in time, no problem."

He looked at Calvin, who nodded.

"By the time the gate locks into place, Calvin should be a good third of the way to the platform. We'll go through the gate one at a time. Skye has chosen to be last." He didn't look at me. Molly gave me a kind smile.

Rives cleared his throat. "All right, let's pack and roll."

Paulo came up as we were ready to set out. His dark eyes burned with emotion. "Skye, I don't think you're supposed to be last." His soft tone was forceful. "I think it's supposed to be me. To make up for my mistake last time."

I hugged him. "Paulo, you're sweet. But I know it's supposed to be me."

He shook his head. "I've heard the island, Skye. You were supposed to *see*, to guide us, to figure out the end. But you're not supposed to die. You were supposed to solve the riddle, remember? I don't think you did."

Anger flared, giving my words bite.

"Yes, I *did. This place is not safe. Look inside.* Well, inside the island is gas. Deadly gas. So is lava, and we can connect them with fire. Riddle or no riddle, I know I'm supposed to be last."

Paulo frowned. "It feels wrong. I need the chance, Skye." He paused. "A second chance. Please."

"It's not about having a second chance, Paulo," I said, frustrated. "It's about making a final choice."

"I know. And I'm willing to make that choice."

"So am I." I lifted my chin.

Paulo almost smiled. "You can argue with me in three days." He took a step, then turned back, his eyes on mine. "It's supposed to be me," he said quietly. "Ask Molly." With a sad smile, he walked away, his pace steady and, if I wasn't mistaken, resigned.

Rives was watching us, arms crossed.

"What does that mean?" I asked, my eyes darting between him and Paulo. *"Ask Molly?"*

"Ask her yourself." Rives pointed to Molly. She stood beside Davey, adjusting a glider pack on his back. It was the last functional glider. I hadn't even realized Davey knew how to fly one.

"Molly!" I ran over, moving so quickly I surprised myself. "Paulo just told me that he's supposed to be last. And he said to ask you. What's changed? What have you seen?"

Molly looked torn. "Skye." She spoke slowly, or maybe I'd just spoken ridiculously fast. "The thing is, my visions aren't clear. The timing of them, how they all fit together. And they change. So I'm interpreting them, and who knows what I'm really seeing."

"What *do* you see?" Rives's voice came from behind me. "Why does Paulo think he should be last?"

"Because sometimes he is," Molly replied. "And sometimes he isn't. I don't know." She closed her eyes, as if willing all the images away. I knew exactly how she felt.

"It's okay," I said. I went to hug her, then stopped myself before I touched her; the visions she got from me were far worse than any others, and they got darker each time. "But if you see something you think I need to know, will you promise to tell me?"

She nodded.

I looked at Davey and Dominic. "Please take care of her, and take care of each other."

"We will do that." Dominic smiled. "And you." His voice softened. "You take care of yourself, Skye. This place, do not give it the power. I will see you in three days."

"Three days," I promised.

I turned back to find Rives staring at me, a crushing desperation darkening his eyes before disappearing altogether.

"Will you please let Paulo win?" His expression was blank. "Let him go last?"

He crossed his arms, fists tight, intensity barely restrained, his entire bearing making it clear this was a final plea. Rives was asking for so much more; he was asking me to change my mind.

If he could read my thoughts, he'd hear the truth.

We can't risk it.

Last time Paulo failed.

It has to be me.

"No," I said sharply. Last time Paulo *lost* time; I couldn't risk it happening again. *I had no choice.*

How could Rives not see that?

Rives turned away, but not before I caught the ache on his face or the pain dulling his eyes.

I sighed. It was going to be a long three days.

CHAPTER 71

RIVES
AUTUMNAL EQUINOX, ALMOST NOON

Skye walked slowly.

Like glacially slow. Like her feet had turned to lead, or maybe she was trying to drag out the trip; I honestly couldn't figure out if her snail's pace was intentional or not. Neither made sense.

After all, *she* was the one who'd chosen today to die.

"Skye," I said for the twentieth time this morning, "we have to move faster. We're not even in sight of the meadow yet."

"I know. I'm trying." Her voice sounded weak.

"I can carry you," Hafthor volunteered.

Skye shook her head. "You've got the fuse. I'm *fine*." For a few minutes, her pace picked up, then lagged again, her expression a spaced-out look. I didn't know if Skye was losing time, but we sure as hell were.

We'd never make the platform by noon. Even midnight wasn't a given, not at this rate.

"That's it." I handed my unlit torches to Hafthor and scooped her up. "We're never going to make it to your farewell party if we don't pick up the pace, which means I'm picking you up." My breath came in spurts.

"Put me *down*," she snapped.

"When we get there," I replied. "But it's nice to see a little spark is still left in there."

She fumed, which made me feel better. And somehow, infinitely worse. Because this was *my* Skye, and she'd chosen death. Death by Nil, *for* Nil, and without me.

I saved my breath for walking. With me carrying her, we made better time. I blocked everything else out of my head except for the ground, the girl in my arms, and the *now*.

Step. Move left. Watch the hole. Watch ahead.

At least I had Hafthor and Calvin watching our backs.

Look around.

Pay attention.

The south lava field stretched before us, black and empty, save for one lone moose. He didn't know it, but his clock was ticking too. At the field's end, Mount Nil rose into wispy clouds, still farther away than I'd like. I wanted to already be there, setting the fuse, laying the line, arguing with Skye.

Changing her mind.

Deep down, I still believed she'd change her mind.

Liar, the breeze whispered. *You know her. And you know you've lost her.*

Out of my head, I snarled.

I forced myself to focus.

Look around.

Pay attention.

Blue sky stretched overhead, clear and stunning. Greenery dotted the horizon like life, like hope. It was an island paradise, a beautiful lie.

Skye, in my arms, was a dead girl walking in every way that mattered.

"Do you hear that?" Calvin asked, looking around. "A voice?"

I shook my head.

"Never mind. It's nothing." He rubbed his head with one hand. "Damn. This place creeps me out sometimes. I can't wait to leave. I'm driving myself crazy."

There were no people in sight, not now, not yesterday. No new people this trip at all, as expected. And disturbingly, as we closed in on the meadow, there was no sign of the other teams. Most should have beaten us, given our poor pace.

But the meadow wasn't empty.

Near the far trees, a rhino stood guard. A zebra flicked its tail in the swath of new growth.

Where were the people?

I had the crazy thought that we'd missed the equinox gate—that I'd screwed up, miscalculated the date. That somehow Nil had stolen time—an entire day.

My sixth sense flared, full-blown worry erupting.

Had we missed the gate?

No, I reasoned, we couldn't *all* have lost a full day. Maybe one person, but not four. Not even when yesterday's detour to see about another of Calvin's voices chewed up time, a wild goose chase around the lava rock until I'd had the sense to call it off.

No, we still had time.

Around us, the clear air felt heavy. Expectant. Like the island was holding its breath, waiting to see what would happen. The stillness crept under my skin; it felt like the moment before a gate flashed, the quiet just before noon. But today no outbounds would flash, not until midnight.

Unless I was one day off.

"Put me down," Skye said suddenly. "Now!"

I set her down, gently. Her soles touched rock as the first tremor hit. For a cold instant, the ground and air blurred, like a dimension had slipped, like the mother of all gates was ready to rise. All four of us dropped to our knees as one. Beneath us, the ground groaned and shifted. A massive crack opened four meters away, an angry split, spilling black rock below, a creepy rockslide crooning our names. We scrambled back, me grabbing Skye and swinging her away from another crack snaking toward her. Hafthor slipped, windmilling as he fought to stay upright; four unlit torches went flying. Calvin reached for them, stumbling and slipping, clawing at rock as he made a mad grab for the torches.

He missed by millimeters; they dropped into a fresh crack out of sight. Gone.

Meters away, the meadow was chaos, a carbonated bottle shaken too long.

A pair of lions sprinted toward the mountain, shining brilliant gold in the sunlight; they streaked past the rhino at the far edge. A whistle blew in the distance, a clear SOS that cut off abruptly. Wolves howled. A honey badger darted out of the low grasses and slid into the crack; the zebra galloped diagonally toward us then cut away, frantic. An elephant sounded behind us, a trumpet of fear.

The quake stopped as abruptly as it had begun.

"Let's move." Hafthor hauled Calvin to his feet. Blood trickled down one of Calvin's arms, mixing with sweat. "I think that tremor was the beginning of something." Hafthor glanced at the mountain briefly before pointing to the ground. "And we do not want to be stuck on this side of that divide today if it grows."

Ten meters away, a massive crack blocked access to the meadow in both directions for a good thirty meters, at least.

Moving parallel to the crack, we headed north, hunting for an access point, all four walking. My eyes went from Skye to the fresh crack in the rock, to our perimeter and then around again. Still no sign of any of the other teams. The crack narrowed enough to cross, putting us at the far end of the meadow.

We leaped across near the decimated rain forest, close enough to make out the individual leaves on new trees and old ones that somehow survived the fire. From here, the mountain platform was a good hour away. And we still had to lay the fuse line, get the torches lit, and get everyone in place.

The Nil clock ticked faster in my head.

I gestured to Hafthor for my satchel, needing my fire bow. "We need a lit torch to keep the big cats away."

"We don't have one," Hafthor said. "We lost them all."

"Seriously?"

Hafthor nodded. Of course he was serious.

"Rives, has the mountain always smoked like that?" Calvin asked, pointing.

Steam hissed into the air near the peak. More steam than usual, but nothing alarming, not yet anyway.

"Yes and no," I said, studying the mountain. "It looks a little hot."

Like Skye, I thought. Her skin still ran hot, like she was on fire. When I'd carried her, I'd begun to sweat from her body heat as much as my exertion.

Right now her skin had faded to a deathly pale, the moons beneath her eyes a dull Nil black.

I passed over my water gourd; there wasn't much left. "Drink. You need it."

Skye shook her head.

"Don't be a martyr," I said. One second late, I realized what I'd said and how I'd said it. "Take the water." My voice was gruff. "Please."

As she lifted the gourd, a knife struck it dead center, knocking it from her hand.

I swept her behind me with one arm as Carmen strode out from behind a swath of deadleaf bushes, her dark eyes flush with island insanity. "You can't do this!" she cried, pointing accusingly at Skye. "You don't understand the beauty of this place. The power, and the future. It's as old as time, as life itself," she crooned. "You can't understand it, not like I do." Her silken tone caressed each word, as if she spoke of a lover. Another knife appeared in her hand as Skye pressed into my back. "And you can't kill it, Skye. Can't hurt it. I won't let you."

"And I won't let you hurt Skye." My voice was hard.

Carmen's eyes slid to me, narrowing in annoyance. "Move," she commanded. She flicked her knife at me. "This is not your fight."

"Wrong," I said. "It's not *your* fight."

"Carmen." Skye's tone was inordinately calm and soft. "It's *you* who doesn't understand this place—its history, and its pain. It's hurting, and

362

hurting others." Skye's gentle voice hardened. "When midnight comes, I will do what must be done."

Carmen's mouth curved. "As must I." She raised her weapon, then cried out as the knife flew out of her grasp. It skipped twice across the black rock before falling into the crack, swallowed by the darkness below. She spun around. James stood behind her.

"You fool! You don't know what you've done!" Carmen yelled, swinging at James. He grabbed her fist and held it tight.

"I do," he said calmly. "You will hurt no one here." He looked at me. "Rope?"

"Calvin's got some."

A few minutes later, Carmen's hands were bound with some of the extra twine.

"Where's Paulo?" Skye asked.

"With Kenji. I saw Carmen and followed her. I knew three would make too much noise so I asked them to stay behind."

A triple danger alert sounded, turning quickly into an SOS call. Make that two. One from past the meadow, by the sea; the other to the south, a chorus of trouble.

Look around, pay attention.

Barks and growls echoed in the distance, a Nil nightmare in play.

"James, do you have a torch?" I asked.

"One."

"Okay, that'll have to do. Light it now. Calvin, I want you to head down to lay the fuse. Go east, avoid the meadow if you can. You may have to tack north slightly and descend near the ruins to get to the coast. Be careful as you feed it into the cave, giving yourself plenty of distance, all right? If you have any problems, blow your whistle two times, both long. That way I'll know it's you. I'll try to get back as fast as I can. James, you stay with Carmen. Head for the platform. Hafthor, you stay with Skye. You two follow Calvin, see what's going on. Stay by the coast, take the first path so you can steer clear of the lions until you all have torches. But don't leave Skye." That last bit was a command. Hafthor nodded.

And then, repeating the past, I ran. Toward the mountain, away from Skye, angling slightly south, following a constant SOS whistle, refusing to look back. My mind had leaped ahead, toward Thad and his crew. I ran in the direction his team should be.

No, I thought, *they should already be at the mountain.* The SOS punctuated what I already knew.

Thad's team was in serious trouble.

CHAPTER 72

SKYE
AUTUMNAL EQUINOX, LATE AFTERNOON

Rives vaulted back over the crack where it narrowed, then ran alongside it, heading back south, the way we'd come, heading toward the SOS whistle that blew from that direction.

I didn't ask Rives which whistle he'd follow. I knew he'd go help Thad.

Plus, we were heading toward the coast, toward the other whistle, so I didn't need to be a rocket scientist to figure out the plan. Now I just needed to figure out how to function amid my crushing fatigue, keep up with Hafthor, and watch out for Carmen. She glared at me, venom in her eyes.

She actually tried to kill me, I thought incredulously.

And she'll try again, a tiny voice said.

"It's not you." I addressed Carmen quietly, keeping a safe distance from her. "Your hate. It's the island, feeding you." *Feeding off you,* I thought.

She laughed, cold and cruel. "As if you know me. You don't."

"And you don't know me. But I know the island, and what it does to people. And it's turning you into someone your own family wouldn't recognize."

"How dare you speak of my family?" she hissed. "Shut your filthy little mouth."

Fine, I thought. But I stopped talking, less for Carmen's sake than for mine.

I'd never been so tired. All I wanted to do was lie down and sleep.

Soon . . . the breeze crooned.

We hadn't gone far when James barked a gentle command. "Trouble on our left. Listen carefully or we'll all die."

My eyes flew to our left. Three lions and three hyenas slunk in our direction, moving silently, eyes intent on us. Each movement deliberate, the lions padded slightly in front, a lioness in the lead; the hyenas skulked well behind. We were outnumbered, six to five, with only one torch between us.

"Calvin, take the torch." James's voice was quiet. As he spoke, I readied my sling, sweeping the ground for rocks. I had only a handful in my bag, which would go quickly.

"I have my spear," James continued. "Look big, make noise. Throw rocks, aim for the cats' faces. And whatever you do, do *not* run."

James widened his stance and waved his arms, shouting. Barely moving, he inched to his left, toward the coast and slightly backward.

We all followed suit, waving our arms over our heads, yelling like crazy people. The lions slowed, possibly confused. Hafthor had surprisingly good aim, hitting two of the lions smack on the nose with rocks.

It's working, I thought. Hope blossomed in my chest.

Without stopping, we yelled, crept left, threw rocks, and made a human racket. Only twenty yards to the cliff's edge, less than ten to the trees. Now I knew where James was leading us: a path down the cliff, putting us near the hot springs and the cavern housing the Pool of Sight. Thick trees were at our backs, fifteen feet away at most.

Without warning, the ground shook. It rolled and shifted, moving like it was alive. Carmen tripped beside me, hitting the rocks with bound hands and rolling.

The lions snarled and sprinted and time slowed and spun. The ground stilled.

One cat leaped at James, mouth open, teeth bared. James froze, his face calm; he watched the lioness fly toward him, waiting. At the last possible second he rammed a spear down her open mouth. Another cat leaped at Hafthor. He grabbed the cat with two hands and head-butted the beast; they rolled on the ground as one. The third one went after Calvin, hissing and snarling at the lit torch. I slung a rock at the cat and missed.

"Help Hafthor!" I cried to Calvin, readying my sling to go again, terrified for Hafthor wrestling a lion with his bare hands. "He needs you!"

"Get behind me!" Calvin yelled.

James wrenched his spear from the dead lioness's mouth. A look of self-loathing crossed his face, then he turned toward Hafthor, bloody spear in hand.

I stepped away from Calvin and aimed for the lion still prowling out of range of the torch.

I slung. Something brushed my shoulder and I missed again. Two hands flashed in front of my face, and wire choked my neck.

"Any last words?" Carmen rasped in my ear.

Are you kidding me? I thought. And then I elbowed her hard in the ribs and pulled out the best Krav Maga move I had. She screamed and relaxed her grip, giving me the opening I needed to slip away. She clutched her side, her face contorted in pain and, strangely enough, confusion.

She stumbled away as I spun toward Hafthor.

He still grappled with the lion on the ground, arms fully extended, hands gripping the lion's mane, a battle of strength and will. Blood slicked across Hafthor's arms and torso like red paint. Hafthor lay on his back, the lion's jaws inches from his exposed throat.

I clutched my rock sling, indecisive. I didn't trust myself not to hit Hafthor. My aim seemed off. Beside me, James jockeyed to get a shot at the animal too; he circled, spear in hand, moving as stealthily as a cat himself. Shouting and hollering and the opposite of stealthy, Calvin waved the lit torch wildly at the other cat.

Carmen took off running, toward the rain forest.

Distracted, the lion darted away from Calvin, toward Carmen. This time I didn't hesitate; I had a clear shot. I steadied my shoulder, slung a rock, and struck the cat on the skull. James closed his eyes as he slid his spear into its heart, finishing what I started. Wrenching his spear out with an angry cry, he sprinted after Carmen.

I wheeled back toward Hafthor in time to see his grip on the lion's mane falter. The lion bit him on the shoulder and clamped down tight.

Hafthor roared almost as loud as the animal.

"Calvin!" I screamed. "Hurry!"

Sprinting over, Calvin pressed the lit torch against the cat's flank. Immediately, the lion recoiled; it released its grip on Hafthor and swung its head around toward the torch. Hafthor hopped to his feet, his compass tattoo destroyed, his shoulder covered in blood and missing flesh. The lion growled, deep in his throat, his fur smoking.

For one crisp second, that visual was so clear.

Hafthor swaying on his feet, dark-red blood running down his arm in rivulets; the lion facing Hafthor, his golden coat smoking, his teeth bared and bloody.

The ground rumbled, a different rhythm from before, a growing vibration that escalated with each passing second.

The smoking lion leaped at Hafthor; Calvin lunged forward with the torch, swiping close enough to actually light the lion's already-singed fur on fire. The hyenas scattered. I glanced behind me and time accelerated: a massive elephant was charging straight at us.

"Run!" I yelled.

Calvin froze. Hafthor yanked Calvin's arm, jerking him to safety; the momentum sent Hafthor stumbling toward me. Blinded by fire and fear, the burning lion charged the elephant. Immediately, the elephant jerked and changed course—straight into Hafthor, passing close enough to me that its heat brushed my skin.

The startled elephant trampled Hafthor and kept going.

The flaming lion disappeared into the trees; the other two lay dead.

I dropped to Hafthor's side. He lay on his back, bloody and beaten, his chest visibly crushed on one side. "Hafthor?" I took his hand. My voice shook. "It's Skye."

His eyelids fluttered. "Skye," he whispered. A relaxed smile pulled at his lips. "I am . . . not lost." He choked as blood bubbled on his lips. He reached up toward his shoulder, as if to touch the skin where his tattoo used to be, a move I'd seen him do countless times, like a personal reassurance; only this time his hand faltered before it ever made contact, his fingers briefly brushing Nil air before falling back to Nil ground. The light left his eyes. The pressure in my hand eased.

"Hafthor?" Tears ran down my cheeks. The ground trembled ever so slightly, and a thin wave of unbridled energy washed over me like an invisible gate, a tangible surge of pleasure and power I couldn't miss, or deny.

Hafthor lay still. I couldn't move, couldn't breathe, couldn't expand my lungs under the leaden pressure of grief and death and *loss*. The weight of pain was suffocating. I would break.

Soon . . . whispered the wind.

I didn't move.

"Skye, we've got to go," Calvin said quietly. He gently pulled me to my feet. I looked up, taking in the shock in his rich brown eyes, the blood splattered across his cheek and chest, the fading torch still burning in his hand. Now he carried two satchels: his, and Hafthor's.

"Skye." Worry crept into his tone. "We gotta get away from those dogs."

All three hyenas were attacking the first lion James had killed; they tore at the cat's lifeless body without pause. "Hyenas," I said, my voice barely a whisper. "Those are hyenas." I looked down at Hafthor. At his empty eyes. For an endless moment, I saw Dex. Then Hafthor and the faces of hundreds of others. All dead. All lost, forever.

I bent down and closed Hafthor's eyes.

"Peace," I whispered. Tears clouded my vision.

Hafthor, gone. Dex, gone.

Rives, missing.

Rives.

He was nowhere in sight. Neither was anyone else, other than Calvin, who stood watching me, waiting nervously. Fear welled, an invisible riptide sucking me out to a place I didn't want to be. For a long moment, there was no air.

You can do this, Skye. Think first, panic later.

Think.

I breathed, and I lifted my chin. I stood. I did *not* look down. "We need to get to the coast," I told Calvin, my tone uncannily calm. "Figure out who else whistled and see if they need help. And then we need to lay that fuse."

We left Hafthor behind. I couldn't match Calvin's long stride, but I held my own until we reached the cliff edge. And then I crumbled to the ground in exhaustion.

"I have to rest," I said. "Just for a minute." A foot away from Calvin, I sat with my head in my hands; it was too heavy to lift without help.

Below us sat the hot springs. The cave entrance we needed was a black hole down to our left. I couldn't see it from where I sat but I could picture it.

"I don't see anyone." Calvin frowned. "They should be here." He took out his whistle and blew two quick blasts. The reply came back right away, faint but clear: two quick blasts. Calvin blew again, a short five-note sequence I didn't recognize. The same sequence returned.

Calvin nodded, his shoulders relaxing. "Davey's all right. Same for Molly."

Calvin's torch went out, leaving wispy smoke. More smoke wafted in the sea breeze.

Look, whispered the sea.

One second, then two.

LOOK.

Glancing back, I gasped.

The trees by the meadow spat flames; they licked at the air, greedy and hot. Smoke billowed from the thickets in massive puffs.

"Calvin," I whispered. "Nil is on fire."

CHAPTER 73

RIVES
AUTUMNAL EQUINOX, ALMOST TWILIGHT

I fought the urge to look back.

To *turn* back.

Rivessss . . . whispered the wind.

Mine . . . Look . . .

I didn't rise to the bait, didn't respond. I just ran.

Get. Out.

Those two words were mine. My plea, my thoughts. My head.

Mine.

I cut around Mount Nil's base and approached the southern cliff edge just as the SOS signal blasted again. I signaled back: *heard and acknowledged.*

Someone repeated my signal from below. A shout mixed with the crash of waves, thunder booming on water, and my gut twisted. No one should be down there, on this side of Mount Nil. Here, lava dripped close enough to scald; the water burned like acid.

I peered over the edge and cursed.

Lava dripped just to the north, a river of oozing black sludge bursting with steaming red cracks as it flowed south, like hell had broken open and spilled out. Lana, Zane, and Thad sat huddled on a rock surrounded by hissing water. Zane had a bloody gash on his temple, big enough for me to see from here.

"Rives!" Thad waved. His arm was bloody too. "Down here!"

Look around, pay attention.

I needed to get them out of harm's way, and get them *up*. I almost yelled *Sit tight*, but it wasn't like they had another option.

I headed south until I found a cliff angle that looked slightly less likely to result in instant death. Slipping and sliding, I managed to get down in one piece.

Pressing my back to the cliff, I worked my way back along the water's edge until I reached the trio. They sat on a rock, trapped by the tide, but they were close enough that they could hop across the water. Maybe a two-meter clearance, at most.

"You're going to have to jump!" I said. "No way around it."

"Can't." Thad grimaced. "Zane busted his ankle. Plus, I think he's got a concussion."

"I'm fine!" Zane raised his hand and tapped his bloody forehead. "A mere flesh wound."

"Right." Lana rolled her eyes as she pointed to his ankle. "Because we're supposed to see bone poking out of your skin." Despite her normal edge, Lana sounded worried.

"I can swing him across," Thad said. "But I need you to catch him."

Getting Zane across was brutal. Keeping his ankle out of the water, trying to keep him upright. But after repeated efforts and a few near-epic fails, Thad, Lana, and I succeeded in getting him across the water. Zane didn't even pass out, which was impressive, because his ankle looked like it'd been smashed between two boulders, which essentially, Thad told me, it had.

Half dragging, half pushing, the three of us even managed to get Zane back up the cliff. We eased him to the ground, then we collapsed, catching our breath. Nothing and no one was around. Just us, panting, and Nil, listening.

My mouth was dry. From thirst, from dread.

"What happened?" I asked Thad quietly. Lana and Zane lay just to our left. "Why were you guys so far south?"

"Zane thought he heard someone. It started at South Beach on our first day out, and we ended up following the voice all the way back to the City. No one was there. Then we turned around, now a full day behind. This morning, Zane started hearing a voice again. A different one, but still. I couldn't convince him it wasn't real."

"Sounds familiar. Calvin heard voices too. But we never found anyone."

Thad hesitated. "We didn't either. At first I wasn't sure, because I thought I heard it too. But then—" He glanced at Zane. "He wouldn't listen. He was frantic. We could barely keep up with him. We were at the base of this cliff when that tremor hit, and we were trapped. I don't remember that much lava being here before, but man, there's a river of it now. The rocks shifted so fast, some slid down. Zane slipped, he went flying. When he fell, he messed up his ankle and knocked himself out." Thad shook his head. "On the upside, he's not hearing the voice anymore." He shrugged. "Maybe he knocked Nil out of his head, eh?"

"Maybe." *Concussions as a Nil antidote? More like a Nil side effect*, I thought.

I knelt beside Zane. "You hanging in there, Z?"

"You know it, Chief." He smiled, then winced. "Sorry I screwed this up. But I really thought I heard him." Pain rippled across his face like a shadow. "And I couldn't have left him hanging if it was him."

"Who?"

"Sy." Zane gave a pained laugh. "But it wasn't him. And I almost walked straight into lava thinking I was seeing Sy. That he was calling for me, for help. Seriously, I nearly barbecued myself. The quake actually saved me. Talk about screwed up." He sighed, his eyes wide open. "Now Garrett doesn't seem so crazy."

"Where *is* Garrett?" I glanced around. I'd forgotten all about the rookie.

"He died," Lana whispered. "It was awful."

"What?" I stared at her.

"Rives." Thad looked incredibly uncomfortable. "It's not good. He walked off the cliff. He was talking to someone, and he literally just stepped off the edge, into thin air."

"Nil made him do it," Lana said with finality. "It's the only thing that makes sense. I think he saw something, but whatever he saw wasn't real."

Like Talla in the gate, leading us here.

Nil's head games had turned deadlier than ever.

Lana rubbed her arms; I realized she was shivering. The breeze blew cool against our damp skin. Daylight was fading fast.

This world tasted stale, the air bitter on my tongue.

Skye.

I jumped to my feet, feeling the pressure of dwindling time, like I was trapped at the bottom of an hourglass and all the grains of sand were pouring down on me, weighty and suffocating.

"We need to go." I quickly slid an arm under Zane's shoulder as I spoke. "Zane, Thad and I will support you, but we have to hurry. We only have a little bit of daylight left. We should light a torch just to be safe. It'll be dark fast."

"I don't think we'll need a torch," Lana said. She pointed east. "The island's already burning."

CHAPTER 74

NIL
TWILIGHT

The island watched the various humans scurry around, their laughable plan underway.

Run, the island thought. Light your fires. Make your stand.

The island would revel in watching the humans burn.

Burning brought the cruelest pain of all. The island recoiled at the memory, then roared at remembered pain, seething with hate and bloodlust and a thirst for vengeance that would never be slaked.

But tonight would be a start.

Tonight, the humans would burn as one, their group death incredibly useful, providing the long-awaited surge of electria powerful enough to shatter the seam forever. The island would no longer be tethered to this shell. It would be free.

And then it would unleash chaos on a new level, in a new world, in their world.

Yes, the island thought, trembling with anticipation as the humans crafted their own pyre. Fuel your fires. We will burn together. But you will be the ones to die.

CHAPTER 75

SKYE
AUTUMNAL EQUINOX, FADING TWILIGHT

The island rocked beneath my feet. I felt shaky and weirdly disoriented. Beside me, Calvin stared at the fire.

Fear washed over me like an icy breeze. It woke me up, like a slap to my cheek.

How long had we been standing there?

The sun was a blood-red ball grazing the water, and we still had to put all the torches in place and set the fuse. *It couldn't have been long*, I told myself.

But we'd had no time to lose. *How could this happen?*

Starting to shake, I grabbed Calvin's arm and shook him too. "Calvin! We need to go!"

He blinked, understanding hitting with the setting sun. Together we scrambled down the cliff, our feet touching the sandy rock at the base just as Molly popped into sight around the corner.

"Skye!" Molly's cry burst with relief.

"Where's Davey?" I asked.

"With Dominic. They're coming, with Paulo and Kenji."

"Anyone else?"

Molly shook her head.

"We heard the danger blasts and the SOS. Who's in trouble?" Fear swelled in my heart; I fought it even as I stared at Molly, dreading her words.

"You." Molly's eyes were sad. "And Hafthor. He's gone, isn't he?"

I nodded.

Molly squeezed her eyes shut, breathing shallowly. "I tried to warn you, but—" She broke off, shaking her head. "I tried." Tears leaked from her eyes. I wanted to comfort her, but I couldn't. I couldn't hug her, or comfort her, or tell her it was okay, because right now, this entire place was definitely not okay, and the pain pumping through my heart would give her a nasty vision of the future—or at least an extraordinarily painful one.

Mine.

I pictured myself walking into death's arms, torch in hand, taking Nil with me. Molly didn't need to see it too. At least I saw myself winning. That visual gave me strength. It gave me the courage to give up what I wanted most: a future with Rives.

But life wasn't always fair, or easy.

Or long, I thought.

And deep down, I secretly couldn't wait to give up the pain of this world. It was too much.

Molly coughed, and her eyes flew open as she sniffed. "Is that smoke?"

"Yes." I focused, because I had to; I fought to think around my pain and fatigue. "We need to lay the fuse and set as many torches as we can. We can't wait."

"About that." Molly turned red. "We lost quite a few when the earthquake hit."

"How many?" Calvin asked.

"All but two," she said, cringing. "But Paulo and Kenji have a good dozen." She turned. "Here they come."

A few seconds later the boys came into sight and we got to work as the last rays of sunlight faded. The wind picked up as darkness fell; it spat sand into my face and grabbed hold of my hair and whipped it around like an invisible bully.

Calvin and Paulo set the fuse line, with Paulo gently feeding it inside the cave. We backtracked, unwinding the line and setting torches to guide Calvin later, but we didn't light them, not yet. We worked quickly, but when we climbed back up, I was shocked at how much the fire had grown.

Flames of orange and yellow tipped with red leaped into the black Nil sky, snarling and hot. Invisible bursts of heat punched us like fists; the entire meadow raged with fire, cracking and roiling and feeding off the wind. Dry grasses, new grasses—all burned with a vengeance.

Rives and Thad's team were still missing, lost in the dark. *To* the dark.

I spun toward Molly. "Can you see them? Rives and Thad?" My voice was pleading, like my heart. "Please tell me they're not trapped in the fire."

Molly's brows pinched together. "I can't see them; all I see is darkness. Which means nothing. This gift is so useless!" she groaned, grabbing her head.

The wind picked up. It howled, streaking past as loud as a scream. Behind us the water crashed and roared with a frightening intensity, the waves churned by the wind and fueled by the crescent moon.

"I hear her again!" Kenji yelled. "I'm going back."

"Back?" I snapped my head toward him.

"I'll come with you!" Paulo shouted.

"No!" Molly cried. "It's no one!"

"We have to be sure!" Paulo was already moving. "If there's even a chance, we have to save her! Be right back!"

"Who are they talking about?" I asked Molly as Kenji and Paulo dashed back down to the rocky beach. I moved slightly north, trying to see where the boys were headed.

"A girl. Kenji heard her all day." Walking beside me, Molly watched the darkness where Kenji and Paulo had vanished. "It's why we were so late. She's behind us. Kenji says she sounds scared. But each time we backtrack, we can't find her, and I've never seen her, not even a glimpse." Molly turned back to the sea, to the dark open water. "I don't think she's real. I think Hafthor was right about his hidden people, at least about something here that we can't see—that *I* can't see—something that likes to play games." She didn't move. "It's the island, isn't it?" she said quietly. "It's toying with all of us."

Like prey, snared in its island web. I thought back to the day we'd arrived, when Nil had shown each of us a different face in the gate. And in that moment I knew we'd underestimated Nil. The island toyed with each of us, pulling from the past to steal our future, messing with our minds with a power we couldn't fathom.

"Yes," I said. "But not for long."

It ends tonight, I thought, my resolve mixing with relief and anger. *By my hand.*

Molly nodded at me, her eyes bright with tears, her smile sad. Then she coughed. The meadow's heat pressing thickly against our faces, like the smoke. She peered at the cliff's edge.

"It's taking the boys too long," she murmured, worried.

Everything was taking too long; time was slipping away, and taking our careful plan with it. The noise, the heat, the darkness and flames—the platform felt so far away, our plan crumbling like ashes in the dark.

Where are all the teams?

Where is Rives? my heart cried.

My name was a dying shout on the wind.

"Did you hear that?" I asked Molly, hope flaring. I leaned closer to the heat. "Someone called my name." *Maybe* I'm *hearing things now*, my rational side informed me snidely.

Then I heard it again.

"There it is!" I spun toward Molly. "Did you hear that?"

She shook her head sadly.

Dominic stepped up beside me. "I heard it. Your name." He smiled. "I do not think we both are imagining that voice."

"Stay here," I said. "I'm going to go to the platform and see if anyone's there."

Molly grabbed my arm, her eyes wide as she jerked back. "No!"

"Why?"

"Oh no," she whispered. She wrapped her arms around her chest, her hands in fists, breathing rapidly, looking between the mountain and the meadow and somewhere I couldn't see.

"Bloody hell," Davey said from behind me. One hand rested on Molly's back, steadying them both. "Do you see that?" He pointed to the middle of the field, where flames spun in a surreal circle.

"A twister. We're about to have a bloody firenado!"

"Run," Molly whispered.

Leaving the cliff's edge, we sprinted across the meadow's south border. The wind whipped mercilessly, screaming and churning; a funnel cloud of fire rose into the night, twisting and clawing as if spawned by hell itself. Fire raged; a rhino cut our way. Dominic shifted cleanly out of its path, and one second later, the wind snatched Dominic off his feet. He flew up into the sky and disappeared.

"Dominic!" I screamed.

The wind howled; the air burned. My skin felt as though it were melting.

"Get to the platform!" Molly yelled. "Go!"

Up the steps we raced, curving around the mountain until we piled onto the black rock. Cooler night air, dark rock. Smoke dulled the crispness of the sky. I could still see the crescent moon winking at me.

The abrupt change was surreal.

Cocooned in stillness and peace, the platform stood in stark contrast to the devastation below.

Hafthor, gone. Dominic, gone.

Rives, missing. Like Thad and Paulo.

My head and heart couldn't accept the terrible reality unfolding in the Nil dark.

Molly stood stone still in shock, Davey's arm wrapped around her shoulder. Soot coated her face, her eyes bright and blinking, against the smoke or visions, I didn't know. I didn't ask.

It was a nightmare.

Walking alone, I went over to the platform's carving and bent down. The diamond eye winked at me, the rings begging to be touched. Gleaming at me was a small bracelet, rough twine holding a raw diamond, a gift from my past. *Happy birthday*, Rives had told me as he'd slipped it on my wrist, his expression radiating love.

I love you, I thought, grieving for what I'd already lost, what I had to give up. *I love you with all that I am, with every last part of me.*

I picked up the bracelet and slid it on. Nil's memories had shown me exactly where to find it; I'd watched it fall as if I'd been standing there myself.

I stood there, alone, until footsteps and shouts made me turn.

Kenji skidded onto the platform, breathing hard. "We couldn't find the girl before a tiger made us turn back. Paulo stayed with Calvin to help light the last torches to guide his run. Paulo says we don't have long. And there was a fire funnel cloud in the meadow, totally crazy. Rives and Thad are coming up now. Zane and Lana too."

Rives.

Relief turned my legs to jelly. Rives was okay. Right now, that was enough.

I leaned against the far wall, resting my shoulder against the same spot where Paulo had waited on the day we'd arrived. He'd asked to be last tonight, but the job was mine. *Our destiny*, his aunt had told my uncle, *it wraps the island from beginning to end; I feel it.* He'd been last before. Now it was my turn. Paulo's ancestors had been with Nil at the beginning, and I'd be with Nil at the end. I'd make sure tonight *was* Nil's end.

And yours, the night whispered.

Yes, I thought. *We'll go down together.* I breathed deeply, aware I couldn't block Nil out. But I could keep myself *in*, as in intact, until the very end: Nil's, and mine.

Rives appeared on the platform with Thad and Zane, his chest and arms streaked with black and red like war paint. My breath hitched until I realized it wasn't his blood; it was Zane's. His temple bloody, Zane's teeth were gritted in pain, his left knee bent, his foot twisted the wrong way, his ankle bloody as he leaned on Rives.

His pain hit me like a wall of heat. Burning, scalding. Choking.

Real.

The crushing, visceral pain tipped my hand; it erased the last self-ish shard of doubt that had lingered in my heart. Zane's pain was a grain of Nil sand compared to the unthinkable suffering of our entire world should Nil survive this night. Because only one of us could win: me, or Nil. And I refused to lose, even though it would cost me everything.

I would be last. It was the only way.

I locked eyes with Rives, a boy covered in soot and sweat and the blood of our friend, a boy I loved more than my own life, and I made my unequivocal choice: I would win.

For Rives, and for his children to come.

CHAPTER 76

RIVES
AUTUMNAL EQUINOX, BEFORE MIDNIGHT

We never should have split up.

Nil had divided us, and damn near conquered us. Gotten into our heads, messed with our minds. The meadow massacre almost did us in. The fire twister didn't last long, but it was long enough.

If we'd been caught in the open, we'd have been roasted alive.

But thanks to Zane, we were slow, buying us the crucial time we needed to stay alive. Then again, we wouldn't have been there if Zane hadn't let Nil into his head in the first place.

Stop with the what-ifs, I told myself. If I kept up that train of thought, I'd get to how I should never have let Skye go to the Death Twin, never let her even get close. *As if I could ever tell Skye what to do.* That thought brought me full circle back to this horrific moment.

To the *now.*

Skye was preparing to sacrifice herself for Nil, and no one could convince her otherwise.

A few meters away, Skye twisted something on her wrist, something that glittered in the torchlight, shining in the dark like the steel flecks in her eyes. With a start, I realized it was the bracelet I'd given her the last time we were here, a birthday present, a symbol of *more.*

Understanding struck.

Nil had pulled us apart, become a wedge between us. And I had let it. I'd played right into Nil's hands.

Merde.

I was a fool.

I strode to Skye, stopping so close I could whisper in her ear if I wanted to.

"Skye," I said quietly. A wild curl blew around her face. I fought the urge to tuck it behind her ear, aware I'd lost the right to touch her.

She lifted her eyes to mine. "I'm scared," she admitted. The torch-light cast shadows on her face, dark and greedy.

"You can't be brave if you're fearless," I said, my chest aching. "And you're the bravest person I know. If you weren't afraid, I'd be worried."

She stood there, nodding, twisting her bracelet, biting the inside of her cheek.

Watching her struggle, the pieces of my heart fused and shattered all over again. My Skye stood right here: the girl I wanted to travel the world with, the girl I wanted to capture on film until we were both old and gray, the girl of my dreams and my future. The girl who had single-handedly chosen to take down Nil, sacrificing herself for *us*, even though the cost was her life. This was the fierce, selfless, stubborn girl I'd fallen in love with. How could I ask her to be any less?

I stepped close enough that I could bend forward and graze her lips with mine. But I didn't. I stood, motionless, as my gaze found hers. Her steel-flecked eyes were packed with questions.

"I'm a fool, Skye." My voice was hoarse. "A bloody idiot, as Dex always said. I love you, Skye. So much it hurts. I can't imagine what you're going through, and I'm so sorry I haven't been there to support you. I'm an idiot for wasting the precious time we had left. You are the fiercest, bravest person I know, and the most selfless. I know that you wouldn't do this unless you thought it was the only way. I just wish it weren't."

A tear streaked down Skye's face, a clear track against the dirt and soot. "I know."

"Please forgive me." My voice cracked.

"There's nothing to forgive. The end is written." Her smile was wry.

"Maybe it is, maybe it isn't. I always thought our future was *ours*. I'm not ready to give that up. To give *you* up."

"But you have to." Skye wiped her cheek, steeling herself against her emotions; I watched her rein it all in. "There's no way out, not for me. Whatever Nil did to me, we're linked. You have to let me go," she whispered.

Never, I thought. I choked out the only words I could. "I love you, Skye. And I always will."

She threw herself into my arms. Her skin burned; her body shook.

"Too much," she whispered.

It's all too much, I thought. *For her. For me. For us.*

With Skye in my arms, I didn't want the moment to end. I wanted the world to stop, right here, right now; I wanted this moment to last forever; I wanted *more*; I wanted it all: Skye, our future, our happily ever after. I wanted a lifetime of these moments.

But it was almost midnight. Our time was up.

Thad blew his whistle, making time slip into a faster gear. More whistles echoed down the line like dominoes; within seconds Calvin would light the fuse and start running.

The black diamond eye on the ground shimmered.

Molly drew in a sharp breath.

"What is it?" I didn't let go of Skye as I spoke.

"The wind!" Molly said. "The fuse won't stay lit. And it's not burning like it should." She blinked, slowly. "It's out."

"It's *out*?" I frowned. Skye went still.

A second later, the shimmering ground took flight. In the center of the platform, a writhing wall of air vaulted straight up into the sky, black on black, massive and powerful. A picture frame of freedom for us, and death for Skye. One doorway, winner take all.

Only winning meant losing.

Skye dropped my hand, regret in her eyes, resolve in the set of her chin.

I couldn't breathe.

"Calvin's running," Molly said. Her eyes were unfocused, then she startled. "Oh no!" Her hands flew to her mouth. "Brace yourselves."

An explosion rocked the ground. We fell to our knees, except for Zane, who was already on the ground. Unaffected by the massive jolt, the gate locked into place. The black dropped away, leaving a liquid wall behind: a glittering doorway, a million grains of silver sand as bright as stars.

Now, it whispered.

"Go!" Thad yelled, pointing at Kenji. Without a word, Kenji hurtled through the gate.

Molly turned to Skye. Tears streamed down Molly's face, but her voice stayed calm. "Paulo chose. He knew what he was doing."

"Chose?" Skye looked lost.

Molly nodded. "He walked into the cave, by choice. The fuse went out, so Paulo lit the gas himself, with the last torch he had."

Horror filled Skye's eyes as comprehension dawned. "He walked into the cave with a lit torch? *That* was the explosion?"

Molly nodded again. Tears spilled from her eyes without pause.

Thad tapped Molly's shoulder. "Molly, you have to go. Now!" He shoved her toward the gate. She stepped into the doorway, then her eyes went wide as she whirled to face us, a shimmering, brilliant version of herself. "Help Dominic!" she cried. And then she was gone.

On cue, Dominic stumbled onto the platform, coughing. His left side was burned from his hip to his calf; his skin glistened with wet blood. "That fire was something else, mon." His front tooth was broken. His smile didn't reach his eyes

Thad pushed Davey toward the gate. "Go! I'll help Dominic!"

Calvin bounded up onto the platform after Dominic, blinking and coughing.

The entire platform rocked as the mountain trembled.

Out of the corner of my eye, silver flashed. Lana jumped in front of Skye, beating me by a split second. An instant later Carmen's knife slid into Lana's shoulder rather than Skye's heart.

"No!" Carmen screamed, wrenching out the knife and lunging for Skye. I caught Carmen by her arms and held her tight.

Lana pressed her hand against her injured shoulder. Blood trickled between her fingers. "I didn't need the Sight to know you were trouble," Lana told Carmen, her voice tired. "Or that this place must end. I saw firsthand what it can do, Carmen. It's evil. And you're just a pawn."

"Checkmate," I said forcefully.

Gripping Carmen's biceps, I threw her into the gate.

"Lana!" Zane said. He'd crawled over to us in the darkness. "Are you okay?"

"A mere flesh wound." Her smile was a grimace.

"Who's hurt worse?" I looked between the two. "Who's stronger?"

"You really have to ask?" Zane pointed to Lana. "She's totally stronger."

I turned to Lana. "Go first. Then pull him through. You got it? And watch out for Carmen on the other end!"

Nodding, Lana strode to the gate. Blood dripped down her useless left arm. She stepped into the doorway. Light glittered across her face, reflecting the crescent moon above. Then, she vanished.

One second. Two.

Thad had helped Zane get close to the gate, keeping himself out of range. "I don't want to throw you in," he said. "Can you make it on your own?"

Zane nodded. He hopped on his good foot into the gate, falling fast into the portal with two thumbs up.

Dominic went next, then Calvin.

Tick tock.

"Rives!" Thad shouted.

I turned around and came face to face with James and a massive Bengal tiger.

"He is next," James said, his hand on the tiger's back. "It is right."

I didn't have time to argue, not that it would've mattered. It was a freaking Bengal tiger. It strolled past me and into the gate as if it owned the place.

Heads up, Calvin, I thought as the cat vanished.

Two heartbeats later, James followed the cat.

It was me, Thad, and Skye.

I couldn't miss the torch in her hand or the tears on her face. This was it. The moment I'd dreaded, the moment I lost everything.

Skye.

Thad squeezed my shoulder, then leaped into the gate. The ground rumbled beneath my feet, ominous and angry.

Skye stared at me. Her torch lit her face with a golden glow, setting the sparks in her eyes on fire.

I couldn't leave her. Not here, not ever.

"No." My heated defiance flooded the platform. "I'll walk in with you. We'll do this together. We'll finish this *together*."

"We are," she said softly. "But you know two people can't go at once. It has to be me."

"No, it doesn't." Fire roared and smoke choked the air. Desperation choked me. "I'll do it."

"You told me once you'd do anything for me." Her voice shook, but her gaze didn't waver. "And now I'm asking you to live. To walk into that gate and let me go. I won't throw you in this time. I need it to be your choice. I need you to do this for me."

I didn't move.

"Please," she whispered. "Go. Do all the things we talked about. Take a picture of the river Seine, the one you were named for, in the place where your parents kissed. Go to the university like you planned. See the world. Fall in love. Live." She pointed at the gate. Tears spilled from her eyes like falling stars. "Go. Please."

Please.

I broke. I broke *for her.*

Because this was how she wanted it to end.

I backed away. "I love you." It wasn't enough, not even close. My voice cracked. "You won't be alone. I'll be with you, okay? To the end."

My eyes never left hers, not when I stumbled as the rock shifted, not when I felt the heat, not when it closed around me, not when it stole my breath. The last image I had was of Skye standing alone on Nil ground, a burning torch in hand, the wind whipping her blond hair around her face like golden flames, her unblinking gaze fixed on me. She lifted one hand to her mouth, pressed her fingers to her lips wet with tears, then held out her hand, offering me one last kiss.

I reached for her, but she was already gone.

The darkness rushed in, severing me from Skye forever. The cut cleaved all the way to my core, cruel and permanent.

To my relief, I blacked out.

CHAPTER 77

NIL
AUTUMNAL EQUINOX, MIDNIGHT

Pain.

Impossible pain.

Searing, consuming, and wholly unbearable; the island twisted and writhed, trapped as it burned from the inside out and the outside in. It fought with the intensity of a different world, a different time; it unleashed the full force of the electria swirling within, using the visceral rush of energy to battle the flames. It roared against the pain, blind fury erupting. Pain mixed with power; the invisible battle raged between worlds, between sides. Within itself.

The past fused into the now.

Now the one called Skye clung to life between worlds, trapped in the seam; she had brought the pain; she had released the power. She had become the keystone—her electria kept the seam from collapsing, from expanding, for she held the power within.

She was the conduit between the past and the future.

She was the one.

With patient deliberation and fearsome rage, the island turned its faces to her.

This was the moment.

The future was now.

CHAPTER
78

SKYE
AUTUMNAL EQUINOX, MIDNIGHT

The burn began like the strike of a match, quick and bearable, reminiscent of the gates I'd taken before, the kind of gate that flips from heat to ice, then brings the sweet relief of freedom.

Not this gate.

The simple flame licking my skin exploded into a solar flare, blistering and burning, as if the match had been tossed into an ocean of gasoline. The fireball engulfed me, as hot as the sun.

I was Icarus, burning.

Melting.

Falling.

The pain was unbearable.

I did the only thing I could: I retreated within.

Within *me*.

White walls, closed room.

I slammed the door and locked it tight, squeezing my eyes closed, shutting everything out. This room—this quiet sanctuary within me—was where I would ride out the end. Where *I* would end, taking Nil with me.

Beyond the walls, the darkness roared. Fire exploded from the inside out and the outside in, ignited by the torch I'd carried into the gate; the door rattled under the pressure. Even here I sensed it: the frightening depth of Nil's fury and fear . . . its hope and its hate . . . and above all, its *pain*; echoes of it all battered the walls around me. It was extraordinary, and extraordinarily terrible.

Nil was being burned alive.

Inside my room, inside *me*, memories swirled like a vortex, drawing me deeper.

A thin boy with my eyes, carving the words Look Inside.

Thad, throwing Charley into a gate, victory on his face.

Lana, tracing a rough 3-2-1-4, her finger lingering on the 4.

A girl named Macy, peace in her soul, whispering, Four chambers of the heart.

The princess, believing.

The prince, returning.

Talla, begging, Choose me.

Me, telling Paulo, You always have a choice.

Paulo, choosing.

My dad, urging, Think.

Rives, saying, Balance reigns.

Rives, vowing, I love you.

Rives, his heart breaking, letting me go.

My heart skipped.

My heart, not Nil's. I'd created this place, inside me, a place Nil couldn't breach, a place where my heart and soul and mind were mine alone. Light blazed around me, soothing, not burning, the light of a new moon, the light of a new day.

The white—the *light*—was mine.

Clarity struck, quelling all thoughts but one: I had the power to choose.

I had the *power*.

Love was stronger than hate, stronger than fear; love turned pain into strength, into a power I could wield. I wasn't alone, I didn't have to die alone, and just maybe I didn't have to die at all. Nil's pain was not mine. I could block it out. I already had, right here, right now.

I would trap Nil in the dark, rather than hide in the light.

I choose to live.

I flung open the door and stepped into the maelstrom of fire. The protective walls vanished; silky darkness converged around me with a choking power: snarling and hungry and cruelly ecstatic; it burned to live, and lived to burn. Behind my eyes, the world churned black and red, like lava, like molten steel. Heat seared my skin; darkness brushed my mind.

And I *knew*.

The darkness had already declared victory; it relished the fight. It wanted to toy and to hurt, to bring me to my knees and break me; it ached to revel in the power of my pain. Images of Paulo and Hafthor, of Dai and Dex and Talla and hundreds of others roared through my head, a silent film infused with painful emotions in levels coldly designed to make me shatter; cruel laughter imbued with hate and power echoed in my head even as it fought to claim me.

No.

My thought was calm, because I'd made my choice. I'd chosen to die; then chosen to live. My future hinged on the *now*. Now the fight was mine.

I would fight fire with fire.

Reaching through the darkness, I reached deep inside, into that place Nil couldn't touch *because it couldn't understand*, and I grasped all the love and light and beauty I held inside my heart—and with all the strength of my human soul, I flung my power into the black void.

Rives.

I pictured his face as he looked back at me with grief in his heart; I remembered his incredible depth of compassion and kindness, his last promise and his fierce declaration of love; I imagined our future, the one he'd given up *because I'd asked him to*. Because I thought I needed to die with Nil for Nil to die.

But my heart wasn't entwined with Nil's, nor was my fate.

Nil wasn't my counterweight.

That was Rives.

Rives! I shouted his name in the dark.

I CHOOSE TO LIVE.

I poured every bit of love I'd ever felt into the fiery blackness around me. Love brought the greatest pain and the sweetest joy; it was the purest source of power I'd ever felt; I wielded it like armor and sword alike. Love offered hope and light and protection and forgiveness, and with my very last breath, I pitted all of mine against the cruel dark.

Love for Rives.

Love for my parents. Love for my friends.

Love for Jillian and Dex, for Charley and Thad. For Hafthor and Paulo.

Love uniting Rives and me; love binding Charley and Thad; love bursting between Molly and Davey. Love shared by others I'd never met, others the island had known, love that brought people home and pulled them *through*. Love wrapped me like armor, absorbing the fire and the pain; walls rose around me of my own creation.

I was bound in light and life and love. I was on fire, and it came from me.

Love cleaved the dark; it revealed a speck of light, still there, dim but present. A girl stood in the dark, smiling.

Talla.

She nodded, once; the flames flickered.

In the deepest part of me, I felt a stillness. Abrupt and unexpected, the barest whisper of time. The tiniest fraction of the *now*.

A hesitation.

It was enough.

Coolness pressed against my shoulder blade, a soothing liquid touch in the midst of cruel fire.

Live.

The hand on my back *pushed.*

I hurtled forward as the fire turned to ice. A thick layer of me stripped away, taking a suffocating weight with it, leaving my entire body stinging and raw and *free*—and then there was nothing.

No dark, no pain.

Just me, tumbling through, wrapped in my shell of light.

No air. No direction.

Rives.

He was my final thought before there was absolutely nothing at all.

CHAPTER 79

RIVES
AUTUMNAL EQUINOX, MIDNIGHT

I came to under another glittering crescent moon.

Black night, black ground, blackness in my head.

I turned toward the gate still writhing in the air like a mirror.

Please turn black, I begged. *Send her through. Send her back, to me.*
Please.

The gate seethed, shifting and rolling, billowing mightily as if a battle warred within. But the color didn't shift. No black, not when I was desperate for it.

The ground rocked. A warning shift.

Thad grabbed my arm. He hauled me away from the gate, as he pressed athletic shorts into my hands.

"Rives! This rock is shaking. Let's go!"

I shook off his arm as I slid on the shorts. Professor Bracken stood nearby, arms crossed, gazing at the gate, grief written all over his face. I couldn't meet his eyes.

I'd broken my promise to him.

I whipped my head back toward the gate. I'd made a promise to Skye, too, and I damn sure wouldn't break it.

SKYE!

"Rives!" Charley cried. "You have to come!"

"No." I stared at the gate. "I promised Skye. I won't leave her," I said. *I promised her she wouldn't die alone.* I didn't count Nil as company.

In my mind, Nil didn't count at all.

I dropped to my knees. I would stay with Skye to the end.

Skye!

The gate writhed, still open. Still taunting me with hope.

"Rives!" Thad shouted. "We have to go, brother!"

I didn't move. With Skye in my soul, I focused on the gate hanging a few meters high, thinking of all I couldn't see; I thought of the darkness, real and cruel and hell-bent on keeping her; I fought it like Skye had done for months, only now I fought for her.

Skye!

Pushing through that blackness, I reached for Skye with my mind, willing her to hear me. To *feel* me, to give her strength, to show her that she wasn't alone.

I hit a wall. Invisible and unyielding, it pushed me back. Repelled me with shocking force.

And my heart told me Skye was trapped behind it.

SKYE!

I love you with all that I am. I am with you, always.

Skye.

I breathed her name, reaching for her with my soul, knowing this was it. My final shot. For her to hear me, for her to beat Nil.

For her to find her way back.

Because if anyone could find a way out, it was my Skye.

Tick.

Tock.

The gate's iridescence surged. I shielded my eyes from the flash. The writhing doorway glowed like a white-hot ember in the night, burning more brilliantly than I'd ever seen. Not reflecting the crescent moon above but lit from within—like a fragment of the surface of the sun.

Something terrible was about to happen. I took a step backward as a crisp thought slashed through my head:

RUN.

I ran.

Still writhing in midair, every speck of the gate turned a brilliant orange-red. Fire red.

And then the gate exploded.

The force of the blast blew me back. I slammed into the ground as flames shot from the gate; they blew past me with a powerful rush of air unlike anything I'd ever felt before. Noise rumbled like a freight train as the ground shook; my ears rang, then an equally massive surge of air roared back the way the first one had come, sucked back into the gate. Branches and rocks and a cat flew past, toward the gate; I grabbed hold of a tree, bracing against the snarling rush of air. Lana slid past me, her hands scrabbling along the ground as she tried to stop her slide. I caught hold of her ankle and held it tight

Abruptly, the wind surge stopped. The mountain was half destroyed; its top, gone. The platform itself had split in two; a jagged crack mutilated the ground, the intricate rings destroyed.

The gate was gone.

Skye!

Hauling myself to my knees, I searched for Skye, first scanning the platform's perimeter, then closing my eyes and reaching with my mind.

Nothing. Just me, in my own head. No darkness, no remnant of Skye.

Around me, trees crackled, their tips on fire.

"Skye!" I screamed. It came out a choked rasp.

"Rives!" the professor yelled. He sounded far away. "We have to go!"

"No!" I threw off his arm. "Not when Skye's still there!"

"She'll take the next one," he said, his iron grip insistent. "She has time!"

I stared at him, stunned. *He doesn't know. He doesn't know Skye brought fire into the gate. That Skye sacrificed herself for humanity's future.*

That she was gone.

"This island is unstable, and it's on fire." His voice softened. "It's time to go, son."

"He's right." Thad's quiet voice sounded behind me. I turned to find him flanked by Lana and Charley. The pair wore matching expressions of shock and grief. "Skye would want you to go. She would want you to live."

I'm asking you to live, Skye had told me, tears in her eyes, resolve in her heart. *To walk into that gate and let me go.*

I'd left her behind. She'd asked me to, but the choice was mine.

Her choice was selfless. Mine had felt forced. And yet I'd have to live with it, with Skye's death on my hands.

The heat intensified. Around us, the trees spat flames.

I stared at the platform until Thad ripped me away.

And then I ran. Through the trees, away from the platform, toward the water and the waiting boat.

Away from Skye.

The mountain rumbled. Behind us, billowing steam filled the night sky, obliterating the stars. The Death Twin burned.

I'd *lost.*

Skye was gone, forever.

Live, she'd said.

How could I live without her?

CHAPTER 80

SKYE
AUTUMNAL EQUINOX, MIDNIGHT

Salty night air kissed my skin seconds before I hit the water. Black night and brilliant stars fought with billowing smoke and spitting flames; below me, inky water glittered like the deepest part of a gate, the sort of darkness with the potential to suck you under forever—the kind of darkness where you could be lost. I struck the water, and went under.

Water as cold as the Crystal Cove pressed against my mouth, dark and searching and wanting more; it wrapped me in ice, as constrictive as a gate and just as deadly. There was no up or down, no right or left; every direction pressed in equally cold, equally black.

All deadly.

I writhed in the gate, burning.

I twisted in the gate, freezing.

I was on Nil.

I was part of Nil.

I was one with Nil.

Birth, life, death.

Time slowed, time stopped. Rewound, sped up, fast-forwarded, and paused; every second I'd lived settled into the *now*.

Now, I was me.

Now, I was *free*.

Think.

I stopped fighting the water. I relaxed, letting myself float, relying on my own body to tell me which direction to go. Then I kicked, hard, with everything I had. When I broke the surface, I barely avoided being slammed by a falling piece of flaming rock; I ducked back underwater at the last minute. Sparks and debris and ash fell around me, fireworks raining from the sky. I strained to make out any sign of a boat. Surely my dad would've brought a boat. The moon and flames glowed across the water, helping me get my bearings, bright enough to tell me that the shallow beach was on the opposite side of the island.

Start swimming, Skye, I told myself. *You can do this.*

I started toward the island's rocky coastline, but the current fought to pull me away.

The Death Twins, our boat captain had called them. And now the deadly current rushing between the islands was pulling me out to sea.

I fought and I swam and when my strength flagged I floated on my back. I closed my eyes, trying to think my way out of this new mess. If I'd made it off Nil only to die at sea, the irony was ridiculous.

Like Uncle Scott, I thought.

But I'm not Uncle Scott.

I started swimming again, fiercely, sideways, out of the riplike current running between the islands, determined to make it back alive.

Someone yelled my name. I stopped swimming.

"Get in," a familiar voice said. It belonged to the last person I wanted to see.

I turned to find Carmen in a canoe, floating a few feet away on the inky water. She wore a gray T-shirt and dark shorts, her wardrobe choices telling me my dad was close.

Why would I get in a canoe with a girl who just an hour ago wanted me dead?

"I won't hurt you," she said quietly, offering her hand. "You have my word."

The shore was still a good thirty feet away, and past the rocks, the island burned. Flames reached for the stars. Even if I *could* make it to the island, no one would be there. No one would stick around for the island finale, which might involve the steaming volcano.

Plus, I was tired. Dead tired.

I stared at Carmen's offered hand. Dad's words rang in my ears. *Sometimes . . . you must take a chance.*

It was how I had ended up on Nil to begin with, and it was how I had survived.

I took her hand.

Carmen dragged me into the canoe, where she handed me a similar pair of shorts and one of my own tank tops. *Thanks, Dad,* I thought.

But I didn't take my eyes off Carmen.

"Why?" I asked as I picked up the extra paddle. "Why help me now?"

"Because you were stronger than me in all the ways that counted. You were right," she admitted haltingly. "About the island. It got in my head. Back on the island, that was not me."

Carmen turned away. I stared at her back, realizing that was her way of apologizing. It was her way of redeeming herself, *for* herself.

She'd given herself a second chance, and it happened to involve me. Saving me after killing me.

Nil wasn't the only place weirdness happened.

Still, I couldn't bring myself to thank her. After all, she *had* tried to kill me, twice.

"Everyone else is over there," Carmen said, her paddle slicing silently through the water with remarkably powerful strokes. My arms were so shaky I could barely lift my paddle, but this fatigue was *mine*, born of *my* experiences, *my* fight to survive, *my* triumph of will to break free. I'd earned this fatigue, and I reveled in it. Because as tired as I was, I was here.

Nil's end was not mine.

We rounded the bend, angling toward the shallow beach. A boat was anchored in deep water. On the beach, a few people milled around. Others were already in canoes, heading toward the big boat. Molly,

Davey, and Calvin were already on the large boat; so were Dominic, Zane, and Lana. Kenji and James were pushing a canoe off the beach with my dad's help. Thad and Charley stood at the water's edge, heads slightly bent, hands clasped. The tiger was nowhere to be seen.

Rives sat alone on the beach, backlit by the island fire. He wore only athletic shorts, his body turned toward the mountain, his face wet with tears.

Rives.

I realized he couldn't see us in the darkness, and no one was looking our way. All eyes were trained on the Death Twin's smoking mountain, or on my dad's deep-sea boat. We paddled silently, gliding over the water. It wasn't until the bow of the canoe struck the beach that anyone noticed.

"Skye!" Charley cried. She waved wildly.

Rives's head snapped toward her. She pointed to me; his gaze followed. Our eyes caught. He stood, his jaw falling open. He watched me walk toward him. He didn't move.

"Are you real?" he whispered. His voice was raw. "Tell me this is real. Tell me Nil isn't still messing with my head. Skye?"

"I'm real." I reached out and wrapped my hand around his clenched fist. "This is real. *We're* real. And Nil is history." I leaned forward and pressed my lips to his. First softly, then fiercely. I smiled as I wrapped my hands around his waist, my lips tingling from Rives's touch. "How was that? Was that real enough?"

"How?" His face still read shock. "The gate closed. It *exploded*. You didn't come through."

"I had a water landing. I don't remember much, but I do remember flying through the air, and waking just before I went under."

With a groan, Rives swept me close, holding me tight. "You make me crazy, you know that?"

"I know." I smiled against his chest. "It's one of my specialties."

"Mad skills," he whispered. He kissed my temple, then my cheek, my neck, my collarbone, as if he couldn't get enough, as if he'd never get enough. Abruptly, he stopped.

"Skye," he said slowly, his voice measured as he held me gently at arm's length. "What happened?" His eyes lingered on my bare shoulders before landing on my eyes. "After you took the torch into the gate?"

"Love saved me," I said simply. "Yours, mine. Ours. Others'. Nil let me live."

"And you're sure Nil is—" He paused, wrestling for the perfect word. "Gone?"

I nodded. "I felt it let me go. The dark side hesitated, or weakened, and the good side won. Or maybe the light overwhelmed the dark, just for an instant. Either way, I felt the seam close behind me. Nil is trapped, between worlds, without access to the power it needs. It's over."

Rives's finger brushed my shoulder blade.

"But it left a mark."

"On everyone," I agreed.

"I mean on *you*. On your shoulder."

"What?" I wrenched around but I couldn't see anything. Then I remembered the cold hand that pushed me through. Had Nil left a mark? A chill crept down my spine. "What does it look like?"

"Like ice," Thad said.

"No, it looks like the inside of a gate," Charley said. She inspected my shoulder blade with a flashlight. "It glitters in the light, but it has to catch the light to be seen. It's lines of silvery light, shaped sort of like a diamond. It's actually really cool."

Thad snorted. Rives didn't look amused.

"Do you still feel Nil?" Rives asked. "In your head? In your heart? Anywhere?"

I remembered the suffocating layer that had peeled away just before I flew through; the same weighty layer that had vanished in the moment before the ice hit, before I blacked out, before the seam had sealed shut. And when I'd woken, I'd felt light. Lighter than I had in months.

I'd felt like *me*.

I went deeper, searching. Nil's memories remained only as ghosts: wispy fragments, dulled by my human ability to access the lingering remnants still in my memory banks. Their weight and substance were gone. My memories were truly mine, just like my mind, and my heart, and my soul.

"Skye?" Rives's worried voice brought me back. "You're scaring me. Talk to me. Please."

I met his eyes, this boy who walked into a gate for me, who gave up everything for me, *because I'd asked him to*. And yet he'd been there, with me, until the end. Until *Nil's* end. And somehow, he'd reached through, to guide me back, just as I'd reached for him. I'd felt him, and so had Nil.

Together, we had been *more*.

And we still were.

"There's nothing to be afraid of." I covered his hand with mine, knowing it was true. "Nil's end is written; it's over, for good. Forever. Our future belongs to us."

Rives's lips curved into a smile, the one that made the rest of the world fall away. "To now," he whispered, his green eyes full of heat and hope.

I pulled him to me, reveling in the love that brought me to this moment. "To now," I agreed, my lips finding his.

Now is just the beginning.

My name is Skye Bracken, and this is the truth.

ACKNOWLEDGMENTS

Writing acknowledgments for the last book in a series brings a heightened case of *oh-my-land-I-need-to-thank-everyone* combined with a hefty dose of *please-don't-let-me-forget-anyone*.☺ But at least I know where to start.

Thanks to God, for with Him all things are possible . . . like creating the fictional world of Nil that I've been blessed to live in for the past five years.

This trilogy—and of course, this final Nil book, with its stunning cover and gorgeous graphics—would not exist without the incredible support, hard work, and tireless enthusiasm of the following people:

Jennifer Unter, my literary agent extraordinaire, who I'm grateful for *every* day. You are THE BEST! Thank you for making my publishing dreams come true, for working so hard to bring Charley, Thad, Rives, and Skye to readers everywhere, and for your unwavering support. Thank you for making this book, and this journey, possible.☺

Kate Farrell, my brilliant editor, who expertly brought this trilogy to life. Four years ago, you took a chance on a debut author, and I'm so incredibly grateful you did.☺ Thank you so much for your enthusiasm, your patience, your wisdom, and your vision; I can't imagine a more perfect editor for this series. All the thanks and Nil love I can send you are yours! YOU ARE AWESOME!

The incredible lovelies at Macmillan and Henry Holt, including Rachel Murray, Brittany Pearlman, Molly Brouillette, Allison Verost, Caitlin Sweeney, Mary Van Akin, Ksenia Winnicki, April Ward, Elizabeth Dresner, Liz Fithian, and the rest of the wonderful publishing team who brought this book, and this *series*, into the world. You lit the Nil fire! The Macmillan #NILtribe is the absolute BEST.☺

The YA Valentines (Sara Raasch, Bethany Hagen, Lindsay Cummings, Bethany Crandell, Phil Siegel, Sara B. Larson, Amy Rolland, Anne Blankman, Paula Stokes, Kristi Helvig, Jen McConnel, Jaye Robin Brown, Kristen Lippert-Martin) aka THE BEST WRITING SUPPORT GROUP EVER. This journey would not have been the same—or nearly as fun—without y'all.☺

Becky Wallace, Tonya Kuper, Lindsay Currie, Trisha Leaver, and Nicole Castroman: I love your brains and your kindness, your generosity and your friendship.☺ How did I get so lucky?

Vivi Barnes, Christy Farley, Amy Parker: I will be a guest chick any day. Road trips and apples and beach getaways on me . . . and we're just getting started.☺

Jay C. Spencer: thank you for going back to Nil in the '80s with Scott and sharing your incredible talent with me.☺

Natalie Whipple, Charles Martin, Laura Stanford, Eliza Tilton, and Jessie Harrell: I can't say thank you enough for believing in the Nil world from the start and in my writing. Your encouragement was huge when I needed it most.☺

My Fierce Reads partners in crime, Marie Rutkoski, Morgan Matson, and Lindsay Smith: I adore you.☺

Artists Maggie Eckford, Gaslight Anthem, The Broods, Snakadaktal, Rise Against, and Silversun Pickups: special thanks for setting this book on fire, inspirationally speaking.

All the booksellers, librarians, and incredible book bloggers (Eli, Nikki, Stacee, Hafsah, Danny, Ivey, Stephanie, Celeste, Jack, Kristen, Jessica, and more!) who have supported the Nil world from word one: YOU AMAZE ME. You are the heart of the #NILtribe, and I truly appreciate everything you do! An island of thanks from me!☺

Speaking of hearts . . . my friends and family, near and far, who have supported me and the Nil world with such love it makes me cry. I am SO blessed.

Sims, Gina, Christy, Mary Caroline, Kelly, Phaedra, Amy, Mary Claire, Leigh, Kelley, Natalie, Kat, Allison, Meg, Avery, Lindsey, Julie, Erin, Heather, Margaret, Isabelle, Susanna, Mary, Susannah, Stephanie, Nina, Lauren, Nicole, Annie, Darden, Porter, Kasie, Laddy, Virginia, Debbie, Rebecca, Michele, Stacy, Lani, Shannon, Angela, Devon, Susan, Rhonda, Sharlon, Jennifer, Pat, and Missy (and my other sweet friends I forgot to mention because of writer's brain), I love you all and am grateful to have you in my life.

My family aka my personal #NILtribe: Ki (best sister ever), Mom, Ryan, Baz, Max, Mark, Jill, Blake, Kerri, Grandma, Bev, Jim, Johnny, and Aymi. I love y'all tons!

My guardian angels, who I miss: my dad, who gave me my first fantasy book . . . this series is for you. Uncle Beepsy, who said there should be more kissing . . . I wish you could have read the final copy. And Penny, who was the proudest mother-in-law ever . . . you inspired me to be the best me.

My boys, Caden, Christian, Davis, and Cooper: I LOVE YOU ALL BEYOND WORDS! Thank you for sharing me with Nil, for your hugs and your inspiration, and for being the amazing boys you are. You make life the best trip ever. I am y'alls' biggest fan, always.☺

My best friend and my soul mate, Stephen, who makes life more. You believed in me and in the Nil world from Day One, and this book—this series—absolutely would not exist without your support. Thank you, my love! I can't wait for our next adventure! Whatever it is, I know it will be awesome—because it will be with you.

And finally, thank you, sweet reader, for taking this journey with me! There isn't enough space to convey how grateful I am for the passion of the #NILtribe. Your excitement, your artwork, your emails, and your generous Nil love have meant the world to me. Over the past few years, meeting you in person and interacting online has been incredible. Nil belongs to you now and so does this book.

And so, to the #NILtribe everywhere: thank you for embracing all things Nil from the start and for staying until the end.☺ This book is for you.